JEFFE KENNEDY

Shooting Star

Thank you for reading!

<u>Credits</u>
Line and Copy Editor: Rebecca Cremonese
Back Cover Copy: Erin Nelsen Parekh
Cover Design: Fiona Jayde

SHOOTING STAR

Not all desires are shiny and sweet—and the dark ones might change you forever…

It's not the kind of obsession a tough Army guy can admit to—a jones for Ava, the pretty-princess pop star. Not just her body, the perfect product that sells all those magazines. Her music.

The critics call her human lip gloss, all style and no substance. To Joe Ivanchan, Ava is the exact blend of reality and fantasy that he can tolerate, the closest he's willing to get to giving his heart after the injury and breakdown that got him out of the service.

But Ava is real. She's a flesh and blood woman with a publicity machine and an album deadline, along with a whole team of handlers paid to shellac a pristine sheen over a damaged, desperate soul. A woman with fears, with secrets, with desires.

When Joe finds himself in an interview to join her security team as her driver, his instinct is to get away. But the woman behind Ava's carefully focus-grouped image is even harder to walk away from. The angry needs tormenting her speak to something within Joe. Something empathetic, protective—and primal…

Besides, even a falling star can light up the darkest night.

Dedication

To the child movie star I won't name
whose long-ago eighteenth birthday debut on the cover of a
men's magazine started this story brewing

Author's Note

This book is a bit of a departure from my others. There's some dark stuff in here that might be triggering, so fair warning. I didn't flinch away from some of the grittier realities. They're in this story for good reasons, which I hope will be clear by the end. It's still a romance with all the hope for happiness and healing that romance promises. I only wish real life worked the same way.

A lot of people read this book over the years I've worked on it and gave me wonderful support and feedback. Some of it I listened to. A lot of it I didn't. So it's not their fault that I clung to a stubborn idea of what this book would be.

So, many thanks to Margaret, Kelly Robson, Grace Draven, Megan Hart, Molly Fader, Sarah Younger, Anna Philpot, Laurie McLean, and Laurie Potter for critique, feedback, discussion, and general support.

Thanks to Megan Mulry, who suggested Sova and Michelle Richter for weighing in on Sovinka.

Thanks to Stacey Agdern (@nystacey) and Elisabeth Lane for weighing on NYC eating spots, and Jessica Topper for rock star inside info.

Gratitude to Ilona Andrews for gifting me with the perfect Russian toast.

Thanks to Twitter and @TheBookNympho, @Twimom227, @JoyfullyReviewd, @RealAng00 for BOB.

Shae Connor came up with Tyler's band name.

Thanks to KitDuluCa (@KitDuluCa) for Greek Orthodox information.

Special gratitude to Sassy Outwater, kickass blind chick and disability activist. Her love of this story kept my faith in it when I needed it most. Thank you, Sassy, for lending me Arlin's spirit. I hope this is a fitting memorial to your first guide dog. All the stuff I got right is entirely due to Sassy's excellent advice.

J. Howard Shannon shared freely about his experiences in Afghanistan, revisiting some dark memories for me. I'm eternally grateful for his insights. Anything I got wrong isn't his fault.

Likewise, a lot of people gave me advice about New York City and the roads north. For the record, I *have* been to the city, and I have driven north through Connecticut up to Maine. (Canceled flight with no connections available for days, long story.) Yes, I took fictional liberties with geography and details. Also not their fault.

Many thanks to Carien who also loves this book and helped me keep my sanity. And to David, who is always steadfast in his belief.

And a shout-out to Romance Writers of America. The 2015 conference in Times Square, with all those flashing, stories-tall digital screens, played heavily into the early drafts of this story.

SHOOTING STAR

by Jeffe Kennedy

~1~

I DON'T HAVE to tell you she's beautiful. All the world knows that.

I knew that much long before I met her, from those sky-scraper-high videos flashing her face in Times Square to the cover of that men's magazine published obscenely soon after her eighteenth birthday. The magazine hit the stands so fast that the shoot had to have happened when she was still a minor. I and all the other twisted perverts of the world had been counting down for that moment, for the little-girl princess to grow up just enough to be legal fodder for our prurient fantasies.

As opposed to the ones I'd had before that. The clock clicked past midnight and she went from forbidden to fair game.

I'd be a liar if I said I wasn't one of those guys. I was. I am. And I'll cop to feeling like a dirty old man for being one of the ones waiting for her to be legal, even though I'm not a hell of a lot older than she is. War will do that to you, make you old before your time.

I got my buddy to bring me a copy in the hospital. I even kept it in a plastic sleeve, to protect those precious images of her. Not that I was obsessed, exactly. Back then I didn't even know much about her music. I'd heard my little sister talk about her, but that was it. Not something the guys listened to.

The guys—we liked her for different reasons.

I don't claim to be some special snowflake, but I always

1

thought something else drew me to her, besides the star-struck, lust-filled awe I shared with so many. I was stupid with the pain management back then, so that contributed. Still, on the glossy pages of that magazine she gazed out with her trademark tawny-gold eyes, as if she saw right through me.

I won't say I didn't scrutinize the fine freckles on those high cheekbones that looked like they belonged on a sculpture of an Egyptian goddess, or where they scattered across the snowy skin of her breasts, a hint of her nipples behind the cloth she held in place. Or that I didn't, like every other het guy out there, study that one pic—the one that showed her back—and the dark mole high on her adorable ass, which was barely covered by the gold-sequined drape of her gown.

Yeah, I fantasized about kissing that little mole. And more.

A hell of a lot more.

But it was never only that. Her eyes grabbed me in that photo, too. Something riveting in that gaze. Calling to me. The way she looked over her shoulder, with her hair in gleaming waves like one of those forties Hollywood movie stars, lips painted with gold glitter, pouting in what was probably supposed to be sexy. I guess it was, for all that, though it didn't work for me. With the expression in her eyes, she looked sad. I had plenty of my own problems, but it still bothered me.

I went over and over that photo spread—and then every one I could find after that—studying her eyes, how they never matched the rest of her expression, the renowned color unfailingly brighter than all the glitter and jewelry they decorated her with. As if, if I looked long enough, I could decipher the thoughts behind them. Not what she was saying to me, some random guy among millions, but what she might say, given the opportunity.

What can I say? I had a lot of time on my hands.

I started downloading her music. People wanted to know

what they could do for me, how to help? An iTunes gift card, man. All through the physical therapy, the hellish weaning from the morphine and all that other shit, I listened to her songs, her sweet voice a constant murmur in my ears. I even went back all the way to the kiddie albums and the inane and infectious bopping of those princess years, the goofy saccharine family movies and that kids' show she started on.

A bubblegum counterpoint to my grim reality. I wasn't going to show anyone my playlist, but I wouldn't give it up, either.

Not long after that magazine spread, she came out with a new album—I told my home health aide to back off and stayed up to midnight to get it when it released. It had some of her own songs on it. With each album over the next few years, she had more of her own stuff. I made a game of it, when each dropped, listening and deciding which were *hers* before I checked the credits. Every once in a while I'd be wrong—and then those would be written by a particular few, the songwriters she must love. Her actual friends, maybe.

Once I was able to work again, I made mixes of her own songs and the special ones, listening while I drove, as long as I had no clients. People seemed to find it funny that a guy like me listened to a pop star known for the rabid fandom of teen—and tween—girls and I didn't have much bandwidth for smart remarks.

Okay—zero bandwidth for static of any kind.

It was never a rational thing, but somewhere in my fucked-up psyche, I figured if the photos wouldn't tell me what lurked behind those too-wise eyes, maybe the songs would. So I listened, over and over, filing away the nuances—parsing the lyrics of her songs the way my freshman lit prof despaired of me ever doing with those college texts. Of course, I'd partied way too much that single year of university and was drunk or hungover most of the time. I never could dredge up a single fuck for those dry, dead poets and their profound thoughts. But with Ava… make fun of pop all you wanted. From that mouth, her words sounded like poetry.

I even went to a concert after I moved to the city. Me, my baby sister—best excuse ever—and twenty-thousand screaming girls. Not that I blamed a one of them. If I'd been a girl, I'd probably have wanted to be just like her, too.

Instead of just wanting *her*, wanting to scrape everything out of her songs and her images, like the melted dregs from an ice cream carton.

Standing there in the front row—a spot I'd paid a ridiculous amount of money to score, on the excuse of it being my sister's birthday treat, not a junkie feeding his jones—I watched her perform, soaking in being so near, working the fantasy that she'd see me and …

Something.

But she hadn't. She'd looked right through me, her eyes so familiar, so like her photos only wilder, more glittering with life. I was nothing to her. Me and ten thousand other sick and twisted guys wanting the princess to look their way. Which, no surprise, but the fury pushed me too near the nowhere zone.

I stayed away after that. No more live concerts, just the music and the magazines. A hobby more than one girlfriend snickered at. A more generous one enrolled me in a fan club of all men, a sweet thought, though I stayed away from that, too. I knew I was one of many, but I didn't need to rub my own face in it. It kind of pissed me off, too, that these other guys mooned over her. Ironic and hypocritical, sure. I never said this was a rational thing.

When I was being honest with myself, I could label it obsession. Not that I spent much time in self-examination. One quote that stuck with me from English—"the unexamined life is not worth living," or something like that. Which summed up my life perfectly. At least before I got injured and then discharged. After that, well… nothing like months of recovery to give a guy time and incentive to think about his fucked-up life.

I only felt close to something valuable, something regal and bright and vivid when it involved her. So I kept my distance and followed my star from afar. Maybe hoping some of her light would illuminate my dark spaces.

Of course, when I got a chance to meet her, I had no hope of refusing.

~ 2 ~

"**A**VA, DARLING, WE need to talk about a driver for you, an expert one who can also function as a bodyguard. Some of your fans can be … obsessive." Her manager steepled his fingers, leaning his elbows on the smudge-free glass table. The faux-concerned, fatherly smile on Dwight's face made his Botoxed lips stretch like a Muppet's. Something she and Katey had once giggled over. Now the sight just made her tired.

And lonely. Seemed like lately she was always tired and lonely.

At the other end of the table, Katey worked Ava's social media on her tablet, clearly not even half listening. At least she was out of bed.

Ava swished her chair back and forth on its swivel, the faces of her "team" reflected in the shining mirror of the conference table. They liked to call themselves that. One big happy "team," patting each other on the backs, running around in matching uniforms, cheering for accumulating hits and growing bank accounts as if someone kept score somewhere.

She'd finally wised up to the reality that there was no team. Certainly not one she got to be a part of. Probably no one else did either and they all just liked to pretend they cared about more than their life trophies.

For a long time, she'd believed her roles in all those shows. Family, togetherness, love. She'd been stupid for a long time,

6

too, about a lot of things. Love lived only in movies, to drive an otherwise listless plot. Need a reason for the heroine to sacrifice her happiness? Love! Need some shiny moment at the end to be the meaning of life? Love!

In the end, nobody was ever on anybody's side but their own.

The real world ran on money and power. And having more drivers and bodyguards in her life would only cost her both. As per usual. She wouldn't win this argument, but she could try to stack it to put a bit more power on her side of the "team" equation.

At least Dwight had waited until the Monday morning meeting—what he likely considered a decent interval after Henry's funeral—before springing his New Plan, but he'd also moved the driver/bodyguard issue to the top of the agenda. She'd label it the last thing she wanted to talk about, but so many issues crowded that particular list.

"Henry wasn't a bodyguard," she said, keeping the hitch of grief out of her voice. "A whatever driver is fine."

"Henry worked very well for the younger you," Hilda put in. Publicist and the voice of reason, Hilda spun uncomfortable truths into cotton candy. "But you're a pop sensation now. More than you ever were before. A superstar. And with recent events, though the situation is well in hand and you shouldn't give any of it a moment's thought, it would be comforting for all of us if you have a driver who can keep you safe. You don't want Katey to worry about you while you're out and about, do you?"

Katey, absorbed in her tablet, didn't look up. No one had told her about Krystal showing up at Henry's funeral because everyone agreed without discussing that she was better off that way. At least they were on her side with that.

"That well-in-hand situation had better be addressed." Ava raised her brows to underscore the point.

"Ava darling, I've explained to you that these things only go so far, we're doing what we can, but unless she crosses that line or breaks the law, we can't stop her from—" Dwight broke off and mopped his brow when Ava glared pointedly. "Besides, there are other reasons for a protective presence, with the photographers and even your fans getting sometimes a little aggressive, shall we say—"

"I have bodyguards. There must be seventeen of those guys in my way every time I want to take a piss alone."

Katey, looking like she'd slept behind a dumpster after an all-night bender, finally looked up from her tablet and rolled her eyes—though for the conversation or Ava's bad attitude, she wasn't sure.

Dwight shook his head, his fond smile Superglued to his Muppet face. "Now, Ava, your fans love your drama, but you can drop the hyperbole with us, you already said you didn't want any of the existing staff to take over for Henry and besides, they have enough to do with their current duties, and we need to choose this person carefully, as he will be with you almost constantly."

Meaning someone to keep an eye on her. More leash-holders. Wonder of wonders. They must be figuring that with Henry gone, Ava would be even less controllable. The possibility held merit. "Katey keeps me company."

"But she can't protect you and she's full-out running your social media." For once, he actually paused, tripping over the words he didn't say. That Katey's meltdown at the funeral had been the worst yet. Not that any of them held Ava accountable—like she deserved—but that was because they cared more about the impact on Ava. Not about Katey's wellbeing. That ship had well and truly sailed. He cleared his throat, doing his shuffle dance. "It's only logical for your driver to serve the dual purpose of seeing that you're protected as you move about."

Hilda broke the jagged silence. "Having a driver who is also a bodyguard means you won't have to have those seventeen guys in your way. One guy only, who does what you direct. Like an assistant. A very capable one."

Hmm. She didn't believe that for a minute, but paring down the entourage would be awesome. "Okay, so…" She had no idea how her staff got hired. "I'll interview some people then."

Dwight spread out soothing hands. "This is not something you need to concern yourself with. The decision has been made, we're only asking you to approve our selection for Henry's replacement."

His *replacement.* Fuck that. She dropped her gaze to the mirroring table, choking back her rising fury. Spewing it would only throw them into containment mode.

"That's okay," she said, in her coolest tone instead of growling the way she wanted to. Grace Kelly, not Amy Winehouse. "I want to be concerned. I'll choose."

"Ava, honey." Betsy was the coaxer, assigned to talk Ava out of whatever tree she'd climbed up. "You don't need to spend your valuable time on—"

Ava spun her chair, her reflection shimmering back from the table. "On the person 'who will be with me almost constantly'? Practically an assistant? How could anyone else possibly choose for me?" How could anyone choose Henry's *replacement* in her life? She produced a laugh to break the icy grip on her heart, to relax them, giving them a warm smile. "Give me six or seven to choose from and I'll pick."

"Ava darling, we already—"

"Oh, come on, Dwight—let's not argue about this. Every minute I sit here instead of recording delays the album that much more." Not that she'd be doing much in the studio besides wasting everyone's time. But she was a professional, if nothing else.

Sparkle, Shirley. Henry used to say that to her and Katey. *That's what Shirley Temple's mother used to say to her, and you gals are just as pretty, bright and talented. Now go on out there and sparkle!*

Too bad she couldn't be recording the song Henry had always asked her to write for him. That had never quite made her schedule. At least she hadn't screwed him out of his life's dream. He'd gotten off relatively easy.

In the movie version of their lives, she'd have written the song as he lay dying, played it for him in some sunny hospice with beaming nurses, and they would have shared a Hallmark moment. He'd have told her she was the daughter he'd never had and angel light would have erased the stink of hospital. But in real life, death robbed you of all of that and left nothing behind. Only null space.

Which was so her. Recently a columnist had called her "human lip gloss," and she hadn't been able to get that out of her head, even during Henry's funeral, when she was supposed to be thinking about him. Henry would have been angry on her behalf. Did that count as thinking about him?

Somehow she doubted it.

But what did you expect of human lip gloss?

She shook off the melancholy, focusing on the current objective. "This is what I want: at least six to choose from, and I'll pick one to be a driver slash bodyguard. I'm not asking for the moon here."

"I think that's reasonable," Betsy put in. Ava wasn't the only one she coaxed.

"Fine." Dwight made a note. "I'll set it up, just to make you happy, Ava darling, but speaking of the album—"

"I'm heading to the studio to record once you're done with your agenda. What more do you want of me?"

"Seriously?" Dwight gave her an exasperated look. "We want what we've wanted for weeks—the album to be finished. We lost most of last week. We're not asking for the moon here."

Because Henry died. She didn't much appreciate the mockery. "It will be finished."

"Not with one and half songs it won't. We're out of time for you to play artist. Pick some other songs and record those. We can do as with the staffing—prepare a list to choose from."

"I want to do my own songs," she replied, clinging to her resolve. A real artist, not Human Lip Gloss.

"Ava darling, I know, but there are about a thousand samples filed in the office from songwriters who would *kill* to have you sing their songs. You would be doing them a favor and you know it. Pick ten and be done. Just for this album. You can make your artistic mark on the next one."

"You've had a hard few months," Betsy put in. "Cut yourself some slack. You can write all the songs for the next album. Give it your best."

"I'll think about it," she said, mostly to shut them all up. Maybe they were right, but it felt like such a … concession. Wasn't taking the easy path what she always did? Slick and shiny. Even though it was only Monday morning, exhaustion dragged at her.

"Let's move on to something else. What's the update on the benefit concert?"

✦ ✦ ✦

"Look at me, what do you see? A stranger who is snappy happy snappy!"

The general ringtone meant someone he didn't know. Could be a spam call. But, as he was currently cooling his heels waiting for a client who'd insisted on leaving for JFK at ten thirty sharp and had yet to make an appearance at ten forty, he tapped off the music and answered. "Joe Ivanchan."

"This is Elise Hart at Hart and McGrath. Your name came up in a recent search to supply a client with a new driver. Would you be interested in interviewing for the position?"

"A client?" That opener had seemed like a spam call for sure and he hovered his thumb over the red disconnect, reconsidering as his sluggish brain lagged a few beats behind. The woman's rapid-fire delivery didn't help.

"Our firm specializes in executive placement services. 'The right person at the right time.'" She paused. Huffed a light breath when he didn't reply. "We're headhunters."

Oh. "I didn't know headhunters bothered with us blue-collar types."

"Mr. Ivanchan," the woman replied in an arch tone, "Hart and McGrath serves an exclusive clientele who demand the very best service in all of their daily needs. Using a sophisticated algorithm, we surveyed the best car services in the city. Your name came up as a highly rated driver for both safety record and customer satisfaction. Your military record is excellent."

Of course—hire a vet and tick off the boxes. He looked like a safe bet that way. On paper.

"Mr. Ivanchan, are you interested in interviewing?"

He tapped his fingers on his good leg, thinking about it. No one had ever just *offered* him a job out of the blue. That was kind of cool, wasn't it? But then, he didn't do great with change. Riding shotgun on the seat beside him, Arlin raised his head in question, and he rubbed the golden lab's ears. Steady as she goes. "I have a good job."

"I can promise this will pay far better than your current employment, with excellent benefits. A single client, mainly local driving, though domestic and international travel may be involved in the future. Well past your probationary period, however, as the client's work will keep her in the city into the fall and through the holidays. There is an additional component, that the driver also be prepared to provide a level of protection, which we believe falls well within your skill set also."

"A bodyguard."

"Standard crowd-avoidance. The candidate should be able to handle aggressive situations with a cool head. You're decorated and numerous references mentioned your sterling record in this capacity. Your experience with situations requiring discretion is a point in your favor."

"My middle name."

"Also a plus in your qualifications," Elise replied without missing a beat. Their interest in his service made a lot more sense all of a sudden. And all of what the headhunter so carefully didn't say spelled out Celebrity Client. He'd subbed in on enough of those to smell that dance.

"Can I ask who it is?"

"As we prefer to match potential employees with clients who will be a good fit, I can release that information, though I'm asking that you treat this as sensitive."

"I can do that."

"The client in question is a young pop star named Ava. Are you familiar with her body of work?"

His ears rang and the blood beat hard behind his eyelids, narrowing his vision.

Her body of work—and that body. Familiar with Ava. Oh yeah.

He'd made himself stay away. He was busy, wasn't he?

Yeah, busy with the music and the magazines, which he kept secret, locked away just for him. If his VA counselor knew, she'd label it obsession.

Arlin whimpered, pushing his chin against Joe's knee, bringing him back to reality. "Good boy. I'm good."

"Mr. Ivanchan?" the voice in his ear rattled too brightly, his brain gone oversensitive, buzzing at the offer of the impossible.

A chance to walk on the surface of the sun. Immolation and annihilation. "Are you interested in interviewing for the job?"

It had never been a question. "Yeah. Sign me up."

~ 3 ~

DWIGHT POUNCED ON her as she emerged from the recording studio. Her manager was about the last person she wanted to deal with, especially if he wanted to discuss the results of the last focus group on this crop of songs. All of them sounded like what she'd sung ten years before. Snappy and lively enough, but not what she wanted to say. Not anymore.

Unfortunately, human lip gloss apparently didn't have much to say.

"Not now, Dwight. I'm off duty and have an urgent appointment with the coldest lemon-drop martini conceived by man."

Rather than annoyed by her brush off, he nodded crisply. "You deserve it, Ava darling, I knew you'd see it my way."

Big red flag there as she never came around to his way of thinking, even when she compromised, which always meant flat-out capitulated. "See what your way?"

He almost didn't say, cagey glance flicking away, searching for an alternative to put her off with. But he held up innocent hands when she put fists on hips and glared. "The driver, Ava darling, I have six guys for you to interview—as per your instructions—but save yourself the trouble and let me do my job, go with our pick. I think you'll be very pleased. Have your cocktail and relax."

Much as she hated to, she relinquished the fantasy of tart

and icy vodka with a sugar-rimmed zing. She owed this much to Henry's memory. And to her own future sanity. Whoever Dwight had such a hard-on for had to be one of his puppets, all tied up with neat strings and ready to report on her every move, and worse. She'd given up a great deal to make Dwight and the label happy. They got to control what they wanted to.

But she had to retain a shred of freedom here and there or she'd lose her ever-loving mind.

What was left of it.

She freshened her lipstick, tucked her hand in the crook of his elbow, the expensive suit crisp, and blew him a kiss. She never went wrong with flirtatious. "I couldn't possibly foist something this important on you. You're always telling me to be more responsible, to think about the consequences of my actions on my career. This is me doing that."

Dwight tried to look pleased, she had to give him that, as he escorted her to one of the several meeting rooms the recording studio maintained. Six men sat around the mahogany conference table, all fish out of water to greater or lesser extents. By definition bodyguard types had to look badass and these dudes all fit that bill. Making a bet with herself, she pegged the slickest, vaguely smarmy guy as Dwight's choice. He'd weighted it to that one, still thinking she had a thing for those blue-eyed blonds. She did. She also had a thing for dark hair, red hair and any shade of skin. If he had nice shoulders and a decent cock, all cats were gray in the dark.

Not like any of them lasted long, and only a few really rang her bell. A skill that never showed on the surface. Though a smart woman paid attention to the clues.

Besides Slick, there was one who could be the IRL version of cartoon Brutus from Popeye; a shifty-eyed Italian stud; a Michael Clarke Duncan lookalike; a Bruce Willis type; and ooh—someone not at all like the usual suspects. Headhunted, maybe, to round out the six Dwight had exactingly delivered.

Unremarkable on the surface. Brown eyes, brown hair, big shoulders. A nose he'd probably broken playing football, or in a fight, depending. A little taciturn, a slightly disaffected, brooding turn on his mouth. How she pictured Jack in Mellencamp's little ditty. Henry played that song in the limo and she and Katey would sing along. A good memory. She'd have dribbled off her Bobbie Brooks for this one, for sure. If she hired him, she might have to hunt up a pair online somewhere—whatever they were—and live out that little fantasy. Dwight didn't much like her fucking the help, but small joys and all.

He stood out from the rest, though he was far from the biggest man in the group. He might be wearing a suit and tie, off the rack and not fitted all that well, but a bit of an angular black tattoo showed above his shirt collar. But more than any of that—he was so clearly *not* what Dwight would choose for her that he stood out like he had a big PICK ME arrow over his head.

Score.

She hugged her manager's arm as she pretended to study the offerings. "Which one do you recommend?"

He side-eyed her, clearly anticipating she'd dump that one first, just to be contrary. She gave him her sunniest fake smile, which always worked, and he flicked his manicured fingers at Slick. *Bingo was his name-o.* "Ava, this is Nathan Wilkins—mixed martial-arts expert, crack shot, professional race-car driver, he's worked for Beyoncé and Whitney-God-rest-her-soul—he's perfect for the job."

Wilkins inclined his head, nearly a bow. "Ava. It's an honor. I'm a huge fan."

She suppressed the impulse to knee him in the nose. "I know what happened to Whitney. God rest her soul," she added, with a bland look at Dwight. She'd canceled a concert when they'd gotten the news of Whitney's pitiable death, her heart breaking and throat too ravaged from weeping. And then from the screaming fight with Dwight who'd acted like she'd canceled the second coming of Christ. "Why'd Beyoncé kick you to the curb?"

Wilkins goggled. Worse, he flushed. Bit of a temper there and not the sexy kind. "We parted ways amicably. She gave me an excellent letter of reference."

She nearly snorted. People always used that word with divorces, too, and it meant the same thing then—that it had been easier just to pay the other person to go away. From goddess Beyoncé to Ava was a big step down and every person in the room knew it.

"I can vouch for Nate's credentials, they're stellar," Dwight said.

Of course they were. As sculpted as his fake nose. "What's your favorite song, Slick?"

"'Shining Star,'" he answered promptly, naming her biggest hit—from when she was sixteen—and flashed her a white grin. Capped. Probably a chin-job, too. Pretty boy. Once she would have liked that. Mostly she still did, depending. "Though it's hard to choose," he added. "I love all your work."

"See, Ava darling? Perfect for you."

A headache throbbed behind her eyes. She needed out of there and she *really* needed that martini. If she waited too long, she'd want the other pills. Or the coke. Vodka was the happy medium, but it wasn't going to happen until she chose one of these guys. It sure wasn't going to be Wilkins. *Power and money,* she reminded herself. *Pick one and you can always fire him later. Just take some fucking responsibility.*

"I'll consider it," she lied. "You two go have coffee and make out or something and let me interview the others. I'll tag you when I've decided."

"Now Ava darling, I really think—"

"Bye, Dwight. Nice meeting you, Slick." She stepped away, dismissing them both, privilege of being a diva and all that. "All right, gentlemen, name, rank and serial number."

✦ ✦ ✦

IMPOSSIBLY, SHE WAS more beautiful in person.

Casually dressed in worn jeans with frayed slashes that gave glimpses of her lean thighs, and an ancient pink Cinderella t-shirt, she looked much thinner than he'd imagined, her face almost odd in its angularity, lush mouth dominating with crisply applied lipstick in her trademark crimson. Rattling lust had him trying to look away from the way the soft cotton clung to her far-from-little-girl-princess curves. It made him feel dirty that he'd seen so much of how she looked without those clothes.

But he wasn't capable of looking anywhere else. The sheer force of her presence burned brighter than the sun, hotter than even her intensely golden eyes.

Abruptly the sense of empty space beneath his feet hit him hard. Too many stories in this building. Too high off the ground. He stood on nothing, and the nowhere zone circled in with a menacing buzz. It had been a mistake to take the headhunter's bait.

The crushing truth of it had begun to grind on him while they waited, the other contenders for the job trading war stories, name-dropping celebrities like reality-show contestants mugging for an invisible camera. All so shallow, grubbing for the next shiny trophy for their shelves. His leg ached with phantom pain, hot and sweaty in the sleeve, and he'd seriously considered ditching the gig so he could go home, shuck the fucking prosthesis and have a good scratch.

He didn't belong in that room.

But he couldn't make himself leave.

Then she walked in, pulling every photon to her and radiating it back. Rendering him well and truly starstruck.

Didn't bother him a bit that Nate "Look at What an Asshole I Am" Green got first bid. That much had been predictable, with all the preening and crowing the guy had done. It gave Joe time to recover himself. Watching her, being in the same room with *Ava*, helped him battle back the nowhere zone, just as she'd done for him countless times in the hospital and after. As if she emanated saturated oxygen like they'd given him in the aftermath, that cooled his overheated brain.

Breathing her in let him plan what he might do to extract himself since he'd been too stupid and starry eyed to plan an exit strategy that didn't involve his complete humiliation. *Assess and observe before taking action, soldier.*

She didn't like the manager, though she clung to his arm convincingly enough. Cranky and restless, she'd dismissed Green with an instant assessment that upped his respect for her. He'd figured her for no dummy, but it could be she was pretty damn smart.

She said she'd think about it, though she clearly wouldn't, all the while scrutinizing him and the others with a laser gaze that pricked him to square his shoulders and come to attention. When she asked for name, rank and serial number, his hand had twitched to salute.

Old habits die hard. Of course, he also wanted to kneel and kiss the naked arch of her foot, which had nothing to do with the army and everything to do with sexual obsession.

"Joe Ivanchan, ma'am," he told her, when it came his turn, "Specialist, 101st Airborne, medical discharge." On reckless impulse—wasn't this all reckless impulse?—he added, "The Army doesn't use serial numbers anymore. Not since World War II and the invention of the Social Security Number."

She put a hand on her hip and cocked it sassily—a move exactly out of her "Hello, Sailor" video—raising her perfect brows, light gold to match her current hair color. "A soldier? How romantic."

He set his teeth at that, dull ugly anger rising at that familiar flip attitude. What he'd been through had been the polar opposite of romantic and fuck anyone who didn't recognize that. Then he caught the assessing gleam behind her flirty smile. There she was, the girl who looked out from behind the lovely mask, the one he'd studied all those times. Baiting him, as she'd baited Green. Only that dipshit had been too dumb to know it. Joe wouldn't be that guy, regardless of how all of this played out. He was fucked up, not stupid.

"It had its moments," he replied evenly, and she gazed back at him with those fabulous golden eyes. *I'm talking to Ava.* The *Ava.*

"And are you a huge fan also, Jack?"

A narrow road there, lined with Ava-flavored IEDs. She hadn't gotten his name wrong by accident, and every one of these guys had fawned over her, naming their favorite songs instantly. Because they'd studied up for the job interview, of course. Not the way he'd studied her, for years, his nonstop coursework in Avaology an endless fascination with no degree and no career prospects. Except maybe this one. Which would crash and burn the moment she suspected the level of his… interest. Let's call it that instead of uglier words. Like obsessed stalker.

"Sorry, ma'am, I'm just a driver."

"And a bodyguard, or Dwight wouldn't have recruited you."

"I can hold my own in a fight. I know how to spot trouble from a ways off." A guy learned that fast where he'd been, or he came back in a bag, not missing a limb and working with a fatally rattled brain.

"And the driving—race cars, the need for speed?"

He choked back a laugh, while the guy who'd said that to her a few minutes before flushed in sullen chagrin. That's what he got for treating Ava like some bimbo who'd love to fondle his biceps. To cover it, Joe shook his head, meeting her gaze levelly. "Only if you count outracing gunfire in an armored Humvee that maxes out at seventy. I have a commercial license and drive for a car service. Not much call for speed in city gridlock."

"Doesn't sound very exciting."

Not compared to these other blowhards, no. "Frankly, ma'am, I've had enough excitement for one lifetime."

"I feel a hundred years old when you call me ma'am." She pouted prettily, but that cagey intelligence danced in her eyes.

"You shouldn't—it's how I'd address anyone in command. Or to be polite to a lady."

Her red lips curved, a hint of real amusement there. "Which am I, Jack—in command or a lady?"

He gave the question due consideration. Something else he'd learned the hard way—never let a superior officer trap you into answering too quickly. Glib answers got you in trouble. "You're the boss, so you call the shots, of course. And my grandmother would take my head off for failing to give respect to a lady. But I won't call you ma'am if you don't like it."

She toyed with a watch on her wrist, that antique one she always wore. The fan sites speculated that it was a family heirloom, but she never answered questions about it. The watch was broken, forever stuck on 10:39—not coincidentally also the title of one of her more famous songs. Not one of his favorites as it sounded like mostly nonsense to him, but what did he know? Fuck all, according to that Lit prof.

She advanced on him, coming around the table so he had to turn his chair to face her. Near enough that her scent, something expensive and probably French, wafted to him, tantalizing. "I don't intimidate you, do I, Jack?"

So much more than she knew. Sweat trickled down his back and his leg ached fiercely. So much power to crush him with her delicate manicured hands—silver sparkles on her nails, like on the t-shirt. But he knew enough about the power of a bluff when engaging the enemy. Sometimes you just brazened it out and hoped you lived through it.

"Respectfully, unless you plan to point an AK-47 at me, I'm not too concerned, ma'am." It sounded damn good, but she laughed, light as wind chimes, shimmying her hips in a sexy dance to an internal song. "All right, you're hired. Thanks guys for your time. If Jack doesn't last out probation, we'll be in touch. Jacky, my boy, you can start now by taking me home."

He almost hadn't heard the rest of her words through the shock, a simultaneous rush of elation and terror flashing an incendiary wipe of his thoughts. Very like staccato gunfire suddenly shattering the monotonous roulette of driving back and forth across Kabul. It would be easier to agree, to give her anything she asked of him, but he found himself shaking his head. "I have to give notice at my job."

"Screw them." She flipped a hand carelessly. "Dwight will take care of the contracts. You work for me now. I call the shots, and I want you to take me home."

His first lesson in how it would be working for her. Most all clients like to indulge a bit in having a driver at their command—even if only for a ride to the airport. Ava was a diva accustomed to having all things her way at the flutter of a careless, self-absorbed whim. She'd want to have him at her beck and call. And she would. *Welcome to your new life, Jack.* Except she could never guess she had him by the balls more tightly than any employment contract could. He'd make sure she never knew it. A woman like her—she'd know exactly how to turn him inside out.

A bad thing as he had nothing left inside.

Only a fool would take a job under these circumstances, which meant it had his name all over it. The only thing that might save him was that she'd liked him pushing back. *I don't intimidate you, do I?* Begin as you mean to go on, his counselor would say.

"Ma'am, I have bookings, clients depending on me. It would be unfair to those people and to my current employer to cut out on them with no notice. These are people who work hard for a living. I can't mess them up like that."

She stared him down coolly, gold fire going matte as chilled metal. "Are you saying I don't work hard for a living, Jack?"

One of the other guys snickered, unfortunately, because she transferred the glare to him. "Why are you still here?"

That got them. The cool demand—not really a question at all—had them scrambling out of the room in almost comical haste. The door shut and Ava folded her arms, studying him somberly. Then flashed one of her radiant, for-show smiles.

"I like you, Jack. I'll make you a deal, if you'll promise me something."

Feeling like he needed the even footing, he pushed the chair back and rose to face her. Not as tall as he expected, though some of that might be the way she filled the room, larger than life. She had on simple, flat shoes, too, like ballerinas wore. In the skyscraper heels she wore on stage, she might be the same height as him. Her mouth level with his.

Easy going there, buddy. "What deal?"

Her smile faded as she tilted her head to consider him, a glossy wave falling over one eye, the thoughtful expression considerably more comfortable to withstand. "Most everyone promises me whatever I want, without asking the particulars."

His fingers itched to tuck the curl back behind her ear, so he stuck his hands in his pants pockets. He was no different than those people. He'd promise her anything, most likely, but it would be beyond dangerous for her to know that. Her thinking he wouldn't might be his only weapon. "Only a fool agrees to a deal without knowing the terms."

"And you're no fool, are you, Jack?"

Was she flirting with him—or manipulating? Maybe the same thing in her world.

"Why are you calling me 'Jack'?" He blurted out the question before he thought better of it. *Whoa, Nelly.*

Her eyes sparkled with amusement, the gleam definitely taunting. "Maybe someday I'll tell you. For now—I want you to promise you'll never lie to me, and you'll answer any question I ask you with perfect honesty. In exchange, I'll arrange to have all of your clients and bookings handled. Even some money to smooth the way at your *former* employer. Plus a hiring bonus to start immediately."

She ticked off the terms with the empty ease of someone who knew nothing about paying bills. The crux of the promise, though, he wasn't letting her gloss over that.

"What does that mean—promise I won't lie to you?"

She regarded him with such cool disdain it pissed him off. "What part didn't you understand?"

"Don't give me that," he replied with some heat. "Why in hell would I lie to you? And what's with this answering every question? Because I'll be your driver and I'll protect you, but I'm not promising to"—*open my heart and soul to you*—"tell you everything you want to know about me." Too much darkness there. Hell, he'd left his family behind to escape all the probing, anxious questions, his mother's smothering concern that only reminded him how much less of a man he'd become.

Ava blinked, long and slow, eyes intensely golden. Looking into him. The image tripped the memory of the owl he'd seen one magical twilight moment with his grandmother, the night before he shipped out. Telling him to move softly, she'd taken him by the hand, her fingers thin and fierce. She showed him the great owl gazing from the wall of her garden, eyes luminescent with the fading light. *Sova*, she called it.

In my village, she'd said, *my brothers and father would carry the claws of the* sova *so that, if they were killed, their souls could use them to climb up to Heaven. Your grandfather, when he went to fight the Afghans, he took my father's claws with him. This is a good omen, Iosif. He is in Heaven now and will watch over you.*

Years later, the first time he saw a photo of Ava and her extraordinary owl eyes, that moment rushed back. Sova. The nowhere zone whined with high white noise inside his skull. He was so not up to this.

"All right," Ava's bell of a voice rang through the dense wind of jumbled memory. "Fair enough. You never lie to me in anything you say. But you should know, Jacky boy, nothing will stop me from asking questions." She caressed his cheek, shocking him to the root of his cock, scraping her sparkling nails over the hint of hard stubble, as he hadn't had time to shave again before coming for the interview. His cock hardened at the caress, as greedy for her as the rest of him; crazed for the impossible fantasy.

She'd dredge that out of him, too. Leave him inside out by the side of a dusty road, nothing even for the ants to eat.

"Do we have a deal?" She palmed his cheek, patting it hard enough to sting a little.

He was a lost man. "Yes."

Her crimson mouth curved, sultry. "Game on. Now get me out of here before I have to kill someone."

~ 4 ~

J OE IVANCHAN WOULD do just fine.

He grew on her by the moment. Definitely not Dwight's puppet—not really anyone's yes man, despite all those "ma'ams." Not a polished pretty boy at all. Up close it turned out his eyes weren't brown but hazel—like sunlight filtered through pine needles. The sharpness of his stubble still made her fingertips tingle and the brusque way he'd tried to put her off only tantalized her. More than that, the dark simmer behind that stoic expression lit her up. What would it take to crack him?

Not much. A delicious little challenge. If she decided to, she could gobble him up in big greedy bites. He'd enjoy it. The Jack to her Diane. She could play that role easily enough so that he'd believe in it. He watched her warily even still, with that hyper-alertness of a man observing the enemy. So interesting that he'd been to war. Fighting for real things. The opposite of human lip gloss.

She and Joe stepped out of the elevator—he a slight step ahead with a protective vibe that also worked just fine for her, especially as it let her assess his broad shoulders. He tensed slightly when Igor and Hulk moved to flank her for the thirty seconds it took to walk through the unsecured part of the lobby and out the back entrance to the car—the overprotective thing that drove her nuts on a daily basis. Like someone would attack her there. Where were they when the bad shit went down?

Nowhere. All for the eternal camera. *Look at us, playing bodyguard. So big and tough.*

Wolverine sat in the driver's seat of the limo, probably napping. She rapped on the window, a little too hard because he jumped before he rolled it down. "You guys are off-duty," she told them all. "Jack here is taking over as my new driver and bodyguard."

"Ava," Igor protested, fingering his phone. Probably he'd already notified Dwight of her movements, which meant she needed to move fast. "Maybe we should—"

"Fuck off?" She made it sweet, with a sparkling smile. Igor earned his nickname as Dwight's evil henchman, though in all fairness he was more broad-shouldered than hunch-backed. Hulk, true to his moniker, mostly lurked and frowned. They glanced among themselves, still not entirely sure of the new protocol. "Seriously, guys. Go hit a happy hour somewhere. Dwight cleared and vetted Jack here. The whole point of having a driver-cum-bodyguard is so I don't have to have an entourage of linebackers with me 24/7. Let him do his job already. I've had a long day. Give him the keys."

Because none of them moved to do it—and she wanted gone before Dwight arrived in time to interfere—she opened the car door herself, rolling her eyes when Igor scrambled too late to do it. Inside the blessed silence of the limo, she dropped her head back on the high banquette. Henry would have passed her a peppermint candy through the window and taken her home.

Unreal that she possessed so little power to tell her own staff what to do.

Through the tinted glass, she watched the men debate, Wolverine with his atrocious sideburns shrugging and handing the keys to Jack, who took them with some reluctance. If they dithered much longer, Dwight would come looking for her and she was out of energy for fighting with people. Did everything have to be such a fucking battle?

Used up my quota for the day.

Thankfully Jack slid into the car, taking stock of the dashboard, then glanced at her in the rear-view mirror. "Want the dividing screen up, ma'am?"

God, it gave her shivers the way he said that, just a flavor of a drawl in it. The same way a hint of that sexy rough-edged temper got to her when she needled him enough for it to show. Real emotions, not artfully faked to entertain. No games with him, just real man. He might be enough to distract her for a while. "No, I want to be able to talk to you."

He set his jaw at that, though he carefully kept his expression neutral and eyes forward. "You'll need to give me your address. The other bodyguards weren't ready to trust me with it yet."

"Other" bodyguards. So he included himself. She'd actually pulled it off. *Go me.* "They're assholes," she said, though Wolverine was pretty much okay.

"They're smart. I could be anyone, holding you under duress."

"If so, couldn't you duress my address out of me?" She deliberately purred the words, just to see if she could get to him. Project Crack Jack underway.

"While driving in New York rush hour traffic? Not likely." He glanced at her again, dry humor in the hazel. He masked it quickly, but a hot glint and the way he looked just a little too long made her sure he'd caught the subtext. "The address?"

"Irrelevant, as I'm not going home yet," she decided.

His brows drew together slightly—thick brows, never waxed—but he didn't argue. "Where to then, ma'am?"

"Take me to your favorite bar," she said on impulse.

She'd surprised him. Then he started shaking his head in a slow, stubborn way that was remarkably sexy for no reason at all. "No can do. I can't protect you by myself in a busy bar. You know that."

Of course she did, but she had hoped he was green enough not to. They pulled out of the studio gates, a few of the paparazzi and some fans lingering on the off chance of getting a shot of her or an autograph. "Besides, there's them," he added. "Take you to a regular bar and they'd swarm the place."

Her phone lit up with a painting of God in all his white-bearded glory, a particularly condescending expression on his face. Dwight, right on schedule. She refused the call. Instead she texted Katey to set up a Twitter diversion, make it seem like she'd gone home for hot chocolate and a chick flick. Once upon a time she'd done all her own social media, but *those* days were long gone. No data plan on this phone—for her own good—just texts and calls, almost all from Dwight and Katey, as fewer than ten people had the number. Katey replied, asking what she was *really* doing. Because everything she could think of to reply sounded too mean and Katey didn't deserve that, she locked the phone and set to work on her new favorite distraction: chiseling away at the Wall of Jack.

"If you take me to a bar *you* like, no one will recognize me, because it will be a place I'd never go on my own" she said in a reasonable tone. "I'm not even dressed up. Hardly anyone recognizes me without makeup and I really want a lemon-drop martini. I might expire if I don't have one. You don't want to be responsible for my untimely demise, do you?"

He flicked a wry glance at her in the rear-view. "The bars I go to don't serve fancy cocktails, ma'am. And if we pull up in this beast, they'll know you're someone. Won't take long to figure out who."

"Lemon juice, vodka, a splash of Triple Sec and sugar. I'll make it myself if they can't. It doesn't have to be your favorite bar. Any bar will do. Park the car somewhere and we'll walk."

"If you know how to make one, why not make it at home?

Or get the staff you surely have to do it." He glared at the stop-and-go traffic, that roughness rising in him as a taxi cut him off, before he tapped his fingers on the steering wheel, visibly calming himself. "You'd get it much faster, too, I bet."

"Because I don't want to go home. You work for me so do what I say and stop arguing." Except that she loved the way he argued with her. Like a man would with his girlfriend. Not like the others did, by turns obsequious and patronizing. She'd annoyed him, but he tamped that down, too. What would it take to get him to explode—and just how hot would it be?

Very hot. Incendiary. She had to have it.

"I won't be working for you long if you get me fired immediately."

"Whatever Dwight claims, only I can fire you. He works for me, too, you know." Her phone lit up again with God's image, so she turned it over. "C'mon, Jacky boy. A small excursion, to make me happy. If there's any trouble, you can take me straight home."

With a sigh, he touched his temple and met her eyes in the mirror. "I suppose if I get fired tonight, I'll still have my other job tomorrow. But I'm not doing a bridge or tunnel this time of day. We're sticking with Manhattan."

"Yay!" She clapped her hands in delight. This was what she needed to clear her mind of the misery of the last months. Just good fun with her boyfriend Jack. And she would be just another girl. "Where are we going?"

"A place I know. Dark. Quiet. They do serve cocktails, so I won't have to worry about you climbing over the bar to show some hapless bartender how it's done. One drink and then I'm taking you home."

He was starting to unbend, forgetting to be all polite. Perfect. "We'll see. And you'll tell me your life story."

"Absolutely not."

"Oh, Jacky. Yes. Yes, you will. You can't resist me for long."
No one could.

He eyed her briefly, then returned his gaze to the traffic. Exasperated, annoyed—though that could be the gridlock—and something else that he blew out on a long breath, before looking at her again. "Do you always get your way?"

✦　✦　✦

TO HIS SURPRISE, she didn't fling back a flip answer to his question. One that he no doubt shouldn't have asked. In the space of barely an hour she'd already gotten him to agree to a number of things he shouldn't have. She was impossible. Both to deal with and to resist. By turns charming gamin and imperious diva, she left him scrambling. In the effort to catch his mental breath, she dragged out of him all sorts of inappropriate responses.

Like this. How the hell had it wound up that he'd agreed to take her to a bar?

Still, even if he lost the job before he landed it, at least he'd be able to remind himself that he'd finally met Ava. More, that he'd had a drink with her.

Maybe this whole thing would be therapeutic. It could let him finally work the fantasy of her out of his system and—who knows?—have a real relationship with a flesh and blood girl, like his counselor always asked him about. Because *that* was so normal. Given all the truly fucked-up marriages in the world, you'd think the shrinks would have a different standard for reassimilating to society.

At least he'd managed not to put his hands on her, even though the demons pricked at him, the ache of desire crawling like the phantom kind. Maybe she was like that in his life—this fantasy girl he'd poured so much thought into. Being in her actual presence was like when he woke up at night, thinking it had all been a dream and his leg was normal. That he was healthy and fine and whole again. When he'd feel happy for a few moments.

Until brutal reality returned.

Don't think about it.

With care, he steered his thoughts from that topic. Some days, it didn't take much to bring back the event in overwhelming IMAX-worthy sound and images, complete with agonizing fear and the smell of blood and bowels. He'd left Arlin at home for the interview—no sense advertising his weakness—so it was particularly important to settle his not-always-reliable brain, especially in traffic like this.

Especially on a day like this one, with the nowhere zone hovering menacingly just past the edge of his peripheral vision. Too much input.

The definition of Ava. Everything that was too much to bear—and everything that sated him at the same time.

Still, it would just be the fucking cherry on the shit sundae of his life if he finally met Ava and melted down into a sniveling weenie in front of her. And that would be best-case scenario.

Fortunately, he had time to wrestle some self-control, as his question had apparently given Ava pause. She frowned over it, looking a little lost and waifish in the big back seat. Then she caught him looking and gave him that movie-star smile, a high gloss one that made him doubt what he'd glimpsed.

"Of course, Jacky boy," she purred. "What's the point of being me if I don't get my way?"

His cell rang. *Look at me, what do you see? A stranger who—*he stabbed it to silent, too late.

"Hey—that's my song!"

"Oh yeah?" *Shit.* "My baby sister is always messing with my phone. I don't know how to change it." A 212 number. Had to be Manning.

"Don't answer it," Ava said, steel in her tone.

"Ma'am, I—"

"I'm asking for an hour. No calls. Just… a little quiet, okay?"

He should turn the limo around. Call Manning back. It would be a simple matter to get an address and take her where she belonged.

Yet she'd looked so genuinely pleased when he agreed, clapping her hands like any of the teens that thronged her concerts. Genuine for an instant, with none of the posing. The real her looking through those much-too-cynical tawny eyes. Reminding him of his little sister, Nona, in a way. He wanted her happy, God help him.

"As you say, ma'am."

Off the main thoroughfares, the traffic thinned and they moved more quickly. He pulled up at a boutique hotel he sometimes chauffeured clients to, so he knew the doorman for a solid guy. He dug a Dodgers cap out of his messenger bag, pulled off his mirrored aviator glasses and passed them back to Ava. Reckless, all of this, but he couldn't seem to stop it. "Put these on or the deal's off."

She gave him an icily imperious stare-down in the rearview. "I've been here. I don't want a fancy hotel bar. I thought I made that clear."

"We're not stopping here. This is to discreetly ditch the car at a place I trust. Then we're walking. *If* you put on the cap and glasses."

"Aye-aye, Captain." She tossed off a cheeky salute in another quicksilver change of mood and donned the cap, looking ridiculously adorable in it. The glasses were big for her piquant face, which helped hide a bit of her unique and too-noticeable beauty.

He had to shake his head at her, suppressing a grin—and the

urge to seize her and taste that tantalizing skin. Just once. "Wait in the car a moment. And wipe off the lipstick, if you can."

"'Please,'" she reminded him archly.

"My apologies, ma'am." Forgetting himself left and right.

But she tilted her head slightly, her face remote and unreadable with her eyes obscured, a strange smile twisting her mouth into something wry. Almost self-deprecating. "I don't know what it is, Jacky boy, but I kind of like how you order me about. At least you're honest about it." She tipped down the sunglasses, blasting him with smoldering gold. "Just remember that you won't win."

He got out of the car before he dug himself into a deeper hole. His buddy Charlie waited politely, only a hint of a raised brow for the unusual circumstances. "Not your usual ride, Joe."

"Special client. Keep it on the down low and I'll owe you. Whatever you need."

"You know you owe me nothing. I'll stash it. Text when you're on the way back and I'll have it ready."

Joe clapped him on the shoulder. "And you didn't see a thing."

Charlie grinned. "Just a cheap-ass, dime-a-dozen car service. I'm supposed to remember them all?"

"Thanks, buddy." He let some passersby clear the sidewalk, then knocked on Ava's window. She popped out immediately, keeping her face averted. He didn't have much experience with real celebrities. Not like those other guys had—or claimed to have during their BS-ing while they all waited—but he should have expected she'd be a pro at passing unnoticed. She tugged at the bill of the cap and smirked. "Good disguise. Everyone knows I'm a Yankees fan. Where to?"

"This way." He started to turn, startled when she slipped a delicate hand into his—one that gripped with surprising tenacity when he tried to pull free.

"It improves the verisimilitude." She made it sound like a dare as she swung their joined hands and pulled him to the sidewalk. "Just a cute young couple out for an evening stroll."

A sweltering stroll, judging by the sweat rolling down his neck. It might be fall, but the summer heat hadn't quite relinquished its grip on the city. But that wasn't what got him. The casual touch lit him up like an inferno and he had to clear his throat twice to get the words out. "At least hold my right hand then."

"To free your gun hand?" With a twirl, she spun in front of him to the other side, hips twitching saucily. Classic Ava dance move. No way someone wouldn't recognize her, if she kept doing things like that. He would have. She claimed his right hand with the same fierce grip. "That's unusual—you're a lefty."

"Not so unusual. So are you," he replied, before he thought better of it, she had his brains so scrambled. That and the attention he devoted to scanning the street and passing traffic for threats. People looked at her, for sure, even not knowing who she was. She simply radiated that kind of intense charisma that drew the eye. But no one seemed unduly interested. Either they didn't recognize her or they were being polite in that weird way New Yorkers had of pretending not to see. One of the things he liked about the city. It helped that people didn't pay him much mind.

"How did you know that?" She squeezed his hand when he didn't reply immediately. "Huh?"

"I noticed you used your left hand more. Besides, a lot of artists and musicians are lefties."

"Are you an artist or musician, Jacky boy?"

"No, ma'am. Just a driver."

"And an Army Specialist."

"Not anymore."

"What does that mean—what are you special at?"

"It's just a rank. Mainly I was good at driving, not getting rattled. Keeping my cool." The vast irony of that. "That's all there is to say about that."

"What about hobbies?"

"Hobbies?"

"Yeah. Do you write novels in your spare time? Watch internet porn? Collect stamps?"

No, just everything I can find about you. He cleared his throat again. "'Fraid not, ma'am. I lead a pretty dull life."

She pursed her lips. She had wiped the glossy lipstick off, but red stained them still. "I think you shouldn't call me, ma'am out here. Not if we're being all incognito."

Paranoid, he scanned the faces around them, to see if anyone heard. "I can't call you by your name."

"True. You need to give me a nickname."

"I'm not giving you a nickname." Still three blocks from the bar he had in mind. He had no intention of drinking while on duty. Really he wasn't supposed to drink at all but a guy did what he could.

"I gave you one," she taunted, moving close enough that the curve of her breast brushed his arm, electrifying him through the layers of his jacket and dress shirt. "Jacky boy," she murmured, sounding entirely too sultry with it.

"I noticed."

"What do you call your girlfriends? I bet an All-American boy like you has so many that you call them all 'sugar' or 'baby' so you don't mix them up."

"Maybe I'm married."

"Nope. No ring."

"Not all guys wear wedding bands." Two blocks to go. Might as well have been miles of desert.

"You would though." She slid the glasses down and peeked at him over the top, the golden brown startlingly bright. Owl eyes. "Because you're a traditional kind of guy."

"I've never been married," he protested, "so I don't know if I would or not."

"Don't lie to me, Jacky boy." She hissed, pushing the glasses back up, but not before he caught a flash of that something sad darkening those brilliant eyes. "Remember—you promised."

"I don't know," he insisted, with the keen sense of relinquishing a live weapon into her hands. How long since he'd thought about anything like marriage as a possible thing? Forever. And he was not *sharing* that with her. He had to think back to the guy he'd been before. Younger, dumber and … okay, traditional in a hometown, don't-know-shit kind of way. "Okay, I probably would wear a ring."

"And you call your girlfriends sugar or baby."

"Both." Not exactly a lie, as he'd had girlfriends back in the day, and called them both of those things, and more. Those careless memories belonged to a different guy. One more block and he could divert her with her much-desired martini, maybe long enough to get his shit together.

"Do you have a girlfriend right now?"

"Not answering that one."

"That's a yes."

"No, that's a not answering. If you want me not to lie, I reserve the right not to speak on some topics. My love life is one." Forever off the table, in more ways than one.

Thankfully they reached the doors of The Bowery, a dark, narrow bar with lots of quiet shadowed tables. Classy, like her. Putting a hand on the small of Ava's back, telling himself to ignore the supple curve of it, to pretend it meant nothing to touch her there despite the savage chewing of the dogs of desire, he guided her to a booth in the back. When he seated himself opposite, she got up and scooted in next to him.

Didn't some guy say hell was other people? Yeah.

"Ma'am, I should be on the outside. And you should face the other way if you're taking off the sunglasses."

"I'll move to the other side and you sit next to me. Your left hand will be clear. Deal?"

"Look—"

"You'll have to manhandle me otherwise. Big commotion. Lots of attention."

He bit back a laugh, covering it with a sigh. How could he be entertained by her when she was driving him up the wall? Sitting next to her for however long it took her to suck down a martini would be torture. "Fine."

She moved, tucking herself back in the dark corner, and he settled in beside her. He couldn't see the door, but that wasn't the kind of attack he needed to worry about. He needed to focus on keeping the lid on. *Adjust your settings, gentlemen; we face a different enemy today.*

"I like this place. Good call," she commented, doffing the glasses and gazing around with bright-eyed interest, then fixing their devastating glow on him. "Interesting that you said 'love life' instead of 'sex life.'"

He groaned mentally at her tenacity. "The one we're not going to discuss? A lemon-drop martini for the lady," he told the waitress who did a rolling stop at their booth. "Club soda with lime for me."

Ava had ducked her face away from the waitress and now looked at him again. Not an idiot about being recognized, even as cavalierly as she behaved. Something of a relief, there, that she wouldn't deliberately out herself. She scowled at him. "You're not having a drink?"

"Club soda counts as a drink."

She wrinkled her nose. "Cute. Have a real drink."

"Not while I'm on duty. I have to stay sharp."

"I suspect you're always sharp. Always on guard, aren't

you?" She propped her elbow on the table, leaning her chin on her hand, the watch face glaring. 10:39. "Which leads back to the topic at hand. It's an interesting man who says love instead of sex. Different than the guy who says the reverse."

"I'm your driver. You don't need to find me interesting."

"And bodyguard," she murmured, making it sound dirty. Then she shrugged, the worn pink cotton tightening over her breasts, spangles catching the light. "What I need and what I want aren't the same thing. Besides, tonight you're my Jacky boy, taking me out on a date. Give me a nickname. Something you've never called any other girl. I want to be special."

He rubbed his eyes with thumb and forefinger, seriously wishing he could have a real drink. Or something stronger. He was beyond a fool to have gotten himself so deep into such dangerous territory.

"Is it that hard?" An edge crept into her voice, and she fidgeted with the watch. "I'll help. Sweetheart."

"Used," he replied without thinking.

"Darling."

"That too."

"Honey." She was tenacious as a pit bull.

How the hell was he supposed to remember? "Probably."

She laughed, too loud, and a little too musically. "Keep it quiet," he urged her, his brain losing the reason for discretion, bracing himself for sniper fire.

"I can't believe this!" She pressed her thigh to his. "You've used up every endearment in the book already and you're only…twenty-nine."

"Twenty-seven." At last, an easy answer, luckily as he couldn't think with her so near. That was in his paperwork anyway.

"No help for it. You're going to have to think up something unique for me." She slipped the hand with the watch under the table, averting her face and fiddling with a cocktail napkin as the waitress set down their drinks. Once the woman moved on, Ava flicked out a pink tongue to lick at the sugar rim, then tilted the glass to let the brimming liquid fill her mouth. "Omigod so good. Might as well flag her down to bring another."

"I thought we agreed on one drink."

"No, you ordered and I ignored. Besides—" She licked her lips and blew him a kiss that went straight to his groin and made the bad plates of his skull expand at the cracks. "*Besides,* I'm not driving." She licked her lips sensually and flicked the half-empty glass a significant look. With a shrug of mental resignation, he signaled the waitress for another. Maybe she'd be easier to manage if a little tipsy.

"Nickname, please, or I'll have to take steps."

Who was he kidding? She was no easier to manage than a Bengal tiger.

~ 5 ~

H E STARED AT that mouth, mesmerized by the crystal grains of sugar, utterly destroyed, bereft of any equanimity to buffer himself. Never in a million years could he tell her the name he called her in his private thoughts, eternally looping back to that night his grandmother showed him the owl. One of his many mental loops, signs of instability when they played too long and hard, crowding out everything else. …*the claws … if they were killed, their souls could use them to climb up to Heaven.*

What about the guys who only died inside? Scrambled, rattled, chopped into pieces and resurrected like zombies of their former selves—what did Russian folklore offer them?

The claws of the sova hadn't saved him, but Ava's eyes… those had brought him out of the depths. Even on flimsy magazine paper, they'd hooked his soul. Maybe not saving him, but at least suspending him far enough above the pit that he could pretend he wasn't plummeting into it at every second. Calling her something besides that would definitely count as lying. She might not know it, but he would. And he couldn't afford to start lying to himself again.

The pit breathed just below his dangling feet.

He was damned already.

"Sova," he told her softly.

She cocked her head, vividly intrigued, innocently unaware of his turmoil. "What does it mean?"

Instead of laying his hands on her as he itched to do with crazed need, he tugged on the brim of her ball cap. "Maybe someday I'll tell you."

"Nicely played." She dipped her chin, as if he'd scored a point in some game, then fixed him with her pit bull stare. "It sounds like Ava."

"Coincidence."

"I think you made it up."

"Nope." He took a deep swallow of the fizzy soda to keep from betraying anything else. If only he could ice his brain as easily.

"Then what language is it?"

"If I tell you that, you'll just look it up. What fun is that?" To his surprise, despite the chilling sense of having exposed himself to her, and the dread buzz of the nowhere zone eating at his cool, he grinned at her, surprised to find that on some surreal level he was having fun.

Maybe it was the sheer relief of calling her that, saying it aloud, like speaking the magic word finally, after having carried it around for so long. Not a symptom of infection or instability. Just a name. If she'd brought vivid life to his dreary world with her music and images, being with her magnified that by thousands.

She pursed her lips—impossibly lovely—narrowing her eyes like focusing the beam of a lamp. "I could just look it up no matter what. I should because it's not in English so that's not playing fair. Jack is at least the same language."

"Then what is it—Jack-in-the-box? Jack and Jill? Jack sprat could eat no fat?"

"Between us, we'll lick the platter clean. The perfect couple."

Couple? *Pull back, pull back.* He edged away, but she caught hold of his lapel, stopping him.

"Don't you think we make a good couple?" She asked, a hot

dare in the set of her mouth.

"I think I work for you." He threw it out there like a distraction, trying not to notice the way she smelled, rich and feminine, those eyes focused on his lips.

She leaned closer. "Kiss me, Jack."

"I can't do that, ma'am." He sounded firm enough that the desperation didn't entirely leak through.

"Call me Sova," she insisted, a bit of a mean edge to it. "That's real. The rest is a lie. I really hate lies, Jack."

She was right. That was real. Sad, too. He nearly kissed her, just to make her smile. Fortunately, the second martini arrived and she released him to lift it to her mouth, giving him a dark look over it.

+ + +

JOE LOOKED AWAY from her, turning the glass of club soda he'd been nursing like it was straight vodka in a careful circle between thumb and forefinger. He should have kissed her. Any other guy would have. And he would, too. She just had to find the cracks. He had a chewy center somewhere under that tough guy exterior. So enigmatic, with his taciturn, even grim smile. Then hints of an unexpected romantic side. *Sova.* What did it mean?

"We should go—you've been out of contact for too long. Your team will worry."

"Fuck my *team*." She didn't want to think about them.

"I'm on your team now." He cast her an opaque look. "Does that include me?"

"No, you're my special pal. What kind of gun do you carry?"

"I don't."

"Really?" How *interesting*. "I thought you military guys were all about more guns, save my ammo, and all that."

His jaw tightened and he gave her a long look. "Not that

you're stereotyping or anything."

"Then tell me about the real Jack. Why no gun?"

"I had enough of them, thank you."

"In the war."

"Exactly." He subsided, mouth set against say more on the topic.

"Why don't you want to kiss me?"

"Ma'am. Enough games. You got your second martini. It's time to go."

"I think I'll have one more."

"Dammit." He glared at her. She liked that about him best of everything, how he forgot who she was and simply showed his annoyance. Brutally honest, even when he tried to prevaricate.

"Don't glare at me like that. You broke your promise to call me sova, instead of ma'am."

He pressed his lips together and rubbed his temple by his ear. "Sova. There—can we leave now?"

"Fine." She could be gracious in victory and he had a point. She'd left her phone in the limo and without it she didn't know what time it was. One reason they'd even agreed to let her keep her phone, since she flat refused to budge on the watch. Dwight would surely be having a royal temper tantrum over her disappearance. Her time away from being Ava had run its course.

She'd have to go home, face Katey, and then tomorrow. And the next day. And the next. Depressing as hell. But… something about the way Joe rubbed his temple, faint lines of strain around his eyes, made her think he'd reached the end of his rope.

She might be brainless diva of a pop princess, but she could smell a meltdown from a mile off, even if it wasn't of the usual variety. Maybe this was the army vet kind. Regardless, cracking him beyond repair wouldn't entertain either of them.

Still, there was the problem of what else she didn't have.

"Only thing?" She smiled and cocked her head, hoping he wouldn't be too annoyed. "When I said you were going to buy me a drink, well… I meant that literally. But I can make sure you're reimbursed. With extra, even."

Yeah, she'd surprised him, but he didn't seem angry. Just dug out a worn leather wallet and a couple of twenties. "You don't carry money—not even a credit card?"

No, they didn't let her anymore. "I'm like the person in a life raft on the ocean—water, water everywhere and not a drop to drink." She tried to sound flip about it, adding extra dazzle to her smile, but he only shook his head and signaled the waitress for the tab.

He guided her out of the dark bar with that hand on the small of her back, a romantically protective gesture that kind of floored her. Though he'd been careful not to touch her in other ways, he treated her differently than the other bodyguards did. Like a real girl.

Joke was on him there.

Whatever the reasons Joe ended up in her preselected group, this wasn't his gig. Not really. Which made him all the more enticing. She'd be in for a hell of battle with Dwight to keep Joe, but it would be worth it, if only because he was so very wrong for the job.

Joe paced beside her with animal grace, arms loose at his sides, sharp gaze scanning the street, the traffic, the faces of every person that passed. He'd maneuvered her to the inside of the sidewalk, ready to block anyone who might approach, expression set in remote, taciturn lines again. War hero face. If she tried to make him hold her hand again, he'd refuse—that showed in the rigidity of his back, the way he held his fingers coiled for action. The way he buzzed with something fierce and feral. She wanted to run her hands over that, dig her nails into it.

Soon enough.

As they approached the hotel where Joe had stashed the limo, it became obvious that the place swarmed with people, a lot of them cops. Her limo sat at the valet stand. The last of the lovely vodka buzz faded, cold reality returning.

"Shit," Joe swore softly. "They found the car. Fuck!" The second curse emerged with razor-edged violence. "I knew better."

"Sorry." Really, *she* had known better, but had succumbed to unrealistic expectations, swept up in the adventure of it all. Practically her superpower, ignoring reality in favor of a compelling fantasy. "I left my phone in the limo, but they can track both if they want to. I really didn't think Dwight would move so fast. A couple of hours was all I asked for." Given all that had happened lately, you'd think he'd cut her that much fucking slack.

Joe ground his teeth, rubbing his temple again. "The car is chipped?" he said, his voice low and still somehow harsh.

"Yes. They'd chip me, too, if I let them. I practically have a satellite dedicated just to tracking me." *Like somebody's pedigreed dog*, she didn't say aloud. *Poor little rich girl.* Besides, he'd seen too much of pitiful Ava already. Time to tighten it up and don a harder shell again. To be Ava. A little damage control to make sure she got to keep her shiny new toy. "Don't worry, Jacky boy—I'll handle this."

✦　✦　✦

IN A QUICKSILVER move, she swept off the hat and sunglasses, running a hand through her hair and shaking the glossy blond waves free. In nearly the same graceful movement, she pulled a tube of lipstick from the coin pocket of her jeans, swiping it on left-handed, so practiced at the move that she didn't need a mirror.

As if she'd suddenly appeared among them like a manifesting goddess, people all around turned to stare, then to exclaim.

And rush her with shrieks of excitement.

Icy chill running down his spine, he tried to step in front of her, but she'd already slipped past him, holding open arms out to her fans. Hadn't he seen her do this very thing in hundreds of news clips and YouTube videos? She was glorious. She embraced her fans—literally—and they loved her for it.

In that moment, he hated her for it.

Bizarrely, her musical laugh rang out, cutting through his terror, along with the trill of her voice as she spoke to people. She'd put the cap back on and was signing autographs, for fuck's sake, that surprised and delighted expression on her face—as if she was forever astonished anyone recognized her, much less worshipped her.

Cold sweat soaked his dress shirt as an array of all the harm that could befall her flashed through his brain in jagged explosions of horror.

With a roar he dimly recognized as his own, he swept her up in his arms, dumping her over his shoulder and ignoring her shrieks and the screams of the fans. All of the sound shrilled over him, disconnected from the emotions that drove them. He put his head down and bulled through the crowd, soft limbs and the sweeping hair of girls falling before his charge.

Reaching the limo, he yanked open the door and tossed her in. A brief flash of her scarlet face and mouth open in a snarl. Then gone.

Safely behind mirrored glass.

One of her bodyguards slammed him up against the car, beefy hands pinning him there by the shoulders. The impact actually helped clear his brain. Sobbing girls and furious handlers. Charlie off to the side, mouth hanging open.

"What in God's holy hell possessed you?" Manning snarled,

ducking his head under the guy's arm. "What in fuck is going on here?"

Joe grabbed at his thoughts. *Take your time. There are words for what you feel. Use them.* Not the right situation, though, to express his fucked-up emotions. "I handled the situation," he got out, biting back the automatic 'sir' that wanted to follow. "I extracted and protected the client."

"You came fucking recommended by Hart and McGrath and you pull shit like this? You don't manhandle Ava."

Thankfully his thoughts were clearing, the nowhere zone receding. Action always helped, even the wrong kind. "Respectfully, she needed it. She doesn't listen well."

The meathead holding him snorted back a laugh and the grip eased up. Manning, however, was not amused. "Beyond that." He waved his hands. "Taking her out of contact like that. What the fuck were you thinking? Where the fuck did you go? Why the hell didn't you answer your phone?"

"I was thinking that I work for her and she calls the shots," he replied evenly.

"Well, you're twice wrong, dipshit." The manager leaned in. A bulldog of a man, he didn't have the height to intimidate, but made it up in ferocity. And spittle. "You don't work for her unless I say so and I don't. And if I lost my ever-fucking mind and actually did hire you, I call the shots, not the talent."

"Understood, sir." He said it partly out of habit, partly to do whatever it took to end the conversation, to get himself home where he could finish the job of getting his head on straight again. The whole gig had been unreal—so much so that it didn't count as a lost opportunity. At least he'd met her. Touched her, even.

Another fragment of the fantasy for his broken brain to ponder.

Probably he should have kissed her instead of wussing out.

He'd had the chance to do what he'd only fantasized about, and now he'd lost his shit in a spectacular way and would never see her again. He'd be lucky if they didn't sue.

He should have kissed her.

He needed to go home.

"I don't think you do understand," Dwight was saying through an eggplant-faced sneer. "I'm having you brought up on charges of kidnapping. When I get done with you, no one in this town will hire you to drive a sidewalk cart. You can go all the way back to buttfuck, Kentucky and no one will hire you there either!"

Seriously—people actually said shit like this? And here he'd thought it was just in the movies. Anyway, he'd had enough. He needed out. "That would be West Buttfuck, sir."

Manning sputtered to a confused halt. "What the hell are you talking about?"

"West Buttfuck—or West Buechel if you're talking to my mama—is where I'm from."

"Do you think I give a rat's ass? You're never seeing your mama again because you'll be locked up for a felony. You'll be lucky if these fine people don't press charges, too." He clenched his fists, and Joe readied himself. He had his worst instincts on a leash again, but one too tenuous to trust himself not to hit back. And once he started down that ugly road, there was no going back.

Manning thought better of it, gesturing to the guard to release him and stalking off to the other side of the limo. He pointed a beefy finger at Joe over the roof. "Don't leave town. Stay available."

The guy sounded like the movie version of himself.

"So much for the down low, huh?" Charlie came up next to him, watching Ava's limo part the waves of fans who lingered, bouncing and calling gleefully as if he hadn't run through them like a linebacker. The blank mirrors of the limo windows reflected the flash of cameras, both amateur and professional, as it eased onto the street, taking Ava out of his world again.

"A word to the wise," Charlie cut through the mist in his head. The man nodded at the professionals, their equipment that looked like it could track satellites. "Soon as those guys figure the photo op is over, they'll come sniffing around you, dig out the story. They got some pretty nice film. You might want to get gone."

Sure enough, with Ava out of reach, a couple of faces already turned in his direction, speculative expressions sharpening.

"Unless you want to make some extra dough," Charlie added cheerfully. "'My date with Ava.' Wouldn't be the first."

"It wasn't a date," he muttered as he turned. Probably he should have kissed her.

"Not that way, buddy." Charlie hit a button and a side door to the underground garage opened. "Take the stairs to delivery and go out the back. Subway's a quick jog."

"Thanks." He ducked inside. "Sorry for the trouble."

"Yeah man—that was something to see. Always the quiet ones."

~ 6 ~

B Y THE TIME Dwight tunneled into the cool interior of the limo, Ava had her earbuds firmly implanted, her head full of Elle King's raunchy bad girl lyrics. No princess image there. No one called Elle human lip gloss. Hulk sat across from her, hulking, while Igor drove. Wolverine had probably been smart enough to clear out of collateral-damage range and had hit some happy hour out there, as advised.

Pretending to listen to the music let her assimilate the afternoon's wild ride. Her heart still pounded from being thrown over Joe's shoulder, the primal thrill mixing exotically with the light vodka buzz. Sure he'd royally pissed her off with that Tarzan routine, but wow—that shoulder. And how he'd looked when he tossed her into the limo, that vein bulging in his temple.

He'd melted down all right, and whatever demons drove him were violent ones. *So* interesting. He gave her literal shivers.

And he was perfect for the job.

Not for being her driver, necessarily, though he seemed to be qualified enough. Driving didn't take all that—no matter what the Mario Andretti wannabes boasted, especially in the city gridlock, as Joe had sensibly pointed out. But even she could admit that being her near-constant companion did require a certain skill set. Being interesting topped that list.

The man interested her and she wanted more, more, more.

She didn't kid herself that she was low-maintenance. In all

honesty, she was about as high-maintenance as a girl could get and she wasn't going to apologize for it. That ship sailed and sank in a hurricane years ago. Joe… he had a knack for both holding his own in a nicely masculine way and simultaneously keeping that maintenance level nice and high.

Despite his propensity to lose his shit—and she'd take some of the blame for what happened—Joe had handled the situation. *Extracted and protected the client,* he'd said as she shamelessly eavesdropped through the cracked window. Damn, if that didn't make a girl feel special. Like a treasure in the quest movie. She needed him. More, she wanted him. Therefore, by God, she would have him. It wasn't just the hard-to-get either. Though his inexplicable resistance added a nice zing.

Dwight would not stymie her on this one. He sat opposite, arms crossed as he fumed at her silently, his lecture subsided in the face of her noise-canceling inattention. In this mood, he'd just follow her up to the penthouse and hound her until she capitulated or threw enough of a tantrum that he'd leave her alone.

Might as well settle it in the car. She pulled out the earbuds.

"I want Joe Ivanchan as my driver."

To her surprise, her manager didn't meet her line in the sand with an immediate and heated refusal. Instead he rubbed his forehead, looking tired. And not at all surprised. "Ava, darling—he's a loose cannon. You saw what happened just now, he lost his ever-loving shit, he could have hurt you."

"He didn't. He protected me. Isn't that his job?"

Dwight returned her stare evenly. "I don't have the energy to put up with your whims, Ava. Fuck him if you have to—God knows I've never been able to stop you there—but don't make me put one of your boy toys on the payroll. Especially someone unstable."

Unusual for him to be so forthright. Maybe Henry had made

them all behave better, just by being present. Or Dwight might be truly fed up. A good time to push for what she wanted then. Hulk stared out the window, pretending he wasn't listening.

"I didn't fuck him."

"I know you, Ava—don't blow sunshine up my ass. You've got that look about you. If you didn't already, you want to, but— listen to me—you had your fun tonight, fine, you deserved to blow off some steam, but be smart about this. Being on your staff puts him too close to you when things go south."

When. Not if. "You just assume things will go badly."

He returned her glare with a pointed one of his own. "You're telling me you think this guy could be the love of your life? C'mon—you're Ava. You could buy and sell him a hundred, maybe a thousand times over. He's a grunt, obviously messed up in the head, maybe a real danger to you. You have the idea you can keep him a leash, but he'll be like one of those pit bull puppies that snaps one day and dismembers the toddler. Only with you it'll be all over the tabloids, and not in a good way— remember what happened before and that unholy shitstorm. Do you really want to put us all through that again? Think about Katey if you don't care about the rest of us."

The slow burn of anger soured her stomach. Along with the bitterness of shame. Her "team" had pulled her out of more than one relationship disaster. Several of which had fed the tabloids for months. None as bad as the Epic Disaster. But she'd paid the price for that, hadn't she? She'd let Katey take over the social media; let Dwight take all his steps to keep her from messing up again. Still, the unfairness of it made her unwilling to back down.

"You know, Dwight, I might be a diva, but you've got it pretty damn easy. If you managed someone like Justin Bieber or Harry Styles, you'd be shoveling girls out of his hotel room on a daily basis. Hell, you'd be picking them out, trolling the pit and handing out backstage passes to the cutest ones like candy, to keep him supplied for the night. And then you'd be worrying about which ones tried to claim paternity."

"Yeah, but—"

She cut him off, fully pissed. "Don't you dare say that they're guys, that boys will be boys. Or that they have *needs*. I have needs. Be grateful you manage a woman and I don't ask you to do that."

"I wouldn't be able to, since your audience is 99 percent female or gay," he retorted.

"Fuck you for that," she said in a soft tone. Of course, he was right. Her fans weren't guys for the most part. Sometimes dads who accompanied their daughters, always easy to spot. Occasionally a guy with his girlfriend. Men didn't take her seriously in general—her music or her person. Joe hadn't kissed her when he could have though. "I'm making a valid point here."

Dwight bit back whatever he'd been about to say. Igor glanced cautiously in the mirror, though Hulk steadfastly stared out the window.

"Look, Ava darling." Dwight sighed. "You've had a long day and you're overtired. Things will look brighter in the morning, tomorrow is another day."

Taking refuge in his clichés. "That worked when I was twelve. Find a new song and dance."

He rubbed his scalp ruefully. "Actually it didn't work so well then, either. You're nearly home. Can we table this and discuss in the morning—when you're sober at least?"

"I'm barely buzzed and you were the one who decided to bring up my sex life." Not love life, like Joe had said. Guy like him should have said sex, not love. Word choice revealed a lot about people, but she wasn't sure yet what that had revealed about him. And he'd had enough of guns. Still waters ran deep.

"So, by all means, let's talk about it. I'm a legal adult with a reasonable grasp on my sanity. I'm abiding by the publicity decisions. I'm also not dead, so if I find someone I want and he wants me, that's *my* choice and you never get to say another word to me about it or I *will* fire you."

He gaped, his hairpiece slightly askew from scratching at it. "You wouldn't. After all we've been through together, after I—"

"I would." She managed to say it gently, with all the seriousness it warranted. No idle threat. "I don't want to do that. Despite our differences, you're a good manager and I want to be loyal to that. But I'm not letting you run my sex life. Clean up after me if you feel it's warranted. You and Katey do your magic to keep it off social media and the tabloid covers. But deal with the fact that who I do or don't take to bed is entirely up to me, as long as I keep it discreet. No one thinks I'm a virgin—that horse left the barn a *long* time ago. Besides which, we're not talking about a lover. This is a conversation about hiring a driver and bodyguard. You offered an approved candidate and I accepted. You don't get to do bait and switch because you happened to give me one I like."

"It's not bait and switch, Ava! That guy came from the agency, but he's borked in the head, you saw! Pick one of the others, one who won't help you hare off without warning anyone."

"No. He's the one I want. At least on probation. I won't fuck him and I won't take off without informing you. But I do want to be able to take some time away. I need that. I'm a woman, not a little girl who needs to be chaperoned 24/7. I'm losing my mind like some zoo animal caged up all the time."

"It's not my fault that Katey is—"

"Don't go there," she cut him off. "Leave her out of it."

He sighed and pinched the bridge of his nose. "Maybe we can work it out with someone besides him."

"No. You vetted him, so I know he passes muster on paper.

Today he proved he could take care of me in any number of situations." *Extracted and protected the client.* "He passed with flying colors."

Dwight shook his head, clearly done. "Don't try to convince me that you pulled this stunt as some kind of test."

"Do you know what the difference is between a circus act and a chorus line?"

His brows drew together. "No, and I don't want to."

"You can fill in the blanks. The first is a cunning array of stunts."

A muscle bulged in his jaw. "Are you done?"

"Today wasn't a stunt any more than I'm a—"

"Fine." He clapped hands over his ears in case she said it anyway. "Trial basis, I'll write up the papers."

She restrained a squeal of joy, though she did indulge in a little seated shimmy of victory, then composed herself. "Thank you, Dwight," she managed to say in a dignified tone.

"Just don't fuck him, okay? Leave the staff alone."

Hulk coughed into his hand, coloring slightly. Like she'd do him. He should be so lucky.

"I said I wouldn't. I never fucked Hulk. Or you."

He ignored that. She had to credit him, and it was a strong reason she hadn't ever fired him—despite everything, Dwight had never laid a finger on her.

"You say a lot of things, Ava. You think about this one, think of your image if nothing else, you're not Madonna with a coffee-table sex book in the making to document your exploits. Your image is about values."

Ah, the irony of that. "Maybe that needs to change."

"Oh yeah." He threw up his hands. "You say that like you don't remember what happened the last time you tried that."

She shrugged, pretending he hadn't scored so deeply. He'd agreed to what she wanted, so she wouldn't call him on it. The limo pulled into the secure garage, Igor getting out to sweep the area before knocking on the window to give Hulk the all clear.

"I'm serious, Ava. This is the advice I earn my 20 percent for."

"Whatever. It's still my career to make or destroy. I want Joe to drive me in the morning. And to the benefit concert tomorrow night."

"What if some of your fans file charges and he's in jail? He knocked down several of those girls."

"Handle it. *That* is why you earn your 20 percent."

"Not everyone can rearrange their lives in at a moment's notice to suit your whims, he might not be available," he warned.

For good measure—and maybe to rattle her manager just a bit more—she kissed him on the cheek before getting out of the car. "I trust you to make it happen."

~ 7 ~

F or Arlin's sake, he'd left the window air conditioner on, barely effective as it was, so his apartment felt blessedly cool—at least compared to the subway platform. Nothing like the heat sink of the city, even in late September. Out on the shore it would be different. There the pound of cool surf against the rocks would soften the air. He should take a couple of days to visit the cabin, decompress a little. Reduce input so his brain could heal.

But he'd made it home without punching anyone, so that was something.

Now get me out of here before I have to kill someone. That smile of Ava's as she said that... It had enough of an edge she might have meant it.

Arlin met him at the door, sheer delight at his return filtered through guilt-inducing woeful eyes at being left behind. Joe dropped to his knees, burying his face in Arlin's fluffy golden fur, inhaling the stabilizing scent of home and peace, accepting the slobbery penance the dog exacted. The sense of vacuum beneath his feet lessened, like he'd sunk back to solid earth. Despite the reproach, Arlin loved him without judging. Let him be only himself.

With the dog, he sometimes forgot what a fucking wreck he was.

"Sorry, buddy. I couldn't take you today. Wasn't driving my

own car." Things might have gone down differently if he had taken Arlin along, but who could have predicted the job interview would not only pan out, but turn into that escapade? And he wouldn't have been able to take Arlin into the bar anyway, not without pulling the service dog card, and he hated going through that routine. Ava probably thought he was a psycho as it was.

And she wouldn't be wrong.

He rubbed his forehead. Hell if he hadn't totally lost his shit back there.

Arlin wriggled, willing to forgive anything in exchange for a run. Though Joe longed to flop down with an ice-cold beer—or a few vodka shots—and some personal time with photos of Ava, he knew he'd be better for the exercise, too. *Healthy choices.* Yeah, right.

"Hang on, buddy. Let me change."

Arlin followed him into the bedroom, dubious woe transforming to dancing-in-place joy when Joe pulled out his running pants and shoes.

Mrs. Lassle, the landlady, took Arlin out a few times a day when Joe had to leave him behind, but nothing substituted for their own time together. Or a good run instead of Mrs. Lassle's leisurely pace. The golden lab was Mrs. Lassle's single exception to the no-pets-over-ten-pounds building policy. He'd had to swallow his pride and show her Arlin's service dog certification, and then only because he'd had no choice if he wanted a place to live.

You'd think a guy who'd faced down what he had wouldn't mind explaining to a stranger why he needed a service dog, but it made him break out in a cold sweat every time. His counselor had made the suggestion that he take an informative pamphlet to hand over with the certification, and that had shut Mrs. Lassle up all right. In fact, he'd picked the apartment in her building over a nicer one because she hadn't kept asking questions, or acted like he might start shooting up the place.

Though she liked to complain about the trouble, Joe knew she secretly enjoyed having the dog around—and she saved him the exhaustion of explaining to the other tenants why Arlin was an exception to the rule, telling them in no uncertain terms to leave the topic alone on the grounds that she could get sued. Questionable logic, but he kind of loved the old lady for it. Now Arlin was practically the building mascot. His impeccable manners and natural charm helped smooth the way, too.

Now that Joe got around on the prosthetic pretty well, he didn't need Arlin as constantly anymore. At least, he told himself he was weaning himself away from depending on the dog so much. Arlin had gotten him through those first difficult months out of the hospital, fetching for him, being a stable pillar against his side when he got dizzy or lost his balance. Making him leave the damn apartment and deal with the world.

Lapses like today, though, showed how fast he danced over the edge of the nowhere zone without Arlin there. Something he didn't care to think about too closely, because facing up to the fact that he might not ever get better than this… He didn't know if he could live like that forever.

Oh yeah? Got any alternatives to that, buddy?

Running would help settle his brain.

Shucking the suit, he yanked on an Army t-shirt—he had enough to last the rest of his life—and nylon running pants. Other guys with the same prosthesis wore shorts and didn't care who saw. Not just about the shorts either—some even posed naked for that Michael Stokes photographer. Not him. He hated for anyone to see it.

Even his mother.

Especially his mother.

He didn't get those guys. Probably they just pretended to be all tough and uncaring, because anyone could see what a messed-up thing that was. Ugly as sin, his mother would say. Another reason he'd never go home to West Buttfuck, Kentucky, even if Manning managed to make good on his threat. Stupid to even think about, though. New York was a big freaking city and one guy couldn't shut him out of every job.

All the therapy had been about facing the reality of his new state of being. *Not less than you've been, just different!* He'd forever hear that in the perky voice of the occupational therapist who'd never quite looked him in the eye. He got it—lies were part of the job for both of them.

He wouldn't kid himself, though, not about that. He'd become the easy target. Predators cull out the weak and the sick. Despite all the technology, the veneer of civilization, human beings still possessed their baser instincts, including the ones that nudged them to shun the weak, to ostracize the sick, hoping to save themselves.

In the end, everyone only wanted to save their own hide.

In the back of his mind, his instincts shrilled at how they stared at him, seeing him like that wounded bachelor gazelle on the nature shows, hamstrung by a lion's swipe and hanging out on the edge of the herd, forever trying to blend in. Never getting to breed. Serving time until he was useful enough to distract another lion with his pitiful death while the others ran away in their glossy health.

Arlin, on the other hand, loved to get his leash on—though Joe never used that fucking service dog harness. It shouted of his weakness and it had to be uncomfortable, though Arlin never seemed to mind. Sometimes Joe really envied the dog, that simple pleasure in life, not caring what anyone thought. Living in the moment and all that.

They headed out, the heat thankfully backing off with the intense autumn sun setting. They'd jog along the sidewalk until they got to the little park and do a few circuits until the good sweat replaced the shaky kind.

He'd come a long way, yes, but the collision with Hurricane Ava had left him reeling, setting him further back than he'd gone in a while. Probably his counselor would say something like that dealing with the amputation and recovery by immersing himself in his obsession with Ava had tied all of those complicated emotions together. He could conjure the words, the psychological explanation for his fuckedupedness, though they meant little so far as actually coping like a normal guy.

Weirdly though, as much as dealing with her had undermined his cool, Ava had also been kind of steadying. Like Arlin was. She'd been so present for him all those bedridden days in the hospital, her voice crooning in his ear, dancing through videos on his tablet, gazing out of photos with those somber owl eyes. *Sova.*

Maybe it was like physical therapy—it left you sore and exhausted but ultimately healthier. That would be a nice spin on the whole shit storm of the afternoon.

He slowed and stopped for Arlin to do his business, then Joe popped the poop bag in the trash can. They headed back at an easier jog, his body finally feeling more limber and relaxed—until they rounded the corner to see Ava's creamy limo idling at the curb out front. Fuck him if his heart didn't actually skip a beat at the sight, the insidious buzz of the nowhere zone vibrating his skull plates.

It was the surprise. He still didn't deal well with surprises.

A burst of panic followed that was grounded in actual reality. She could never see his place. They'd lock him up for sure.

To his relief, not Ava but Dwight Manning emerged from the car at his approach. It went a long way toward confirming what a personal nightmare it would be for Ava to see how he lived that he was actually relieved to see the little shit.

"Joe." Manning held up a hand in greeting. "Nice looking mutt."

"Golden Labrador—from a breeder. Thanks."

"My bad, my bad," the other man replied, rocking from heel to toe and back again.

"Here to make a citizen's arrest?" Joe sounded good to his own ear, the light press of Arlin against his good leg a reassuring presence.

Manning lifted both hands in a palms-up shrug of peace. "I was pissed before and I'll apologize for it."

Joe darted a glance at the opaque car windows. "She in there?"

"No." Manning raised his eyes to the sky. "Thank the heavens, she's safely ensconced in her penthouse for one more night. I have maybe twelve hours before I have to start panicking again." As if reminded, he pulled out a roll of Tums, thumbed three into his mouth and eyed Joe, crunching loudly. "Ava wants you hired."

Totally unexpected after the day's debacle. "What happened to you calling the shots, not her?"

He made such a rueful grimace that Joe felt a glimmer of unexpected sympathy for the guy. "Tell you what—after you've worked for her for a week, you can buy me a drink, or twenty, and tell me what you think about that."

Joe could just imagine. With a little distance from the gravity well of Ava's charismatic charm, however, he could also reconsider the wisdom of subjecting himself to working for her. He'd resisted the invitation to kiss her, but barely. If she suggested it again, he didn't know what would happen.

Who was he kidding? He'd cave at the least quirk of her sparkly-tipped little finger.

"I appreciate the offer, and you coming all the way out to Brooklyn to tell me, but I think I have to decline."

Manning leaned against the limo, folding his arms and studying the sidewalk. "You know, an hour ago I would have danced a jig to hear that. I think you're trouble, I think you're whacked in the head, and I'd pay good money to have you well away from Ava."

"But? I don't see you making like a happy leprechaun."

The man snorted. "No wonder she likes you, both of you, contrary as fuck. Thing is—she wants *you*. And keeping Ava happy is my job. She thinks having you as her driver will do that, so I'm here to make it happen." He pulled a money clip out of his inside jacket pocket, peeled off a hundred and held it out. "First off, she wanted you reimbursed for the drinks. Plus extra."

Numbly, Joe took it. "It wasn't anywhere near this much."

Manning shrugged. "Plus extra," he repeated. "Besides, if you drive for her, you'll need petty cash for when she wants stuff. Just keep a record."

"Why doesn't she carry her own money?"

Manning put hands on hips, staring at the sidewalk and shaking his head. "You have no idea the history we're dealing with. And I don't have all night. Let's talk what it will take to get you on the payroll. You make, what—seventy-five K as a driver?"

"A bit more, if the tips are running hot." And if you extrapolated a really good month over the whole year, but no sense adding that.

"I'll double it. Plus the other perks Ava promised." He sounded a bit disgusted about that. Joe flinched a little, thinking of her purred suggestions and outright demand for a kiss, but realized Manning meant her other glib guarantees. He'd wondered if Ava knew what that would cost. Probably not, if they kept her as sheltered from reality as it seemed.

But the money was better than good. Pretty much an offer he couldn't refuse, even if he could bring himself to walk away from the chance to see her again. Who knew? He'd probably be out on his ass inside of a week.

"I'll give you ten grand up front," Manning added, clearly mistaking Joe's hesitation. Call it a hiring bonus. And if you don't last a full month, I'll give you the full month's salary on top of that."

"Generous," was all Joe could think of to say. Particularly in light of their earlier encounter.

"Not exactly." Manning smiled without humor. "I figure you won't last the month, so it's a short-term investment."

"Gee, thanks."

Manning shrugged, unconcerned. "I got an eye for people and I think you've got deep cracks. But Ava's brought you home like a dying baby bird, so I'm letting her keep you. You'll at least keep her energy occupied."

He had no response to that, so he ruffled Arlin's ears. *Deep cracks.*

"Think of your job as petting the golden goose and keeping her safely in her cage. That's what I do. Those priceless eggs she lays is what it's all about. You'll learn to do whatever it takes. There's one caveat to all of this, however."

"What's that?"

"You still report to me. If she talks you into spiriting her off someplace again, go along within reason. Keep it out of the papers and offline; keep me informed at all times. And fucking her is strictly off limits. You do it, you're gone." Manning might not be a big guy, but the look he leveled at Joe reminded him of his high school girlfriend's dad, the one who'd promised to shoot him and dump his body in the Ohio River if anything happened to his daughter.

He decided not to touch the bit about sex. That would never happen, for any number of reasons. "Agreed—as long as she knows I'm reporting to you on her movements. I promised not to lie to her."

Manning cracked a grin at that. "Did you? You'll break that promise soon enough. Ava doesn't really want to hear the truth—she only thinks she does. Mark my words, you'll be far better off telling her what she wants to hear."

It put his back up, to hear Manning talk about her that way. She was far sharper than her manager gave her credit for.

"Does that piss you off?" Manning chuckled, not nicely. "Did I insult your lady love? Word to the wise, buddy—she'll break your heart if you let her. She won't even mean to. She's like a toddler with expensive toys. One minute she loves them, the next she breaks them just to see what happens. Take my advice—idolize her if you can't help yourself, but don't be stupid."

That he believed. "Understood."

"All right then." Manning tapped the window and took the file folder that was handed out. "Let's get your John Hancock on these documents. Including a non-disclosure agreement. That should be no surprise. Shall we go up to your place?"

No way he could let Ava's manager see his apartment either. "Something wrong with the hood of the car?"

Manning gave him a disgusted look. "No, no—why wouldn't I want to stand out here on the city street. Let's sit in the car at least. Climb in and let's get this shit signed so I can have a goddamned drink."

Amen to that.

~ 8 ~

"WHERE HAVE YOU been?" Katey demanded, meeting Ava as she walked in the door. "It's been *hours*. I've been tweeting about chick flicks, fielding movie suggestions, picked one, and then pretended to be you watching it. I hope you appreciate me." She waved her tablet in demonstration.

"Bless you." Flush with the success of her power play, she impulsively hugged her sister, her too-thin bones sharp to the touch, guilt similarly spikey that she hadn't given Katey a thought while she'd been out. Of course Katey had been waiting for Ava to come home to the quiet and empty penthouse.

"Ugh." Katey ducked away. "You smell like bar. Disgusting."

"What movie did you watch?"

"You mean what did *you* watch? I don't exist, only you do. *Black Swan*."

A pain stabbed behind Ava's eyes. Katey had a knack for payback. Not that she didn't deserve to do it, but… ouch. Ava kept her tone nonchalant. "Oh, yeah?"

"You know, we started to watch it once and then you bailed. Natalie Portman is this oh-so-perfect, neurotic ballerina with a psycho mother. Remember?" Katey stared her down. She had in the green contact lenses that never looked quite right. Too YA alien book cover.

"Vaguely." A lie, which Katey knew. A poor choice of one because Katey smiled, enjoying herself.

"She's the star. The prima ballerina dancing in *Swan Lake*. She's perfect as the white swan, but she has to dance the black swan, too, and she can't because she's so sexually repressed. But that's not you, is it?"

"Katey… I don't have the energy for this." Great—now she sounded like Dwight.

"Yeah. You've been working all day, being the superstar. Not like me. Sitting around on my worthless ass."

"You're not—"

"Did you remember Winona's in it? She plays the has-been. The aged-out little princess. She runs out in front of a car because she can't handle being a nobody."

Okay. Ava took a deep breath.

"Anyway, you never saw the end. Natalie kills herself. Because she knows she'll never be anything more than she is at that moment. Maybe you could say she kills the image of herself. The one she wants to destroy. The one she hates." The unnatural green of Katey's eyes caught the glint of the hall sconces.

"Kates—why do that to yourself? It's not healthy."

"For you, of course." Katey pushed back her limp blond curls. She hadn't washed her hair in days and it showed. "Everything's about you."

The moment hummed between them and Ava didn't know what to say to end it.

"Anyway." Katey shrugged it off, going listless. "Now you never have to run the risk of actually seeing it. It wasn't like I had anything better to do. You're welcome."

The cocktails soured in her stomach, but Ava nodded. "Yes—thank you." Katey still blocked her way and touching her again could be iffy. The impulsive hug had been wrong-headed.

"I mixed martinis. Want one?" Katey offered, breaking the stilted silence. A peace offering of a kind.

"Sure."

"And dinner is waiting. A bit dried out now, but … whatever."

"I can come help plate it up."

"Don't make me feel useless." At least with that remark Katey moved, tossing the tablet onto the coffee table in front of the big screen. She'd frozen it on an image of Natalie as the dying white swan, blood spreading through her pristine beaded costume.

Deliberately ignoring it, Ava flopped onto the white leather couch that faced the view of the Hudson instead. The city lights were emerging like stars as the evening darkened. "What horrible thing does Celine have planned for our gastronomic punishment?" she tried, keeping it as light as possible.

"Not bad tonight. Sea bass, roasted brussels sprouts with a jess a glahze of 'oney. You weel lahv eet." Katey called back from the kitchen, mimicking the nutritionist/cook's French accent mercilessly. They had dubbed her Celine for her dramatic ways. A good sign if Katey was trying to be playful.

And the food didn't sound too bad. Better than yet another salad, but not at all appetizing either. Why hadn't she ordered bar food when she had the chance? Nachos. An artichoke dip. A cheeseburger. Something. A lost opportunity.

But she'd played it well with Dwight, hadn't she? There would be more time with Joe. Maybe even a chance to have a cheeseburger.

Katey set the tray with two perfectly sugared lemon-drop martinis on the crystal coffee table—along with an insulated shaker that would contain refills—and a plate of Celine-approved cocktail snacks. Low-fat cheese, grapes, celery with hummus. Joy. Why hadn't she ordered food? "So? Spill." Katey raised her brows, the wrong green unsettling in her hollow face.

"Spill what?" Ava snagged a celery and chomped before swigging from the martini glass, swallowing her disappointment.

The ones at the bar had been better, even though Katey had used a much higher grade of vodka. Those had been… brighter. More vivid.

Katey sniffed, pursing her mouth in hurt. "Fine. Be that way. But I know you slipped the leash. Dwight called looking for you. Four times."

"What did you tell him?"

"That he's your keeper. I'm just your good twin," Katey said, her tone making their old joke a pointed reminder.

They obviously weren't twins, but the family resemblance put them close enough that, in her better days, Katey had stood in as Ava's doppelgänger in real life as well as online, particularly if they needed to divert the paparazzi or get Ava in and out of a concert on time. She hadn't asked Katey to do it, all those surgeries and the other work to "improve" herself. By the time she'd realized how far it had gone, well… Well, Katey wouldn't ever be the star she'd sacrificed to be.

Anyway, water under the bridge. These days that simply wouldn't be possible, at least not in real life. Katey continued to live as Ava's alter ego, her virtual self who scintillated online, her physical body haunting the penthouse like a banshee walking the moors and wailing Ava's sins to the world. Black swan to her white. Or vice-versa. It could be hard to sort.

I'm just your good twin.

Regardless, if not for Ava, Katey might be living a normal life, not a vicarious one. Ava owed her the story of her day, at least, much as something about the encounter with Joe made her want to keep it a special secret, just for herself. Katey would eventually know all of Ava's business anyway.

"Dwight showed me his approved group of drivers to replace Henry."

"Oh." Katey sobered, tears welling up. "Right—we talked about it at the Monday meeting. It feels too soon." Katey had been missing Henry too, the one steady figure since the early tumult of *Tween Hangout*, when she and Ava had both been brand new starlets. "But you have so many places to go," Katey added. "The show must go on!"

"Dwight is determined, so I had to do something—at least try to pick someone good."

"A bodyguard, too," Katey offered with scorn. "You know they'd never hurt you."

Ava wasn't having that conversation again. They'd argued about this enough times, always culminating in Katey getting hysterical. So she shrugged it off. "You heard them in the meeting. I'm not planting my flag on that hill. They want someone to drive me who can also handle crowd control? Fine. Whatever."

Unhappy, Katey nevertheless dropped the topic, nibbling on a grape. Celine's meal management kept Katey out of the danger zone, but she still barely ate. Old habits—and ambitions—don't just die hard, some never do, like shuffling zombies. Healthy fitness turned into a gaunt monstrosity. Determined to set a good example—and keep herself from going down that dark path—Ava took several hummus-laden celery stalks and munched, pretending they were nachos. Joe probably liked that kind of thing, a good, greasy cheeseburger, French fries and a beer. She should have made him take her to do that.

"And?" Katey prompted.

"And what?"

"The drivers. Are you tracking this conversation?"

"Of course I am. It's just been a long day." One with unusual experiences, which didn't happen often. "Do you know what 'sova' means?"

Katey leaned forward and took the nearly-empty martini out of her hand. "No more booze for you until you've eaten real food."

"I'm not drunk," she snapped. Dwight had thought so, too. It took way more than that to give her a buzz. Her liver was practically titanium.

"Just cray-cray. I'll get our dinner."

"I don't want any fucking sea bass."

"What do you want?"

A cheeseburger. "I'm not hungry." So much for being a good example.

"You said you already had two martinis and you just slammed that one. I bet you haven't eaten anything since the salad Celine sent with you for lunch."

She hadn't eaten that either. Too nauseated by the songs they'd trotted out for her to record and—let's face it—too depressed to face even delightfully prepared and balanced greens. Why hadn't she ordered a cheeseburger? Dropping her head against the couch, she stared up at the skylights, feeling a few tears leak out of her eyes. Maybe she *was* drunk.

She wanted to ask if Katey thought she was human lip gloss, but she was afraid to hear the answer.

"Just tell me what happened today." Katey sounded exasperated enough that Ava would have to tell her something. But she didn't want to talk about Joe. Even though she'd have to eventually. She just needed some time to come up with a solid cover that wouldn't betray her unusual interest in him.

"Dwight and I had a fight, and I threatened to fire him."

Katey didn't say anything. Ava rolled her head to find her sister sipping her drink with a thoughtful expression.

"What's that look?"

Katey shrugged her shoulders a little. "Not that I'd argue for you to keep Dwight on our good ship Lollipop, but you've never threatened to fire him before. Are you just in the mood to get rid of *everyone* these days?"

Okay, that hurt. Ava pressed her lips together, swallowing

down a meaner reply. Katey was too fragile for that. "That's unfair," she said instead.

Katey looked away. She didn't apologize, but came back with a different tack. "Then what did you fight about?"

Ava huffed out a sigh, impatient with herself. "The stupid driver."

"You didn't like the choices?"

"No, I approved of one. Not Dwight's top pick, of course, but a guy he found to fill out the lineup. I hired him and sent Wolverine, Igor and Hulk on their way so Jack could drive me home. Only I had him take me to a bar instead, so we could talk. Like an interview."

Katey choked out a laugh. "No wonder everyone was having fits."

"It was a couple of hours and I'm a fucking grown woman."

"One that can't be trusted on her own," Katey pointed out. "Or are we pretending we don't know what happens when you slip the leash?"

Katey was certainly out for her pound of flesh tonight, exacting due penance for being left alone. Ava poured herself another martini, even though it wasn't quite as good with all the sugar gone from the rim. If she got up to do it herself, Katey would be hurt, with those 'don't make me feel useless' remarks, and hell if she'd ask Katey to wait on her.

"Tell me more about Jack." Katey wriggled on the couch with a hopeful smile. Both a peace offering and a request for a distracting story. "No nickname for him—or is that it?"

"Joe in reality. Jack to me." *My Jacky boy.* She felt the smile curving her lips, which helped banish some of the gloom. She was a moody shit these days.

Katey cocked her head. "He looks like Jack Nicholson?"

"No! Gods, no. He's way younger and hotter. War vet. Muscles like whoa and all intense with it."

"Then why 'Jack'?"

She didn't want to tell Katey, which wasn't fair. They shared all those inside jokes—had created most of them together. But the whole Jack and Diane thing felt… okay, kind of silly. And also precious in some way. Katey would make cracks about it, riffing on the theme and Ava just couldn't bear that thought. Could she make something up?

"Uh-oh." Katey made a horrified O of her mouth, drawing out the sounds like they had on *Tween Hangout*. It irritated Ava no end. Clearly she had no sense of humor today.

"What? There is no uh-oh."

"You're crushing on this guy. Are you going all blue collar on me? What about Mr. Wonderful?"

"Haven't you read your own tweets? Mr. Wonderful and I are over."

"Uh-huh. Until you have make-up sex tomorrow night."

"You know how those benefit concerts are—whisk me on stage, whisk me off. I probably won't even see him. And I wouldn't do him anyway. Not after what he did with those pics."

"He swore it wasn't his fault."

"Yeah, but who believes him? He was pissed at me and did a gotcha."

"You did him since the Epic Disaster."

"I shouldn't have."

"Well, you're not famous for your good judgement," Katey replied in a lofty tone, all smug certainty. "So finish the story— you got recognized? I saw the pics all over Instagram."

Ava winced. "Yeah. I probably looked like hell."

"Cinna will have a fit and read you the riot act, but the ball cap was a cute touch. Jack's?"

"Yes." She'd left it and the sunglasses in the limo, dammit. "He has this protective vibe, didn't want me to be recognized."

"So, the fight with Dwight was because you slipped the

leash?"

"That, sure. And because I want Jack to be my driver and Dwight was all 'no way' and 'fuck him if you have to but I'm not paying him to be your boy toy.'" She left out the incident where Jack lost his shit and tossed her in the limo. No need to worry Katey.

"So…?" Katey sucked on a stick of celery suggestively, raising her eyebrows. "Did you? Fuck him?"

Katey was a virgin still, for really good reasons, but she loved to hear about Ava's exploits. Usually a small price to pay, to make up for everything. It shouldn't irritate her, the way her sister was being all salacious.

"Oh, right. I fucked him in the back seat of the limo."

"Wouldn't be the first time," Katey pointed out.

"Well, I didn't. He drove me to a bar. We talked. He didn't even kiss me when he had the chance."

"Maybe he plays for the other team."

Not the way he'd looked at her. "I don't think so. He wanted to, but wouldn't."

"Inn. Terr. Ess. Ting." Katey drew out the word, chiming on the final syllable.

"Don't toy with me."

"It's just that not many guys—and by that, I mean, no one ever—turns down a shot at the beautiful Ava." The bitterness oozed out with that. Not that Ava blamed her.

"Mr. Wonderful sure did. And Brown-Eyed Boy and His Hotness. Oh! And don't forget Sir Lancelot."

"All *after* you broke their hearts—"

"Or they broke mine—"

"And you wouldn't have taken them back anyway." Regardless of everything else, Katey always had her back. She took each rejection to heart, as if they'd dumped her, too.

"I tried to take Mr. Wonderful back." Lead singer of one of

the hot boy bands, Tyler of the pretty blue eyes and black hair had been her first. Both of them fifteen, but he'd already cut a swath through the girls by then. Losing her virginity to him at a hotel they both stayed at during a concert tour had been the first time she'd slipped the leash. And Katey had helped her do it.

"You did take him back. Twice," Katey pointed out ruthlessly.

"One and a half times."

"Only because he bailed on you before you even got a chance to have makeup sex."

"Yeah. Bastard."

"Yeah."

They sat in rueful silence. She snagged her glass and refilled it yet again. Katey didn't say anything, but raised her eyebrows pointedly, so Ava took some cheese, too. Flavorful, but not like what she wanted, the greasy sharp cheddar melting over a rare burger. Ava's phone lit up with the image of God. The walking cliché in all his omnipotent glory, so she handed it to Katey.

"Hi, Dwight. Yes, she's sitting right here, eating her dinner. No, she's not having any more drinks." Katey rolled her eyes. "Oh, really? Okay—I'll tell her. I don't know on that, she hasn't said. Fine, fine. I'll ask her." She clicked mute. "He says you have to pick the remaining songs tomorrow so they can look the list over and schedule what session musicians they'll need to bring in for next week."

Her stomach clenched, too empty, too full of vodka and sugary lemons. Fucking around wouldn't destroy her career— this album would. Once everyone heard it, she'd be lucky if her fans didn't hunt her down in the street and bludgeon her to death with their earbuds.

Katey waited a beat more, then thumbed the sound on again. "She says she's thinking it over. Hey—I'm just the messenger. You know you can't rush her creative genius. Okay, I'll remind her. Yet again." Katey's eyes found hers. "Yeah, I think you're right. It might be exactly what she needs."

"Thank you," Ava said on a sigh as soon as her sister hung up. "What was all that?"

"You gotta pick the songs, Aves."

Ugh. "I will."

"Or I can pick them for you." Katey's eyes glittered, the green a little too poisonous for comfort. Would Katey go so far in her need for revenge as to sabotage the album? Not something she wanted to find out.

"I'll do it. What exactly do I need?"

"Apparently Dwight caved as he always does for you and got your Jack to sign on the dotted line. He'll be here to pick you up bright and early tomorrow. Eight. He says he did this for you, so you owe him."

"That's practically dawn!"

"Yes. And he said you'd better not be hungover because you're already four weeks behind schedule on recording."

"Oh, forgive me if the death of someone who was practically family put his precious calendar out of whack."

Katey pursed her lips. "You were behind before that."

She knew it. She'd lost it. Lost the magic. If it had ever been her to begin with instead of something she stole. Everything those nasty articles and reviews said stuck with her, sniveling through her brain, leaving their slime trails behind. Created by the marketers for her looks and voice, Ava had been relentlessly groomed and packaged. The walking, singing, dancing Barbie Doll. They might call her the Talent, but everyone knew what she really was—a product. Now the time had come for the truth to emerge. She was surface. The dressed-up plastic doll with nothing inside.

And she couldn't be anything else.

"The label will gut you if you miss another drop date." Katey didn't sound as gleeful as she might have, a consideration Ava appreciated. Either that or she'd become so truly pitiful that Katey bypassed an opportunity to poke at her.

"I won't miss the drop date." Ava dropped her head back on the couch. Too much vodka. That must be why the room spun like a psychotic carousel. If they'd made fun of her before this, the reaction to the upcoming album would be a gluttonous feast of snark.

"Come on." Katey stood and set her sticky empty down. "Let's go raid the kitchen and I'll make you something to eat. Something Celine would clutch her heart over, and you can tell me more about this Joe Ivanchan."

Ava trailed behind her, mostly for lack of impetus to do otherwise. "Can you even cook?"

"YouTube is a marvelous thing, dahling, and I've had time on my hands. What do you want?"

"A cheeseburger."

Katey pounded a fist to her heart, in true Titanic style. "Red meat—in Celine's kitchen? Quelle horreur!"

"Nachos?"

"Oh, right." Katey rifled through the cabinets. "Can I sell you on a close facsimile? Kale chips, hummus, veggies, with melted low-fat cheese."

Better than sea bass. Still. "Will you have it, too?"

"I already ate my supper, like a good girl."

Probably she had, under Celine's watchful eye. "Okay. I have a stash of cherry sours, too."

Katey shook the bag of kale chips and the container of homemade hummus like pompons. "Sugar high for the win!"

For just that moment, it was as if they were girls again, and none of the intervening years had happened.

If only.

~ 9 ~

J OE WAITED FOR Ava.

He glanced at the clock. 8:30. Manning had said she'd be ready at eight, but he doubted that meant much to Ava, even if she'd gotten the memo. Arlin perched next to him, ecstatic to be included and back in his position at shotgun.

Joe wasn't risking his first real day on the job without the dog's steadying presence. He'd explain him somehow.

The waiting didn't bother him much. At least the underground garage was dim and quiet. He'd be spending a lot of his time waiting for her, as he would for any client. That was part of the job. A skill he'd acquired through those long hours, days, weeks and months of waiting for something, anything to happen. At least now when he gave in to boredom and actively wished for something, anything to happen, it wouldn't involve getting his skull rattled and his leg blown off.

Keeping the paparazzi off Ava would be like escorting grade-schoolers through a crosswalk compared to that.

Fending off her mercurial flirtations and demands, however, would be like navigating land mines riddling the only source of water for miles. After a while, the thirst became more important than any other consideration. Either way you died. It became a choice of fast or slow.

"Why did I agree to this?" He asked Arlin.

The dog gave him a canine grin, tongue lolling as if he

laughed in answer. He ruffled the dog's ears.

"Some help you are." Maybe she'd be all business today, yesterday's pass at him simply a whim on her part. Or part of the job interview. *Kiss me.* Her lashes had feathered over her tawny eyes as she'd dropped her gaze to his mouth. He'd nearly obeyed—both her and the clamoring hounds of lust—before he yanked himself back, grasped reality again.

Not that his fevered brain hadn't replayed the moment over and over, his eyes popping open to jerk him awake all night, unsure whether any of it had been real or more lurid dreams. Twice he'd grabbed his phone off the nightstand to leave Manning a voice mail saying he'd changed his mind.

Three times he shut off the glaring light, unable to bear the sight of the slowly passing hours.

He must have fallen asleep finally, because dreams took over—identifiable mainly because he did kiss her. More, he pushed her onto the sticky bar table, took her right there, even though she screamed. Screams that echoed in his brain like the agonized cries from the hospital.

No wonder he couldn't refuse the opportunity to be around Ava a little bit more. He was clearly fucked in the head, that some part of him wanted her that way.

Okay, he'd already known he was fucked in the head. Just not like that. Gut churning from it, he'd awakened at 4:30 and decided against trying for more sleep. Dreams got longer and more vivid towards morning, even without the morphine drip and pills. Better not to let them have the chance to dig in their claws too deep.

He should bail, do the right thing for them both, but he couldn't bring himself to. Just your typical chickenshit coward. Arlin leaned into him, no doubt sensing something of Joe's distress at the memory of those cold-sweat dreams, then laid his head on Joe's knee. How the dog knew remained a mystery, but

Arlin always did. Joe stroked the silky ears, reflecting as always how odd it was that soothing the dog calmed himself. They calmed each other, he supposed, and that was the point. It wasn't that he thought all those therapists didn't know their jobs, but how they'd figured out a dog could keep a guy on the steady... beyond him anyway.

But then, no one had ever called him a rocket scientist.

At least the early wake-up had ensured he got to the job in plenty of time to thoroughly learn the car and compose himself. He'd brought his eReader, but the words kept blurring on the screen, replaced by the images from his dreams.

Ava, tawny eyes blind from desire.

Ava, sparkly nails dragging down his chest.

Ava, under him, screaming his name when he ripped away her pretty dress and—

"Jacky boy!" Ava's voice rang out, calling his name like a song.

Shit!

Shaking off the dregs of the potent fantasy, he hopped out of the car, moving fast to open the door for her. Fortunately, she'd only just emerged from the elevator, flanked by the big bodyguards whose names he'd learned, but couldn't help thinking of as Igor and Hulk, as Ava dubbed them. She had a canny knack for sizing people up and slapping a descriptive moniker on them. Hopefully her calling him 'Jack' meant something positive and wasn't shorthand for 'Jackass' or "Jack shit."

Or worse. Though considering the direction his thoughts had been going, he likely deserved that, or worse.

She strode ahead of her escort, glorious even in the sterile garage lighting, gliding with her dancer's grace on endless legs, carrying a thermos that glittered with pink and white rhine-stones. Or diamonds—what did he know?

In full glamorous mode today, she wore make-up and heels, scarlet red skyscrapers that shouldn't have been possible to walk in. Otherwise she wore entirely white—a sinfully short, tight skirt, and a lacy shirt over some kind of tank top that shoved up the pale curves of her breasts. And pearls. A simple strand over the wings of her collarbones and little ones in her ears. They looked like what his grandmother wore to Liturgy. Well, they *should* have been that prim. On Ava they became seriously seductive, begging him to taste the difference between the jewels and her shimmering skin.

Rein it in, buddy.

"Good morning, Ava. You look lovely today." There. That sounded like a gentlemanly thing to say. His grandmother would be proud. Or at least not ashamed.

"Thank you, I was feeling virginal." She widened her eyes as she said it, pursing lips that matched the heels, and feigning innocence in such a way that he felt the impact of her sensuality as palpably as if she'd grabbed him by the balls. This close, the shadows under those eyes so artfully made up, showed like old bruises.

"Except for the shoes," he noted, rattled enough to blurt that out before he thought better of it.

Though he yanked his gaze away from what he couldn't unsee, and held the car door open, she lingered there, catching his gaze by pointing one toe so they could both admire her slim foot in the artistically arched curve of the shoe. "Well, there's a bit of a slut in every good girl, don't you think, Jacky boy?"

He nearly choked on his own spit. Behind her, Igor and Hulk seemed not to hear, placidly waiting for the transfer of custody. He envied their studied nonchalance, wondering how long it had taken them to acquire it. "Ah, I wouldn't know, ma'am."

"First 'Ava' and now 'ma'am'—are you going back on our

agreement already?" She glared at him coolly, regal as an ice queen and slightly taller in those impossible heels.

"No, Sova," he replied in a quiet tone. She had to know the guys were listening. "Just keeping up appearances."

She wrinkled her nose, a wry twist to her full mouth. "God I hate that word. *Appearances.* Don't fret that I'll forget about those. After all, that's all I am." She folded herself into the car with practiced grace, disappearing behind mirrored windows and leaving a cloud of her expensive perfume behind.

"Don't fuck up today, Ivanchan," Igor said. "We'd ride along, but she doesn't want it. Consider this a test. Manning says to keep her on a short leash. Take her straight to the studio. ASAP—she's already late. Straight back here for prep. Then to the benefit concert. Agenda's in the dash computer; he'll text you any changes. Simple."

Oh yeah, it sounded easy, put that way. Simple instructions that did not factor in the force of nature that was Ava. Or how fucked up it was how they talked about her. *On a short leash.*

He let himself back into the limo, to find Ava halfway through the window to the front, hanging over with her ass in the air, an over-the-moon Arlin licking her face like it was ice cream. Probably tasted that good, and not that he blamed the dog, but he sent up a brief prayer of gratitude for the tinted windows that hadn't let anyone see what her short skirt surely revealed in that position.

"A puppy!" she squealed, her voice muffled by sloppy dog kisses. "You brought me a puppy!"

"This is Arlin." At least he hadn't needed to make excuses, right?

She lifted her head, owl-eyes curious, not blinking as the dog slurped her ear. "Why'd you pick that name?"

"He came with it." Service dogs always did—because they were trained to answer to their names. Not something he planned to explain. "Why don't you sit back and put on your seat belt so we can go? I'm sure you don't want to be late." 8:45.

"It's not like they can start without me. Besides, I'm busy saying hello to my newest fan. Aren't I? You seem like a very discerning dog. What's your favorite song, baby, huh?"

Don't fuck up today.

"Maybe if we get you there soon enough, you can get enough work done to take a break later, maybe help me take him for a walk."

"I would love that! We could go to the park." She continued making slobbery noises at the dog, then stopped. "But I have the wrong shoes. Let me run back upstairs for some and—"

"Sova," he said, adding some sternness to it. "If I don't deliver you within a reasonable amount of time, Manning will figure I can't do my job and I'll get fired. Work with me here."

She heaved a dramatic sigh and looked at him again, scratching Arlin under the collar with her white-tipped nails. Different than the day before. She'd smudged the crisp line of her lipstick. Only inches away. Close enough for him to kiss and smear it beyond repair.

As if she read his mind, that mouth curved in knowing sensuality. "Why wouldn't you kiss me yesterday? It's been suggested that it's because you play for the other team."

He managed not to laugh in her face. "That's not why. I told you I'd had girlfriends." Back when he was still a man worth having. Whatever.

"That's what I told Katey."

"Who's Katey?" He asked, even though it played into her delay tactics. He had no idea how to coax her into budging.

"My sister—she's my personal assistant, personal martini-maker and personal minder. She lives with me. I told her all about you last night."

"Ah."

"She wants to meet you. Want to come up? She's awake. You'll have to eventually."

Another gambit to go back upstairs, though she had that edge to her voice, talking about her sister. "No," he said evenly. "We have to go to the recording studio."

Her generous lips took on a mutinous twist, a bit of a sulk, more temper. "I don't *want* to go to the studio. Am I not my own person? I don't have to do things just because other people think I should." She sounded petulant enough to grate on his nerves, but her expressive eyes flashed with something deeper. Something he recognized, from the haunted gazes of men he'd served with. That look a guy gets when he's got to go back out there and the dread is like a cloud you can barely see through.

Arlin, sensitive to such things also, leaned into her hand and she rubbed his ears, much like Joe did when he needed the comfort. It had taken a lot for him to admit to needing help, even when he couldn't move on his own and obviously had to have assistance just to stay alive. Sometimes sympathy was the worst thing to get. *Pet the golden goose.* A swift kick had done more for him than all the petting in the world.

"Get a grip, Ava. Sit down and strap in. I mean it."

She stiffened, her golden eyes shocked—and maybe a little hurt. "Sova," she snapped back. "You promised."

"Not if you're going to behave like a child. You're not going to the recording studio because anyone is making you. This is your goddamn job and you're lucky to have one that's fun and that you love. Do you think those people out there slogging along the streets, hurrying to get to jobs they hate, are going because they *want* to? That's why they call it work and why people pay you to do it. You ever notice people don't pay you to do the stuff you want to do? That's why. Otherwise we'd all be sitting by the pool, drinking margaritas and raking in the dough."

"And that's what I am to you—a job. Something unfun that

you wouldn't do if you didn't get paid."

9:01 "We'll debate this as I'm driving you to the studio." He pointed at the back seat. "Sit. Stay."

She drowned the smile at his joke with a stiff sulk and didn't move. "No. I want an answer first. An honest one. I want to know what you really think."

"You're procrastinating is what you're doing."

Dipping her chin in acknowledgment of the score, she didn't back down. "Got it in one and I'm a master of procrastination, if nothing else. Now answer my question or I won't sit *or* stay."

"Do you promise you will if I answer?" This was like negotiating with Nona to stay out of his room when she was eight.

"Yes. I promise."

There was the smart reply and the honest one. Not at all the same thing. The honest answer was the way to go, but would put even more power into her willful hands. The smart one would hurt her feelings and—despite her bravado and careless ways— he couldn't bear to do it, not for that reason, just to save himself.

"It's not just a job to me. Driving is how I make money, sure, but I can drive anyone. *You* are not just anyone."

"Am I special?"

He pulled back saying that she was special, all right, like his Army buddies would have. His heart grabbed, losing a few beats. She reminded him of Nona now, somehow young and uncertain. "I think you're wonderful." He said it too fervently, but she didn't seem to notice. At least he managed to stop there.

"You mean that," she breathed, moving closer. "Kiss me, Jack."

He put a hand to her shoulder, holding her off. "Absolutely not."

Her eyes snapped with temper again—far better than that little girl lost expression. "Why not? You think I'm wonderful."

"If I kiss you—or anything else—Manning will see to it I

never work in this town again."

"Did he actually say that? God, he's such a fucking cliché!"

He did for sure, though he wasn't going to offer that fuel to her fire.

"That's not a good enough reason." She leaned harder into his bracing hand, reminding him of Arlin, who panted between them, poised for the opportunity to slobber on Ava again, but too well behaved to try it without an invitation. "It might be true that he said that, but that's not the reason you won't kiss me. He's not here."

"Maybe I don't want to. You have dog slobber on your lips, after all."

"Liar."

Well, yeah. That was the thing about trying not to succumb to denial. Honesty got a guy into trouble. "Don't push me, Sova."

"Silly Jack—pushing is what I do best. Ask anyone."

Sweat slid down his back. Arlin whimpered, so he stroked the dog, reassuring them both. Ava observed the exchange with interest.

"What's wrong with him?"

A desperate man, he improvised. "It makes him nervous to have you crowding us."

At least it backed her off. She moved away, though she didn't retreat through the window, so he still couldn't start driving. 9:13. "I think you do want to kiss me, but you're being all noble about it. It goes against your principles."

With a rush of relief, he seized on that, nodding. "Exactly. Now I answered your question and you made me a promise."

With a thoughtful purse of her lips, she stroked Arlin's head and—thank God—sat back and even put on her seat belt. Seizing the opportunity, he started the engine and guided the long car to the doors that opened to the code he tapped in, then risked a look at her in the mirror after easing into traffic. She had her long legs crossed, the bedazzled thermos wrapped in her hands, sipping at it. Definitely pensive now.

"Did Dwight tell you not to fuck me?" she asked, still not looking up.

He nearly choked on his own spit. "Not exactly," he temporized.

"Then what? I want to know everything he said to you, *exactly*."

No way was he telling her all that. "He said you were off limits, which is common sense for business associates anyway."

"Oh, really?" Interest sharpened her voice and he flicked a glance to find rearview full of her tawny eyes. "No other caveats or warnings?"

"Only that you'd break my heart if I let you." He tried to make it sound like a joke, but she didn't smile. She was all bored diva now.

"I probably would. I have a knack for it. You can ask anyone that, too. Or read any of the gossip rags."

He didn't say anything to that. Oh yeah, the gossip rags said plenty about her. She'd broken his heart a thousand times before he ever met her, with every new love affair, every breakup rebound, each poor choice. All those boys who treated her like a tramp.

"Of course, I can't break what I don't have." She said it idly, even playfully, but her gaze had gone as predatory as a lion's. "Maybe I'll make you fall in love with me."

"Only so you could break my heart?"

She laughed, lightly. "You'd enjoy the ride, Jacky boy."

Highly debatable. Not that the adrenaline junkie in him wasn't into the idea. The guy he'd become, who'd had to pick up that junkie's pieces in those long months in the hospital, had learned that the crash and burn wasn't worth it. Or the risk of addiction. Like the morphine, the -contins, the -condones, taking Ava up on the offer would soothe the broken edges in him, dull the pain for a while.

Then exact a heavy price.

There wouldn't be a gradual tapering off with her, no helpful VA therapists to walk him through withdrawal. If he let Ava into his bloodstream, the inevitable dumping would be cold turkey. Something that might cost him all the progress he'd made in the last couple of years of recovery.

"Let's make a deal," Ava broke into his thoughts. "I go to the recording studio and do my goddamn job"—she imitated his accent flawlessly—"and then you take me out for a cheeseburger on the way home."

Straight back here for prep. "You have the benefit concert tonight. I have to get you home to get ready."

"Oh. Right." She shifted on the seat, deflated and restless at once. "But you'll drive me?"

"That's the plan."

"Arlin, too?"

He surveyed her in the mirror, taking in her hopeful expression. It helped that she liked the dog. He didn't have to explain why he needed to keep Arlin with him as much as possible. Particularly key after the spectacular loss of his shit the day before. "Sure, if you like."

"I like." She was quiet a few minutes. "Jack?"

"Yeah?"

"Did Dwight tell you anything in particular… about people who might show up tonight?"

"No. Something I should know?"

She shrugged it off. Fiddled with her watch, studying it. Finally sighed. "Probably not, if he didn't mention. Just—don't leave me alone, okay?"

"You got it."

He thought she might say more, but she didn't, staying quiet for the rest of the short drive. When the studio gates swung wide and they passed in, some of her sparkle dimmed. But neither of them mentioned it.

~ 10 ~

THE LIMO DOOR opened and all the flashbulbs went off. That moment always dazzled her—and disoriented. No matter that she'd been doing it most of her life, no matter how she braced herself for the onslaught, reminding herself to smile—eyes wide, face relaxed—that first burst of lights from everywhere at once always startled her. Of course, it took only one photo of you looking like a deer in the headlights to teach you to do better. Practice, practice, practice.

So she had her smile in place when Joe opened the car door. He stood well to the side so as not to block the cameras, as Dwight had drilled him, scanning the crowd while offering his hand to for her to grasp as she rose, to prevent any clumsy accidents. *Knees together, swing your ankles, find your footing*—Joe's hand was so warm and steadying like his presence—*stand, pause, pose, sparkle.* She chanted the old advice to herself, warding off that one careless moment that would allow the opportunistic telephoto lens to snap an upskirt.

God knows they all tried for it.

All too fast, Joe's steadying hand relinquished her to the crowd. They chanted her name and screamed—avid faces all lit up from phones and the enormous tunneled eyes of TV cameras. She paused often, making the slow parade of smiles, waves and poses, obligingly turning to face those who asked. This part she could do in her sleep. Be the image. Cross ankles and turn just so to create the skinny starlet silhouette. Smile and wave. Become the photograph. Human lip gloss.

She should stop fighting this craving to be anything else. Take the easy path and record the songs they handed her. They already had her lined up to sing two of them tonight, to whet excitement for the album drop, fast approaching. Get paid for doing her damn job, which she didn't have to enjoy. She might be human lip gloss, but the fans adored her. That should be enough for anyone.

Every girl's dream.

An entertainment reporter, Candy Conway, met her partway, microphone in hand, the minotaur of a cameraman behind her. She and Katey used to make up stories about the monsters with cameras for heads to scare each other, back when they shared a princess pink bedroom with matching twin canopy beds, in that first decent New York apartment.

"Ava! You look gorgeous! Who designed your gown?"

She couldn't even remember what it looked like, but she knew better than to glance down. Hilda had drilled her in the answer. "Atelier Versace—you know how I love her."

"And she must love you because she always brings out the fabulous for you. Such a good cause tonight—are you excited?"

"I sure am, Candy! I can't wait to share my new songs with all my fans, both here and watching at home." A tremendous cheer went up and she waved to the crowd. Then caught a glimpse of flaming hair.

Was that?

Surely not, no. Not possible. Dwight had said he'd take care of it, and this had to be less than 1500 feet. And where the hell was Joe? She looked for him and spotted him to the side, out of the camera line of sight, scanning the crowd. Of course he didn't notice anything. *Because it's okay. She can't come any closer.* The lapse, though, rattled her enough that she missed Candy's next question. "I'm sorry—what was that?"

The reporter's eyes sparkled with malicious glee. "I asked how you felt about seeing your long time on and off again sweetheart Tyler, tonight. Will you be taking him home tonight? Or perhaps some other lucky young man?"

Spiteful little bitch. But she smiled, glossy and pretending not to notice the toxicity. "I'm not taking anyone home tonight."

"But Tyler—"

"Tyler is a good friend of course, but that's all. Anything more is ancient history."

An arm snaked around her waist, expensive aftershave coiling with it, a kiss to her cheek, rough with perfectly groomed scruff. "Aw, Ava—you know those who forget history are doomed to repeat it," Tyler said, looking squarely into the camera. "I've never stopped thinking about you. Don't break my heart by saying you've forgotten how good we are. Even you aren't that cruel."

"Tyler, you devil. You're wrinkling my dress." She kept the words playful, flirting for the avid eye of the camera and the reporter clearly determined to milk every bit of the ambush. "But you may escort me in and make your case. What do you all think out there?" She gave the camera a saucy wink. "Does Tyler deserve another chance? Tweet me with your opinion!"

Katey would pick that up and run with it. Looping her hand through Mr. Wonderful's Armani clad arm, making sure Joe followed behind them, she muttered through her fixed smile. "That was low, even for a snake like you."

"I told you before—it wasn't me." He flashed her his movie-star grin, the girls in the crowd screaming as he did. "We always made good press, Ava darling. You've been a busy, naughty girl. What aren't you wearing under that sex-goddess gown?"

"You wish you knew."

"Don't I just. Give me a chance to find out. We were good

together. Our fans love us together. You said you believed it wasn't me, forgive and forget. Were you lying?"

She kept the smile in place, mentally sighing. "No. Water under the bridge." Photos on the internet that never washed out to sea, but whatever.

"That's my girl. My people want to talk to yours about some dual appearances. I said I'd pitch it to you."

Just business. She could handle that. "Sure. After the show, though."

"We have connecting dressing rooms. It could be like old times." He waggled his eyebrows. He'd always had that boyish charm going for him.

She laughed, right on cue. "You get five minutes."

"Score."

"But the door stays locked."

"You don't want to do that—you can't resist me." He bussed her on the cheek, to more shrieking delight, and handed her over to the stagehand assigned to escort her backstage.

THE SHOW WENT fantastically well. Of course, it could hardly not, with the crowd beyond hyped at the sight of so many celebrities. Tyler and Four4All whipped the audience into a frenzy and she rode that wave, hitting them with "Shining Star" first, then one of the new songs, which sounded pretty much the same to her ears, but they greeted it with the same rapture. This was always the best part, performing for the fans. She took a pause, talking to them before the third song, part of her trademark.

In the beginning, it had been easy to talk, because they all felt like friends. Like they loved her. These days Katey and Hilda wrote it out for her ahead of time, light and meaningless banter.

Her brand, after all. When they first took that away from her, after she'd phrased some things badly and the words had gotten picked up and broadcast everywhere, it was supposed to be just to help her through the bad publicity. After that they only wanted to keep helping her, just to lighten her load. One less thing to think about. Then the whole Epic Disaster happened, and everyone had freaked, so she'd handed everything over.

Now she repeated the words they gave her, barely paying attention to what she said. None of it held much more import than her empty lyrics. All designed to please and never offend.

She sang the other new song, and they cheered for that, too. Though doubtless some critic our there made more snarky notes. A list, probably, of all the key words: bubblegum, candy, empty-headed, lip gloss.

But she'd done her damn job. Joe waited for her just offstage with a solemn smile and a nod. No Arlin. Joe had said it would be easier to leave the dog in the limo with Wolverine in the pickup line.

"Great job, Ava darling!" Dwight hustled up. "See? They ate up the new songs, was I right or was I right. The new album will be a smash hit, then you can take break, come back, write all the songs you like and everyone will be happy."

He went on like that and she led her little parade to her dressing room, wishing her manager would shut up for two seconds, just long enough for her to put a couple of thoughts together.

Rounding the bend, she stopped cold at the sight of flaming hair. The scent of Chanel enveloped her, her stomach cramping so hard she thought she might vomit, and she broke out in a fine, chill sweat. "Mother."

Hulk and Igor were on the door, faces dark. Dwight pushed past her preening mother to confer with them and venue security, hands waving, but Ava couldn't seem to hear anything at all. Krystal's makeup was layered on, her body easily ten pounds heavier than when Ava had last seen her. "Hi, baby girl. No hug for mama?"

"What the hell are you doing here?"

"It's a free country. And I'm your mother. You can't close me out. I gave birth to you. I *made* you. You don't exist without me."

A dank mist rose behind Ava's eyes. She couldn't do this. Joe's hand cupped her elbow, his steady presence warm behind her. He hadn't left her alone.

"Sova?" he murmured close to her ear.

"Make her go away," she begged him.

"You love me," her mother insisted, tears spilling down her cheeks. "You don't even know why you're angry at me. What did I even do to you? I think you don't even know. Enough of this hissy fit."

Her teeth hurt, the throbbing spiking to her temple, tears springing to her eyes. "Just… go away."

"See? You can't even explain. You used to be such a loving little girl. I don't know what happened to make you such a little bitch. You're buying into your own press, listening to the wrong people. You should listen to your *mother*."

"I can't. I just can't. Get her out of here."

Hulk and Igor didn't move, regret on their faces, the venue security guy saying something she couldn't hear over the roar in her ears. Joe, however, took action, stepping around her. In the shadow of his wide shoulders, she took a calming breath, marginally better. "Ma'am," he said in that slow drawl, the command clear in it, "I'm going to have to ask you to leave."

"It's a public venue," Krystal spat at him. "You can't make me do shit."

"I have a restraining order," Ava told Joe, panic rising, making her heart pound and her vision go scarlet black. "She shouldn't be here."

"She can't enter the dressing room, Ava. That's private." Dwight came around to take her arm. "Come on inside. That's all you have to do. Just walk inside."

"Even if you've hardened your heart against me," Krystal raised her voice, still weeping. "You can't decide for your sister. Even if you've forgotten how to love, she's not a monster. I wish she'd been the star, not you, you nasty whore. You have no right to keep her from me."

"I have every fucking right!" Ava knew she was losing it, spiraling into the rage place her mother always took her, but she was beyond caring. Flashbulbs popped, people shouted with excitement. Dwight yammered in her ear, a mutter against the crashing of voices in her head. "You stay away from Katey. Stay away from both of us!"

"I made you, *Ava*, and I can destroy you just as easily," her mother shrieked. "You're nothing without me!"

The guys pulled her past Krystal, too close, the perfume choking her and she tore away from them, launching herself at the beast who birthed her, scratching at that traitorous bitch. "You stay away from me, you fucking harpy! I'll kill you. I swear to God, I will!"

Then she lifted into the air, constellations of bulbs flashing through her brain, and she flailed against the restraining arms.

"Sova. Okay, Sova. Enough of this. I've got you."

She collapsed against him, sobbing. Vaguely she was aware of Dwight ushering them into her dressing room, the door sealing off the bright lights of the cameras, the frenzied babble of voices. "Where the hell is the car?" he demanded.

"Still bringing the car around. It's a crush out there," Igor said.

"Shit! And that crazy dingbat will be giving interviews. I can't imagine the pictures they got. Along with that priceless sound bite. Ava! Calm your shit down. Put her here, Joe."

Dwight pressed something into her hand along with a chill glass. Vodka on the rocks. She swallowed down the pill, head still jangling. It had been better when Joe held her.

"What are you giving her?"

"Do me a favor and shut the fuck up, Ivanchan. I want her out of here. Without further photo opportunities. She looks like hell."

"We're working on it." Igor sounded remarkably calm.

"Tyler—what the fuck do you want?" Dwight again.

"We were supposed to meet and—hey, Ava." He had his arms around her pulling her close, that expensive aftershave taking her back. They'd had good times together and now she sniffled against his tux, the waterworks returning. Being held was definitely better than being alone in that cold hard chair. "What's wrong, sweetheart?"

"My horrible mother is here and I just can't..." Her throat closed down.

"Shh. Let me help you. We can sneak out through my dressing room. Just like we used to do. Remember Copenhagen—and those chocolate-dipped strawberries?"

The memory was one of the best. She'd lost her virginity to him that night, and it had been everything a girl could want. Tyler had made it romantic and perfect.

"You're even more beautiful tonight. What did the Twitter poll say?" he asked, kissing her under her ear, just where she liked it.

"What?"

"About us? I bet they voted yes to us as a couple. You can't fight the fans."

She didn't know what the poll said. Or care. Tired. She was tired and miserable.

"Let me take care of you, Ava darling."

"Okay," she sighed, twining her arms around his neck.

"Let's do this people. No mistakes." Dwight taking charge, talking to Hilda on his phone to handle the spin. Tyler draped his topcoat around her, spiriting her out the other end of the hall, then helping her into the limo, handing her a fresh vodka.

"Get her home," Dwight ordered from a distance. "I'm going back in to deal with damage control."

"But what about—"

"Just drive her home. How fucking hard is it?"

"Whew," Tyler laughed, raking his hair back from his forehead. Mr. Wonderful, boyishly handsome, eyes sparkling with fun. "That was like old times, huh? Remember in Paris that time, when the paparazzi mobbed us and we jumped in that cab?"

"Mais oui!" She giggled. She'd been maybe sixteen. The cabbie hadn't spoken English, but he'd driven round and round the city while they made out in the back seat until they dared sneak back into the hotel. She'd been off the leash for hours that time. She'd also been coked to the gills. Something she wished she didn't miss—sex on coke had been amazing. So much easier to let go and just ride it. "That was a great night."

"The best." He toyed with the ripped strap dangling over her shoulder, brushing her skin. Her nipples, hard from the cold, sent sparks of delight as the silk moved across them. "I'm afraid this dress is trashed."

"Yeah." And she'd broken three nails, down to the quick. It seemed remote now, the whole scene, chilled behind vodka and whatever Dwight had given her. Valium, probably. Better the soothing fog than … she wasn't going to think about it.

"You were astonishing tonight. I've never seen you look so beautiful. I've never stopped thinking about you, Ava." Then his mouth was on hers, his hand on her breast. *Like old times.* "I've missed you so much."

Yes. Yes, this was what she needed. Not the coke, but this,

the rush of performance, the roaring crowd, the clean burn of sex. Tyler had his hand up her dress, pressing against her stocking-clad pussy, murmuring outrageously dirty things against her skin.

Oh yes, just like that.

~ 11 ~

J OE KEPT HIS eyes on traffic, not looking in the rear-view mirror but keeping the window down between him and the passenger compartment. His job to make sure she was okay, not to sulk like a jilted boyfriend at the prom. By the sounds that grated on his psyche like a cosmic cheese-grater, Ava was having a fine time, indeed. He kept one hand on the wheel and the other buried in the comforting silk of Arlin's fur. If he could drive a disabled vehicle with his leg gone and his buddies screaming, he could keep steady through knowing the sun of his obsession was banging another guy a few feet away.

Fucking Tyler, too.

He breathed into the pain, letting it flow through and out. *Just a phantom limb, buddy. You're feeling an injury in a place that no longer exists.* That, hey, who was he kidding? That never existed.

This had been the danger of working for her all along. He'd known this. When she'd been a remote star, the fantasy had stayed immaculate and complete. He'd been no more able to get close to her than he could fly to the sun. Then meeting her, talking to her... hell, *flirting* with her—it had made him get all kinds of ideas.

Stupid, wrong-headed ideas.

The more fool he for even thinking about having her. Even though he'd tried to wrestle down those fantasies, his stupid heart hadn't received the memo. The worst of it was, he'd known better. Hell, he'd been warned.

She'll break your heart if you let her. She won't even mean to. She's like a toddler with expensive toys. One minute she loves them, the next she breaks them just to see what happens.

No, that wasn't the worst of it. The worst was she didn't even know he was there.

Which he wasn't. He'd maintained pretty well through the red carpet walk, despite the crowds, and even the unexpected arrival of Ava's mother. The guys—especially Manning—should have warned him about that. Restraining order? Definitely should have warned him. But through all of that he'd been fine. Now the nowhere zone buzzed loud in his head, sucking him into the nothing, erasing him. Arlin licked his hand and he rubbed the dog's ears.

He pulled into the underground garage and sat there a moment idling before he killed the engine. The other guys were still back at the concert venue. He'd have to be the one to open the door, to extract her from whatever compromising position he'd find her in, to get her upstairs and safely home. To do his own fucking job.

And then he was quitting.

Getting out, he ignored his aching leg and knocked on the window, giving them a moment while he scanned the garage for trouble. Then he opened the door, standing well back as he had when she stepped out onto the red carpet, so glorious, like the sun itself. And, like Icarus, he'd flown too close and now plummeted to the earth.

The pain when he hit bottom would be epic.

Their laughter emerged first, then Tyler staggered out, reaching back in to help Ava, the short dress tangled far too high up on her hips. Her formerly perfectly coiffed hair was rumpled in mad waves, crimson lipstick smeared. Tyler wore a fair amount on his mouth also. Joe took over with a hand under her elbow.

She blinked at him blearily, mascara smeared from weeping, a puzzled frown between her finely arched brows. "Jack?" She looked over at the limo, as if surprised to see it there.

"Thanks, dude." Tyler grinned at him. "She's kind of a hot mess."

Joe throttled back the urge the punch the punk kid in his too-perfect nose. "I need to get her upstairs."

"Cool, cool. I'll call my people and come up to wait for them. Unless you want to give me a lift?"

"I have to stay with Ava."

In the elevator, Ava leaned against him, weaving a little on her feet. In her skyscraper heels, she'd be eye-to-eye with him, if she hadn't dropped her head on his shoulder. "Jacky boy—what are you doing here?"

"You're fine, Ava. You're home."

Tyler slouched against the elevator wall, hands in pockets. "Nice dog, dude."

"Thanks. How much did she have to drink?"

He shrugged. "Some vodka. Just a couple. Not much. I think her manager gave her a chill pill after her mother showed up and…" He flexed his fingers and made a meowing sound, cackling. "Cat fight—gotta love it."

Joe stared at the laughing, slender kid, doing the math and realizing they were close to the same age. Didn't even seem possible.

The elevator doors opened, revealing a literal penthouse. That was, of course Ava lived in one, but knowing and seeing were two different things. He'd never felt more like the rube from Kentucky than he did stepping into that palace of white, glass and chrome. The perfect icy setting for her golden beauty. Restraining himself from gaping, he muttered his mantra to himself. *Be cool. Be cool.* It had worked on duty in Kabul—it ought to work with celebrity-shock.

And Ava, her dress torn and bloodstained, sagging against him, hardly looked the remote goddess at the moment. Her fingers clutched at him, pulling him close.

"Don't tell Katey," she urged.

"What?"

"Just don't say what happened."

Two women met them immediately, one older and a younger one who must be Katey. She stood back, though, reminding him of a fawn looking to its mom for the signal to run. Though Ava's sister must be close to the same age, she looked ten years younger. The baggy sweats she wore swallowed up her painfully thin frame and she tugged the over long cuffs over her hands, but not before he caught the angry red of suicide scars.

"Well if it isn't Mr. Wonderful," she said, and at first Joe thought she meant him, but Tyler tossed her a little wave.

"Always a pleasure, little Kates."

"I'm Hilda, Ava's publicist," the older woman said. "Katey, let's get Ava comfortable. Show Mr. Ivanchan the way. Tyler, I've called your people and set out refreshments for you in the living room. This way." Hilda took Tyler off, no doubt to square away what *his* story would be.

But Katey didn't immediately move. "Nice to meet you, Jack" she said, so softly he pretty much had to read her lips. She didn't look directly at him, all her attention riveted on Arlin.

"And this is Arlin," Ava inserted, weaving only a little in the circle of his arm. "Can she pet him?"

"Sure." It seemed surreal to be having this conversation after all that happened, but he'd go with it. "He likes his ears rubbed, Katey."

The fey girl edged closer, then folded to her knees, reaching out to rub the dog's golden ears. Arlin grinned at her, tongue lolling, and she smiled—transforming her from a ghost of a girl into one a bit more alive, though she still seemed more Nona's age.

"Arlin," she said, then glanced up at Ava. "Remember when we wanted a puppy?"

"Yes." Ava shook her head, giggling a little too loud. "We campaigned for months, making our mom watch every dog movie ever made, cutting out puppy photos from magazines."

"We even tried that hunger strike." Katey giggled, too, very like Ava's. "Which lasted until Henry took us for ice cream."

"How'd it turn out?" he asked, going along with it. They must have been cuties, caving to the offer of ice cream. But both girls sobered.

"No go," Katey sighed in that wraithlike voice again. "Well, we had one visit for a few days—maybe a week—but it didn't work out. The breeder took Violet back. At least Ava got a song out of it."

"'Violet' is about a dog?" One of his favorites, sad as it was. He'd always figured it was about someone she loved who died. A grandmother or something with that old-fashioned name.

Ava's face had gone gray and she sagged against him. "I need to sit down."

Katey gave Arlin one last pat, and stood. "We'd better put her to bed while she's pliable. This way."

Joe helped guide the staggering Ava to her room, sitting her on one of the chairs. Katey crouched to unbuckle her heels.

"What happened?" Katey asked.

He hesitated, pretty sure Ava had meant she didn't want her sister to know about the mother's arrival at the concert. Katey flashed him a frustrated look. "Not at the venue—that's all over the internet. Going to take us *weeks* to get that off the breaking gossip click-baits. I don't know what you guys get paid for, if not to stop shit like that from going down. What did she take?"

"Tyler said Dwight gave her a 'chill pill'—along with vodka."

"Fucker," she muttered. "Ava, honey? I'm going to get you

something to help."

"Okay." Ava smiled brightly at her. "Did you hear me sing?"

"I did. You were awesome."

"Are you sure? Those new songs…"

"Are amazing, just like you. Everything is wonderful."

"Thanks! I love you, Kates."

Katey gave him a pointed look. "I've got this. You can go already. Jack."

✦　✦　✦

JOE COULDN'T SAY he was exactly surprised to get Manning's message to pick Ava up at ten the next morning—the later hour no doubt a concession to the debacle of the night before—but he hadn't expected it, either. Friday morning, and all. You'd think they'd give her the long weekend to recover.

Guess not.

Really, he'd more than half expected to be given notice that he wouldn't work out. Which would have been ideal, as it would have saved him having to tell them that he quit. Neither eventuality would be two-weeks' notice or anything, but technically the probation meant they could fire him and he could quit anytime.

Hell, who was he kidding? He'd likely end this job fired on the spot just as coldly and easily as Katey had dismissed the help. Kicked out of Ava's life as abruptly as he'd entered it. Good to remember his place.

It would be smart to leave now, under his own power. But though he thought he'd been certain of the decision, composed the message countless times during the dragging hours of the night, he couldn't walk away. No more than he'd been able to stop thinking about Ava from the first moment he'd laid eyes on her picture. Arlin gazed at him with those soulful brown eyes that seemed to look right into his heart, seeing everything about him, assessing his state of mind.

She emerged by 10:15, bracketed by Hulk and Igor, something about the image putting him in mind of a prisoner being marched down death row. No glam today, she was back in the faded jeans with ragged holes that showed tantalizing glimpses of her slim thighs. Probably designer and artfully distressed, but they—along with the little tank and a big shirt hanging on top—made her look like a waif. Like her sister. Even in the dim of the garage she wore big, dark sunglasses, and she'd tied her hair into some kind of messy knot.

No lipstick, which seemed like the worst harbinger of all.

Hulk said hello to him while Igor helped her into the back, pre-empting Joe. No shenanigans. While he should be grateful she gave him no trouble and simply buckled herself in, the defeated, listless Ava made him gloomy. The sun hidden by deep overcast.

Telling himself he respected her privacy, he drove in silence. Probably he should've had the dividing window up, but he hadn't expected this from her and it seemed rude to put it up now. She would do it if she wanted to. Not like she hesitated to do what she liked—the night before had been evidence enough of *that*. Excellent lesson for him on his role in her life. Distant planet in her solar system, easily eclipsed in her interest.

He was lucky she'd dropped her flirtation with him. Much better this way. He could keep professional distance this way, and maybe even his job.

Once he had them in the stream of mid-morning traffic, he chanced a glance at her in the rear-view. Hard to tell with those huge sunglasses, but she seemed to be watching him. Her generous mouth quirked to the side at him looking, verifying it.

"I know I'm a fuck up, but I don't even rate a good morning?" Her voice sounded raspy, like she had a cold. Or like she'd been crying.

"Good morning, Sova," he said. Nice and polite. Just a driver. "Great concert last night."

"Oh, don't you start with me, too." She turned her face away to look out the side window. Then pulled off the glasses and rubbed her eyes. Deep shadows stood out beneath them, purple dusk on a winter day.

Not sure what he'd said wrong—or what to say right, he held his tongue. Arlin's tail thumped on the floorboards and he reached down to ruffle the dog's ears.

"So now I get the silent treatment?" She gave him the stare-down in the mirror again, reminding him of Nona at her wounded and defiant eight-year-old worst, with eyes bloodshot from tears and a stubborn lift to her chin.

"I don't know what I said wrong." He kept it even keeled, not playing into her thing.

"Just… don't be obsequious, okay? I get enough of that. A guy like you—I know you hate my teeny-bopper pop songs and that's fine. Don't pander to me, though."

He opened his mouth to reply, not sure how much to say to her about that, but she plowed on.

"And that shit with my mother, well… All I can say is welcome to my world."

"You have a restraining order against her?" He asked, figuring that for neutral enough information.

"Yeah." She sounded weary. "For the fuck-all good it does."

"You could have told me." Should have, if any of them had the sense to give him a decent briefing. "I'd have been on the lookout for her."

"Yeah, well, I'm not in the habit of dragging out my dirty laundry for every guy who wants to know."

"Fair enough." He concentrated on traffic, not pointing out that he wasn't just any guy, but one supposed to be her bodyguard. This job got crazier by the minute. He should really extract himself.

"I'm sorry." She raked her hands through her hair, caught the knot, and yanked out the comb-thing holding it, impatiently tossing it on the seat. "I feel like utter crap and totally crazy. She does that to me."

"Mothers have a way." Though privately he suspected the pills and booze had more to do with it. Plus whatever Katey had given her to level her out the other direction. He understood going for chemical assistance—but he also knew all too well that it only dug the hole deeper.

"I hate her." Ava offered it like he might be surprised. "I mean, I know it's cliché. Everyone hates their mothers, right? Especially stage mothers, yada yada. But I really just … hate her guts." She finished on a heavy sigh, bruised eyes finding his, waiting as if she'd asked him a question.

"Have you talked to someone about it?" He asked, since he had no answer for her.

She laughed, brittle and too loud, picking at the frayed threads on her jeans. "You mean, like a psychiatrist or something? You don't seem like the kind of guy to suggest counseling, Jack. Shouldn't you be telling me to man up and walk it off? Cause that's what I'm doing. I don't want to talk about my miserable childhood and all my feelings about it. I'm doing what you told me to yesterday—going to work to do my fucking job."

No way he was tromping through that boggy territory with her, talking about his own perverted feelings and what the therapists had done for him—and what they hadn't managed to do. He cast about for something to cheer her up. "Hey, it's Friday, anyway. TGIF, right?"

She flicked her eyes up, lip curled in a snarl. "Hi-ho, hi-fucking-ho. I told you—ditch the coddling and cajoling already."

He nearly responded in kind, about done with her attitude,

but that shadow behind the tawny gold grabbed him, reeling him in as it always had. Shifting gears then. "All right. Enough of the BS then. Tell me why you're dreading today so much."

She tucked one leg up under her, leaning forward with a flicker of interest. "Dread. Now that's an interesting word for it. Why pick that one?"

"I've seen enough of it. It shows in your eyes."

"Really?" She tilted her head, thoughtful. Then opened her phone, did the reverse camera thing girls did to fix their lipstick and take selfies, studying herself. "I don't see it."

"Maybe it's harder to see these things in yourself."

"Or I don't know what it looks like, the way you do."

He nodded slightly, waving the city bus into his lane. She was quiet for a full minute.

"Where do you think dread comes from?"

"Dammit, Sova—I'm a driver, not a psychiatrist."

"Did you just make a *Star Trek* joke?" She actually smiled a little.

"Maybe." He gave her a little grin in the mirror, happy to have lightened her mood, if only a little.

"Nice. But you don't get off that easily. You brought up dread for a reason, so don't pull out the hulking 'I'm just a dumb guy' act. Why dread instead of fear?"

Of course she couldn't leave well enough alone. For her, though, he dragged his thoughts back to those days in Afghanistan, the daily climb into the driver's seat of the Humvee, the dull sense of foreboding settling in with familiar unease. The oppressiveness of it. *Depression is anger turned inward*, his therapist always said. Seemed like fear could be the same. "Maybe fear is sharper—more acute. A reaction to something real. An existing threat. Dread isn't like that. It's like this formless cloud where you're afraid of something that hasn't happened and you don't know what it is, looming somewhere in your future."

Silence. He glanced at her in the rear-view, to find her watching him, unpainted lips slightly parted. "Yes," she breathed. "That's it exactly."

"What are you dreading, Sova?" He asked as gently as he could, as he'd wanted to all those times he'd gazed at her photograph, trying to decipher the emotion behind her golden eyes.

She hesitated long enough that he thought he'd misstepped, that she wouldn't answer. "So many things. Some formless, like you say; some so perfectly vivid they feel like they've already happened. Right now though... today I think it's the looming and inevitable moment everyone discovers I'm a fraud."

"That will never happen."

A light laugh, with a caustic edge. "Don't be so sure. Tick-tock, coming closer with every passing minute."

"I am sure, because I know it's not true. You are no fraud."

Her mouth twisted, bitter and unhappy. "You just bought into the marketing, Jack. I'm the Barbie Doll, all shine and no substance. Airbrushed and packaged. I'm the aging child star still clinging to the fame other people created for her. Singing songs they hand me, like glorified karaoke. I'm one mediocre album away from one of those 'whatever happened to' features."

He didn't believe that, but clearly she did. "You're recording other people's songs for this album—not your own?"

"That's the business, Jacky boy. I'm the puppet with the record company's hand up my ass, making my mouth move."

She said it in her flip tone, but the hollowness under her sculpted cheekbones as she stared numbly out the window got to him. He wanted to tell her that he knew she wrote plenty of the songs she sang. That he loved those in particular. That her words spoke to him when the supposed poets didn't, how she reached inside him and gave voice to all the shattered bits and the stupidly hopeful pieces, making him feel not quite so stupid about it. How sometimes he listened to her golden voice and stared at her face, feeling like maybe she could somehow save him… All of which sounded weird and awful and stalkery.

So he didn't say anything at all.

Arlin panted up at him, brown eyes full of some message he couldn't read.

Then they were at the studio and she was getting out of the limo, Manning taking her arm and talking away at her with all the words that had escaped Joe.

~ 12 ~

THE MUSIC CAME out as hollow and ashen as her cold, black heart. She sang the songs, working through them doggedly. She didn't need heart—or to feel anything—for them to be good enough.

Good enough. That should be her brand. Good enough for lip gloss.

It's pop music, for Christ's sake! Stop mooning like you're some kind of artist. Just repeat the chorus, shake your pretty ass. Nobody cares about anything else. Her mother's words echoed in her head, louder than ever since seeing her again. Ava's nails bit into her palms and the high note went flat.

The others—the session musicians, the sound engineers—oh yeah, they were all pros. All keeping their expressions carefully blank, concentrating on their jobs, doing their damnedest to earn their paychecks, to make the label happy. *All these people trudging to their jobs.* Probably all thinking that if they could get through lunch and the endless afternoon, they could have that cold beer and be free of her for the weekend. If only she could do that, too. *TGIF.*

Taking a moment, she pulled her lipstick out of her pocket, swiping some on just to feel like her more powerful self. *Sing through the scarlet gleam.* She bore down, lifted the song into her cheekbones and forehead the way her dogged voice instructors had tried to teach her. Flat again.

"Cut," she said, dropping into speaking voice mid-croon and shoving the mic away.

One of the session musicians—she didn't look to see who—muttered an expletive. Andy Goldsmith, her sound engineer, scrubbed a hand through his wiry red hair, making it stand out in wild tufts. "Ava, let's—"

She grabbed back the live mic. "It's shit!"

Everyone winced as the feedback whined painfully.

They all hated her and she couldn't blame them. She hated her, too. She pushed the mic away again, choking back apologies that wouldn't do any good anyway. Besides, Andy had already muted it. *You're a star and stars never apologize. Sorry in one hand, shit in the other—see which fills up first.* "I can't do this today."

"Ava," Andy tried again, sounding tired. "We've got it already. We've got umpteen tracks of four new songs with you singing your heart out. Enough. Let me mix them already. You're absolutely right that—"

"That they're shit?"

"Enough with that." He glared around at the others, who all studiously looked elsewhere. "You're a pro. You know as well as I do that not every track is going platinum. It's okay for some songs to be the B-side. It's why B-sides were created."

"And now they no longer exist, so what does that say?"

"More's the pity." He pulled off his headphones and tossed them down. "I can't work with you when you're like this. No one can."

Even though she'd known it, hearing that still hurt. "Fuck you, too, Andy."

"Take the rest of the day, Ava," Andy said, clearly as done as she was. "We'll finish, fill in the holes on these four. I'll work them over the weekend. If I need more from you, I'll let you know, but my gut says you've worked them to death. Let's put them to bed already. You come back Monday and we'll do the other songs next week. When we're all fresh. Get some rest. Do something fun for Christ's sake."

Her stomach hurt, thinking about it. All the fight drained out of her, leaving sick sadness behind. They wanted her gone and who could blame them? She'd kick herself to the curb if she could.

"Right." She pulled off her headphones, pulled her heels back on. Glanced around at the musicians. Most of them she knew, had worked with before. Dren, one of her backup singers, gave her a sympathetic nod.

"I'm really…" She broke off the near apology, perilously close to actual tears. What the hell. First she slipped and fucked Tyler again, which she'd sworn she'd never do, and now she was melting down in the studio.

"It's not a thing, Ava honey," Dren said. "We're good. Andy's right. Go rest. Have you some fun. Bring us back that Ava magic."

Unable to bear a moment more of their sympathy— somehow so much worse than the anger she deserved—she strode out. She craved the chill of vodka and valium with an intensity that carved through her gut. Last night had been the first in a while and even that small taste left her starving for more. Valium or some nice, sparkly cocaine.

In her head, she knew that's why so many did it. When the high of the music abandoned you, leaving you broken on the rocks, you'd reach for anything. She'd seen enough of that to swear off, at least for a while. Seen too many of her cohorts and heroes go down that path. Whitney hadn't been the last straw, but her death had been part of it.

No, she wouldn't do the drugs again—not the hard stuff anyway—but sometimes she missed those days with a fierce ache. The coke made everything sparkle more. It wasn't a high so much as the glorious feeling of invincibility. She never felt like a fraud then, didn't have to face those expressions of dark-eyed pity. Another diva going down. Dwight would get it for her. Had obliquely offered here and there. Just a little pick-me-up, whatever it took to finish the album.

And the album after that.

And the six after that. Until they found her dead in some hotel bathtub. All alone.

She scrubbed furiously at the hot tears.

"Planning to walk home?" Joe had her elbow, stopping her just before the glass doors to the street. "Sova?"

She'd forgotten him there, Arlin at his side. He searched her face with concerned hazel eyes, a bracket of a frown between his thick brows. He looked so strong, his shoulders broad in the suit jacket—and like he actually cared—that she flung herself into his arms, sobbing against his chest.

He froze a moment in surprise, and she braced herself for him to push her away, but his arms came around her, holding her tight, exactly the way she needed. Burying her cheek against his lapel she breathed in his scent and exhaled spurts of weeping. *Never cling to a man because they'll always leave you. I'm the only one who loves you, the only one who ever will,* her mother's voice cut through her head, but the words had less power as long as Joe held her, cupping her head and stroking her hair, murmuring that everything would be okay.

She pulled it together, aware that Arlin pressed against her leg and that she'd smeared lipstick on Joe's white shirt. Her turn to be the psychotic clown. Like mother like daughter. Letting him go, much as she didn't want to, she stood on her own feet, finger combing her hair. Jack handed her a handkerchief, of all things. The old-fashioned kind, of almost transparent linen, with embroidered initials in one corner.

Wiping her nose, she peered over the top of it at him. "I know I look like hell."

He gave her that solemn half-smile. "I'm not sure it's possible for you to be anything but ravishing."

"That's my Jacky boy." She tried for sassy, but it came out watery. "But don't lie to me. I'm a fucking mess."

"Look, you're done for the day." He put an arm around her to steer her back to the elevator to the underground garage, leaving a hand lingering at the small of her back. "C'mon. Let's get you that cheeseburger."

"Cheeseburger?"

"Isn't that what you wanted yesterday? But you had to go to the benefit concert."

He closed his mouth on saying more—he hadn't in any way mentioned the night before, a perfectly discreet driver and bodyguard—but the guilt and shame wormed through her. It wasn't like Joe was her actual boyfriend as she'd pretended, if only for a few hours. Probably Diane wouldn't do another guy in the back seat of Jacky's car. She should apologize, but for what exactly? Maybe that's why stars never apologized. They were such caricatures of themselves, none of them knew what the real transgressions were. Still, here was Joe, offering to take her out for a cheeseburger.

If she had been that normal girl, he'd have been the perfect guy.

"With French fries?" She'd aimed for flirtatious and landed on sniffly.

"And a chocolate malt. My treat."

"Strawberry."

"Absolutely."

He handed her into the back of the limo with that chivalrous courtesy that she'd bet he used with every girl, making every freaking one of them feel like a princess. With savage jealousy, she contemplated those numerous baby's, sweethearts and darlings who'd had his attention before. Who hadn't needed to pay him to put up with them.

"You want Arlin with you?" he asked.

"Can I?" She felt watery again, that he'd offered.

"Sure thing. Go on, Arlin."

The dog bounded into the back seat, a wriggling mass of furry joy, slurping her cheek. "Hey, now," Joe tapped the dog on the head. "Manners, please."

Arlin sat politely, tongue hanging and eyes rolling up at the instruction, as if he found his master *far* too serious and persnickety. Joe got in the front and started the car, heading out in his steady, careful way.

"Where are we going?"

He gave her a cheeky grin. "Best cheeseburger in the city. Enough comfort grease to fix you right up."

"Okay." She used her phone to check her face. Not that awful. Not glam either. She hadn't had the heart to doll up today. Hell, she'd been doing well to get out of bed. Probably wouldn't have without Katey dragging her. Joe's cell rang—a boring generic ringtone, not *Happy*, which he'd said his sister put on there. Maybe Ava would put it back, just to annoy him. He tapped the dash to see who it was. Dwight, checking up on her.

"I'd better answer," he told her, smile gone.

"Put him on speaker."

He hesitated, so she said it more crisply. The diva, not the trainwreck. "I won't let on I can hear, but I won't have you talking around me."

With a press of his lips and a slight head shake, he punched it to speaker. "Ivanchan here."

"You have her contained?" Manning snapped without preamble.

"She's in the limo, yes. We just left the recording studio."

"She have a total meltdown or what?"

Joe met her eyes in the rearview and she raised her brows

back at the assessing look. Couldn't wait to hear this answer.

"Why aren't you asking Ava herself?

"Just answer the fucking question already."

"No meltdown. Goldsmith said they had enough to finish out the tracks so far and let her go for the day, so she'd be fresh for Monday. Something about getting a little more from the musicians and doing a final mix. Not my area, though, so you might talk to him. Or Ava."

She shook her head, though he had his eyes on traffic and not on her.

"I talked to Goldsmith. He says she's off the charts. Like, commit-me-already."

Joe still didn't look at her, but the corner of his jaw firmed with unhappy tension. She stroked Arlin's ears and he shifted to rest his silky chin on her knee. So Andy thought she was certifiable. After all this time. All that fake patience. "Look, Manning," Joe was saying, "I'm not comfortable with—"

"Suck it up. I don't give a shit what makes you comfortable. You talk her out of her tree, or whatever is going on. She wanted you, so she gets you. Deal with this. We don't have time for her to go off the deep end. Get her whatever she needs to be in that studio bright fucking early Monday morning, ready to do the rest of the album next week. I want it done. Tell her that."

Arlin sighed in pure pleasure, gazing up at her in adoration.

"Yes, sir," Joe said.

"And keep me apprised. I want updates."

"Okay. Right now I'm taking her for a cheeseburger, French fries and a strawberry malt."

Dwight was silent so long she thought maybe the call dropped. "You're fucking kidding me," he finally said. "This is why I pay for a nutritionist?"

"You said give her what she wants. That's what she wants."

"Whatever, kid," he sighed. "Do me a favor and keep her

out of the public eye—please, God, no photos, especially after last night—at least until the cray-cray wears off. If she needs to medicate, tag me and I'll get it to you."

"Yes sir." Joe kept his voice neutral, even obedient, and punched off the call. Just a soldier taking orders, but the rigid line of his shoulders gave him away. Pissed. At her or on her behalf?

He shot her a hard look in the mirror, anger in it, but maybe not directed at her. "Doing okay back there?"

"Sure!" She gave him her glamour smile. "Everything's ducky in cray-cray land."

"If you're crazy then my grandmother is a Rockette."

"Was she—a Rockette?"

He blew a laugh through his lips. "Grandmother Ilona? What an image. No. Definitely no."

"Because it's possible, right? I mean, Rockettes fall in love and have babies like normal women, too. Then those babies grow up and have babies, and boom! There you are, some guy has a Rockette for a grandmother."

He laughed for real, some of the tension leaving him. "You have a point there." Then he sobered. "That put me in a bad spot, that you heard all that."

"Don't fret yourself, Jacky boy. I've been hearing that and worse my whole life. It doesn't really matter if it's to my face or not. I'd rather know what they're saying about me and what your instructions are."

He flicked her one of those hard looks. Offended. "I don't have any—"

Her phone rang and Katey's face—in her better days—popped onto the screen. She answered, cutting off whatever Joe had been about to lob her way. Some things she was better off not hearing. "Hey Kates—problem?"

"What I was going to ask you. Dwight wants me to reel you

in."

"Shocking. What yummy worm are you to offer?"

"He told me to line up whatever it takes."

They let that settle between them. "More than cherry sours," Ava finally said, but Katey didn't laugh.

"Well, what the hell—is this about last night?"

Ava paused, assimilating the bitter edge. "I guess you know, huh?"

A burst of sound, then her own voice, shrieking, "You stay away from me, you fucking harpy! I'll kill you. I swear to God, I will!" Pause. Then again. "You stay away from me, you fucking harpy! I'll kill you. I swear to God, I will!"

Her head pounded and she rubbed her eyes. "I was—"

"They're making memes of it everywhere. Some are pretty funny though overall Hilda is having a shitfit. I'm making a file. I'll show you when you get here."

"We're, um, getting burgers and malts. And French fries." Silence. "You want us to bring you some?"

More silence. Finally, "you know I can't eat that junk."

"Just this once—"

"And you shouldn't either. Fried food gives you cellulite. Some superstar you'd be with big ol'saddlebags pouching out from your short shorts."

"Gee, where have I heard that before?" Because Katey sounded just like their mother.

"Fine. Not like the golden girl can do any wrong. But I'm telling you, Aves, Dwight is pissed about this latest fuck up."

Ava stared dully out the window. She really didn't want to see the folder of memes. In the background, Katey had the clip on a loop. *You stay away from me, you fucking harpy! I'll kill you. I swear to God, I will! You stay away from me, you fucking harpy! I'll kill you. I swear to God, I will! You stay away from me, you fucking harpy! I'll kill you. I swear to God, I will!*

"Okay, well—"

"Did Mom ask about me?" Katey interrupted.

"You're asking me now?"

"Yeah. I'm asking you now because you were no better than a fucking zombie this morning. Which I might point out was only a couple of hours ago. Did she ask about me?"

Ava pinched the bridge of her nose, with no idea which answer would be better. "She was crazy acting. Nothing she said made any sense."

A long pause. "What did she want, anyway?"

"What do you *think* she wanted, Katey?" Ava snapped, losing her fragile grip.

"I was just asking." Katey sounded wounded. Now she'd sulk for hours or maybe all weekend. "You don't have to yell at me. It's not *me* you're mad at anyway."

Shit. "I'm sorry, Kates. I just—"

"Save it. Go eat your feelings and then come barf it up like you always do." She clicked off.

"That was Katey," she offered into the silence, though Joe hadn't commented.

"So I gathered." His tone was neutral enough.

"I don't do that—the bulimic thing."

His eyes flicked to hers in the mirror. "It wouldn't be my business if you did."

"I just don't want you to think…" What? That she was as fucked up as she obviously was? "You haven't said anything about that incident last night."

"Also not my business." No glance this time. Just the reserve.

And how would she explain any of it? It made her exhausted to contemplate trying. And lightheaded. "Are you driving me to Siberia for this amazing cheeseburger?"

He chuckled. "Ten more minutes."

"I'm starving is all."

"It's not even noon yet."

Wow. She'd flamed out faster than she'd thought. "I'm an artiste," she proclaimed loftily. "We are not bound by the dull constructs of the average boring human. Isn't that right, Arlin? Yes. We eats when we wants."

Arlin, of course, didn't reply, but he licked her hand and somehow, somewhere in his doggy brain, she felt sure he understood.

✦ ✦ ✦

OKAY, IT *WAS* the best cheeseburger she'd ever had in her life, even if Joe did make her eat it in the limo. Following Dwight's orders to keep her out of the public eye, but it annoyed her more than usual because she really wanted to be one of those girls sitting at the park benches under the trees, flirting with their boyfriends.

At least Joe had agreed to climb in back with her, after banishing Arlin to the front where he watched them with bereft longing.

"Don't even think about it," Joe admonished and Ava wasn't sure which of them he was talking to. Probably both. Arlin didn't get to have human food and Ava didn't get the point.

"I'm on a super strict diet all the time—that's all Katey meant—so this is a treat for me. Arlin should get to have a treat, too."

"He does get treats—just not human food."

"You and me, Arlin." She shook her head sorrowfully. "Always on a short leash."

Joe gave her an odd look at that. "Doesn't it bug you, that they say that?"

"Whose side are you on? You're the one holding the other

end at the moment." She didn't want to think about it right then, really. They had the radio up, playing a great rock mix. The cheeseburger dripped with greasy goodness, the meat nearly as melty as the cheese, and the strawberry malt tasted of sugar and sunshine. There were even chunks of real strawberries. The fries left her fingers shiny and her mouth singing. Ava swirled a fry in the ketchup, then the mustard, popped it in her mouth and added a suck of strawberry.

So good.

Jack was staring at her, those lines paired between his brows. She chewed and swallowed. "What?"

He looked down, shaking his head and adjusted the paper wrap on his burger. "Some things a guy just can't take."

That caught her hard, almost painfully. She'd disgusted him with her behavior. It shouldn't matter. She didn't care about this rando guy who worked for her. Even if he did have a cute dog. "I don't blame you a bit, Jacky boy."

"Exactly. Who puts mustard on their French fries? It's disgusting."

In surprise, she laughed. Then clapped a hand over her mouth to cover the half-chewed muck, shocked at herself, then nearly choking on it. Jack thumped her back, eyes crinkled with amusement.

"Fortunately I know the Heimlich."

She cleared her throat with some of the malt. "Do you? Will you patch up all of my boo-boos, too?"

"Basic first aid, I can handle." He polished off the last of his chocolate malt. He'd eaten faster than anyone she'd ever seen, the double cheeseburger and extra-large fries gone in a few bites. The malt, though, he savored, sitting sideways on the seat, sun in his hair and lightening his eyes so the hazel glimmered green, watching her. "What's the plan?"

"Plan?"

He gathered up the detritus of their meal, neatly tucking everything into the one bag. "What do you want to do? You have the weekend off. You're supposed to kick back and relax." *Do something fun for Christ's sake.* "Do you want me to take you somewhere?"

"Take me somewhere?"

"You know—go somewhere for the weekend?"

"Is that what people do?" They'd done that in *Little Girl Lost,* the family vacation before her movie mom died.

"Sure—why not? You don't want to sit around while your sister plays last night on a loop, do you?" His eyes held unexpected sympathy. And no, she didn't want to and Katey would do exactly that. Going away from all of that…

"Katey doesn't travel," she said.

"So?" He shrugged, in that fatalistic way of his. Maybe like his Grandmother Ilona did. "Doesn't mean you can't."

No. No, it didn't. She'd feel guilty, of course, but a couple of days away from those sharp-edged barbs and accusations would be… a miracle really.

"And you'd take me?"

"I am your driver. My damn job." He slanted her a grin. "Seriously—Manning gave me my marching orders. Give you what you want so you can get back in the studio. Seems like it would be good for you to get away. So, pick your spot—within driving distance."

"I have no idea how to decide. I've never picked a place to go to before. And how far is 'driving distance'? You pick. Somewhere without cameras, if such a place exists."

"Oh, it exists. I know the perfect place. One question, though."

She braced herself, not sure she wanted to hear it. Not sure she could deal. But she pulled out an easy smile and an insouciant hair flip. "Hit me, Jacky boy."

"Do you have any other cars besides this one?"

~ 13 ~

HE'D SURPRISED HER with that—both what he'd asked and the possibility of there being another car. Of course, he'd shocked himself with this whole impulsive plan and was blindly forging ahead at this point. Her misery made him crazy and he'd do whatever it took to make her smile again. The real kind.

Something, too, about the way the sister had jabbed at her, layering salt in the wound... No way he'd feel okay thinking about Ava, so obviously raw and floundering for some kind of purchase, suffering that all weekend. She needed to heal and toughen, not bleed more.

She blinked her golden eyes in real puzzlement instead of that fake stage flutter she pulled out, reassessing in a way that made him wonder what she'd thought he was going to ask. "Why would I have another car?"

"So I can take you away somewhere," he explained patiently, "without you becoming an immediate spectacle. One of the fundamentals of keeping a low profile is not being recognized."

She wrinkled her nose at him, a practiced gamine expression that nevertheless charmed him. "I know that, silly. But I don't have another. At least I don't think so... What do we do?"

If her question hadn't carried the weight of potential disappointment, he would have teased her. Would have said how the plebes of the world did this thing called 'renting a car.' But she was too fragile for any but the right kind of teasing.

"No big deal," he reassured her. She wanted him to take over the decisions for her? He could do that. God knew he could plan a road trip, but not in the ostentatious limo. "I'll take care of it."

He punched in a call to Manning. Fortunately, the midday traffic remained reasonably light, but it would thicken up soon enough and he wanted to be on the road north before everyone else in the city got the same idea.

"What do you need?" Manning answered with the question, sounding less than belligerent for once. Clearly all in on getting Ava handled, whatever it took.

"I'm taking her on a road trip and I need a rental car. Something fun, but not too high end. Convertible, maybe." Might as well live it up.

"Fine," Manning agreed without rancor. "One of the guys will meet you with it at her building, along with a credit card and petty cash. I don't have to tell you to pick someplace discreet, do I?"

"Nope. I'll check in, but otherwise you won't hear a thing."

"I'd better not. Hilda and Katey have their heads together on soothing the meme madness anyway. You should take at least one other guy along for backup."

"No, Dwight." Ava called from the back seat. Glasses on and jaw firm. "We agreed. One guy. Driver and bodyguard combined. No one else comes along."

Manning muttered something incomprehensible, but almost certainly vile.

"What's that?" Joe asked, winking at Ava in the mirror.

"Yes, Ava, whatever you say, Ava." Manning's sarcasm coiled out caustically. "But this is it. No fuckups. I don't want to hear anything about or from you beyond what's already out there until Monday morning."

Ava gave the dash a middle finger salute.

"You hear me, Ava?" Manning demanded.

"She heard you," Joe confirmed. "Consider it handled." And he clicked off while the getting was good. So far as that went.

✦   ✦   ✦

AVA SAID SHE could pack her own stuff—laughing at his caution to keep it simple, nothing fancy—so he waited with the limo in the garage to make the trade. Better than facing that penthouse again. Or holding his tongue and temper if Ava's sister lit into her. No telling what the deal was there—or why Ava put up with it—but he'd stay clear of that battle lest he come out as collateral damage.

Figuring it would take a while, he went to take Arlin to do his business and stretch his legs. To his surprise, Manning himself waited for him with a zippy little Alfa Romeo convertible.

"Not exactly low profile," Joe remarked.

Predictably, Manning scowled. Handing Joe a zippered document case, he surveyed the car. "She's Ava—not some hillbilly prom date," he said.

"What, her ass can't touch less than leather seats?"

"Exactly." Manning didn't crack a smile. "Something to bear in mind. She's way out of your league. Take her away. Don't fuck her, no matter what she tries. I tucked a little candy pack in the case there, should you need it. There's not enough to cause problems, but plenty to manage her mood. Just keep her away from any coke. Her ID's in there, too, just in case of trouble, which—should you need that—you're fucked and you can consider yourself fired and sued. With any luck you can tuck her up in a posh suite, give her a candy treat, and she'll sleep all weekend."

Joe refrained from commenting on that, or on the array of

sedatives Manning had thoughtfully included. "Why didn't you brief me on the restraining order?"

"Which one?" Manning shot back. "There's probably two dozen. Her mother is the wimpiest of the bunch. A star like Ava accumulates those things like a comet trail."

Huh. "Does she know about all of them?"

"Why should she? God above, Ivanchan—are you really this much of a rube? Your good ol' boy routine works for our girl, so I'm going with it, but keep in mind that this is a job. Yours is to keep her safe, which means don't worry her pretty head with extraneous shit. Understood?"

"Yes, sir," he drawled, and tossed off a salute sloppy enough to be insulting, though Manning had already headed for the elevator.

✦　✦　✦

"IT'S LITTLE," AVA peered at the two-seater dubiously. She'd changed into tight jeans that stopped below her knees, along with the pearls again and a white tank, with a denim jacket over it. She'd also donned a black wig that made her look like some femme fatale from an old noir flick, especially with the leopard-print scarf she'd wrapped over it. The mirrored glasses swallowed her piquant face, so that only her lips—now cotton-candy pink—showed.

"Not every car is big as an airplane," he replied, with what he figured was admirable patience. In the jump seat, Arlin laughed at the joke, but Ava stuck her tongue out at him. Resigned to the wait, he stowed her bag in the trunk and arranged the snacks the dramatic nutritionist had pressed on him. Who knew they made chips out of kale? At last Ava got in the car, reaching for the seatbelt without being told.

"Funny boy," she commented when he seated himself. "Just

don't roll this thing and kill us."

"Scared?" He started, then revved the engine—very nice power—just to yank her chain and she flashed him an annoyed golden glance, then softened.

"With you, Jacky boy? Never."

She fell asleep before they made it past the Cloisters, dropping off like a little kid, practically mid-sentence. Probably due to the combination of the perfect autumn sunshine, the huge meal that still sat heavy in his own gut, the late night, and more than a little emotional hangover. Hopefully Manning hadn't pressed any more sedatives on her.

She'd picked the radio station, setting it to the same one she'd played for their limo picnic, so he left it there. Normally he'd have synced his phone, played one of his Ava mixes—but that wouldn't be the thing. Even if it wouldn't prompt questions about why he had the playlist in the first place, he didn't know if she even liked listening to her own stuff. But even if she did, she wouldn't want the reminder today, given what had happened.

She have a meltdown or what?

He didn't know what to call what she'd had, and he thought he'd seen every kind of human misery and failure to cope. She'd gotten on that mic, pulling her diva act, everyone kowtowing to her and he'd figured it would be fine. Then she'd blown her intro, not once, but five times. In fact she never hit the timing exactly right, like she couldn't hear it, even though Goldsmith had cued her precisely and obviously. The more she tried and failed, the more she fragmented, high notes going flat, caving in on herself.

The temper tantrum had been almost a relief after witnessing that. Not only for him. It had showed on everyone's faces. That and their determination to hustle her out of there.

He understood Manning's haste to give him whatever he asked for, to hand off the problem of Ava for the weekend. Her manager had to know better than anyone how close Ava was to cracking altogether. A weekend away wouldn't be enough to put her back together enough to finish this album, but he didn't know what would be.

Maybe she was right. Not that she was a fraud. But she might be done.

Time would tell.

So, they'd do it the only way he'd found that worked—one day at a time. Take the break, don't fret the future. She probably needed months, but he'd give her at least a low-key weekend, something totally different from her posh life and boy-band hottie hookups. She needed a dose of reality. No, he wouldn't fuck her. Not even he would be that stupid. But he could show her a little platonic romance. Maybe then she'd see how guys like Tyler just used her and left her even more broken.

That's what she needed from him. Even what she wanted. *Just a cute young couple out for an evening stroll.*

When he turned off the turnpike onto the coastal highway, the change of speed roused her. She pulled off her sunglasses and blinked sleepily at him, a red mark on her cheek where the frames had dug in.

"Sorry to wake you," he told her. "We're not there yet, if you want to nap some more."

She frowned, then looked out the windshield at the beach town going by. "I don't nap."

"Okay." Whatever. His mom was like that, too, insisting that she couldn't nap. "Since you're awake then, I need to stop at the store. We can put the top up and you can wait in the car with Arlin."

The dog, too, had crashed, snoring belly-up in the jump seat.

"Store?" She was still fuzzy, peering around her. "Do you even know where we are?"

"Yep. No worries." He patted her on the knee before he

thought better of it and she covered his hand with hers, trapping it there and giving him a smile. A real one. So he left it there, rather than risk making her sad again by pulling it away.

"A grocery store?" She studied the sign as he pulled into the little lot, as if she'd never seen one before.

"People get food at them." He couldn't help teasing her on that one and she slapped the hand he'd rested on her knee. At least it let him snatch it back. The flex of her lean thigh muscle had been nearly too much. *No touching her.*

"I know that! Why are we getting food?"

"Well, Arlin needs more than kale chips, for starters, and the place I have in mind does not have an in-house nutritionist and cook. Staying or coming in?"

"Coming in," she said. He caught a flash of the eyeroll before she donned the glasses again.

"Stay, buddy. Not this time—sorry," he told Arlin.

"You could lie and say he's a service dog." Ava pointed at the sign on the sliding glass doors. "One of my costume gals does that with her Pekinese, so she can take it everywhere."

"Don't get me started on that," he muttered.

"What?"

"Nothing. Sure you don't want to wait in the car?"

"No." She gave him a scornful look. "This is fun."

"That would be a first. Okay then—make yourself useful and push the cart."

With no protest, she did, following him around the store as he loaded the cart. He kept an eye on the other shoppers, but no one looked at Ava twice. She could have been any of the polished, designer-clothes wearing Connecticut women stocking up for a weekend of lavish entertaining.

"Anything you want, Sova?"

"Like what?"

"I don't know. Cookies? Lemon-drop martini makings?"

"Are we leaving civilization?"

"Pretty much." He snagged a package of cake pops and handed them to her to put in the cart. When he turned back from rejecting some bakery brownies as too plastic-looking, she was still holding them, frowning. "No on the cake pops?"

"I've never seen these. Why 'birthday cake'?"

"Because it's delicious. You'll see." He took them and tossed them in the cart. "Lemons and sugar, right? We'll stop at the liquor store for the rest."

"You sure are in a happy mood all of a sudden." She sounded accusing and he wished he could see more of her face. But she was right—he was happy.

"We're going to one of my favorite places in the world." *With the woman of my dreams.* And he wasn't going to think any further past it than that. He bagged the lemons and tossed them in the cart. "So, yeah. I'm happy. You'll see why."

"Where is it?"

"Surprise."

✦ ✦ ✦

IT TOOK ANOTHER hour to get there, plus a little extra time at the liquor store. A squall came through, forcing them to put up the top. Unfortunately not before Arlin got wet enough to fill the small space with eau-de-wet-pooch. "Sorry," he said, when Ava waved a hand in front of her face.

She cocked her head at him. "Don't be. This is what people do, right? They go to the grocery store and their dogs get wet and smell bad."

"Have you really never been in a grocery store?"

"Of course I have. Long time ago, when I was little. Before... you know. Everything."

"You don't have to talk about it."

She rolled her shoulders and stared out the rain-splattered windshield, her hands pressed palms together and tucked them between her thighs. "I don't mind. I mean—my whole life is all out there in the fan stuff, right? I got my break doing *Tween Hangout* when I was seven. Katey was on it, too."

"Weren't you a little young to be on a tween show?"

"Well, yeah, but that's the business for you. They dress you up to be older than you are until you turn eighteen, then they try to freeze you there any way they can. Plastic surgery. Creams galore. Acupuncture. You name it."

"You've had plastic surgery?" He asked it carefully, though the idea kind of pissed him off. She heard it in his voice anyway.

"Upset to find out the fantasy isn't real?" she mocked lightly. "I had a nose job when I was six. Katey, too, plus a bunch more stuff. If I showed you a photo of her from before, you wouldn't recognize her." She trailed off, an edge to her voice. Shaking it off, she adjusted her wig. "I was lucky to have only that. Though Dwight has been making noises lately about me getting a maintenance face lift."

He chewed on that, finding himself angry as hell in fact. "You're twenty-two."

"But I don't look eighteen anymore." She waggled a finger in an excellent imitation of Manning, then dropped her hand. "Sorry to disappoint. Something to remember about me, Jacky boy—I'm all surface and no substance. Like a cubic zirconium: flashy and totally inauthentic. I'm no natural diamond, but a manmade fabrication." She said it with her usual acerbic wit, but also sounded sad enough that he reflexively reached over to give her hand a reassuring squeeze. A lapse in judgement brought on by the too-intimate feel of the small car and the pouring rain. For all that, it still could have been brief, and quickly over, but she hung on.

"I'm not disappointed," he told her firmly. "I've got so

much plastic and metal in me I'm practically a Borg." And what the hell had possessed him to admit that? He plowed on, hoping she wouldn't notice the slip. "I'm just... appalled. Who gives a six-year-old a nose job?"

"An ambitious mama," she replied in a light tone, but grip on his hand tightened.

"I mean, what kind of plastic surgeon would?"

"Oh, there's always someone who can be bought, if you want it bad enough. And Mother wanted the dream. Even before *Tween Hangout*, it was the toddler beauty pageants. As far back as I can remember."

He had to slide her a quick look, to see if she was teasing him, but her expression was dead serious. "Like that reality show?"

"Omigod, yes." She laughed, finally releasing his hand to smooth her wig. With the top up, she'd taken off the scarf and glasses, but she kept messing with the hair, like it irritated her. "That's not public info, by the way. But Kates and I used to watch that show *religiously*. You have no idea."

"Because..." He considered his phrasing. "It reminded you of good times?"

She gasped theatrically. "God, no! The show is appalling, but not anything close to what it was like to live it. I still have weird nightmares about those pageants."

"Then why watch?" He glanced at her, trying to read her face. Personally, he avoided all war movies, anything with explosives. Too risky that the nowhere zone could descend and... well. Not good. "If it was that bad I'd think you'd—" There he went, slipping again, but he couldn't think of another word for it. "You know, trigger," he finished, sorry he'd gone there.

"You're an interesting guy, Jacky boy," she murmured, giving him a thoughtful sidelong look. "I guess you'd know about that.

Yeah. Triggers. Fucking things. I dunno—with that show, there's this whole other aspect, watching those little girls go through what we did. The awful mothers having their fights, screaming at their daughters and each other. The dresses, the makeup, practicing the dance routines, the fucking unbelievable pressure. It's kind of reassuring, in a way. Like… it wasn't just something I made up. It *was* horrible. It helps to know I'm not crazy. Not about that anyway."

She shrugged, more of a wiggle in the seat, then set her hand on his thigh. Squeezed. Electricity shot straight to his groin and blue-screened his brain. "You don't feel like a Borg. All delicious strong muscle here. Do you work out?"

Too much to hope that she'd missed that. She was changing the subject to avoid the pain of discussing it—a trick he recognized well—but he was in no position to hold her feet to the fire. It took everything in him to master the mad rush of need her slim hand ignited. He blew out a long, even breath, counting the beats with the windshield wipers. *Answer the question. Don't think about your cock.*

"Yes. I run, lift weights. Other stuff, rowing machine." For the life of him he couldn't remember what else. "That kind of thing."

"Mmm. Paid off." She slid her hand along his quads, turning in her seat a little to watch his face. *Keep your eyes on the road, buddy.* "Was that because of the Army or did you before that?"

He had to clear his throat, keep the tone casual, not a growl of lust. "I played sports in high school, so I did some then, but yeah, really got in the habit in basic training." That helped to level him, thinking about all of that and not her hand much too close to the hot zone. "Then on tour, there's a lot of down time. Working out is a productive way to fend off boredom, gives you the illusion of progress."

"I like that—the 'illusion of progress.'"

Okay, he could do this. Conversation. "Believe me, when you're doing the same patrols for weeks on end, living a war that goes nowhere, accomplishes nothing, the illusion of progress can be what saves your sanity."

"And then you got hurt."

The flash. The staggering impact of heat and sound. Screaming. The agony. His bad leg flared with remembered pain and he had to shake it off.

"Sorry," she said, pulling her hand away.

"How did you know?" He thought he didn't limp and she'd touched the good leg.

"You told me." She widened her eyes when he glanced over. "Medical discharge."

Oh right. He was a fucking idiot. She put her hand back, even higher. His suit pants were far too thin, the heat of her fingers burning through.

"Ava…"

"Oops. That's a penalty for using the wrong name." She inched her hand higher, flexing it on his thigh and he stopped her by covering it with his, trying to catch his breath and cool his raging brain. "How were you injured?"

"A, uh, explosion. IED." He couldn't talk about that. Especially not with her slim fingers, wiggling beneath his, sliding determinedly higher, setting fire to his brain. *Don't fuck her, no matter what she tries.* "Stop this now, Sova. It's not safe."

"Answer me this and I will." She nudged closer, inching up her hand, leaning in close enough that her perfume swamped him, nibbling at the corner of his jaw. "Jacky boy, does *everything* work?"

"Ava…" The edges of his vision went black.

"Uh-uh, that's another penalty." Quick as a snake, she cupped his hardening bulge. His eyes nearly rolled up in his head and he focused them with fierce determination on the road, tightening his hands on the wheel. Good thing they were on a nearly deserted lane. "Oh my, yes. Yes, this seems to work just fine. Is this for me?"

"Okay, enough," he definitely growled it now. "Or I'll break my promise not to wreck us."

"Then pull over."

"No. Stop this now. We're not doing this."

She laughed softly, a warm siren song, not releasing him from her tenacious grip, instead encircling him with practiced ease. She stroked him and he groaned. "That's not how it looks from here."

His body made the decision before his brain processed it, hitting the brakes and crunching onto the shoulder of the tree-lined two-lane. He killed the engine and turned, putting a hand behind her neck and taking her mouth in a ferocious kiss.

Just as he'd fantasized. Much harder than he'd planned to.

But she tasted so damn sweet and those luscious lips parted, dragging him under, pulling him into her, that slim hand tight on his cock. He made a ragged sound and she murmured agreement, nimble fingers undoing his belt buckle and plucking at the closure of his suit pants.

"Fuck me, Jacky boy," she said into his mouth. "Right here on the side of the road. I need it."

The rain roared against the windshield. Or that was the driving desire against his skull. He kissed her with a sense of desperation, needing to feed on that mouth. She freed his cock and it sprang free with a blast of blood to his ragged brain.

"Holy shit," he gasped.

"The holiest." She bit his lower lip and squeezed his cock. "Jacky boy," she purred. "I'm going to—gah! Arlin, gross."

"Arlin!" He echoed, wiping the dog slobber from his mouth, just as Ava was.

She screwed up her nose. "Guess he wanted in on that very

hot kiss."

Arlin's tail thumped against the seat back, his head still thrust between them, hot doggy breath filling the space. Saving him from disaster yet again.

"The stopping woke him up and he figures it's time for a pee. I'd better take him out, even though we're nearly there."

She raised an eyebrow at his still throbbing cock, sticking out of his suit pants, between the tails of his dress shirt. "Like that?"

"Pass on that, thanks." He tucked himself back in—not at all comfortable, but with a sense of reprieve—and zipped up. He got out into the pouring rain and tipped the seat forward for Arlin to leap out. Ava got out, too, tipping up her face to the rain and holding up her palms to it, like some kind of sculpture of an Egyptian goddess.

"You'll get wet," he warned her, really wishing she'd stayed in the car.

She shot him a smile that was pure sex. "You already did that to me, Jacky boy. How close?"

For a crazed moment, he thought she meant how close he'd been to coming in her fierce little grip, which was much too damn close, but the sparkling amusement in her golden eyes—all the brighter with that black hair—informed him otherwise.

"Ten minutes, maybe." What the hell had he been thinking, taking her away alone like this? That she wouldn't try to blow him in the car, that was for sure. He should've been smart and tucked her away in that posh hotel suite, nicely sedated while he drank himself to oblivion in the bar. Not too late for that.

"Hmm…" A smile teased her lips, long lashes dark against the shadowed curve under her eyes.

"What?" Arlin had finished, returning to sit politely at his ankle.

"I'm trying to decide if that's too far or if I should hop up on this hood, shimmy off these crops and let you do what you please."

The image electrified him—and, fortunately, kicked his brain into rational thought again. *Keep her out of the public eye—please, God, no photos.* He shook his head emphatically. "No."

There. A solid decision.

"I thought you promised to give me what I want," she pouted, amping up the wattage. Amazing how sexy and gorgeous she could look soaking wet, her wig slightly askew from his hands. Though he wanted it off her, wanted to see *her.* She boldly eyed the vicinity of his erection, though he'd closed his jacket over it. "You like the idea."

Resolute, he opened the car door for Arlin to hop in, then held it for her. "Not a factor."

"It is if it means I can seduce you into forgetting your better judgment." She sidled up to him, rubbing against him like a cat, threading her arms behind his neck. "I want you to fuck me, Jacky boy, and I won't take no for an answer."

He managed not to kiss her again, manfully lifting his chin, which only meant she dragged her avid mouth along his throat, scraping with her pearly teeth. He was a lost man. Too late to take her to a hotel. She was right—she could seduce him easily, and not only because he'd promised to give her what she wanted.

Of their own accord, his hands slipped around her narrow waist and she leaned into him, her lush breasts soft and her nipples hard. She fit against him perfectly. The feel, scent and taste of her, all perfect.

One weekend, and he'd deal with the fallout later. His MO.

"Say yes, Jack," she crooned, sucking lightly at the skin under his jaw.

"Not in public," he gasped, setting her away from him. "Line in the sand there."

"Oh, Jacky boy." She raked him with her intense gaze. "You

should know by now that I'll push you past every line you think you have."

He didn't bother to tell her she already had.

~ 14 ~

JOE DIDN'T GET back in the car right away—thinking he could cool off, probably—so she flipped down the visor to fix her lipstick. Holy God, the man could kiss. And that cock. Nothing at all wrong with the man. Her fingers still tingled from it. They seriously needed to get out of this tiny car and into bed where she could explore him at her leisure. She straightened her wig, surveying the drape of it critically. Her Cleopatra wig, Katey called it, for how exotic it made her look—and a bit of a snarky reminder that Elizabeth Taylor had been a white woman playing an Egyptian, a fraud just like Ava.

And, like her Barbie façade, it made her itchy from wearing it too long. Jack's Diane wouldn't wear a wig. Enough of that shit. Impatiently, she pulled it off and threw it on the console, then finger combed through the curls plastered to her scalp, hitting tangles immediately.

Joe let Arlin into the jump seat, then slid an opaque glance at the discarded wig as he arranged his long legs in the driver's seat. He had to adjust the pull of his pants twice. Still hard for her. Atta boy.

"Is that wise?" he asked. No cranky like a man with blue balls.

"There's not a soul out here and didn't you say there's no one where we're going? Who's to see?"

"Or you could wait ten minutes more and not risk it." He

143

checked all the mirrors, then pulled onto the road. That meticulous, slow-paced thoroughness of his shouldn't turn her on, but it totally did. Of course, as hot as he'd made her with that demanding, possessive kiss, it could be difficult to tell *what* was doing it for her. It just did.

"I'm all over itchy. I've had it on for *hours*—I can't bear ten more minutes." For anything. "My current hair is way too long for extended wig-wearing."

He burst out in a laugh that warmed her from the toes up. "There's a right hair-length for that?"

"Of course, dummy. I wore this wig on the 10:39 tour, which meant my real hair was super short. Like buzz cut." She tugged on a stubborn tangle. Might have to wait for her brush.

"How short? I don't remember seeing photos of you like that."

She stopped messing with her hair, giving him a long look. Well, surprise, surprise. "You've seen a lot of photos of me, Jacky boy?"

He snorted, but didn't look at her. "There are twenty-story videos of you in Times Square."

"Yeah, but besides that."

"What do I know? I just never saw you with a buzz cut." He shrugged it off. Something, though, about the studious way he watched the road and so carefully did not look at her nudged her intuition.

"No, sirree, you wouldn't have. I wore another wig, one that looked like me, until it grew back enough for extensions." She gave up, flipping the visor back into place, wrapped her fingers in the mess and tugged. "Maybe I should cut it all off again."

They'd scream at her for it, but they did that anyway. *This is it. No fuckups.* Dwight meant it. She might be done. Breach of contract. Everything she'd sacrificed for, gone. She could shave her head then and no one would care. Just her and Katey, sister ghosts in some kind of made-for-streaming age-swap of Grey Gardens.

"Don't cut it."

She grabbed onto Joe's words like that rope in *Poltergeist*, dragging herself back from the hell behind the TV screen. "Why do guys always break out the 'don't cut your hair' business?" She said it flippantly, searching for the earlier playful vibe. What she got for thinking too much.

He pulled into a driveway that tunneled into the trees and ended at a weathered, ramshackle house. Killing the engine, he looked out the windshield. He took a deep breath and let it out slowly. Then looked at her, his gaze not soft, but intent and hot. Somehow very green all of a sudden. "Because it's beautiful. *You* are so fucking beautiful, Sova."

"What happened to not in public?" she breathed, transfixed. The way he said that…

He grinned, lopsided, as if off balance. "We're here."

She peered through the rain-runneled windshield. "Here?" she said to no one, as he was already out of the car, tipping the lever for the seat. Arlin bounded up onto the deck that seemed to wrap around the place—and looked decrepit enough to collapse under the dog's weight. But no, Joe followed, her suitcase and a grocery bag already in his arms. She got out and put her hands on her hips, glaring at him when he returned for another trip.

"Here?" she demanded.

"God, you're gorgeous when you go imperious. Yes, here."

"I thought you said ten more minutes."

"You lost track of time." With his head still in the trunk, he held out the bag from the liquor store. "Take this in, would you? I can get the rest."

Glaring at him—a worthless effort as he didn't even look— she snatched the bag and stalked up the rain-slick wooden steps, her ballet flats skidding a little. Total death trap. Then she made it around the corner and stopped, awestruck.

The place perched on an outcropping over the ocean, the waves dashing in gray white fury below. No other houses in any direction—just jagged cliffs, trees and water. A set of ramshackle steps led down to the rocks, snaking back and forth on their way.

"Incredible spot, huh?" Joe paused beside her, his hand briefly settling on the small of her back, then went inside.

Every time he did that, it made her heart turn over a little. It was sweet. Sweet in a way that nobody ever was to her. So she followed him into the house.

It looked like it had been last decorated before she was born, with a plaid upholstered couch and ancient kitchen with cracked linoleum and yellowed curtains at the windows. Not a rented cabin or resort. Framed photos on the mantel of the fireplace where paper crackled, burning into the logs of a just-lit fire. A wall heater cranked and popped in the effort to dispel the chill. Like a family house. She didn't at all know what to think of it.

"What is this place?" She asked, a little nervous about the answer, and added the liquor sack to the group on the kitchen table, which Joe was rapidly emptying, putting things in the cabinets. Arlin crunched his way through a bowl of kibble, water waiting beside it.

"My grandparents' place. Summer cabin. It belongs to the whole family now—each of us bought in and takes turns using it."

"Someone should take a turn at fixing it up." She picked at the linoleum on the table. What the hell?

He tsked. "Such a snob, she is," he said in an exaggerated Russian accent. "For what you don't like this furniture? This is perfectly good couch. The freezer still makes ice. Don't talk to me about changing what works already."

She crossed her arms, leaning a hip on the table, the unexpected playful side of him helping defuse her nerves. He grinned at her, so different than his usual reserved demeanor. "Your grandmother?" she guessed.

"Got it in one." He pulled out a saucepan, dumped some olive oil in it and started the stove warming. "I don't suppose you know how to chop garlic?"

"Not one of my mad skillz, no."

"Then make those martinis you bragged about being so good at."

She watched him a moment, still in his suit, slapping a cutting board on the counter, then mashing a garlic with the flat blade of a butcher knife. "You're cooking?"

"You might not be hungry now, but you will be later and the sauce is best if it simmers a while."

"What are you making?" She looked around the tiny antique kitchen. No juicer, for sure. With a sigh, she picked up the bag of lemons and began washing them in the sink. Cinna would kill her if she ruined his repair on her French manicure already, but whatever.

"Spaghetti and meatballs," he said. "Family recipe."

"Pasta is a traditional Russian dish?"

"Ah-ah." He dumped the garlic in the sizzling olive oil. "My mother's side is Italian. I swear I come by this honestly."

She found a paring knife and rinsed the garlic leavings off the cutting board, then cut a few of the lemons in half. "Measuring glass?"

Jack reached over her head to an upper cabinet and handed her one from an impressive array. "Jeez—how many shot glasses does one family use?"

"Russian," he reminded her. "They don't believe in adding anything to the vodka."

"I guess that means a martini shaker is right out." She held the lemon over the shot glass and squeezed as hard as she could, rewarded with three drops. This would take all night.

"Fraid so. We'll improvise. Here." He took the lemon from her hand and squeezed it over the shot glass, about ten times more effectively than she had. Strong hands. She needed them on her. Now.

"How much do you need?" he asked, glancing at her, then paused.

"A lot," she answered, wetting her lips so he'd have to look. Sex would settle her down. Time for him to pony up already. "I think I need a lot."

He caged her against the counter, mouth hot on hers in a flash. Just as he'd done in the car. Zero to sixty. Joe might not be a race car driver, but he ran fast once he made up his mind. From teasing and chopping garlic to nearly violent sexual fury. She hadn't been kidding that he made her wet before. She went there again, immediately, her vulva clenching as if she already had him inside her. Sizzling garlic and the bite of lemons filled her head with a swimming haze of desire, as she gave herself over to his mouth, to the weight of his muscled body crushing her against the sharp edge of the counter.

When he released her mouth, she dropped her head back, clutching his shoulders as his mouth trailed down her throat, a path of liquid fire arrowing to her groin.

"I love how you do that," he growled between kisses.

"Do what?"

"You just…" He bit the side of her neck and she sagged against him. "Like that. You melt. You take me in."

"Come on in, Jacky boy," she urged him.

He groaned and let her go. "*After* the sauce is started." Then deflected her punch with his shoulder, laughing.

"Really?" She leveled her best glare at him.

"Told you—it's better for the simmering." He winked at her,

then held up his hands in a gesture of surrender. "Just don't use the paring knife."

"Make yourself useful and squeeze me one and a half shots of lemon juice," she snapped and began rummaging for something to use as a shaker. Stopped. "Jack?"

He turned at her serious tone. "Sova?"

"Why are we here?"

To his credit, he didn't deliberately misunderstand or deflect her. "It was the best I could think of on short notice. You'll be left alone; no one would think to look for you here. And…" He hesitated, looking over her shoulder into some middle distance only he could see.

"And?"

His eyes came back to hers, somber and moss dark. "It's always been a good place for me, when I was… feeling cracked. You know?"

Oh. Her turn to look away.

"But we don't have to stay," he added. "If you don't like it, we can go find a resort or hotel. I have the credit cards from Manning and—"

"No." She hugged her arms around herself, surveying the worn kitchen, the rain and surf crashing outside. She didn't feel like herself in this place, and that was maybe a good thing. "I like it. And after the billing this marinara sauce has gotten, how could I miss out?"

"Okay." He smiled at her, a bare twitch of his stern lips, something sad in it. "But say the word and we can go."

"Not before I've had my martini. I've never worked so hard for one in my life."

No martini glasses either, but amidst the assortment of plastic cups, chipped juice glasses and water bottles, she found a full-belled couple for red wine. The rims didn't sugar perfectly, but they worked. Arlin had retired to snore belly-up by the fire and

Joe was wrists deep in a bowl of ground meat he'd been doctoring with all sorts of ingredients. Who knew meatballs had more than meat in them? Then again, she probably hadn't had spaghetti and meatballs since the *Tween Hangout* days. Before that it had been the kind from a can. She and Katey would eat them with crackers and cream soda. Once they got the TV gig, though, it was all balanced diets and daily weight checks.

Eyes on the prize. The camera adds ten pounds and nobody wants to look at a fat girl.

"Ready to taste?" She held up the frosted concoction. The ice in the freezer—in plastic molds no less—had looked a little questionable, but that's all there was.

Hazel eyes locking on hers, he paused in his kneading of the meat and parted his lips, so she held the rim against that enticing curve, tipping the glass gently. "Mmm." He swallowed. "Tart, sweet and with a kick. Reminds me of someone I know."

"Ha!" She set his glass down where he could reach it when his hands were clean, then hitched herself on to the counter to observe and drink her own martini. Not bad. Not her best effort, but decent considering the tools at hand. The alcohol hit her system with a sweet kick, indeed. Funny that she hadn't been craving it till now. After the day she'd had, she'd normally be obsessing over having a drink. Of course, Dwight had made that crack about getting her medicated. She watched Joe work, the rain a steady patter outside. He'd shucked the jacket and rolled up his shirtsleeves. His forearms flexed as he shaped the meatballs, setting them in neat rows in an oiled pan. Clean, efficient, steady—same way he did everything.

It was weird, being with a guy like this. No press outside. No Katey waiting for her to return to their room. Grocery stores and wet dogs. The kitchen curtains had blue checks, like she'd pictured at Henry's sister's house. The white had yellowed, yes, but somehow okay for all that. Something that had been tight in her uncoiled. Not exactly relaxed. But better. *It's always been a good place for me, when I was… feeling cracked.*

Still, it felt like a lie to let him believe her sweet. Earnest Joe who'd said she was beautiful and meant it. "I'm not, you know."

Joe cocked a brow at her. "Not what?"

"Sweet." She swung her toes. The leather flats were water-logged, so she kicked them off.

"Why do you say that?"

She snorted for his dissembling. "Oh come on—you know it's true."

"No, I don't."

"You can ask anyone."

"I'm asking you." He cast her a glance, eyes going to her toes, then washed his hands and put the meatballs in the oven to bake. Giving the sauce a stir, he grunted in satisfaction and covered it, then took up his martini and drank. "What makes you think you're not sweet?"

"Jack."

"I'm serious. You have your sweet moments."

"And my raging bitch moments."

He grinned, seeming not at all bothered. "Those are pretty spectacular, too."

She shook her head, laughing. A curl fell in her face, remind-ing her what a tangled mess her hair was. Something else she'd forgotten to think about. She pushed at it, annoyed not to look her best, but Joe nudged her hand away and ran his fingers along the curl, rapt expression on his face. He coiled it around his finger, then leaned in, brushing her lips with his. All tenderness this time.

"Sweet," he murmured. "My sweet and lovely Sova."

When he said it like that, she almost believed him. She luxu-riated in the kiss, letting it infuse her bloodstream along with cooling vodka and bright lemon. He tasted of sugar, too, on top of the tomato sauce he must have been tasting as he cooked. Unwilling to let him go, she wrapped her legs around his lean hips and dug her heels into his firm butt, pulling him closer. He groaned, a rumble in his chest, and deepened the kiss. Stealing her breath.

Because he liked it, she gave over to him, letting him plunder her mouth. As soft as she could be. And he—he was hot and hard, pressing against her crotch. She might not be able to squeeze a lemon, but her dancer's legs could squeeze a man well enough. She held him there, tight against her, grinding against the hard length of his erection, so prominent in those light-weight suit pants.

He'd let go of her hair and braced his hands on the counter, one still holding his martini off to the side.

"Jack." She pulled her mouth away and he simply went for her neck, finding that exact spot and sucking on it, so her eyes practically rolled up in her head. "Jack—if you don't put your hands on me soon, I'm going to have to hurt you."

He pulled back, hazel eyes burning as he stared into her, then dropped his gaze to her breasts. Shaking his head slightly, he took a deep breath. "Look…"

"Dwight told you not to fuck me, didn't he?"

"Yeah." He sighed. "Sorry."

"Why? He told me that, too. And he's not here. Just you and me, Jacky boy."

"He has a point, though, that—"

Being on your staff puts him too close to you when things go south. She didn't want to hear it. "You're not backing out, dammit!" She clutched her own glass, contemplating smashing it against the side of his thick skull.

"No, I'm not." He breathed a laugh, though his eyes were shadowed. "The look on your face. It's just that—" He shook his head again, rubbed a hand across his forehead. "Your martini will get warm."

"What martini?" She tossed the last of it back, delighted that his riveted gaze followed her every movement. "Better do the same with yours."

"What the hell." He drank it down, shook his head slightly. "More punch than a straight shot. Where are you going?" He put his hands on her hips, stopping her from sliding off the counter.

"You want to do it here?" The niche of counter she sat on, between the fridge and stove, was awfully narrow, but...

"No, Sova. Hold on."

He moved her hands to the back of his neck again, picked her up, holding her tight against him, and headed out of the kitchen. Finally! Riding him like that, she felt the difference in his gait between right and left. Not exactly a limp—just a different bounciness. His injury?

"So strong and manly." Because his ear was right there, she nibbled on it.

"Because I can carry a bit of a thing like you? I bench press three times your weight."

"Braggart." She bit his ear sharply to punish him, well rewarded when his hands vised on her.

He carried her into a room on the other side of the cottage from the kitchen, a corner room that faced the same view as the front deck, with additional windows on the side. It wasn't glam, but it was a huge step up from the rest, with a big brass bed and a lace coverlet, the walls painted in shades of cream and blue.

"This is pretty," she commented, unwrapping her legs so she slid down his body.

"My mother," Joe said, backing her to the bed. "Possibly the one person who can stand up to my grandmother. Family lore is she dragged out the specter of bed bugs. All the mattresses are new."

"I love your mother." Her breath hitched as he dragged the

jacket off her shoulders, leaving her in the camisole. She reached to pull it off, but he stopped her, his face hard, jaw tight.

Okay then.

~ 15 ~

AVA RAISED HER arms languidly over her head, her expression coy, the pretty tank riding up to reveal her flat belly. Instead of seizing her obvious invitation to pull it off immediately, however, he delayed. He wanted to savor her. If he was going against all common sense, not to mention direct orders from his boss, he wanted to save up this memory to replay in the dark days that would surely follow.

Her skin was soft as snowflakes, and just as cool. She held still for him, golden eyes wide and uncertain as he trailed his fingers from her wrist down the pale and delicate skin of her inner arm. He avoided the curve of her breast, brushing down her rib cage instead, until he reached the dangling jewel in her belly button. He groaned mentally. So many times he'd studied that piercing, the various jewels she threaded through it. Jacked off to the sight.

Holding her by the hips, he pressed his mouth to her skin there, inhaling her. Losing himself in her.

"Jacky boy," she breathed, plucking at him.

"What's wrong?" He lifted up, searched her face. She looked afraid. Of him? "We don't have to—"

"Don't even." She blew out a breath, puffing the fine strands of hair that curled around her forehead. "It's just that I'm thinking too much. Can we speed it up?"

Right. Okay. He hadn't been with a flesh and blood woman

for so long that… But she was spot on. Speed would help make sure she didn't see anything she shouldn't.

She kissed him, drinking him in and he lost the train of thought. Her mouth fed on him, hot and avid. Yanking off her tank top, she tossed it aside and arched back in his grip, humming with approval as he lavished kisses on the rise of her breasts over the lacy bra. He licked and nibbled his way down her midline, pausing to tug again at her belly-button jewel with his teeth, rewarded by her erotic cry at the sharp sensation.

"Harder! Faster," she demanded.

Sinking to one knee and holding her by the hips, he ran his tongue along the skin over the waistband of her jeans. With an impatient sound, she undid the button and zipper, pushing at the jeans. He brushed her hands aside and tugged the pants down for her, leaving her panties in place. Balancing with her hands on his shoulders, she kicked out of the jeans, squirming restlessly when he held still, just looking at her.

"So beautiful," he told her, as a kind of explanation. And she tossed her head, scoffing.

"Everybody's seen it all before. There are plenty of photos of me wearing this little—or less."

"Not in Times Square."

"But you've seen more than that, haven't you? You know more about me than you let on."

She'd find out eventually, but he'd rather preserve the fiction, at least for that night.

"A photo of a beautiful woman and one in the flesh, one you can touch"—he curved a hand over her hip, tracing the line of her thigh muscle—"two miraculously different things."

"Okay, enough poetry." She pulled him up, yanking at his dress shirt in her impatience and sending at least one button tinkling to the polished wood floor. She raked him lightly with her white, sharp nails and he hissed, vision going red. Worse when she bit his nipple with her pretty teeth. Despite himself, he growled, gripping her pert ass. She bit him harder, sinking her teeth into the bulge of his pec.

"Ava, dammit!" If she kept pushing him, he wouldn't have any control left.

She fluttered her lashes, peeking with pretended innocence through them at him. "Did that hurt?"

She made him crazy. He loved her that way, with all the cracked insanity left to him. "Paybacks are hell."

"Promises, promises," she taunted, then brushed her gorgeous tits against his bare chest, nipples hard through the lace. "So far all I've heard are a lot of promises and very little action." She raised up a bit on her toes and bit him on the lower lip.

He lost it. With a snarl he pushed her back on the bed, falling on her like a wild animal that snapped its leash. He wanted to devour her. He filled his hands with her, vising on her breasts, then tearing the flimsy bra away so his teeth fastened on her nipple. *See how she likes it.* She screamed with pleasure/pain, even that registering in his addled brain as musical, arching into his mouth, digging her nails into his back, the pain of it intensifying his need. He found her other breast, tormenting that, too.

He snapped her panties, cupped her pussy, the skin there even softer, hot and hairless, his fingers skidding through her slickened flesh. *God, yes.* She had his cock freed without him realizing, wrapping him in a fierce grip, her slim hips lifting. Golden eyes like molten metal.

"In me, now," she demanded.

"Condom." He freed himself of her hands, and reached for his pants pocket. They draped low on his hips and with a start he realized he'd nearly forgotten. Nearly let them fall.

"I have an implant. Do me, Jacky boy. I can't wait." She writhed in gorgeous abandon.

"Hold on," he muttered, pushing her back on the bed and

using it to pin his pants in place. He got the fucking condom on despite clumsy fingers, and shoved her knees back, splaying her wide. So fucking beautiful, pink and slick and sweet. Goddess. Woman. His.

Arching, she toyed with her nipples. "All for you, Jacky boy."

A sound came out of him that he almost didn't recognize as himself, and he pushed her knees back farther, lifting her hips from the bed with the force of it, and sheathed himself in her. So tight, she seared him, his brain frying helplessly with what she did to him.

She screamed, then clawed at him, demanding more, and he fucked her, snarling her name. Fire raked his chest, so he grabbed her wrists, pinned them to the bed. She writhed under him as he pounded in and out of her.

Too fast, too soon, way too violent, the climax took him, practically locking him up. The convulsion of it made him throw his head back, teeth clenched. For a few dazed seconds, he could only suffer in its grip. When it let go, relief coursed through him instead of satiation. It hadn't been any kind of release, burying himself in Ava's sleek body. Instead the hunger for her still burned with even more scorching intensity.

It didn't help that Ava lay pinned under him, golden eyes wide, panting and watching him with a raw, vulnerable look on her face. *Shit.*

He let go of her wrists, where he'd held them brutally against the bed, and tried to pull out of her slick, hot clasp. But she wound those phenomenally strong legs around his hips and held him there, slid her arms around his neck, and pulled him down as she wriggled against him, lithe and sinuous, the points of her nipples still hard against his chest.

"Don't go yet, Jacky boy," she crooned in his ear. "You feel too damn good."

"Ava," he managed, trying to lever himself up.

"Sova," she corrected him, with a nip to the side of his neck. Sharp little teeth on her and no compunction about using them.

"Dammit, stop that." Since she wouldn't let him go and he was too off-balance not to crush her—and his bad leg threatening to give—he rolled onto his back, bringing her with him. Not easy with her squirming and nipping at him, not unlike holding a feisty cat. Sharp claws, too. It wasn't easy to keep the bad leg away from her, but he managed.

She sat up, straddling him, still keeping him inside her though he'd softened, and rocked her hips, the movement sending a seductive shimmy through her body. The pretty lace bra still hung half on her, half ripped off, and her white breasts, her skin like the demure pearls she still wore—God! Those perfect breasts—showed red marks from his fingers. Maybe bruises later.

He scrubbed his hands over his face. "Shit. I am so damn sorry."

"Nothing to be sorry for," she practically purred, smoothing her hands over his chest, tracing a scratch mark as if proud of her handiwork.

"You didn't even come." Because he'd lost his head. He'd never treated any woman that badly, not even when he was younger and stupider.

She shrugged, breasts bouncing with it. "I don't always. Doesn't mean I don't like the sex." She circled one of his nipples with her nail. It stung, tender from her bite. "There's more to sex than orgasm."

"That sounds like an excuse and I'm not sure that counted as sex."

"Oh, hella yes, it surely did." She tilted her head, pursing her lips. "I liked watching you lose it, Jacky boy. That was the best part."

Heaven help him. "Okay, I'm sure that's not what a guy wants to hear was the best part."

"Well, the best part so far." She gave him an arch look as she drawled the last two words. "How's that?"

He put a hand over hers where it rested on his chest. "So far? Does that mean I get another chance?"

"Silly." She rocked her hips. "I plan to keep you busy all weekend."

Might as well. Not like he could unfuck her. "I promise to do right by you next time."

"You already did, so promise kept. Besides, there's always Bob, if I need him."

Irrational jealousy crawled through him. So many other guys. "Who's Bob?"

She smiled, a genuine one, wide and delighted. "My battery-operated boyfriend. Always hard, never lets me down."

"Ouch. On that note…" Putting his hands on her vigorous hips, he tried to lift her off of him, but she clamped down with her thighs and held on.

"Not yet."

"I have to ditch the condom, or it'll leak into you."

"Implant—remember?"

"Don't tell me you don't think about STDs."

She snickered. "Don't tell me you have one. You? Mr. By the Book."

"Okay." He could concede that. "You know this about me, so let me follow this rule."

"To make you happy, Jacky boy." She patted him on the cheek and let him move her then, though she watched his softening cock emerge from her with something akin to fascination. Not helping him with it, though. Collapsing on the bed when he let her go, she stretched, sinuous as a cat in the sun. A fortunate moment of distraction that let him pull up his pants before she saw. She dragged the ruined bra off her shoulder and tossed it across the room, eyeing him as he moved into the adjoining bath.

"Sorry about your underwear," he told her, looking at himself in the mirror as he washed his hands, warming the water to soak a washcloth for her. "I'll replace it."

"Are you kidding? I can afford a lot of expensive lingerie. Having it ripped off of me means I've achieved full value for my shopping dollar."

He had to laugh. Who would have guessed she'd be funny? She possessed a certain bawdy wit that didn't come out in her songs. Which made him wonder what else got glossed over. *All shine and no substance.* Maybe that was true of her image, but not of her. Returning to her where she still lolled naked, a goddess of sex on his mother's bedspread, he held out the washcloth. She levered herself up, raising a puzzled brow before taking it.

"It's warm."

"Did you think I'd give you a cold cloth to clean up with?"

Totally unselfconscious, she spread her legs and wiped herself. With no hair there at all, her luscious folds showed pink and tempting. His cock stirred at the sight, hardening slightly, making him glad he'd buttoned up his pants before facing her again.

"I didn't think you'd hand me a wash cloth at all. You're the first guy who ever has."

"What?" A grind of anger started behind his eyes. Only partly at the image of the other men who'd been with her, though that annoyed more than it should. He knew that about her. Hell, he'd been driving while she did one of them. What really got to him was that they'd been such shits to her. And he wasn't any better, the way he'd fucked her with no tenderness, zero consideration. "How hard is it to wet a washcloth?"

She pointed to the tissues on the bedside. "The decent guys at least hand you the box."

"You wouldn't know a decent guy if—" He managed to stop himself. And because he wanted to punch something, he shoved his hands into his pockets. "I'd better check the marinara."

"Hey." She held out a hand. Sitting there naked, her blond waves in disarray, she looked adorable and still managed to be imperious enough that he took her hand and sat when she tugged him down. "What made you so pissy all of a sudden? Most guys are happy after they get laid."

"I'm not angry at you." He tried giving her a reassuring smile.

"I know *that*, silly. And don't get me wrong—the sullen, angry vibe totally works for me. Don't go check the stupid sauce. Work that energy off on me." She trailed those long nails over one of the bloody furrows she'd left on his chest, the sting making him hiss and grab her wrist.

"It's not stupid sauce." Then he groaned, because she grabbed his other hand and put it between her legs. So slick, searingly soft. His cock finished the job of reawaking, as painfully hard as it had been before. He'd tried to take control of himself, distract his mind with cooking and doing something caring for her. So much for platonic romance. He'd meant to give her softness and nurturing, but the little head seemed to be doing all the distracting. "You're not sore? We—I went at it pretty rough there."

"Feels good." She met his gaze very seriously. "A little sting just makes it more real. Rough is good. Do it again. You said the sauce needs to simmer." She rocked her hips on his hand, sighing when he pushed a finger inside her. "You never even took your shoes or pants off. At least let me get you naked."

"We don't need to do that." He pushed another finger into her tight channel, loving how she arched with it, leaning back on her elbows and spreading her legs for him. "I'm fine as is."

She opened one eye and frowned. "What—getting you naked? Yes, you will."

To distract her from that path, he curled his fingers inside her, but she pushed his hand away and straddled him. "What's the deal?"

"Look…" He should have anticipated having to explain this. Wasn't this why he'd stayed away from women, from relationships, from sex, full stop? Something about Ava, about the sheer unreality of being with her at all, had lulled him into this fantasy realm where he … what? Was still whole. Not this messed up vet with a split skull and a missing leg. "You don't want—"

"Do you have scars or something? Because I don't care."

Scars. He nearly laughed. If only it were just scars. He could live with that. "You don't care because you have zero idea what you're talking about," he fired back at her. "It's not pretty, Ava. Trust me on this."

She went still, her face smoothing into that neutral mask. She could be one of her photos, but for the wild hair and less than pristine makeup. "Maybe you *should* go check the fucking sauce, Jack," she said, even and calm. Way too quiet. The unblemished surface of the road with an IED beneath.

"Sova…"

"No, no. It's all good. Go make yourself useful." Sliding off his lap, she flounced into the bathroom—not easy to do naked, but her butt twitched with vigorous disdain—and slammed the door shut.

<h1 style="text-align:center">~ 16 ~</h1>

AVA TOOK STOCK of the damage, examining herself in the unforgiving fluorescent light. More of that harsh reality for her. Her hair was totally out of control. And the makeup—Cinna would have a total meltdown if he saw her like this. The smearing of her eyeshadow revealed the way one of her eyes tilted down at the corner. And the lines around her mouth—were they deeper?

The rest didn't show so much. Funny how that worked. She looked like she'd been thoroughly fucked, as she had, but no more than usual. Kind of laughable to feel so wounded as plenty of guys had treated her far worse. It wasn't like Joe had hit her or treated her like a slut afterwards. He'd even been all gentlemanly, which was weird right there. Maybe that's why it had hit her so hard. She'd gotten lulled into forgetting who she was. Seduced by a warm washcloth of all things. So what if Joe thought she was so shallow and vain that she couldn't handle the sight of a few scars?

Probably a fair assessment. She was hardly the poster child for internal beauty.

She clearly wasn't any good at the whole not-having-actual-sex part of sex. Not a role she'd ever played beyond a few kisses. Always that good-girl image. Who could blame her for being a rank amateur at the rest—where the hell did people learn this stuff? Somewhere in with dealing with wet dogs and grocery stores, probably.

"Sparkle, Shirley," she said to the mirror and pasted on the smile she could generate no matter how she felt inside. For some reason this time, though, it looked all wrong, so she let it drop away.

She needed to shower. Polish up that surface so Joe would forget being peeved with her. So he'd want her again with that delicious rawness of his. Thankfully the shower had shampoo and stuff in it. Not her special ones that Cinna had blended for her, but hopefully Joe's Italian mother who hated icky mattresses wouldn't mind her son's shallow mistress copping her bath goodies. But she couldn't face seeing Joe just yet, so no venturing out to raid her suitcase for the little travel bottles.

It's not pretty, Ava.

Because that's what she was all about, wasn't it? Pretty, pretty, ballerina. Dress me up, keep me in the box. Mint condition. Don't show me anything else.

The words ran around her mind as the hot water soaked over her skull. A tune teasing with it, echoes of the gospel choir winding through, bright notes of hope, threaded through with grief over the past. It actually felt good, despite all the turmoil. She hummed a little as she shampooed, surprised that she wanted to. Good sex maybe. She let it roll around and just be. *Don't scare it away by seizing hold. Don't overthink.*

Once she would have jumped out of the shower and written it down, or recorded it on her phone, not caring about the suds and the dripping. That was before she'd lost the spark. And her phone. Since then, every time she tried to write the words, a hint of melody down, she lost it immediately.

She stayed in long enough that the water started to get cold. Cabin living, apparently. Then rummaged through the cabinets in a vain search for product. It would take some doing to comb out her hair without it. Who was Joe's mom that she didn't have mousse or gel? Surely not everyone lived like that.

She'd have to risk finding her suitcase, wherever Joe held it hostage. Cracking the door, she peeked out, more than half-expecting him to be sitting there on the bed, staring at the door, waiting for her. Guys did that, getting annoyed if she took too long in the bathroom. They never listened when she pointed out that spectacular results required intensive effort.

Instead, he'd left her blessedly alone and—hallelujah!—her suitcase sat on the bed instead.

He was a good guy. No wonder he was careful of subjecting himself to her. Pretty ballerinas have sharp and pointed toes.

Humming still, she found her makeup bag and hair stuff, then took her time to fix up properly. She'd been too hungover and depressed that morning to suffer much primping and then in too much of a hurry when she grabbed her things than to do more than just spruce up. It was kind of nice to do her own full makeup, the way she liked it best, rather than what the focus groups picked.

Satisfied that she looked halfway human again, she dressed in a silk and lace peignoir the color of good champagne. It was one of her favorites, making her feel like a Hollywood glamour girl. Suitably armored, she wandered out to dazzle Joe into loving her.

He'd built up the fire in the fireplace, and it crackled cheerfully. But no him and no Arlin.

Going to the side window—not exactly panicked, but…she peered out at the driveway. The little car was still there, so they must have gone for a walk. Pouring rain and dark as hell, but they must not care. Ridiculous that after worrying that he wouldn't leave her alone, now she was disappointed that he'd just, what? Taken off for however long. Some bodyguard.

Shrugging it off, trying not to feel too sulky about it, she went to make more martinis. He'd been busy while she cleaned up. All the lemons had been juiced and put in a glass measuring cup on the counter. With plastic wrap sealing it. He'd even put a couple of rinds in a baggie, presumably so she could sugar the rims and add a bit of peel. Vodka in the freezer, icing. The wine glasses and makeshift shaker washed, dried and waiting in the freezer also.

He'd paid attention to her whole method and set things up for her to make more, even after she'd stormed off. Why that felt like some kind of profound gesture of affection, she didn't know. Especially after all the rest.

It just did. And she felt kind of bad for mentally criticizing him for abandoning her. She was fine, wasn't she? Just weird to be totally alone. She needed to find her stride with this guy, that was all. Just a different type, but under it they were all the same, right? All gray in the dark.

The spaghetti sauce smelled amazing. Kind of magical that he could slice up tomatoes, toss in garlic and onions and have it smell like that. Experimentally, she stirred it.

Then jumped back as if caught red-handed when front door banged open, letting in the roar of ocean, rain and wind—along with a drenched Joe, who blocked the door with his back to her. "Uh-uh, buddy. Shake there. I mean it."

"Need a towel?" she called out. She knew that line, at least, even if it was usually said to her.

He glanced over his shoulder, did a double take. "Wow. I mean, that would be great."

Mission accomplished. Pleased with his reaction, she retrieved several towels, for man and dog, from the bathroom she'd used and held the stack, feeling kind of domestic and wifely, while he pulled one off and used it on a disgruntled Arlin. After setting the dog free to flop down on the rug with a groan, Joe took a fresh towel from her, and dried his own hair, taking her in. He'd put on running clothes and dripped with sweat as well as rain.

"You glammed up," he said.

"Not really." She tried to shrug it off, but the look in his eyes made her a little giddy. That was better. *This old thing?* "But thanks."

He gave her a bit of a funny look. Okay… that hadn't been meant as a compliment. Well, fuck him then. She hadn't done it to please him, but to make herself feel better. Exactly. But what the hell was wrong with him? Done with the wifely domesticity, she set down the stack of towels and went to get her martini. Never paid to step out of your usual role.

"I just mean," he said, shrugging out of his jacket and hanging it up on a peg by the door, "that you didn't have to do it for me. You look gorgeous no matter what. And we're the only ones here. You should be comfortable."

She gestured to the gown. "Comfortable."

He sighed. "I'm sorry. I seem to be saying everything the wrong way."

"No worries, Jacky boy." She gave him her best smile and posed in front of the fireplace. The warm light made the champagne silk gleam and should be transparent enough to show the silhouette of her body.

Even if she was a fraud in every other way, at least she knew how to look beautiful. She might be all surface, all about the pretty, but she did it damn well. A finely honed skill for lo these twenty years. He'd want her again. He wouldn't be able to help himself. She'd make sure of it.

✦　✦　✦

SHE LOOKED SO eye-scorchingly beautiful—like she'd stepped out of a movie—that he couldn't quite seem to spur his brain into rational thought. The run had helped, the exercise, fighting the wind and freezing rain, all of it had done a fair amount to bleed off some of the energy, the explosive emotions gutting him. The dull, threatening buzz of the nowhere zone behind the sense of unreality. But walking in and seeing her like that ... slammed him right back to where he'd been.

Like his photo collection had come to life, mocking him with the clawing need for her.

He hadn't cooled anywhere near enough. His blood raged, brain spinning with images of seizing her, kissing her senseless, destroying that careful, glamorous poise. He wanted her pinned and naked again, rumpled and smeared and screaming.

All so wrong. Not things he should want. Hell, he wasn't supposed to want *her* in the first place.

He'd talked himself down, he'd thought. They'd eat by candle light, or by the fire. Have more martinis if she wanted or open the wine. Then, if she still wanted to, he'd make love to her the way she deserved. See to it that she came first, maybe several times, if he could find her rhythm. He'd be gentle, reverent. A goddamn gentleman the way he was supposed to be. Her employee, not a guy acting like he somehow deserved something from her.

Not a ravaging beast or pouting man-child.

He wrenched his gaze off of her, because if he looked a moment longer, that pretty gown would be in shreds, too. "I'll take a quick shower." *As cold as possible.* "And then we can eat."

"Oh, goody. Pre-dinner entertainment. I'll watch."

Tenacious as a pit bull, with her lovely smile full of sharp little teeth—and her words chilled him more thoroughly than any shower could.

"That's not a good idea." He regretted the words instantly as her face iced to that perfect mask, made the more uncanny because her seductive smile remained perfectly the same, while her eyes went cold. He preferred her pissed off instead. Going to her, he put deliberately gentle hands on her arms, skin smooth as chill marble warmed by the fire. She tilted up her chin, watching him, no hint of emotion in her gaze. Her expensive perfume combined with the whatever flowery something she put in her hair to make it smooth and gleaming again.

"Look—I'd just rather shower alone, and…" He trailed off at the fury burning in her golden eyes. Had he thought a moment ago that he preferred it?

"*You* look, Jacky boy." She spoke smoothly, as elegantly as she'd posed. "I don't know what you think my life is like. I—I'm not this…whatever, fucking, glass thing… *Doll*, that you…" Her composure and voice broke on it. She ducked her face and drank from the martini, but not before he glimpsed the tears in her eyes.

Not anger, but hurt. He was a world class jackass. Obviously why she called him Jack.

"Sova." He took the glass from her and drew her into his arms, holding her as he had that morning when she sobbed in the studio lobby. He was supposed to be helping her rest, not stressing her further. "Don't cry. I'm sorry."

She pulled away, swiping at her nose with impatience— though not enough to smear her lipstick. "I really don't do this," she said, her voice broken and watery, still not looking at him. "Cry, I mean. Rarely ever. Except at sappy movies, which isn't real. You won't believe me because I've been a blubbering fool today, but this isn't me."

"Hey. You *are* you. I'm only sorry to be the cause of it—cry as much as you want to."

"It's my party," she sang softly, her voice warm gold on even those few notes.

"And you've had a rough few days."

"I don't know how you can say that to me. You're the one who's had a rough life. I'm just… spoiled. Stupid. Whatever."

"That's not true." He drew her into his arms again and this

time she softened, laying her cheek against his chest. "You're a sensitive person. Artistic. The world is hard on people like you."

"And you, Jacky boy?"

"Head and heart hard as a rock. Ask anyone."

She laughed softly. "It has been a hard few days. Hell, a hard few months."

"That would do it." He rocked her, like they were slow dancing and she sighed a little. "I don't think you're a delicate doll." Maybe he had thought that some, before he met her. Now she was all vivid mercurial reality. Far from mint condition, too.

She tipped her head up to look at him, eyes soft and lashes damp. "I know you have no reason to trust me, that I'm all shallow, frivolous and careless, but I—I've seen some shit. Dealt with ugly before. I can deal with seeing your scars."

Was that what she thought? "You're not shallow or frivolous or careless. I knew that before I ever met you. The songs you write—you have depth, this tremendous heart." He struggled to put it into words, then noticed she had the oddest look on her face. "What?"

"You've heard my songs?"

Shit. Screwing up left and right. He needed to cool the emotional crap and start thinking before he spoke. She had him gutted and upside down. "Of course I have." He kept it light. "Everyone has."

"No." She shook her head slowly. "Not big tough Army guys."

"Even big tough Army guys have little sisters who play your albums nonstop." It came out a little belligerent, but better that than the desperate sense of lethal exposure.

She narrowed her eyes, however, not buying it. Never think she's a bimbo, no. That was it about her eyes and the owl, far too old and wise. "And you paid attention to which songs I actually wrote myself."

"I don't know why not. It's not a secret, is it?"

"If anything, the label overplays that, because it makes me seem more *genuine*. You'd've had to study the liner notes to know for sure."

He tried to shrug it off. "I was interested and too much time on my hands." All those days in the hospital, killing time inch by inch. "Why do you put that stuff out there if you don't expect people to read it?"

"*People*," she mused over that, with an odd emphasis. "Industry folks, yes. Fans, some, depending. Most *people*, though, they assume I write them all—and that each one is a true story about my life. Fewer people figure that someone else writes them all for me, which was true for a long time. Probably the majority don't give it a second thought. Why do you?"

She'd never let it go until he gave her a satisfactory answer. He moved restlessly, as vulnerable as if she had seen his leg, but she held on, not letting go. "Okay, I'm kind of a fan. Sue me."

"My biggest fan?" She had that teasing tone, like when she'd asked the guys for their favorite song.

"I have no idea how to measure that," he answered, the honest words scraping him raw.

"Oh. My. God." She stared at him. "You're completely serious." For once she wasn't paying attention to her studied expressions, her thoughts showing clearly in her face as she processed that information. When she finished on a frown, he braced himself. "You lied to me about not having a favorite song," she accused him, not teasing in the least.

"No," he corrected in a firm tone. "I didn't answer. Besides—that was before I promised not to lie to you."

"But now you have promised. What's your favorite song?"

"I like them all."

"Liar."

"I'm not seven. It's possible to like many things equally well, at the same time." He tried to step back, but she wouldn't let him.

"Now you're just stalling. Tell me."

"Why?"

"It matters to me. Tell me. The truth, too."

"Pinocchio."

Her lovely mouth parted in surprise. "Really?"

"Yes, really." He put his hands to her wrists to disengage her. "I should check the sauce."

"No." Her mouth firmed, her expression unexpectedly grim, grip fierce on his shirt. "The fucking sauce can burn. Why that song?"

The thing was, he didn't know. How could anyone explain why certain notes and words hit you like a bullet, shredding you in a moment? This was why he flunked English Lit. But her gaze burned into him, so he said the only thing that came to mind.

"When they cut those long strings
When I take the hard fall
I'll cop to the lies I made them tell
The ones I told you
The ones that aren't true
None of it's real
Not even to you."

She absorbed that, barely breathing. "Did you take the hard fall, Jacky boy?" she finally whispered. Too discerning. Not what he'd expected her to say.

"The hardest." Because it was her, and the moment felt like all those times he'd looked into her eyes, listened to her voice, trusted her with his pain and secrets, he added, "Only instead of becoming a real boy, I became the puppet. Metal and plastic. None of it's real."

"What are you telling me?"

"My left leg. It's gone." He managed to say it matter-of-factly—and to take advantage of her shock to unknot her hands finally. Not wanting to see more of her reaction, he moved into the kitchen, aware that she frowned after him, watching.

"I can't even tell."

"Prosthetic."

"Oh."

He risked glancing at her. She was watching him all right, studying his non-leg. He needed to say something, to defuse the moment for them both. "That's part of why I work out. The stronger I am, the better shape I'm in, the easier it is to work the prosthesis. This is almost ready—are you hungry?"

"You're trying to divert me. That's kind of like a lie." She sounded dangerous.

If only. He braced his arms on the counter, hanging his head between his locked elbows, pacing his breathing, holding off the vertigo of the nowhere zone by sheer force of will. He needed to get a serious grip on himself, alone here with Ava, who depended on him. What the hell had possessed him to reveal all that? Before he realized she'd approached, she'd slid up between his arms, soft, fragrant, radiantly beautiful. Like gold come to life. Kissing him with long, sweet coaxing kisses that made his head spin.

"Let me see you, Jack," she said against his mouth. "Give me that."

He wasn't sure he could face it. The ugliness and the pity. The way his mother had literally screamed at the sight. But Ava had a stubborn streak as vivid as the rest of her passionate nature. She wouldn't drop this and he didn't know how to effectively refuse her.

"Why?" The question came out as a desperate bid to divert her.

She looked at him seriously. "How about this—why don't

you want me to?"

Wasn't that obvious? "I'm not whole. There are scars and the stump is—it's awful and ugly and—" His chest hurt trying to explain it to her, heart thumping in rising panic, the sense of space opening beneath his feet. Arlin padded over to lean against his good leg. *Shit.*

"What's happening, Jacky boy?" Ava asked softly, looking at Arlin, then searching Joe's face. "Are we having a little diva meltdown?"

He laughed, though it came out hoarse. "Nothing so artistic. I just get worked up sometimes, thinking about it. I'm fucked up, Sova. More than you know. You should stay away."

"Fuck that. This is something I'm actually an expert at. What calms you down?"

He tried to think. Say something besides *her.* "Different things. Meditating. Listening to your music." The admission leaked out through the growing cracks.

"Wow. I had no idea." She caressed his face, trailing soft kisses behind her exquisite fingers. "What about sex, Jack? That always works for me."

"I don't think that—"

"Shh. Let me do something for you. If you don't like it, tell me and I'll stop, okay?" She kissed him before he could reply, took him by the hand and led him into the living area, seating him in his grandfather's armchair by the fire. "No talking otherwise. No thinking."

Softly she began to sing. One of her own songs, a love song, another of his all-time favorites. As if she'd looked into his heart and knew. Sometimes he'd listened to it in the dark, imagining she sang it for him. Now, firelit and beyond lovely, she did sing it to him, pulling the T-shirt off over his head and running her hands over his chest.

Why haven't you been where I was looking?
Not there at the dance
Not there at the party
Leaving me to dance alone.
Where have you gone that we never met?

In a kind of trance, he watched as she knelt, a golden goddess of light and song, stroking his skin and easing down his pants, just onto his thighs. He'd worried sometimes if he'd be able to get it up with a real live woman. Being with Ava … was somehow in between. Her images and music taken flesh. Those glossy red lips. Her slim hand on his cock, so sweet. As the song trailed off, she wrapped her mouth around him.

He'd put a hand on her head, to stop her. He had to stink of sweat, but he lost the thought in the exquisite clasp of her mouth, the sight of her scarlet lips around him, her molten gold eyes gazing up at him. Instead of pushing her away, his hand wound tighter into the silk of her hair. His heart thudded in a heavy rhythm, not in the panic of the nowhere zone, but with huge and urgent lust.

She made a sound of animal satisfaction and gripped the root of his cock, pulling hard on him, driving him up fast and furiously. His brain fogged out completely and he thrust into her mouth, desperate for more. Not what he meant to do, but she controlled it. Controlled him.

And he was helpless under her hands.

She made him come with wrenching speed, hot eyes never leaving his face. His vision went black, with crimson on the edges and he held onto her hair to keep himself anchored to the earth, calling out incoherently.

~ 17 ~

SHE LICKED HIS cock gently, cleaning up the last drops of semen and bringing him down slowly. Joe lay back in the armchair, head tipped back to show his tanned throat and jutting Adam's apple, breathing harder than when he'd come in from running, sweat glistening on his skin.

Not much beat the utter pleasure of sucking off the right man, watching him come apart.

And Joe—oh, he made out like he was so calm and collected. But the man was tightly wound. Maybe even more than she. Of course, he had real reasons for his crazy. Still, when he let go, he did it in spectacular fashion.

When he opened his eyes and raised his head to look at her, she smiled. A sexy curve of her lips for him. "You come like a man who hasn't been doing nearly enough of it, Jacky boy."

With a ragged laugh, he released his death grip on her hair, caressing her with a rueful smile. "You have no idea. Did I hurt you?"

"Not in any way I didn't enjoy. A good hair-pulling always adds to the pleasure."

"So far all the pleasure has been mine," he said, in a wry tone, his thumb tracing her lower lip.

She kissed it. "Totally wrong. I got to do exactly what I wanted."

"Sorry I'm all sweaty."

"A little man stink never hurt me." Keeping an eye on him, she moved back a little to untie his shoelace on his good leg. "But let's get you that shower you wanted." And finish this while he was still relaxed. She pulled off his shoe and sock. Turned to the other foot.

"Sova." He'd tensed, hands on the arms of the chair down, wariness in his gaze. But he didn't do more than that, so she kept going.

Though it looked similar at a glance, the shoe was different, clearly adapted to the curved metal of the prosthetic foot. She'd seen photos, here and there, but hadn't paid much attention or seen one up close. Joe's prosthesis looked light years beyond those horrible wooden and plastic things people used to be stuck with. Or the peg like the villain had in *Pirates*. Light and graceful, like something out of sci-fi, it had spring to it. Oddly sexy, in fact.

Or maybe that was Joe.

He was watching her quietly, face blank, braced for her reaction. She slid her hands up his calves over the running pants, muscled calf on one side, streamlined metal on the other. He flinched and made a noise when she reached his knees, the bulge where the prosthetic leg met his body.

"Hurts?" She asked, fairly certain it didn't. Not physically anyway.

"Not like how you mean," he answered, confirming it, his voice strained. Keeping calm though. One skill she did possess—she knew how to talk someone out of a meltdown. Practice, practice.

Rising up on her knees, she ran her hands up his gorgeously muscled thighs, then took the waistband of his pants and tugged gently, meeting his gaze. He hesitated, then lifted his hips so she could drag them down and off.

Sitting back, she looked at him. He'd braced himself again,

hands digging into the armrests, the tension almost audible in her ears, a dark harmonic to that melody that still rattled round her brain. *Pretty ballerina and GI Joe. Velveteen worn away. No longer new. No longer real.*

"You are a hella gorgeous man, Jacky boy." She crooned it a little, the way he liked, and it did settle him. Sliding her hands up his muscled thighs, she murmured her pleasure. "Like one of those Michael Stokes photos. You should model for him. Those pics would sell like hotcakes. I'd buy one and hang it over my fireplace."

He laughed mirthlessly, more a huff of strangled breath. "You're unreal."

"I know it. I keep trying to tell you. But I do know packaging and you are quite the package." She traced fingers over a ripple of scar tissue that ran up his thigh from under a white sock. "Fire?"

Nodding slightly, he tapped one that looked like the ripple of a wave on the shore of his tan skin, smooth and free of his dark hair. "This one. These others from shrapnel." He brushed his fingers over the divots in his firm flesh.

"But there's no pain?"

"Not real pain." He touched his own leg, tracing the various scars much as she had. "It's weird. I can feel stuff in some places and not others. Here it's numb, but right next to it I have pretty good sensation."

Something else she understood. It never seemed to make sense, where you could feel and where you went numb. "What do you mean by 'not real pain'—that it doesn't hurt much or that the pain isn't real?"

His lips quirked in that wry smile. "Both? Where it hurts most is the part that's not there. They call it phantom limb. Some brain thing where you keep getting the emergency signal, even though the injury is long over."

"A memory of pain that's so vivid you can't tell it apart from reality."

At last he touched her again, laying his hand over hers. "You know something about that, Sova?"

Yeah, she did. Abruptly it became hard to hold his gaze, so she sat back surveying his prosthesis. "Do you wear this whole thing when you shower?"

Holding her gaze, he shook his head. "It's important to keep the … stump clean."

"The stump." She shouldn't laugh, but it sounded like such a brick of a word.

Joe, watching her closely, caught her amusement. "The guys, docs and so forth, usually call it the BKA—below knee amputation."

"Better than stump, for sure."

"I didn't expect you to laugh." He had a strange look on his face. Hard to say what went on in that hard head of his.

"I'm sorry—it's awful of me."

"Don't be." He took a breath. "Laughing is better. My mother screamed."

Ava caught her breath, horrified. Fucking mothers. "She didn't."

Surprising her, he cracked a grin, and shook his head at the memory. "Full-throated, bloodcurdling shriek, horror-movie style. Followed by inconsolable sobbing. Brought half the nursing floor running."

"Oh, Jacky boy. I am so, so sorry about that."

"It's not a big deal." He lifted her hand and laced his fingers with hers.

"It is. She made your pain, your loss be all about her." She knew plenty about that syndrome, too.

"You don't know my mother. It was… just really hard on her." His chin puckered, and he swallowed hard, squeezing her hand. "Her son, her perfect boy, a cripple!" He pulled out a hint of drama for that, rolling his eyes. But not quite covering how much it had wounded him.

"Is that why you moved to New York?"

"In part." He shrugged. "It was a lot of things. I should get in the shower, so we can eat."

"Okay." She waited. "You going to show me the rest?"

"Will you give me any peace until I do?" He was teasing her, more at ease again. A relief.

"No. And there could be a significant reward for you." She blew him a kiss, along with an exaggerated eyelash flutter.

"I take off mine, you take off yours?"

"Done." She rose to her feet and shimmied the peignoir off her shoulders so it slid to her feet, leaving her standing naked in the pool of silk.

"Holy Mother of God. Give a guy some warning. You almost stopped my heart." His gaze raked her, head to foot and back again, his expression sending a pulse of moisture between her thighs. That and the way his heavy cock stirred in its nest of dark hair. She kind of liked that he wasn't all manscaped.

"You've already seen me." But she liked his reaction. Liked it a whole lot.

He shook his head slowly. "That doesn't change a thing."

"Your turn."

"Come on then." He pushed up and stood, a fine manly figure in the firelight, and took her hand. He moved gracefully, the curved metal bowing and straightening as he walked.

"Do you even need to wear shoes?"

"Yeah. Both to keep an even tread on both sides of my body and to protect the prosthesis."

In the bathroom, still sweet and steamy from her shower, he braced himself against the wall, and shucked off the plastic cup that clasped his leg and dropped it to the floor. With only a hint of hesitation, he pulled off the sock, tossed it on the counter, then looked her in the eye, gesturing to his leg. "In all its stumpy glory."

She bit her lip, more than a little tempted to let out a blood-curdling scream. Somehow he predicted her, read the mischievous impulse in her face.

"Don't you dare," he warned. But not pissed. Nearly laughing.

"Or what? You already got your reward." She did a little hip swivel shimmy for him. Already at half-mast, that brought him all the way to fully erect. Quite the sight to see. His face tightened with good honest lust.

"Or I won't be responsible for the consequences."

She sidled up to him, stopping a whisper away from the tip of his cock. "I like the sound of that. What would you do to me, Jacky boy, if I said you could do anything at all?"

A hundred dirty thoughts flashed through his eyes, hot and sharp. Good. Not thinking about the leg at all. "Uh-uh." He shook his head, reining it back. "Next time is going to be about you."

Resolutely, he reached over and turned on the shower, bracing himself on the sides to hop in. No steam. He'd turned on cold only—and gurgled at the shock of as he stepped under the spray, shaking his head like Arlin shedding the rain.

"Isn't a cold shower pretty cliché?" She leaned against the wall, enjoying the show as much as she'd expected. He had a great ass. Firm and bitable.

He ducked her a hot hazel glance under his arm as he lathered shampoo, standing impressively balanced on one foot. "With you looking like you stepped out of a porn movie? I'll grasp any straw available."

That made her laugh. "You need to watch better porn."

"Now you're just fishing for more compliments."

"Always." She kept it light, but a bit of tremor fluttered at the edge of her voice. Probably not loud enough for him to hear. "You know me—flattery is the air I breathe."

He glanced at her, a curiously opaque expression, then ducked his head under the water for a final rinse, shampoo and soap suds streaming down his lean form. Not sure what she'd said wrong, she fixed up a little with the things she'd left on the counter, wiping off the smeared lipstick and recreating the crisp lines. Restored the smooth waves he'd crumpled with his grip on her hair.

When he turned off the water, she remembered. "Oops. Left the towels in the other room. I'll get them."

"Do me a favor and put the gown back on while you're at it."

She glanced over her shoulder, catching him ogling her behind. "The cold water didn't do the trick?"

"Maybe a dip in the Arctic might… but no. Have pity on me. I'm a weak man."

Probably the least weak man she'd ever met. Funny how he was the same age as Mr. Wonderful, but Tyler seemed like a boy where Joe was totally a man. But she donned the peignoir again, retrieved her martini—warm, but totally worth it—and dropped off the clean towels. From the doorway, she watched him dry off. Particularly careful with his stump, which looked like soft baby skin, folded over and neatly tucked up. He pulled on the sock he'd set aside, and then the prosthesis. Studiously ignoring her all the while.

"Mind grabbing my bag from the bedroom?" He still didn't look up. "Gold's Gym."

Without comment, she did, bringing it back to him. She hadn't thought about him needing to pack, but they hadn't stopped wherever he lived. "You just happened to have it with you?"

"You never know when a gorgeous pop star might kidnap you for the weekend." He grinned at her then, a dark curl falling over his forehead.

"Ha. You're the one who carried me off to this godforsaken cabin in the wilderness and had your way with me."

Standing before the mirror, he combed his hair, then pulled out deodorant, rolled it on. Fascinated by his ritual, she finished her martini. She hadn't had much occasion to watch a man do this sort of thing. Usually the sex was hot and fast—and then they parted ways. Almost always to separate hotel rooms, separate handlers. How many men had she fucked who weren't in the business? Hard to say. Not many, for sure.

Joe was stroking his chin thoughtfully, but watching her. "I'm a little rough. Want me to shave?"

Hmm. She really wanted to watch him shave, but she also wanted the sharp bristle of his shadow. Possibly on her inner thighs.

"Let me see." Slipping between him and the counter, she toed up and kissed him, taking his breath in a long woosh. His arms came around her and he returned the kiss with interest, deepening it, taking her mouth with that delightful savagery of his. Oh yeah, the prickle of his whiskers definitely added to it. A little bite to sharpen the dreamy pleasure.

She bit his lower lip. "Keep it."

"You'll get whisker burn on your face if I do." He ran a finger along the bow of her lip. "Already have, in fact."

"All the more reason. Mark me up now and give me a day or so to recover for the camera. Besides, that's why God invented makeup."

"Funny girl." He pulled out some boxer shorts and a pair of jeans.

"Jacky boy?"

He eyed her warily. "What?"

"Just the boxers. Don't cover up."

With a grimace, he studied her. "Why is this so important to you?"

A good question. "I think… You know how I asked you never to lie to me?"

"You mean, that you browbeat me into promising?"

She supposed she had, at that. "Okay then, yes. This is like that. I don't want you to pretend to be someone else with me. I don't want you to hide anything. Just be you." She wasn't sure where that came from, but it seemed vitally important. Joe in all his real guy presence.

"Like you pulling out the beauty routine?" He waved a hand at her face. She reflexively glanced in the mirror.

"Is that how it reads to you?" Absurdly, it hurt. And pissed her off. "There's a difference. This *is* who I am." She bracketed her face, deliberately vogueing. "Don't tell me you're one of *those* guys, the ones who go on about how the womens are betraying their trust with all the tricksy makeups."

He blinked at her. "You used that in a song."

"Yes." It took a little steam out of her that he recognized it. "Not those exact words, but—"

"What about the rest of the lyrics?" He interrupted.

Her turn to pause, processing the abrupt turn.

"You know," he said. "*But the face I wear is not the girl I am. You deserve my mask since you won't see me.*"

"I know my own fucking song."

He took her wrists, lifting them over her head and pinning her to the wall, deliciously strong, simmeringly annoyed with her. "What about me, Sova? Is the mask all I get—does the honesty go only one way?"

His gaze had her trapped as surely as his grip did. But she knew her limitations. "I never promised you honesty, Jacky boy. Don't get your expectations up. There *is* no me. Dwight warned you, right? When he told you not to fuck me. I'll break your heart." She sing-songed it, playful, but he didn't relent.

"Is that so?" His eyes roved her face, a bit wild. "You're assuming I have a heart to break."

"Oh no, that's me. All of my ugly is on the inside. I don't have a stump to show you, but it's a scarred shit show in there. Consider the gloss my prosthetic. A prosthetic candy heart." She had to say it. Fair warning and all, though it made that rotten place ache, the one that eased when he'd called her sweet. She writhed against him. "So you might as well take your fill of this while you can. That is what you get."

His jaw flexed and a growl rumbled in his throat. "You might regret taunting me," he said very softly. His own warning. Once that sent an illicit thrill through her.

She licked her lips, then bit the lower one. "Do your worst."

With hot flash of his gaze, he transferred her wrists to one hand and yanked a sash from the fuzzy bathrobe on the back of the door. With quick efficiency—and taking advantage of her shock—he whipped it around her wrists, lashing them to the hook for hanging towels. Bending, he bit her breast through the silk of the peignoir. Hard enough to make her squeak and try to pull away. He laughed, a dark sound, and held her fast, moving his hot mouth and tormenting teeth to her other breast.

"Jack," she gasped, "I—"

He paused, visibly wrestling with himself, not looking. "Too much?" he gritted out.

"No. I—" She clamped down on admitting the weakness. Whatever he could dish out, she could take. "Never."

"We'll see," he breathed and dropped to his knees, parting the sheer skirt, shoving it up around her waist and putting his mouth on her. Leaving her to stare at herself in the mirror, her face startled, lipstick smeared from those devastating kisses. Her mouth worked in an O as he thrust two fingers into her and sucked hard on her clit. Driving her as fiercely as she'd done to him earlier. She tugged at her wrists, struggling, and he snarled a warning, looking up at her, mouth glistening with her fluids.

"You stay still and take it. I'm going to make you come."

"We'll see." She hissed it back at him, wanting to sound mean, but it came out wobbly. When she'd told him to do his worst, she'd wanted him to take, not this… He'd changed tactics, placing a tender kiss on her mons, fingers stroking in and out of her gently. Too soft. Too sweet. Was that panic on her face? He slid a tongue into her folds, a long, slow lick that unraveled her. That drew a rough gasp out of her. "Jack…"

"Mmm. You taste sweet as wine, Sova," he murmured. "So hot. So vulnerable. What do I want to do to you? I want to take you apart. Piece by piece, until I reach that sweet, chewy center inside that candy heart."

She sobbed. A moan of exquisite pleasure, a thread of despair. She'd never watched herself like this. Never felt this sensation, of being so … opened. So far from the Ava she saw on screen, perfectly polished, poised and glamorous. This woman gasped like a fish, her face a rictus of emotion she'd never glimpsed on herself. He'd laid her open with a few words and that unrelenting mouth. She was coming apart. Even weeping again. The pleasure too keen-edged. Not even the scrape of Joe's stubble on her tender inner thighs could cut it.

She wanted to tell him to stop. But she couldn't admit defeat.

"I've got you, Sova. So sweet. So lovely. Let go. Give yourself over."

She couldn't have withheld, even if she'd found the resolve. With a cry, she gave in. Her seams unraveled, threads flying. Not an explosion, but a collapsing. A crumbling into a million tiny pieces of emotion and sensation. A song sung in the dark early morning hours, for no one at all, except someone who might be out there somewhere to listen.

Where have you gone that we never met?

Then she was weeping in earnest, dimly aware that he untied her wrists, picked her up and carried her to the bed. Sitting on the edge, he held her, rocking her and whispering reassurances. Apologizing.

"Don't apologize," she got out. "It's not you. It's me. A cliché, but true." God—who cries during sex? Someone pitiful, for sure.

"I still hate to see you cry."

"Lucky you." Maybe three times would be the charm and make this the final meltdown of the day. She had no idea what was going on with her anymore. Okay, maybe ever.

"At least we're taking turns." He gave her a crooked grin and kissed her on the nose. Too sharply sweet. She crawled off his lap, and knelt on the bed, determinedly wiping the tears away and seizing some fucking composure.

"Now I'm hungry," she told him. And she really was, she discovered. Though she shouldn't be. She'd eaten probably four times her calorie allotment for the day at lunch alone.

"How about this—you get under the covers and I'll bring you dinner in bed."

It sounded nice. Cozy. And, Lord God above, she was tired. As if that orgasm had drained the last of her fight. "If I do that, I'll be asleep in no time."

"So?"

"So." She lifted a shoulder, aware of venturing back onto dicey territory. "I should probably wash my face. Bad to sleep in makeup, you know." Cinna would never speak to her again.

He regarded her steadily. "So, wash your face. It will take me at least that long to boil the pasta."

"The sauce is probably mud by now."

"I have my ways." He headed off for the kitchen, singing a

fragment of the song she'd sung for him earlier. Wearing only his boxer shorts, the gleaming metal of the prosthetic an elegant extension of his body. His sterling character. Heart of steel.

And hers was glossy red, a sugar candy shell over rotten black corruption. Crack it a little and watch the pus ooze out.

~ 18 ~

H E PUT THE pasta water on high, letting it get to boil while he dealt with the sauce. It had thickened considerably, but not beyond repair. *Better too thick than not thick enough*, his mother always said. Opening the Malbec, he added some gradually, stirring over low heat, feeling his mother's eagle eye over his shoulder.

He hadn't thought of that debacle in the hospital for a long time. Had put it all out of his head, or thought he had—particularly the part he hadn't told Ava, how his mother had bewailed the loss of his manhood, the wedding she'd never plan, the grandchildren she'd never have, making the assumption so many did.

Hard to tell what Ava really thought about the stump. He'd challenged her pride, so she'd act as if she didn't care regardless of her true feelings. She had so many faces, slipping from one role to the next, forever tap-dancing her routine. The moment he thought he had a glimpse of something raw in her, she covered it swiftly, an emotional shell game, swapping out one lure for another, intellectual sleight of hand and deft misdirection. Effortlessly manipulating him so he forgot what he'd been trying to pay attention to in the first place.

He just had to remind himself that none of this was about him really understanding her. At least, not for her it wasn't.

The meatballs had dried out some, but the sauce would make

up for that. He added them to the pan, letting them simmer in the marinara to soak up the juices while he boiled the pasta.

Funny to be in this place, site of so many years of family memories, with Ava—the sun of his obsessions. And then her evoking that other life on the high desert hills of Afghanistan, the one that exploded in pain and fire. A collision of his several worlds, all fractured in his brain, stirred up by Ava's insistent curiosity. He hadn't really told her that part, about not being right in the head. That he might never be again. But that was long term and this wasn't. All the images and emotions slipped and slid around each other in his head, shifting to form a new pattern. One he wasn't at all sure of.

Slim arms wrapped around his waist, making him start only a little—*a friendly, buddy, nothing to be concerned about*—and Ava leaned her check against the bare skin of his back. "I'm sorry I'm so psycho."

He patted her hands and didn't move, not sure what brought on that apology. "You're not."

"We both know I am." She let him go and picked up the Malbec, pouring some into one of the glasses he'd set out. Bemused, he looked her over. She'd scrubbed her face so it shone pink and moist—and donned fleece pajamas scattered with cupcakes in every imaginable color, many of which would never be found on a real cupcake. Sipping her wine, she raised her brows and gestured at the PJs. "Kates must have packed them. My favorites. For being *comfortable*."

She looked different with no makeup at all. Younger. More… something. Not wanting to make her self-conscious as he had no doubt she'd done it for him, he smiled, then concentrated on the food. "Perfect."

She sat at the kitchen table, fidgeting with her wine glass. "I figured spaghetti in bed was a recipe for disaster. Your mother would never forgive me if I ruined her pretty room."

Light conversation then. He could do that. "Well, it's every-one's room. Whoever's got the place for the weekend or whatever generally takes the master. We only use the other rooms if a bunch of us are here."

"And this was your weekend anyway?"

"No, but nobody uses it this time of year as the weather is nasty and it's not Thanksgiving or Christmas, something like that. Mostly we come in the summertime." He blanched the pasta and dished it into big bowls, dressing it with the marinara and meatballs, sprinkling a generous helping of sharp cheddar on top, and set the bowl in front of her.

She frowned at it. "Cheddar on spaghetti?"

"Don't knock it until you've tried it, oh ye who eats things like kale chips."

"Kale chips aren't awful. Better than rice cakes."

"I don't plan to find out." He set his bowl and the Malbec on the table, grabbed a couple of candles from the sideboard, lit them and killed the fluorescent kitchen light. Topping off her glass and filling his own, he raised his glass. "Women are the typhoons with gentle names. Let's drink to our typhoons storming only in bed."

"Gallant. Not at all sexist." She raised her brows at him.

"My grandfather's favorite toast. Probably not the best choice, but you had me thinking of him. How about—to the woman who lights up my world."

With an odd smile, she clinked her glass to his and drank, eyes luminous in the candlelight. "You're a romantic guy under it all, aren't you?"

"I thought you had me pegged as traditional."

"They go together." She forked up some of her pasta, giving him an astonished look while she chewed and swallowed. "Omigod, this is so good."

He grinned as she dug in, absurdly happy to be able to feed

her. She looked like a refugee from some teenage slumber party movie and yet perfectly right at his grandmother's kitchen table. Not so much Ava anymore. *Sova.* In another lifetime, maybe he'd be whole and they'd have met in some normal way. *Where have you gone that we never met?*

"So, how many girls before me have gotten Jack's Romantic Weekend Special?"

He mentally stumbled. It never paid to daydream around her. "A gentleman never tells."

"Ah, ah, ah—we've established you are no gentleman. Not in the sack, for sure."

Ouch. He put his fork down. "I apologize for how I—"

"Shut up. You know I love it. I take it back—I'll bet you were a perfect gentleman with these other girls. You make the spaghetti, pour the wine, light the candles and afterwards you take them to bed and *make love.*" Her voice went saccharine on the last, mocking. "Using condoms every time."

"There's nothing wrong with making love. And using condoms is common sense."

She eyed him, that gleam of mischief in the purse of her lips. "Bareback is better. Everyone knows that."

"Old habits die hard."

"You mean you've *always* used a rubber. Your entire life?"

"I'm not that old. But no—in a few long-term relationships, we dispensed with protection after a while."

"Like how long?"

"One was eighteen months, another just over three years, but long distance for most of it. And an eight-monther." All of them *before*, but he didn't care to confess that.

She smiled, pleased, and he belatedly recalled he'd initially refused to tell her about his personal life. But they'd moved beyond that, hadn't they? Far beyond.

"I meant, how long is 'a while'—what's the Jack Rule for

dispensing with protection?"

"I leave it up to her to decide."

Ava folded up her legs under her, pushing her half-filled plate away and keeping her wine glass. "I decided already."

Treacherous territory. "Aren't you going to finish that?"

She puffed out her cheeks like a blowfish. "I'm stuffed. I can't believe you already finished yours." He took her plated and started in on it. "And that you eat so much."

"That's Army for you—you learn to eat as much as you can, as fast as you can, when you can."

"So, you figure I'm diseased?"

He nearly choked on the meatball. *Danger ahead.* "No. I never said that."

"Something."

"Well, do you have unprotected sex?"

She shrugged, studying her wine. "Sometimes. It's not something I think about."

"You should. Or your lovers should." It rankled to think that boy band Tyler would have blown that off the other night. He should have put a stop to it. His place or not. Funny how they both pretended like it hadn't happened. No—that it didn't matter. Which it likely didn't to her. Still. "That's insanely self-destructive."

"Oh, Jacky boy," she replied softly. "That barely registers on the Ava scale of self-destructive."

She meant it, somber with a grimness behind it. The way she'd talked about her ugly insides. *A prosthetic heart.* It hurt his own that she could think such a thing. Getting up, he grabbed the box of cake pops and handed her one, just to make her smile. It matched her PJs. She nibbled at it dubiously, considering him. "I'm going to be ten pounds heavier at the Monday morning weigh-in. Celine is going to have a conniption fit."

"You have to weigh in every Monday?"

"Ha! I wish. Every day. So my diet can be appropriately adjusted. Every one of these—" she held up the cake pop, the sparkles on it glittering "—means another meal of kale chips, possibly ten. Salads forever." She made a face.

"I think you should be able to indulge once in a while. This is a recuperation weekend, right? You deserve to indulge. Even the body builders have treat days."

"Hmm." She sounded unconvinced. "Answer my other question. How many girls have you brought up here?"

"That I was sleeping with?"

"Why does that matter?"

"Well, when I was younger, we'd come up for a few weeks in the summer and I'd bring whatever girlfriend I had at the time. There's bunkbed rooms downstairs, one for girls, one for boys. It was basically one big party."

"Sounds like something out of a teen movie."

"We never put on a show in the old barn or anything. Beach volleyball, swimming, surfing. Lots of lobster bakes and barbeques."

"My all-American Jacky boy." She yawned, hugely.

He got up to wash the dishes. "Why don't you get in bed, Sova?"

"That's a Russian word, I'm betting."

He shook his head. "Not telling. You could always Google it."

"I'm not allowed internet access."

He laughed. When she didn't join in, he glanced over his shoulder. She still nibbled on the cake pop, picking off the sugar crystals in small nips, watching him owlishly. "You're serious?"

"I'm surprised Dwight didn't warn you, though I suppose it's just SOP now. Really I gave it up voluntarily. It's all Katey."

"None of it's you?"

She shrugged. "Nope. I can't be trusted."

He turned back to the dishes. "That's just crazy. Of course you can be trusted. You're a grown woman."

"Oh, Jack, you're so… I don't even know the word. Not naïve. Innocent maybe."

"You say that after what we've done together?"

She laughed, not in amusement. "See? That you can even say that just proves my point."

"Hmm." A silence fell, broken only by the rush of water and clanging of the pots.

"If you're a fan," she said, and he tensed for the salvo her idle tone promised, "then you know about the Epic Disaster."

"Uh, no. Is that with capital letters?"

"Funny boy. The naked pics on the internet. Of me."

Of which he'd searched out all of them and had them printed on archival paper. "Wasn't there debate about whether your head was photoshopped onto some other girl's body?"

She laughed, nearly genuine, but with that edge. "You've seen me naked in real life—what do you think? Or do you plan to claim you never saw them?"

That would be the safest route.

"Remember your promise," she taunted, as if she could read his mind.

"So what?" he shrugged. He'd have to let the one pan soak, with the way the sauce had baked on. "Bad publicity is still good publicity, isn't that what they say?"

Ava snorted. Poured more wine. "If only. Anyway, since you're so carefully not asking, yes that was me, and the pics were on my phone and somehow got *off* my phone. And then I had the unfortunate Twitter fight with Mr. Wonderful about it because I know it was him, even if he insists to the end of the earth it wasn't."

He dried the clean dishes. *Listen*, his counselor had always said in group. *You don't have to say anything back, just let people be heard.*

"Nothing to say?" Ava asked, insistently poking. Clearly those principles didn't apply to her.

"'Mr. Wonderful' is Tyler from Four4All?"

"Yeah. Old nickname. We should change it, but that's against the rules."

"You and Katey?"

"Right. The nickname game. Once we pick one, it sticks, or it gets too confusing. And you're changing the subject."

He wiped off his hands and turned to look at her, so girlish in her cupcake PJs. "No, I'm just listening." And not asking why she'd fuck a guy she thought had done that to her.

She gave him a dubious look and sighed, twirling the wine glass by the stem. "Anyway. I forget why I was telling you that."

"No access to the internet."

"Oh, right. So, that's why I can't be trusted. I mean what kind of idiot lets a guy take naked pics of her and then fights with him about it on a public forum?"

He leaned back on the counter, studying her, not sure what to say. Mostly wanting to punch that fucking Tyler. Uncomfortable that he'd treasured those pics. What if that happened to Nona? "I think you trusted him. You called him 'Mr. Wonderful' for a reason." Though it escaped him what it could be. "You're not an idiot for thinking he cared about you enough not to betray you." And ouch, speaking of betrayal.

"Yeah, well…" Her eyes filled with tears and she ducked her head, pinching the bridge of her nose. "He says it wasn't him."

"And you believe him?"

"I don't know. Depends on the day. If it wasn't, then the answer is even worse and I can't think about that."

"Okay." He finished putting the dishes away, happy to have a reason not to face her.

"Are you… planning to sleep in that bed with me?" She

asked it casually, but sounded a little lost.

What answer did she want?

"Do you want me to? Or I can sleep in another room."

"The boys' bunkroom?"

"No thank you—did my time. There are other, much more comfortable choices."

"I don't, usually, sleep with someone else." She had a funny look on her face and he couldn't tell if it was because she did or didn't want to share a bed with him.

"Totally your call. Whatever make you happiest."

"Of course you shared a bed with *them*," she said, "these innumerable other girls you brought up here for cozy romantic weekends. That's what normal people do."

Jealous? It didn't seem likely. "First of all, there's no such thing as normal. Second, they're not innumerable. If we count since I've been an adult, I've been up here twice with just me and another woman. Finally, yes, we always slept together, but you and I don't have to."

"Because this isn't a real thing," she replied, and poured herself more wine. "This is about you tending to me. *Doing your damn job*. Holding me when I cry, listening to my tragic tales, giving me cake pops and sex. Lather, rinse, repeat."

"The perks are excellent," he tried for the joke, but she didn't smile.

"I wish you loved me. Like real people do." She sounded wistful, maybe a little drunk. "That's what would make me happiest. If I wasn't Ava and you weren't my handler *du jour*. That you'd brought me up here for romance and long walks on the beach. That I wasn't some self-destructive diva you're cautious of dipping your wick into because God knows who else has been in there."

"Sova." He snagged the chair with a foot to bring it closer, sat in it and took her hands. "It's not like that. When I was on tour, you wouldn't believe the shit guys contracted. Protection is common sense. I don't care how many men you've been with, but I will take care of you the way I would any woman I went to bed with." He took a breath. What the hell—he couldn't compromise himself any more than he had already. "And it's not just a job to me. I brought you here because you were miserable and this is the most peaceful place I know. I wanted to share it with you. I'm not interested in handling you. I just want you happy."

She searched his face for something. The truth, maybe. "I know I asked you to be honest with me, but could we… pretend? For the rest of the weekend, let's say that I'm just this girl you met and you brought me up here for a romantic getaway."

"It doesn't work that way. You are—"

"Oh Jack, believe you me—I don't forget who I am. I'm asking you to help me put on a show in the old barn. Make believe. Look, here I am with no makeup, like you wanted."

So much wrong with that, but hadn't he been daydreaming that very thing? Never mind that he simply filled the role for the couple of days. She looked so miserable, desperately on edge. What could it hurt? He tucked a curl behind her ear and she leaned into the touch like Arlin left too long alone. "Of course," he told her, saying the words before he consciously decided. "But be warned—Arlin will sneak up on the bed during the night, even if I tell him not to."

She smiled, a hint of that girlish joy in it that she and Katey had shared, talking about their puppy Violet. "That would be cool."

"I'm going to take Arlin out for one last whiz. Why don't you get in bed and I'll be right there?"

"Okay." She drained her wine, then gave him a dazzling smile. "My Jacky boy."

Arlin wasn't enthused about the excursion, though the storm had tapered off. They were in and out pretty quickly, then Joe banked the fire, locked up and turned off the lights. By the time he got back to the bedroom, Ava was out cold, one hand tucked beneath her cheek, looking more like an angel than any living woman had a right to. Also shadowed and wounded.

He killed the light and doffed the prosthesis. Just as well she'd seen how his leg looked, given where they'd ended up. Not what he'd expected at all. Being careful with the covers, he slid in beside her, shifting close enough to scent her, to feel her warmth, but not so as to disturb her.

To his surprise, she turned and snuggled up against him. Not waking though. Putting a gentle arm around her, he gathered her in. She was naked, all hot, sweet woman.

He lay there for a while before he slept, listening to the ocean. Wondering how this had come to pass.

And where the hell it would land him in the end. A hell of his own making, that was for sure.

~ 19 ~

H ER EYES FLEW open, staring into the impenetrable dark. Where the hell was she?

"Hey!" The shout came again, from right beside her. That's what had wakened her. Joe, in bed with her, thrashing. Strangling out another cry. One of terror and violent aggression. Not thrashing exactly—he was trying to punch something, his arm tangled in the sheet. "Hey you!" he shouted, voice thick, guttural and filled with anger, riddled with fear.

She laid a hand on him, finding him slick with sweat. He stilled immediately, coming instantly awake. Then heaved a weary sigh.

"Was I shouting?" he asked quietly, as if they could be overheard in the dimness of the night. "Hi, Arlin. Good boy. I'm fine."

The dog whined a little, whuffing in the dark. Probably licking.

"I think you were trying to punch someone," she said.

"Sorry. A good argument for me not to sleep with another person. Happens sometimes. Did I hurt you?"

"Nope. Scary guy was the other direction. Nightmares?"

"Yeah." A shadow of his hand shifted to scrub over his face. "Sorry I woke you."

"It's okay." She ran a hand over his ridged abs. Definite argument in favor of having a man in your bed all night. "Will you be able to go back to sleep?"

"Not for a while. I'll go in the other room."

"No—don't."

"It could happen again. I should go sleep somewhere else."

"Stay. Why waste the opportunity?" She trailed her hand down, finding he still wore his boxers—and that he was hard. Slipping her hand inside, she grasped him. "Or this."

With a groan—and only slight hesitation—he rolled to her, thrusting into her hand, warm mouth finding hers in the dark. His hands roamed over her, stroking her skin, both soothing and arousing. Like he took comfort in her, soaking in the feel of her. It was different this way, slow, lazy. Almost dreamlike.

Making love.

His hand slid between her legs, stroking her slickness, and she opened for him, savoring his caressing touch, then turning onto her back and urging him into her. With a murmur, he put her off, reaching to the nightstand for one of his so-important condoms. To hurry him along, she scratched at his back. Laughing, he turned back, pinning her to the bed with his strength.

Then slid into her, stretching and filling. Deliciously sweet. Cake pops and sex.

He moved over and in her, a darker shadow, taking his time, dropping kisses on her lips, face, shoulder, breast. She hadn't figured on climaxing, but the pressure built surprisingly fast, growing and burgeoning. He put a hand under her hips, lifting so the angle intensified, levering himself up to hit that sweet spot.

"Joe..." She sighed out his name, dissolving, clinging to his strong shoulders as he followed after, shuddering.

"My lovely Ava," he whispered in her ear.

"Stay with me, okay? Don't go."

"But what if—"

"I don't care. I need you here."

He cuddled her close. "So beautiful. So precious to me."

Believing him, in the way only the shadows of night allowed, she fell back asleep with him still holding her.

✦   ✦   ✦

HE WASN'T THERE when she awoke in the morning. No weight of Arlin on the bed either. She fought the strange sense of loneliness, and yes, disappointment. Stupid, since she always woke alone. When had he left though? Gray light filtered in the high window, along with the sound of softly falling rain.

She rolled over, more than half contemplating going back to sleep rather than face the day. And him. What all had she said? Gut-wrenchingly vulnerable things. She rolled her eyes at herself and a foil-wrapped package on the bedside table caught her eye. A sticky note on it said, "good morning, Sova" in ball-point ink. Interesting to see it spelled out. And to see his neat, efficient printing. Unwrapping the foil, she found a damp washcloth, still warm. And smiled.

The rare times she'd spent an entire night with a guy, she'd once or twice awakened to roses or room service delivery. This—this simple thoughtfulness—seemed exponentially more romantic. Maybe because there weren't handlers waiting in the outer suite for them. She kind of wished she hadn't asked him to pretend, so she could believe he really did care. But then she'd been drunk, hadn't she? Maybe she'd only imagined that conversation. That was it. She'd never begged him to like her.

So precious to me.

Fine. She didn't care if she'd dreamed it, or if he'd said it only because she'd asked for the fantasy. She'd take it. Suspend disbelief for two more days.

Grabbing her PJs, she headed into the bathroom. With teeth

and hair brushed—a just a little makeup, mostly to cover the shadows of weeping and perk up her color a bit—she pulled on the PJs and went to find Joe. If he was even there and not out running or something crazy like that. But no—he was sitting by the fire, drinking from a mug, and reading on his eReader, Arlin at his feet. Hearing her, he looked up and smiled. He did that pretty much every time—smiled when he spotted her, naturally and easily, without any agenda behind it. Like he was just happy to see her.

"Sleeping beauty awakes," he said. "There's coffee in the pot. Or I can make you some tea."

They wouldn't have a Keurig or espresso machine, of course. "Coffee is good. What time is it?"

"About ten thirty."

He'd left a mug out for her next to the pot, along with cream, milk, sugar—and a cake pop on a little saucer. She doctored her coffee, carried the plate into the other room and sat cross-legged on the rug in front of the fire. "Breakfast of champions?"

"My sister's favorite thing to have for breakfast. She always saves a slice of her birthday cake for the morning after, as a special treat."

She bit into the sparkly pastry, savoring the spike of creamy sweetness. "How old is she?"

"Nona? She's seventeen."

"Big age difference."

"Mom had something like five miscarriages between me and Nona. They'd nearly given up when she was finally born, but Mom really wanted a girl."

"Why?"

"Most women want a daughter, don't they?"

"I guess I wouldn't know."

He paused at that. She supposed her tone had been a little

biting. "Maybe it's just my family," he continued, watching her, feeling his way, "a girl to carry on her legacy. Learn the family recipes and keep the old photos and such."

"You know the family marinara recipe."

His smile flashed. "True, but I don't think it counts to my mother. And Nona is the one learning to scrapbook, not me."

It sounded like an alien planet. "'Nona' is an unusual name."

"Short for Ilona. She's named for both of our grandmothers. Ilona Regina Ivanchan. Quite the mixed-ethnic mouthful."

"'Joe' isn't Russian."

"It's really Iosif—for my grandfather. But Joseph for simplicity."

The coffee and cake pop tasted surprisingly good together, the fire warm and his company … restful. "I'm not named for anyone. That must be kind of comforting, to feel like you belong to something that continues on like that. Something real and meaningful."

"Isn't Ava your real name?"

"Actually it is. You thought it was a stage name?"

"It's a popular name. A good one. Perfect for the stage."

"Exactly. Did you know it means singer as well as referencing Eve? My mother is the epitome of the long-term planner. Pisses her off, though, that it's such a popular name now. It was unusual when I was born. Old, you know. Ava Gardner. Eva Gabor. Me." She rolled her eyes for her mother's ambition—and all the poison that had come along with it.

He nodded thoughtfully. "Probably because of you that it's so popular again."

"Which is weird to think about. Your family's way is better. Name your kid after her grandmothers, not some tarted up TV princess."

"You shouldn't say things like that about yourself."

She shrugged that off with a little smile. Her naïve Jacky boy.

Sweet though, to be pretending for her like this.

"If you're finished with your coffee, we could go for a walk," he said.

"You don't have to offer that." With an internal wince for her wine-sodden self, she regretted saying those things to him the night before. Her personal "I'm just a girl standing in front of a boy asking him to like her" moment. *Notting Hill* was her go-to comfort movie. Sure her favorite scene, the one she played over and over was the stupid birthday party. Meeting his friends and hanging out. The most unrealistic part of that whole movie. But the one that made her cry every damn time was the whole groveling scene, giving him the Chagall and asking him to like her. At least Julia had known Hugh loved her once and probably still did. Ava was that much more pitiful that she had to hire someone to pretend to romance her. The low rent Anna Scott. Glum thoughts.

"Actually, I'm going regardless." Jack set aside his eReader and stood, stretching. As if he'd been waiting for the cue, Arlin went from apparent dead sleep to bouncing, prancing life. Jack grinned at the dog and patted him on the head. "See? But we'd love for you to join us."

"I'll get dressed then."

"Walking shoes, not heels," he called after her. "If you brought any," he amended when she cast a glare over her shoulder.

"I know about walking on the beach, Jacky boy." In theory, anyway. This one had rocks, right? And it would be cold and wet. It always seemed cozier in the movies. Maybe it would be okay. Couldn't have fantasy romance weekend without the love montage.

Thankfully, Katey had packed her cross-trainers, so she didn't have to eat her words. Her sister had a talent for predicting what Ava would need. The jeans, t-shirt and cotton sweater to go over it should work. It wasn't raining all that hard, but it looked pretty damp and dreary all the same.

"Here," Joe said, looking her over when she emerged and opening a hall closet, "you'll want a windbreaker." He handed her one in a vivid, startling orange, along with a black knit cap. "And this for your ears."

Ugly, but at least no one would possibly recognize her in such things, and there wouldn't be an actual camera following them for the love montage. "Do you take care of everyone—or just me?"

He gave her a quick grin and pulled a similar watchman's cap over his own ears, which made him look somehow dangerous and dashing. "We keep a closet full of nasty-weather gear here for a reason."

"Which doesn't answer my question."

Arlin barked impatiently at the delay and Joe raised an eyebrow. "There's your answer. Let's get moving. You have cake pops to work off."

"I wouldn't if you didn't keep feeding them to me," she grumbled. "Do I have to wear my sunglasses?"

He cocked his head, considering. "Put them in your pocket. I doubt we'll see much of anyone out and about in this weather."

"Doesn't that make them smarter than us?"

"No, ma'am." He offered his hand and she took it, warm as he laced his fingers with hers. "We all need the exercise," he added. "Besides—that means I can let Arlin run off leash."

"What if we do see someone?"

"Then you put on the glasses and I call Arlin to me to get on his leash."

"Both of us well trained."

He cocked a brow at her. "Well, Arlin is, anyway. Come on—it will be romantic."

She tried to think of the right reply as he tugged her out the door and locked up. She'd asked him to play the part, so she couldn't criticize him for doing so. But the regret gave it all a tinge of bittersweet, because now she couldn't pretend to herself that he meant any of it. Caught in her own game.

No less than she deserved.

~ 20 ~

I T FELT GOOD to get out into the salt-spray air. He felt better overall than he had in a long time. Coming to this place had been the right idea, precarious as the choice had been. Ava wanted him to pretend to romance her, and he could do that. A relief, in a way, not to have to pretend the reverse, that he didn't love her to an unreasonable, even insane degree.

And the amazing sex with her…yeah, it definitely cleared the mind. Along with everything else.

Ava hung back, tugging on their joined hands, her wide golden eyes fixed on the staircase to the ocean walk. "I promise they're safe," he assured her. "We check them out and shore them up."

"Who's we?" She edged closer to him, holding his hand in that fierce grip of hers.

"Me, my dad, my uncles, my brother and sister, a few cousins. We check it every year." And had a big family fight the first time he went to help after the injury and his mom had a crying fit about it, screaming at his dad to stop him.

"You have a big family."

"A dramatic one, too."

She picked her way down the slick wooden steps, though he didn't get her trepidation, as sure-footed and graceful as she was, but she settled into her easy stride once they hit the paved path that followed along the cliffs. "Not actually beach," she noted, looking around with interest at the wildly churning surf. The stiff breeze brought pink to her high cheekbones, blonde curls tossing at the edges of the black watch cap, eyes bright, their own sun against the gray sky.

"The cliff walk is much easier than the actual beach. There's sand, but lots of rock outcroppings, too. If we want a vigorous uninterrupted walk, this is the place to be. Besides, the views are better. We'll go down to the sand at a couple of places. Arlin will want to swim."

"Brr."

"No kidding. He's a dog of steel."

They walked in comfortable quiet for a while, Ava keeping up easily on her long legs, holding his hand and drinking it all in. She'd relaxed some, put aside what ate at her. For a few minutes there by the fire, she'd started to sink into the dark place, but he was getting better at seeing the signs and diverting her.

"Me, I don't have a big family," she said, gazing out at the lighthouse on the point. "I don't really have anyone."

"You have all your fans—that's a huge family."

She glanced at him, rolling her eyes dramatically. "You don't believe that bullcrap, do you?"

He thought of himself, those lonely months, edged with desperation and the certainty that his life had ended, that no one would ever love him again. His imagined connection to her. "I do believe it," he said slowly, thinking out loud. "Maybe you don't always feel it, but when you sing to people, we hear you and answer. You light up people's lives, give them a reason to wake up in the morning, to get through a tiresome work day." Losing body and mind. "Your fans, they love you. It's real. You must feel it when you go among them and hug them, sign whatever they offer you."

She was quiet, her face remote. "Is that what love feels like?"

He laughed, then snuffed it when she didn't join in. "It's a kind of love," he said. It certainly was from him. Wasn't it?

"I mean…" She worried one of her eyeteeth with her tongue. "How do you *know* what love is supposed to feel like? You know, the directors and acting coaches tell you how to *look*. 'Oh, touch his arm, make your eyes wide and damp, purse your lips.' They make the light all soft and play weepy sounding music, but they can't say how to *feel* it. How the hell are you supposed to know it?"

"I don't know. How do you know that you feel mad or sad?"

"Aha!" She bounced on her toes, stabbing a finger into the air. "Because you pitch a fit and someone tells you not to be mad. You cry and they say, 'don't be sad.' No one ever tells you when you're being—what?—loving, I guess."

"When your parents, or your sister, hug you and say they love you—that's telling you, in a way."

"But if you don't get that?" She sounded genuinely curious, if a little hollow.

He'd seen her mother in action, but now he really wondered what the hell kind of childhood Ava had. "Other people then."

She shook her head. "No one has ever said that they loved me when it wasn't a line in a performance. Or shouted by a fan, which I guess you're saying counts."

He squeezed her hand, wanting to tell her loved her, but that would be coming from just another fan. "I'm sorry for that, Sova."

"Are you?" She cocked her head at him, curls whipping across her eyes. "Maybe it's not a bad thing. I think a lot of people lie when they say it. You know, just because they're supposed to. At least I'm not kidding myself—I know I'm following a script."

He hadn't thought of it that way.

"But you," she continued, "you love your family and they love you. You think you all really feel it, mean it when you say it?"

"I do." He mulled it more. "Yeah, we mean it."

"How do you know?" She was insistently curious.

"Because even when we're mad or upset, the love is still there. Even when I wanted to throttle my mom for screaming at the hospital, I loved her."

"Hmm. I don't think it worked that way for us. But then there's just me, my mom, and Katey. And… well, when we're mad or upset, it's like, that's all there is."

"Ah." He said nothing more, uncertain whether she wanted him to ask more. "Sad that your father died."

She flashed him a golden sideways glance. "Read my official bio, did you? My mother's high school sweetheart who tragically died young. Leukemia, I think she decided on as suitably romantic." She snorted. "Want to know the real story, Jacky boy? Dwight would make you sign a non-disclosure."

"I already did. Very thorough." Near as he could tell. He didn't even bother to run it past a lawyer, since it so obviously promised to eviscerate him for breathing a word about anything to do with Ava to anyone. Not that he would want to. Or that anyone would believe him if he did.

"Ah. Good to know that my secrets are safe with you in a legally enforceable way." She said it lightly, but that bitterness had snuck back in. Enough that he stopped, turned her and pulled her into his arms, kissing her forehead because she didn't lift her chin.

"Hey." He waited for her to look him in the eye, then kissed her again, coaxing and gentle. Her lips tasted sweet from the lip gloss she'd swiped on. "You have my secrets, too, remember? And you don't even have to keep them." He hated that he'd had a nightmare with her there, one reason he hadn't slept with anyone, but maybe it worked out that she knew something of him, too.

She sighed and leaned against him, tucking her head into the fold of his shoulder. Then stirred restlessly, pushed away and took his hand again, pulling him along. "It's too cold to stop." Arlin, waiting with ill grace, barked in agreement and set off trotting.

"So, this is the story. It may shock you to discover there is no tragically lost high school sweetheart. In fact, Mommy Dearest did not attend much of high school. It's hard to tell."

"Hard to tell?"

"Sometimes she'd tell stories." Ava twirled a hand in the air. "But they always changed. Never the same one twice. Or the same one on the surface but all the details go wonky. I swear I recognize some from movies. Like I said—just hard to tell. After a while you begin to doubt your own memory, too, particularly when she insists she never said any such thing. We're pretty sure she ran away from home before she had a driver's license. That seems to be a recurrent theme, because she never did learn to drive. Ironic, huh?" She slid a glance at him, brows raised.

"So neither did you?"

"Bingo. Of course, I never needed to. I was a kid and then I had the same driver since *Tween Hangout* until you. Henry. Probably no one mentioned him." She faltered. Kicked a stone in the path so it skittered off. "You know, I think he would have liked you."

"What happened to him?" Though he figured he knew.

"He died." She gazed out at the sea, her voice neutral, another breath on the wind. "A stroke, they said."

"I'm sorry." If he'd been her driver since *Tween Hangout*, then she'd known him for fifteen years or more.

"Yeah. Thanks. You know the crying thing? Before Henry died, I just never did. Not for real. Only in movies or when watching them. Since then… I'm a waterfall. I don't get it. So not me."

"My—" He caught himself before mentioning his VA counselor. "I always heard it's better to get the emotion out than repress it."

"Leads to nightmares?" She slid him a glance, not at all fooled.

"Sorry about that."

"Don't be. I told you I didn't mind." They were silent a moment and she took his hand. A kind of apology, maybe. "He loved Shirley Temple movies. He'd always tell us to sparkle, just like her mom would say. Sparkle, Shirley."

"A good memory."

"Yeah. *Anyway…* I was talking about my father."

And father figure—or grandfather figure—it occurred to him, though she might not realize that.

She leaned in, speaking in a fake conspiratorial whisper. "Ship in the night."

"One-night stand?"

"If that. Probably more like ten-minute stand, knowing her. She'd moved to LA, wanted to be a movie star, dontcha know. Worked it I don't know how long. Long enough to figure she didn't have what it took, so she stalked the stars. Did the groupie thing. *You* know. Those guys are so irresponsible, they don't use protection." She sent him a sunny smile. "See? She needed a stalwart man like you, to insist on safe sex 24/7."

"Don't start."

"Anyhoo," she continued as he hadn't spoken, "when she was high she'd say it was Brad Pitt or Val Kilmer or even Hugh Jackman—and everyone knows *he* doesn't sleep around. A couple times she claimed it was Axl Rose, which would be kind of cool and also explain my personality flaws. But it was *always* someone fabulous. Both trophy and meal ticket."

"But she didn't go for paternity?"

"Nope. Which tells you something right there."

He wasn't sure what. Ava glanced at him, then rolled her eyes.

"Jacky boy—*she* doesn't know who the fuck it was. If she'd had even a wild guess, she would have gone for his pocketbook for sure. She was probably blind drunk or doped out of her head, so much cum dripping out of her she left a slime trail behind."

He managed not to flinch, mainly because Ava was watching for it, golden eyes hard and mocking. He also didn't know what to say, so he squeezed her hand and went for one of the counseling phrases that they'd coached them to use in group therapy. "That must have been difficult for you."

Empty words—and she made a scoffing sound, shrugging it off. "Why? I wasn't there." But her mouth relaxed from its bitter lines.

"So where does the meal ticket come in?"

She pulled away and pirouetted, finishing in a snazzy pose. "You're looking at her. Mom claims she carefully chose my dad for looks and star quality, her personal breeding experiment. Only in her world the perfect child is a pretty one who sings and dances. Of course, if she'd wanted to breed a super-scientist or athlete, she would have needed different genes of her own." She snorted at her own joke, staring out at the sea, face going remote.

"Let's go down here," he said, turning her toward the steps to the empty beach, loosing Arlin to race ahead, ears and tongue flying as he beelined for the water. A little quieter here, in this cove shielded from the bigger waves, but the wind bit harder close to the surf.

She stepped along the edges of the foam, hands buried in pockets, face down. Even like that she looked larger than life, slender and vibrating with personality. She caught him studying her. "Looking for the resemblance to one of them? Pick your male celeb—or also-ran—of the mid-nineties."

"You'd think the eyes would be a clue."

She shook her head. "Mom's eyes are brown, mine are just a weird lighter take. Katey… she thinks my eyes are what did it."

"Did it?"

"Cracked the difference between us. Why I got lucky and she didn't."

"What do you mean?"

~ 21 ~

WEIRD TO BE discussing this stuff. At all, but especially with a guy like Joe. Though maybe that was why she could. He listened, and not just waiting for her to get done talking so he could say something. In fact, sometimes she'd figured he wasn't going to reply and then he'd come out with some thought on what she'd said that showed he'd been pondering it the whole time.

He'd found a stick, throwing it into the surf for Arlin, who flew through the waves like some kind of golden dolphin-dog, grabbing it and bring it back, everything poised to do it again. A simple way to live. Enviable.

Her nose was cold and chill rain coated her face, but she wasn't miserable. Not even thinking about her mother and Katey and all of that. She wasn't sure what she felt. Maybe it was like her own phantom limb had quit screaming for a while, and so she just felt relief.

Joe threw the stick again, slid her a sideways look, stuck his hands in his jeans pockets and shook his head. "I love your eyes—they're amazing and gorgeous, no doubt—but it seems to me that it's *you* that made the difference. Your voice. Your songs. Your talent."

Warmth fizzed in her. "My number one fan," she teased, but he didn't smile.

"You joke, but yeah, you have that impact on people. You're

a star for a lot of reasons, but I don't think any of them are luck."

"You're wrong there. Never underestimate the power of serendipity. First there's the genetics, and—"

"Katey's your half-sister then?"

"Funny that, huh? We look so much alike—I'm not even a full year younger than Katey—but so far as we know, it wasn't the same guy. We both look like *her.*"

"Doesn't she have red hair?" He grimaced when she gave him a surprised look. "I saw her at the concert, remember."

Ava laughed, delighted with him, and caught him by the belt loops, turning him to face her. The kiss slid cold and wet on the surface, with melting heat beneath. "Oh Jacky boy," she spoke against his mouth, then kissed him again, hard and fast, before letting him go to receive Arlin's freshly retrieved stick. "We all color our hair. God only knows what my actual color is, or Katey's. Our mother… yeah. Zero idea there. Maybe it was brown? It's not like we have scrapbooks full of family photos."

He reached out and took her hand, his cold and wet from the stick, just holding it. She must sound pathetic and she hadn't meant to. "Anyway," she said.

"You were telling me about Katey," he prompted. "Why wasn't she given the prophetic name?"

Not a dumb guy, by any stretch. "Oh, but she was! Katharine, as in Hepburn. But it didn't work out so well for Katey." She wasn't sure she could talk about that, or her culpability in it all.

"What happened to her?" When she didn't answer, he pulled her hand, still laced with his, into his pocket, then turned her to face him, doing the same with her other hand. "I should have given you gloves, too. Your hands are cold."

His eyes looked like the evergreens tossing on the cliffs, his dark brows and lashes accentuated by the black watchman's cap.

How had she ever thought him not particularly handsome?

"I saw the scars on her wrists," he said gently, "but you don't have to talk about it if you don't want to."

Her throat abruptly thick, she looked past him to Arlin digging at something in the sand. "She didn't mean it. I mean, not to actually die. 'A cry for help' they said. And I guess it did help. Mom wanted her to have another plastic surgery, to fix her chin, and she didn't want to." She met Joe's eyes again, watching him try not to look naïve and shocked. "She'd had so many surgeries and she just … couldn't anymore."

"There's something wrong with her chin?"

"Was. It was too pointed, caught the camera shadows wrong. She was up for a big part. Could have made her career. But she had to lose weight, fix the chin."

"She looked skinnier than you are."

"Ah, yeah. This was years ago—for *Little Girl Lost*."

"Your big breakthrough role."

"Exactly." How could she have missed that he was a fan? He knew every damn thing about her career. "Good illustration of my character, Jacky boy. Katey gets called back, top choice, has to lose fifteen pounds and get the surgery. Cuts her wrists. The director, Wilson Alan, stops by with flowers while she's laid up. She was sleeping, so I auditioned."

He took a beat. "You what?"

"You heard me. Put on a skimpy outfit, all the cosmetics, sang, danced, performed that monologue—you know the one— I had it memorized 'cause I'd helped Katey with it. And I got the part. Katey tried to make it up. Lost the weight, nearly managed to kill herself then, got the surgery. But it was too late. I made my career over my suicidal sister's body."

He shook his head. "I'm sure you're exaggerating."

"Not a bit. If anything I'm tempering it. I'm a stone-cold bitch, Jacky boy. Don't ever forget it."

"You were like fourteen when you did that movie."

"Thirteen at the start. Twelve when I auditioned." She watched his face as he struggled to excuse her. Probably a good thing she'd asked him to pretend to care about her, to want to romance her. Though it had been foolish to tell him this whole sordid story. She wasn't at all sure why she had. At least she hadn't told him the worst part.

"So young. I—"

"Oh, Jacky boy. Don't try to excuse me for it. I was never young. When I was five years old I bashed Katey over the head with her own tiara because she won some fucking contest—I can't even remember what now, Little Miss Fucking Wonderful Something—and she had to have stitches. Her first surgery, thanks to me." And her mother had praised her winning spirit.

He pressed his lips together, looking pained. So, she patted him on the cheek.

"It's okay. There's nothing to say." She'd been talking way too much, making her stomach twist. "Kiss me."

He did, quickly warming to it. If nothing else, he wanted her. Even windblown and wearing a horrible jacket, she turned him on. The press of his hard-on confirmed it, and she rubbed her pelvis against him to encourage him. He murmured something sweet against her skin as he kissed the corner of her mouth, her jaw. She tipped her head to the side, allowing him unfettered access. That was better. More sex and less talking. "You're a hell of a kisser, Jacky boy. How about we duck over to those rocks over there and…"

That stopped him. "Not in public. No way." He yanked back and she kicked herself for reminding him of reality. Hopefully that's all it was.

"Fine. Let's go back to the cabin then. You can service me there."

He only gave her a sidelong glance at that, something knowing in it, and whistled for Arlin. "Not yet."

Oh? "Then what's next on the romantic weekend agenda?"

"We stop at this little place, get the best clam chowder made on this planet to go, take it back to the cabin, eat it by the fire and drink wine."

"There has to be sex involved in this scenario."

"I think that can be arranged."

Keeping her hand in his pocket, he turned them back up the sand to the path. It was an amazing thing, that trail that led sometimes right through people's back yards. She'd never known there were places like this. Not for real. People in those houses with the lit windows, making spaghetti dinners and giving their kids cake pops. Hugging them and saying they loved them like they didn't even have to memorize the lines.

They walked in silence that felt pretty much okay, Arlin dashing ahead, then coming back to check on them, then dashing off again. She nearly asked Joe what he thought of that whole story, but really she didn't want to know.

So she didn't break the silence either.

✦ ✦ ✦

THE CLAM CHOWDER place turned out to be a short distance from the cabin, part of a little dock and shopping area she'd never have guessed was there, tucked into a cove fringed with tall trees. She put on her sunglasses, just in case. Not worried so much about being recognized, but more because she might not be able to take it if she was, if some fan shouted that they loved her.

Normally she kept her shit together in public and only lost it dramatically in relative private—or online—but there was a first for everything. The way her life and career were in a current death spiral, this would be the time.

She prowled around the shop, perusing the few shelves with groceries and souvenirs, while Joe paid and waited for them to package it up. More people there, eating in the cramped dining area, the windows fogged over. It would be cozy to grab that corner table, bump knees with Joe and get their wine buzz on watching the harbor. But he got that *look* when she suggested it, so she let it go. Especially when one woman stared at her too long, then leaned over to say something to her husband, who turned to look even as she thumped him on the shoulder.

Ava averted her face, made sure her sleeve hid the watch, and put back the cheerful red mug she'd picked up—with a stylized crab on it that she liked—then went to wait on the sidewalk with Arlin. Such a well-behaved dog. He greeted her with a polite lick of her fingertips and resumed sentry duty, always with an eye on where Joe moved about inside. Bright pots of flowers shuddered in the chill wind. Not dead yet, but soon to be. Hanging on to every scrap of life.

What had possessed her to tell Joe that story? Not just hers to tell either, but also Katey's. Though she hadn't spilled all of that tale. Not the worst of it.

She and Katey hadn't been this long apart in forever and she hadn't thought about her until this moment. It had been a relief, frankly, not to think about her sister—which just showed what a selfish, horrible person she was. And yet… she dreaded going back to it all. Monday morning no longer seemed so far away. *The dread is like a cloud you can barely see through.* As if he sensed her mood, Arlin diverted his attention to her, leaning against her leg, a solid, warm reminder of the here and now that strangely helped the dread cloud dissipate.

"Ready?" Joe's voice made her start.

She nodded falling into step, Arlin pacing between them. "Those people in the café may have recognized me."

"They won't know where to look, even if they do tip someone off. No one would expect it to be actually you here."

No. People like her didn't do these things, picking up take-out chowder and walking on a chilly beach, opening up the dark, corrupt corners of their psyche.

As Joe had promised, they picnicked on the rug before the fire—which, she had to admit, worked for the love montage—and finished the Malbec from the night before, then opened another. It *was* the best clam chowder she'd ever tasted. Creamy, rich, with a bit of sherry Joe had them add to give it a little bite. When they finished, he took their cardboard containers to the kitchen and came back with the remaining cake pops.

"No way." She had to laugh, though. "Are you medicating me with sugar?"

"And sex." He cupped her head the way he did, affectionate, but also deliciously commanding, holding her still for a kiss. "Aren't those my marching orders?"

"I don't know. What were Dwight's confidential instruc-tions?" She'd meant it to be teasing, but he stilled. Guilty as fuck. "Not sugar and sex, I'm betting. Didn't he slip you something for me—a little candy pack maybe?"

His face hardened. "You don't need that shit."

"No? We could share. Free drugs. Better than a Saturday afternoon wine buzz."

"Don't think it, Sova. I know what I'm talking about. You don't need to be messing with that shit."

So protective. It shouldn't give her such a thrill. "You're a little late with that warning. Been there. Done it. Have a big pile of regrets." Too many. *Do you have unprotected sex?* She wouldn't tell him that half the sex she'd had she couldn't remember. Maybe more than half. How would she know when she couldn't remember? "But I'm surprised. My All-American Army boy has tried drugs?"

He looked way too somber, staring into his wine. "Think

about it. I had an amputation. Burns everyfuckingwhere. My brain got rattled. A bunch of other shit. They put you on a morphine drip and wean you off of that with more painkillers. So yeah—Oxycontin was my best friend for a few months. Some guys never kick it."

Shit. She felt like an idiot. "That was stupid of me."

"No. Why would you know? Not something that you'd have to think about."

Not in her pretty little world, he meant. Which made her laugh, harshly enough that his head jerked up, his eyes narrowing on her. "What?"

"I've probably done way more drugs than you, Jacky boy."

He made a dismissive sound. "I'm not talking about a little coke or a Valium here and there."

"Are you kidding?" she asked. Apparently the confessional mood had stuck. "I had my first drink at nine, began smoking pot at ten, and did cocaine at twelve. I used for a long time. Still do some of it, as you'd know if you peeked into that candy pack. Not everything's on the fan sites. Dwight does his best to keep his princess shiny, clean and appropriate for family entertainment, but there's old gum stuck under the table."

"It's not candy, Ava."

"Don't I know it. But it keeps me off the coke. That's the one thing that just…" Hoo boy, she couldn't continue. "I dunno. Maybe everyone has their poison and that one is mine. I had to give it up because too much really bad shit went down. Including the much-regretted Epic Disaster Tweetstorm."

"I never read anything about you doing rehab."

"And no you wouldn't. I quit on my own." One of the few things she was proud of herself for. "Katey helped. We called it Martha Stewart's Rehab-at-Home."

He laughed. Shook his head. "It sounds like hell. I have an idea of what you went through."

She watched him rub Arlin's belly. Maybe he did know at that. "Sometimes I wonder what it matters, you know what I mean?"

He sobered. "No, I don't."

"Why didn't you just give me the pills and tuck me up in some hotel? I'd lay money that's what Dwight told you to do."

"Because you deserve better than that."

"Oh, Jack—you have no idea what I deserve."

"I do know drugs." He held up the wine. "I shouldn't be doing this. Or encouraging you to."

"Like you could stop me. We can't give up all of our vices or we'd just be miserable rocks."

"I guess we have that in common," he mused, seeming a little surprised. "But the alcohol doesn't fuck up your mind the same way. And you need yours, for your music, to write those songs."

"But I don't. The new album… None of it's mine. All of the songs are ones they're feeding me. I'm just the marionette who sings them."

He regarded her steadily. "Then change that."

She laughed, but he didn't crack. "Oh yeah, right, like it would be so easy."

"Not much is harder than quitting a coke habit cold turkey."

There was that. "You know what the worst part is?"

"What?"

"I've never stopped wanting it. That never completely goes away. Even though I *know* I don't want to go back to that, when I start to… like yesterday … Shit! I cannot believe I'm crying again."

"It's good to let them out." He wiped a tear off her cheek, then stroked her damp skin. "Tell me the rest."

"Part of Therapy Weekend?" She huffed out a breath, impatient with herself. "I start wanting it again, like part of me eternally believes that's the answer. That if I can mute the pain long enough, I can make it through a session and not care if I suck. If I could coke up, just grab a little of that sparkle, I'd believe again. Even though I know they're lies. Does that make any sense?"

"*Give me the crystal snowflake, show me the shadowed wood, allow me one more mistake, and I'll be gone for good.*"

"Snow Angels. You know that one, too."

He shook his head, laughing under his breath. "I listened to that one a lot, when I was kicking the oxy."

"Who are you, Jacky boy?" She breathed the question, asking in earnest.

"Just a guy." He shrugged his shoulders, tightening the dark green t-shirt across them.

"My guy."

"For as long as you want me."

"Do you mean that—every word of it?" Too late she realized that she'd asked him to pretend and tried to think of a way to pull it back. To stop him before he told the truth and ruined it all.

"Of course." He'd smiled saying it, then caught something in her expression. Sobered. Scooted closer to cup her face in his big hands. "I mean every word of it, Sova. I'm yours as long as you want me. Truth."

"Good. I want you. You know what I want?"

"You have that look in your eye that doesn't bode well for me."

"Pfft. You've faced down armies, bombs and AK-47s—what could lil' ol' me do to a big, strong man like you?"

"Now I'm really afraid."

She tugged at his t-shirt. "Take this off."

With a bemused twitch of his lips, he did, tossing it aside. Then waited while she looked him over. He really had a fine physique. She'd never cared much one way or the other. A guy was a guy and she tended to gravitate to pretty faces. But Joe's chest … manly. With hair and defined pecs. Tracing the tattoo on his left pec, she glanced up to find him watching her. "What is this—Russian alphabet?"

"Yeah, Cyrillic. My grandfather's name and rank. He fought in Afghanistan for the Soviet Union back in the eighties. A weird circle for me, to be back there, fighting pretty much the same war, because of the one he fought."

"I'm not much for history." The letters made their own pattern, forming a circle.

"They were fighting us. The U.S. poured money into fighting the Soviets, battling communism. Part of the reason we're fighting there today is a direct result of that."

"Hmm. You didn't mention him fixing up the cabin."

"No. He didn't make it home. That's when I got the tattoo—to celebrate that I did."

The tattoo felt like the rest of his skin. Close her eyes and nothing. Open them, and the memorial to the man who'd died where his grandson lived shone clear. Full circle. Joe could have died, too. Killed before she ever met him. Unreal.

"How long ago was your injury?"

He watched her gravely, the firelight gleaming warm on his skin, the black hairs glinting with red flame. "About four—no, five years ago now."

"You were fighting in these big wars while I was a coked-up teenager."

"I was just a kid, too, Sova. Flunked out of my first semester in college because I partied instead of studying. Figured I'd better get some goddamned discipline or I was going to waste my life, so I joined the army. You can imagine how my grandmother and father reacted to *that* news. Losing my grandfather wrecked their lives—they managed only by leaving and coming to the states. My dad was sure I'd get myself killed. Nearly did."

"Did you get some goddamned discipline?"

"Yeah, I guess? But then it took time to recover, and I finally took the driving job because I knew how to do that. It didn't demand too much of me."

"Demand too much how?"

"Just… more than I can do. Leave it at that." He sounded sad.

"Take the rest off," she told him.

He raised an eyebrow. "Bossy, all of a sudden." But he complied, pulling off his running shoes and shimmying out of his jeans. "Boxers, too?"

"You'd better believe it." She picked up the discarded jeans and unthreaded his leather belt from the loops.

Jack narrowed his eyes, naked but for his prosthesis. Like some elegant and exotic animal, with a clawed foot. "I haven't been strapped since I was a kid, if that's what you have in mind. It was *not* sexy."

"Your dad beat you with a belt? Lie back and put your wrists up by that fireplace stand."

"Russian, remember? Very old school. It wasn't a beating so much as a few licks to get my attention." He grinned up at her unrepentant as she crawled around his head to wrap the belt around his wrists, looping it around the iron bar built into the brick fireplace. "I was a bad kid. Ornery. Hot-headed."

"I'll just bet you were. You're still a little hot-headed."

"Not so much. Certain golden-eyed divas bring it out in me more than usual."

She loved that, being able to push his particular buttons. Not admirable of her, most likely, but she enjoyed it and planned to enjoy him. "Can you get free?"

He tugged at the belt, looking at it. Met her eye. "If I tried hard enough, but I won't. What do you plan to do to me?"

"You did it to me. I wanted to know what it was like, to have you at my mercy. To torment you." She licked along his throat, salt and bristle, sharp with the sweet. He groaned, low in his throat. "But it's not fair that you could get free. I couldn't have, last night."

"You just don't know how to tie knots the right way."

"Will you teach me?"

He laughed, then sucked it in when she lightly bit his nipple. He was hard—had been since he undressed, maybe even before that—but she planned to make him wait a long time for that. "I think that would be against my best interests. The smart soldier doesn't hand his enemy a weapon."

"Am I your enemy, Jacky boy?" She swirled her tongue in his deep navel, whorled by silky hair, carefully avoiding the weeping head of his cock. "I thought we were friends."

"You, Sova, are the ultimate double-agent." He caught his breath as she ran her tongue along his hipbone, dragging her teeth along the sharp ridge. "You're too good at knowing how to get inside my head and using it against me."

"I am?" That pleased her, knowing she got to him as much as he seemed to be able to intuit her. "Stay right like that. I've got something for your head. Do you promise not to break free?"

He stared at the ceiling, jaw set, looking a little wild, a bit desperate—and ungodly gorgeous in the firelight. "All right, I promise not to break free while you're gone, but no promises for later. I'm not giving you that much power."

Fair enough. "I'll be right back."

~ 22 ~

H E LAY THERE, on the rug his aunt Maria had braided, butt-
naked and attached with his own belt to the firepost.
Bound by a promise. And—might as well face it—his own
helpless lust and inability to refuse a gamine-faced woman her
least request when she got that mischievous sparkle in her eyes.

She returned from the bedroom. And he nearly choked on
his own tongue.

The sight of her made him bitterly regret his promise. She'd
donned black lace—thigh-high stockings, g-string and barely-
there push-up bra. Along with those red come-fuck-me heels
she'd worn before. She posed, all white skin, long legs and
golden eyes, then slowly turned, letting him see everything, her
slim hips moving to an internal song.

"Sova," he got out. "You're killing me."

"Oh, Jacky boy," she purred, "I've barely gotten started."

✦　✦　✦

A LONG, LONG while later, they lay twined together, scraps of
her black lace scattered around them. She'd teased him into
losing control entirely, breaking free of his belt and tearing the
taunting lingerie from her hot body, making her beg in turn for
the release she'd denied him. In the aftermath, he couldn't regret
it. Especially with the replete sensation of having emptied

himself of all worry and tension. Ava, too, her lissome body draped bonelessly against his.

"There's something to be said for sex as a sedative," he said, his voice somewhat hoarse from growling and shouting at her to let him come already.

She rolled onto her back, letting her arms fall to the rug. "Amen, Brother Jack."

He propped himself on one elbow, drawing the line of her curves with one finger, from the glasslike edge of her jaw, down the slim column of her throat, around one pink-tipped breast, then across her flat, nearly concave belly. Her naked pubis rose prominently from there, between the sharp parentheses of her hips. All velvet-smooth, flawless skin. "Do you wax off all your body hair?"

Cracking her lids, she studied him, owl eyes in the night. "Electrolysis. Started getting it at puberty, as soon as the hair grew in. More credit to my ambitious mama."

It seemed an obscenity to do to such a young girl, though why that stood out to him of the crumbs she'd dropped about her childhood, he couldn't say. He'd seen far worse done to girls—and little boys—in Afghanistan. Valuable commodities, used and abused, until there were only tatters of human beings left. He should know better than most what cruelties people were capable of. This was a small thing, and yet… "Why would it matter, if you had pubic hair or not?" Unable to stop touching her, he caressed her bare mound, rapt by its softness.

"Legs, arms, pits. It shows in photos." Her voice sounded dreamy, her skin resilient, soaking in his caresses. "And disrupts the little-girl image. Also, it's just standard in the biz. Nobody has body hair. Not even the boys."

"Even the guys?" And here he'd thought he was worldly, beyond being shocked by anything.

Her generous mouth curved with playful amusement.

"You're one of the few lovers I've had who goes natural. Most of them are manscaped, at least."

Manscaped. Definitely not an image he'd wanted in his head. Especially with some of the boy band guys she was rumored to have slept with. And Tyler, who she'd fucked right in the limo. He'd looked like such a wimpy, arrogant teen, too. To imagine him… no, no, no. "Why would any guy want to be all hairless?"

She reached over and tugged on his cock. For once, it didn't rise to her least suggestion, exhausted by her voracious attentions—and those ugly imaginings. "It makes the peen look longer, the balls bigger. You know how guys are about that. More is better."

"Not all guys."

"Your new hashtag?" Her smile turned wicked. "You just think that because you have no concerns in that department, Jacky boy. You're unusually blessed."

"Thank you, I think."

"You're welcome. The pleasure is all mine." Catlike, she crawled over him, pushing him onto his back. "I wonder if I can get another rise out of you."

"If you have any mercy, not yet. Give me a thirty-minute nap, at least."

She leaned down, kissing him sweetly, her hair falling around his face, a glittering veil of gold. "I suppose you've earned it, and I got to sleep in." Draping herself over him, she snuggled against his chest as he cleared his mind, saturating himself with the feel and scent of Ava, naked against him as he'd so often dreamed.

✦ ✦ ✦

WHEN HE WOKE, the room was dim and the fire low, embers glowing dark red. The air too chill. Ava. Had she left?

But no. There was her voice, soft and throaty, singing a song he'd never heard, with a deep, almost bluesy sound.

Ballerina, GI Joe
Talk to me, my boy. You have to know.
The velveteen has worn to none.
Full fucking circle,
Shattered to the bone.

She stopped and a pencil scratched. Then silence. He held quiet, holding his breath to sleep patterns, at the thrill of being present for something both auspicious and fragile, like the birth of a new star. He'd never understood it, how a person could create something from nothing. It seemed miraculous. Though he waited to hear more, the stillness stretched on so long that he couldn't quite stay unmoving on the hard floor. He had to shift, twitch to the right to relieve that catch in his bad hip…

"Oh, Jacky boy," she crooned softly, almost an extension of the song. "Are you awake?"

Making it ostentatious, he blinked and yawned, deliberately slurring his voice. "Mmmph." It might bother her, to have been overheard in a private moment of creation. For himself, he'd tuck it away in a secret corner of his heart, that he'd been present as Ava spun a new song out of thin air.

And if there was something of him in it? Unsettling and amazing. *GI Joe, shattered to the bone.* Was that him? At least she didn't have anything in there about his fucked-up brain. Though only because he'd narrowly avoided confessing that part, too.

He sat up, ran a hand through his hair and surveyed the shadowed room. Found her, naked still, curled up by the dying light of the fire, a memo pad in her hand. She watched him with lambent eyes, her hair in disarray, and flipped the pad dismissively. "I was messing with something."

Say something or not?

"I kind of heard the tail end. Sounded great."

Her mouth quirked. Not quite a wobbly smile, and she shrugged that off.

"I mean it."

"You know, I was thinking." She set down the pad and pencil—the ones his grandmother took from her bank and used to make grocery lists—and hugged her knees. "I used to bring my guitar everywhere I went. I mean … every-damn-where."

"The Gibson that Joan Jett gave you."

"You know that story?" She shook her curls, gold catching the bloodred of the embers. He crawled over to add logs to the fire. "What am I saying—of course you do. I don't know why she did it. I was just this punk-ass pretty princess when she guested on the show."

Maybe she'd seen something of that same sorrow in Ava's eyes that he had, but he didn't want to suggest it. Or her shining talent.

"Yeah," she continued, "that guitar. Time was, I never had it more than an arm's reach away. Now … here I came on this trip with you, a whole weekend away, and it didn't once cross my mind that I should bring it."

"I think we can agree you had a lot of other things on your mind yesterday."

"Okay. Sure, fine, whatever. But it wasn't like I thought 'oh, it's a small car and I won't need my guitar for only two days.' It didn't even occur to me to grab it. And, once upon a time, that would have been my *first* thought. Neither did Katey, and she always packs everything I need—she's almost psychic that way."

"Nothing wrong with wanting a break from it all."

She frowned. "You're nice about petting me, but that's not the point. When did I stop thinking about my guitar?"

"I don't know." He pulled on his boxers and jeans, retrieved his belt. "When did you?"

"Well, that's what's weird. I don't know. I've been thinking about it and I'm not even sure exactly where it is."

"I'm sure Katey knows. I can call her and ask, if you want."

"No—don't." She sounded tense, no longer reflective.

"Okay." He got his shoes on and Arlin appeared from no-where, with his keen doggy telepathy for an imminent walk. Speaking of psychic.

"You're going out? It's raining really hard again."

He knew that. The thrumming of it on the pitched roof had played a counterpoint to her melody, though she might not realize that she'd incorporated that timeless rhythm. Part of that natural ability to create. "Just to get more logs from the woodshed, let Arlin run himself around. I won't be long."

She nodded, picking up the pad and looking at it, a faint line between her brows.

"Or I can go out longer, give you some quiet and privacy."

Her eyes flashed gold up to his. "What for?"

"So you can finish writing your song. I don't want to distract you."

Making a face, she tossed the pad aside again, and rose to her feet, stretching her arms over her head. Slim, pale, like a sculpture of a modern dancer. If he had any artistic talent, he'd want to capture her like that—in metallic paint maybe. Or fashioned from copper wire.

"I'm not going to finish writing that song," she was saying. "It's barely even a song. Just fragments of things."

"Isn't that where you start, with pieces, and then you weave them together?"

"You mean back when I actually wrote songs? More or less."

"So do that."

"Jacky boy…" She laughed without humor. Looking an-noyed, in fact. "There's no point."

"Of course there is. This is what you do—you write songs

and you sing them. You're recording a new album. Finish this one and use it."

"You don't get it, Jacky boy." She planted her fists on her hips, cocking them with irritated attitude. "It's crap. I could never use it, even if I did finish the fucking thing. On this or any album."

"Why not?" His own annoyance rose to meet hers and he blurted before he remembered to pull it back. "Because it's about you and me?"

Her mouth quirked, a bit of a sardonic tilt. "Someone was only pretending to be asleep."

"No." He took an even breath, mastering his temper. "I was trying not to disturb you, interfere with your creative flow or—"

Her harsh laugh interrupted him. "Creative flow? What a romantic view you have of me. My career is about package and gloss, not art. I can't use that song, G.I. Joe, because it's off-brand. It's bluesy rock, not pop, it's not family values, it's not *Ava.* You have a lot to learn about the realities of the business."

"Whose voice is that?" He shot back. "Is that what Mama Krystal used to tell you?"

She looked so abruptly stricken that he cursed himself and took a step to comfort her—when Arlin's yip warned him. Followed by the sound of a car door and raised voices snapped him to full alert. In two strides he was at the window overlooking the drive.

Shit.

"Is it the press?"

"If only. Go get dressed. My family is here."

~ 23 ~

"I THOUGHT YOU said—"

Joe flashed her a hard look, full of simmering warning and implicit command. "I fucked up, okay? Unless you want my parents and grandmother to see you naked, you'll want to get dressed. Shit. And my baby sister is here, too. I'll try to get rid of them, but…" He raked his hands through his hair, growling an impatient noise for the impossibility of that. Spotting the tatters of her lingerie scattered around the floor, he moved quickly to gather it up. "Fuck it all to hell. Just stay in the bedroom and I'll think of something. I won't let them know you're here. I'll say it's someone else."

Like which someone else? The jealousy nearly kept her there to ask, but the thump of boots on the deck and the sound of voices sent her scurrying back to the bedroom. Closing herself in, she rummaged through her suitcase. What did one wear to meet the family of the guy you'd paid and manipulated into being your lover, because you might have lost your mind otherwise? No, no—if he couldn't get rid of them they'd just play it like the cover. He worked for her and she was just taking some weekend down time.

In their family cabin. Where she'd been fucking their son silly.

How did normal people *do* this?

Kates had packed outfits to cover most contingencies, but

nothing looked right. Probably no etiquette book covered this anyway.

From down the hall, voices raised in surprise and welcome. They'd all be hugging, because that's what normal families did. Maybe his dad thumped him on the back and his mom kissed his cheek and said he looked too thin. Maybe that was just in the movies. A rumble of what must be Joe's explanation, exclamations of dismay. Another man's voice, like Joe's but deeper, sternness in the tone.

Abandoning the fantasy of dressing in some ModCloth pretty-prim frock, she instead pulled on a slim black skirt, knee-high boots, camisole tank and a pink cardigan. And her pearls. The watch, of course, she never took off. She looked like a nice girl, not a slut. Close enough. She was attempting to make order of her disarrayed hair—what the hell had Joe done to her to put those snarls in it?—when she answered the brisk knock at the door, calling to Joe to come in.

"How did you know it was me?" He appeared in the bathroom doorway, gruff, irritated, and utterly charming. Arlin stayed close to his side, leaning against his leg. "It could have been anyone."

"It sounded like you." She went for pink lipstick as the more demure choice.

He frowned at her words, shaking them off. "What are you doing?"

She arched her brows at him in the mirror, decided they could be darkened a bit and picked up the brush to do that. He had his arms folded. Not. Happy. At. All. "As instructed, sir— getting dressed."

He dismissed that with an abrupt hand gesture. "I mean the makeup and everything. I told them you're a girl they don't know and that you're asleep, not feeling well. Once they all turn in for the night, we can sneak out—or we can go super early—

and I'll take you somewhere else."

A girl they don't know. "Nice resort hotel where you can stick me in a fancy room and sedate me?"

He set his jaw. "I never said that."

"Are you ashamed for me to meet your family, Jacky boy?" It shouldn't matter, but it did. Such was life. Her life.

He all but audibly ground his teeth. "You're not supposed to be here, remember? No one can know."

"What, are they going to run off and sell photos to the *Daily Star*? 'Singer found in illicit love nest with hot Army vet. Family is horrified. We never imagined that slut would corrupt our stalwart Joe, says grandmother.'"

"Would you stop?"

She turned to face him. Leaned back against the counter. Folded her own arms. "Stopping."

He blew out a breath and raked a hand through his hair. "I'm sorry—I'm handling this badly."

"Okay, let's try this. If it's really important to you to maintain this fiction, I'll go along with your story. I'll stay in here, be quiet and we can sneak away later."

He nodded, mouth in a flat line of determination, and moved to go. She stopped him with a hand on his sleeve.

"I'm not done. I don't think I should have to cower in here, hiding like we're doing something wrong. We're consenting adults, not hurting anyone, and I'd..." She had to take a steadying breath. *I'd love to go to your baby sister's birthday party.* "I'd really like to meet them. I promise to behave. Or," she hastily amended, "if I feel the crazy coming on, I'll excuse myself to the bedroom."

He softened, touching her cheek, then tucked a curl behind her ear, his fingers brushing the pearl stud there. "You're not crazy, Sova. You might think *they* are, however."

"You came from them. How bad can they be?"

"You have no idea."

"Look, if you're worried about what they'll think, don't tell them we're involved."

His mouth quirked out of that line. "Is that what we are?"

"I mean the extra tending, not the driving and guarding. They don't have to know about what we do privately. Maybe they won't even recognize me—"

"Oh, my sister will."

"Nona?"

"Who else?"

"Then tell them the truth. You're minding me for the weekend and brought me here for downtime. The press have all the hotels staked out or something. You told the cover story to protect my identity. I said they could be trusted. All there is to it."

"All right." He let out a breath, still tense. "A workable plan, I guess."

"Let's do this thing."

"If you're sure."

She was. Nervously excited, but whatever. No one needed to know if she extended her fantasy of the weekend in her own mind, pretending to meet her boyfriend's family instead of her employee's. "How do I look?"

A genuine smile as his eyes caressed her face. "Gorgeous, as always. No matter what face you're wearing, you're always beautiful. Radiant."

It took her breath away, her heart lurching with unexpected tender feeling. Without words to respond, she tucked her hand in his, Arlin leading the way, tail high. She didn't even mind very much when he dropped her hand at the end of the hall, putting a shepherding hand on the small of her back instead. She liked that just fine, too.

They were in the kitchen, unloading groceries. The mom and

grandmother bickering about where to put things, a man and teenage girl at the table. The girl glanced up as they walked in, then bolted to her feet, spilling hot tea on the table.

"Holy shit—you're Ava!"

"Language, Nona," the mom said without temper and turned, assessing Ava, with eyes as snapping black as her hair.

"But Mom!" The girl, a lankier version of Joe, eyes greener and hair dark like her mother's, waved her arms wildly enough that her dad good naturedly ducked to the side. "Ava! Mother-effing Ava in our cabin. Omigod, I have to tell Betsy. She will absolutely—hey!"

Jack had neatly nipped the phone from her hand before she could do more than thumb it on, tucking it in his pocket. "No texts. No pics. You don't get your phone back until we're gone."

"Don't you trust me?" She pouted, but her avid gaze remained fixed on Ava. "I just—"

"No."

"But—"

"No."

"Maybe you should introduce us to your friend, Iosif," the grandmother interrupted. A tall woman with steel-gray hair and Joe's hazel eyes, she examined Ava with piercing intensity. "I know your mother raised you with better manners than this." The mother in question muttered something.

Joe gave Ava a private I-told-you-so look of long suffering, and led her around to his grandmother with that hand at her back.

"Everyone, this is Ava. I'm working for her, and brought her here for some quiet and downtime away from the city, so we're relying on your discretion. Ava, this is my grandmother, Ilona Ivanchan."

Ava offered her hand and the woman took it, not shaking it but holding it between her own in a firm grip. "What's your family name, child?"

That gave her pause. No one asked her that. "I don't really have one." Krystal had used several over time. For *Tween Hangout*, Ava and Katey had used "Simpson" because everyone thought it sounded nice and they liked to play the pair of them as twins. Later her mother had gone to court to have her legally named only "Ava." *Like Madonna or Beyoncé. You're a star, baby. You have to stand out.*

"A person should have a family name," Joe's grandmother was saying. "Or you forget what you come from. Only fake people like movie stars have only one name."

"Grandmother, she *is* a movie star," Nona piped up, but they all ignored her.

"Who are your people then?" Ilona demanded, still not relinquishing her hand.

Joe touched the small of her back, like he wanted to pull her away. "Grandmother, let's not—"

"Did I ask you? No. Quiet when your elders are speaking."

He pressed his lips together and cast her another of those speaking looks, both sympathetic and clearly letting her know he thought she should have stayed in the bedroom.

"I don't know who my people are," she said, truthfully enough. The meeting-the-family fantasy wasn't going at all well. How did people do this? "I never knew my father and my mother's family is dead. She doesn't talk about them. I guess I don't come from anything." Which maybe explained why she felt so hollowed out anymore.

Grandmother Ilona studied her, keen eyes in a stern face with a blade of a nose. "Plenty of orphans in the world and a sad thing it is, too. Everyone comes from something, child, even if they don't know what it is. Remember that." She nodded at Joe. "She'll do, boy. Eyes like the sova. Watch what she sees in you."

"Sova?" She cast a glance up at Joe, who'd put on his neutral face but looked pained with it. "What does that mean?"

"Your eyes are yellow and too wise, like the owl that carries souls to Heaven," his grandmother replied instead, touching the cross at her throat. A jingle of Arlin's collar as Joe ruffled the dog's ears. "The sova visited young Iosif before he went to fight the war that killed his grandfather. He lived to find you. Perhaps you have some Russian in you."

"I just work for her. That's all I—"

"I have eyes in my head, too, young Iosif. And more than a hint of the sight. Watch the talons, my boy."

"Okay, Mama Ivanchan—enough with playing Baba Yaga." Joe's mother smoothly edged her mother-in-law to the side. "I'm Regina, Joe's mother. We're pleased to have you visit."

She wasn't pleased at all, raking Ava with her dark eyes, holding herself with regal disdain. Making it seem as if Ava had intruded uninvited. Which, technically, she had. Into the woman's bedroom, no less.

"Very nice to meet you. We, I mean I, can move out of the master bedroom so that—" Joe made a little inarticulate sound and she broke off, her face going hot. Had she blushed over sex before in her entire life? Of course, she'd met very few mothers at all, much less bare hours after driving one of their sons to screaming orgasm on a rug a few feet away.

"Nonsense," Regina said, with a reproving glance at her son. "We'd only have to wash the sheets." *Ouch.* Not fooled for a second. She turned back to putting the groceries away. "Speaking of washing, Joe, you left spots on my good baking dish and you know how I feel about that."

He rolled his eyes at her back and turned Ava to meet his dad, who grinned and shrugged good naturedly. There was Joe's smile, his boyish charm. His father came around the table and enveloped Ava in a bear hug, smelling of pipe tobacco and peppermint—not like Henry, but also so like him that it gave her heart a wrench. "You're just a bit of a thing. Pretty, too. We're always happy to meet a girl of Joe's. A singer, are you?"

Nona pretended to strangle herself. "Dad! All of you! We have *the* Ava in our cabin and you're all just—Augh! I can't even."

"It's okay," Ava told her. Then followed her instinct and hugged Nona, too. "Jack brought me here to chill for the weekend. He's my bodyguard. And driver." *I'm not his girl. Keep that reality firmly in mind.*

"You mean Joe," Nona corrected.

"She calls me Jack," her brother inserted, giving Ava an inscrutable look.

Nona looked between them, dawning disappointment scrubbing at the edges of her bright enthusiasm. "Then you're not…" She slid her eyes to her mother. "Seeing each other?"

Well, hell. She should have realized how difficult this would be. This was why Joe had wanted her to hide in the bedroom. You couldn't tell a teenage girl you were just fucking her brother because he was available to take the itch off, because it was hell of a lot easier to bed a guy who'd work for her for a few weeks than add yet another complication to her life. Joe didn't say anything, letting her take the lead. Clearly prepared to follow along with whatever tone she set. Time to get a grip on herself and play the role she knew. *Sparkle, Shirley.*

"No, we're not." With a practiced gesture, she tossed back her hair and aimed a dazzling smile at all of them. "He was covering for me. Part of his job. I needed to hide for a few days and Joe brought me here, because he thought it would be relaxing for me. Private."

Joe's mother made an *mm-hmm* sound over by the sink. Nona, however, only nodded, her world back in order. Joe's dad seemed surprised and disappointed, however, tucking his hands in pockets. "Well, that it is. That it is. Sorry we've gone and disrupted that for you."

"Why *are* you here?" Joe broke in.

"Your sister has fall break and your grandmother wanted to see to some things before everyone comes for Thanksgiving," Regina called from the kitchen.

"I wrote it on the calendar," Ilona added.

"The one hanging in your kitchen?" Joe retorted. "Thanks, Grandmother. You all could have told me."

"What should it matter to us if you're here or not?" she replied.

"I keep telling you we should use a Google calendar," Nona said.

"And nothing stops you from picking up a phone," his mother said.

Joe sighed and scrubbed his forehead. "Look, I'll put the sheets in the wash and get us packed up, so I can take Ava elsewhere."

"Nonsense!" His mother called out. "I'm heating a lasagna I brought. You'll sit and eat. Your girl can keep the master, we'll take the guest room and Mama Ivanchan can take the room Joe *usually* has."

"What about me?" Nona protested.

"Bunk rooms for us, squirt," Joe tossed over his shoulder.

She groaned theatrically. "*So* not fair."

He roughed up her carefully styled, purple-highlighted hair, ignoring her yip of indignation. Met Ava's eyes across the table and gave her a deferential nod. All business. "Anything I can get for you, Ava?"

"Thanks, I'm fine." Though she really wanted to have a martini. Or ten.

He nodded again, something of a salute in it. "Dad—I was just about to bring in some more firewood. Want to help me?"

"Sure, sure. We've more things to bring in from the car, too.

I was waiting for the rain to let up, but might as well get it done."

"All right." They shrugged into jackets and Joe pointed at Nona. "No bugging Ava. Leave her be or I'll skin you."

"I'll take care of that," their mother said. "Our guest can go sit in the living room and Nony can get in here and help her grandmother with the salad."

Nona sighed heavily, dragging her feet, but went to do as instructed.

Feeling a bit bereft, and quite unwelcome, Ava also did as she was told. By the fire, she found the memo pad where she'd jotted down the lyrics to the song that kept circling her mind. Only words now. Pretentious ones, too.

The velveteen has worn to none.

Full fucking circle, shattered to the bone.

She'd made a few notes to indicate the melody, but couldn't get it to play in her head. Could be she'd lost the thread of it. Crap anyway.

Time to play pretty ballerina. At least it was second nature.

~ 24 ~

AVA WAS ACTING funny. Joe noted it to himself with a mental salute to the humor of that thought. Arguably, Ava never behaved in any way that could be called even-keeled for very long. She could be imperious, devastated, mischievous, furious, fiercely sexual, playful—all one after another. A mercurial, ever-shifting kaleidoscope of a woman.

No, the irony was that it took her being polite, cheerful and carefully on-brand to make him seriously worry about her. Of course, he'd taken her by surprise with this FUBAR situation. Royally screwed what was supposed to be much-needed downtime for her. He could've picked up the phone, called to check the fucking calendar, but no—he'd been so focused on her. Okay, on fulfilling the fantasy of having her in that place that had always meant so much to him that, well…

He'd fucked up. The nowhere zone buzzed in the distance. Surprises. You'd think he'd learn to manage them out of his life.

And now Ava sat beside him, a bare foot away—which might as well be ten thousand miles, so impossibly huge was the distance that separated them—answering his baby sister's rocket-speed questions, while his mother sent him betrayed, accusing stares for bringing a stranger there, and his father pretended he didn't notice. A headache, like a tiny bright star, was forming between Joe's eyes. A worse sign, Arlin nudged at his knee under the table, leaning into him. The dog had been glued to him for the last hour, which helped, even as he worried that Ava would notice.

For the moment, though, Ava was deep into a story about doing the half-time show at the Super Bowl. He'd never really seen her in full entertainer mode. There'd been that one time on the sidewalk, when she revealed herself and talked to her fans, signing autographs, but that had been short-lived. With his family, she'd shrugged on her superstar persona like a mink stole.

Effortlessly charming and graciously ignoring his mother's barbed comments, Ava regaled them all with her glamorous stories and effervescent wit. Answering Nona's questions with enthusiastic patience. Beyond reproach—and not at all the woman he'd come to know in the last few days. Another irony there, that he greatly preferred Ava snarking, weeping or even in a full snarly rage, rather than this faultlessly delightful character she presented.

Pretty ballerina.

With the vicious bitterness of regret, he wished they'd had another day, the time he'd promised her they'd have. No—the time he'd selfishly wanted to have with her. Maybe this was better, for her to have dinner with an admiring fan, to remind her of what she meant to people. She certainly behaved seamlessly, a polished surface with no hint of the cracks that led to her darker emotions. Why then did he hate seeing her like this? Twisted that he'd rather have her weeping over that horrible mother of hers or snapping mad, dressing him down for liking a song she called crap.

But he did. And he couldn't take another moment of this … persona.

"Arlin needs to go out," he said, standing. "Be back in a few."

"Watch your balance on that slick deck." His mother

frowned in concern. "You could pitch right off those cliffs with that bum leg."

"I'll be fine, Mother." Even after several years, she didn't have a clue. But he wouldn't let it irritate him. Arlin understood, nudging him with affection.

"I know you think you're the same as ever, but—"

"Reggie," his dad said, quietly, but firm. "Enough."

His mother pressed her mouth shut. "Fine. Don't listen to your mother. I suppose no one plans to help me with the dishes?"

"I'll help," Ava surprised him by saying. "I've been being pretty lazy, letting Jack do all the work."

His mother, however, gave her a look just short of contempt. "And have you mess up those pretty nails? I don't think so. You go sit in the living room. Nony, why are you still sitting there? Clear the table."

Ava stood and picked up her plate, but Nona took it from her with a warning head shake and eye roll. For a second, hurt and anger flicked over Ava's face, the shadow of an airplane, racing over the ground at the speed of sound, there and gone, replaced by the serene stage face. "I'll go with you then, Jacky boy."

"It's still pretty stormy out there."

A dazzlingly fake smile. "I could use a breath of fresh air."

"Why do you call him 'Jack'?" Nona wanted to know.

"Because he's a jack of all trades. Bodyguard, driver, cook and dishwasher."

His mother sniffed in disdain. "I hope you're paying him well, is all I can say."

"Mom!" Nona sounded aghast.

"On that note, maybe a walk *is* in order," Joe declared. Without wasting any more time, he located the windbreaker and watch cap Ava had used that morning, along with some gloves.

He managed to get them out the door without more trouble. "You want to stay up on the road or…" But Ava, hands in pockets and head down, was already headed for the steps to the beach. *All righty then.*

They made it to the cliff walk, then walked without speaking for a time. The storm had backed off some, but the waves crashed below, foamy surf catching the moonlight, the rest disappearing into black. On the point, the lighthouse flashed its regular beacon.

"Your mother hates me," Ava finally said.

"She doesn't know you. She just doesn't like being caught by surprise and she's territorial. I tried to warn you."

"She doesn't believe I'm not fucking you. What she is, is protective."

Wishing he could touch her, he shoved his hands deeper in his pockets. "Yeah. Always has been. Only got worse after the … after I came home."

"I'll bet. I wondered if that bugged you—what she said about the 'bum leg.'"

He set his jaw against the irritation of it, determined not to let it bother him. Not to let the nowhere zone eat at the ground beneath him. "It is what it is. Go on, Arlin, enough already. You sniffed that spot ten times."

Ava gave him a sidelong glance. "Your sister seems sweet. And your dad."

"Yeah."

"Your grandmother, though—scary. Not in a bad way, but…"

"And now you know."

"You've been calling me 'owl.' Not exactly romantic, Jacky boy." She wasn't annoyed though, a half-smile—a genuine one—playing on her face in the light of the lamps along the walk.

"I was under pressure at the time."

"And?" she prompted.

He gave up. "Your eyes remind me of that owl's, yes. Big and golden and looking right through me."

"I take it back," she decided. "It is romantic. In a different, warped, poetic kind of way. Just like me. I like it."

"Are you going to tell me why 'Jack' now?" he asked, not really sure how to handle her response, or why it added to the ache in his head. She could have been telling the truth to Nona. Somehow he didn't think so.

"I said what it is inside."

"Uh-uh." He knew her at least that well now. "That was a nice cover story. Gonna tell me the real reason?"

"Nope."

"*So* not fair," he muttered, imitating his sister, which at least made Ava laugh. Then she caught him by the arm and tugged him into an alcove of rocks, wrapping her arms around him.

"What's crawled under your skin?" she asked.

He pushed at her, but she didn't let go. "Nothing. Let's keep moving."

"We're not on a forced march. Talk to me, Joe."

"Now you're calling me Joe?"

"Why are you so pissed? I'm sorry I slipped about the master bedroom. I'm not used to lying about stuff like that."

"I didn't ask you to lie." Okay, he did sound pissed, even to himself, and his head pounded, the rock like sand beneath his feet. Arlin came back to check on him. "It's okay, Arlin buddy. Go smell that one pee spot again about a dozen more times," he snapped.

Ava turned her penetrating gaze back on him. "I rest my case."

"About what?" he bit out.

"You never yell at Arlin. What's your problem?"

"Ava, I—"

"Sova," she insisted. "At least when we're alone." And she stretched up to kiss him.

He didn't want to kiss her. At least, so he thought. But the press of her lips, the sweetness of wine on her breath, the searing heat of her opening mouth pushed him over the edge. He had to put his hands on her, up under the windbreaker and that ridiculously prim pink sweater she'd put on. How that and the pearls could rattle his brain, make him even hotter for her than the devastating black lace number, he didn't know, but he lost all sense in a red haze of sheer lust.

She gasped encouragement in his ear as he found her breasts under the tank, naked and nipples hard, pinching them the way she liked. The rhythmic flash of the lighthouse illuminated her face, then shadowed it again, her eyes beacons that burned into his soul. Her whispered chants of his name, urgent cries for more and moans of desperate need formed another kind of song. One of ragged desire. She had her gloved hands on his rigid cock, the rough knit as stimulating as her avid grip, and he had his hands up her tight little skirt, then into her slick heat.

Picking her up, he put her back against the rock and she wrapped her legs—with those sexy, shiny black boots—around his waist, guiding him into her. At the last moment, he recalled he had no condom with him. "Wait, I—"

"Fuck the condom!" she hissed. Then laughed. "Fuck me instead."

He couldn't resist her. Had lost all sense of keeping himself in check. He slammed into her welcoming sheath with a sense of returning home, shuddering as she clamped around him, his knees going weak. Glorious, her skin against his, velvet hot. She sank her teeth into his shoulder, electrifying him. Once, twice, three times … and he lost it, the climax taking him hard in a vengeful grip. As if he hadn't come a several times that day already, with no consideration for her. She cried out, too, however, convulsing, her voice full of triumphant satisfaction.

Staggering a little—*you could pitch right off those cliffs with that bum leg*—he untangled one hand from her hair and turned so he braced himself against the rock. Ava panted against the skin of his neck, clinging like a cat he'd rescued from a tree, all sharp claws and shivering trust. His head swam and his balls ached. Too much to sort out, that he'd had her in public, or she'd had him, rather, where anyone could come along. Without protection. With his family a short walk away, believing the lie that Ava wasn't the sun of his universe, his unending obsession and likely his damnation.

It seemed he couldn't care about any of that anymore.

Ava moved, pressing a warm, wet kiss under his ear. "Better?"

He laughed, raggedly, sliding free of her and setting her on her feet. Then rummaged in the shadows for the watch cap he'd pulled from her hair sometime in the frenzy. Oddly, the nowhere zone had retreated. Enough that he stood on rock again. "That was for me?"

"You seemed like you needed a ping on your pressure valve, yeah. Though I needed it just as badly." She adjusted her panties back into place. "What—no warm washcloth? The time I really could use one, too."

Rummaging in his pockets, he found a handkerchief and gave it to her. With a funny expression, she took it, then gave him a warm smile. Not the dazzling superstar, but a soft and genuine twist of her mouth, that made her look almost quizzical. "You never cease to surprise me, Jacky boy."

Uncomfortable, he finished arranging his clothes. "Hanging around you, I'll have to remember to keep a supply."

"For sex and tears clean-up. Wise. We'll add it to the job description." She finished wiping herself, pulling her skirt down over her slender thighs, white above her boots in the moonlight and the flash of the lighthouse. He held out his hand for the soiled cloth and, with an amused smile, she gave it to him.

"Wouldn't want to forget it in the jacket," he told her, putting it in his jeans pocket. He whistled for Arlin and she let him lead her back toward the cabin, though this time Ava looped her arm through his.

"I'm sorry I muffed things with your mother," she said after a time. "Times like that I wish I was more normal. That I knew how to do things like meet a guy's mother."

He put a hand over her gloved one on his arm. "Sova, that *was* normal. My mother acts like that to every girl I've ever introduced her to. I guess we both have awful mothers."

"Oh, Jacky boy." She shook her head, the swipe of the lighthouse catching the gleam of her hair. "I don't want to play I-can-top-your-pain, but you don't know awful. She loves you and worries about you. And, fortunately," she added in an arch tone, "I *am* paying you well."

There she went, pulling on a role again. Along with forever reminding him that he worked for her. She'd asked him to pretend, but never let him forget the truth. It irritated him enough that he asked without thinking, "Do you even know what you're paying me?"

"A figure of speech. I assume it's a lot. Dwight was supposed to make sure of it." She had an edge to her voice that he couldn't quite pin down.

"But you don't know the numbers." Just like she didn't carry money.

"What exactly are you busting my balls for here, Jacky boy? If you want a raise, due to excellent performance above and beyond your job description, then—"

"Whoa. Now who's busting balls? I never said that." In fact, fuck her for saying it. The nowhere zone rushed up as if it had never backed off. Too much. Too late. Instead of clutching his skull like he wanted to, to hold the plates together, he pulled away, fisting his hands. *Keep it steady.*

"Then what?"

"What the hell," he ground out. "How can you not be looking at your own finances?"

"Because I have people, Jack. People who take care of things for me, just like you do, I might point out."

"You don't have to point out anything. I'm fully aware of that."

"Then what are we fighting about?"

He didn't know. Brain rattle, crash and burn. Arlin pushed his head under Joe's hand. Shit. He wasn't going to lose it. *Maintain, soldier.* "I just think you're capable of more," he finally said, uncertain if the words even came out right.

She resettled her cap on her head. "It's adorable that you think so highly of me, but I'll remind you that you've known me less than a week. Give it time and you'll understand."

"Understand what?"

"To manage your expectations. I've given you plenty of warning. Told you what I did to Katey, though I don't know why."

"You were a kid—of course you don't know why."

"I mean I don't know why I told *you*, of all people. You don't even understand that I was never a kid." She was harsh and scornful, her voice like her mother's had been that night.

His head throbbed, heart pounding in a staccato, painful beat, the chill greasy sweat popping out of his pores. Arlin moved into him, full body, and Joe gave in, letting his crouch collapse into a sit, the chill, wet stone biting immediately through his jeans. He buried his face in Arlin's golden fur, so silky, smelling of rain and warm life. Arlin's heart beat steadily, a serene rhythm. An echo of the surf, the lighthouse, the surge of all the emotion.

Another comforting weight pressed into his other side, slim arms wrapping around him while the scent of flowers wove in with salt spray.

Ava. With him all along.

She sang in his ear, a throaty purr.

"When I cut those false strings

When I pick up again

I'll eat the lie I never told

The ones you told me

The ones that aren't true

One day I'll be real

Maybe even to you."

He'd never noticed before how the cadence of that song fit the rhythm of the sea, too. And of Arlin's heart. And his own heart—it beat for Ava and had ever since they restarted it in the hospital. Nothing changed that.

Finally he had enough breath to say—without facing her—"I never heard that verse before."

"I never recorded it. Crap, dontcha know." She said it without irony.

"You don't believe that."

"I don't know what I believe anymore." Her hair was damp silk on his temple, her lips a warm press. "What's going on here—some kind of PTSD thing?"

"Something like that." The nowhere zone.

"What can I do to help you?"

He laughed, a rasp of aching humor. "I'm pretty sure that's not in *your* job description."

"I am a woman of many talents. And I know a meltdown

when I see one."

"I'm sorry." He dug his face into Arlin's fur, to scrub away any telltale signs of dampness that might not be rain.

"Don't even. Paybacks are hell, right?"

"It's not the same."

"Isn't it? I wonder." She threaded her fingers through his hair, also soothing. "Arlin is more than a pet, isn't he? You need him."

"Yeah." He rubbed his knuckles over the dog's ribs, just the way he liked it, and Arlin sighed in pleasure, a whuff of warm breath.

"Service dog and all."

He searched for how to explain, so still hadn't replied when she continued. "But he should have the outfit that says so, and he doesn't. That's why you were all peeved when I suggested it."

"I was peeved because people abuse it."

"Hmm."

"What?"

"I dunno, Jacky boy. I think you don't tell me everything you're thinking."

He lifted his head, finding her so close, face luminous in the moonlight, eyes shadowed for once. "I didn't lie to you." Not exactly. Sure, he'd needed Arlin's constant presence at first, but he didn't anymore. Only when shit like this happened. Maybe he would be forever the weak member of the herd. The nowhere zone his eternal stalker, waiting to take him down.

"I didn't say that." She was subdued, thoughtful. Not playing her roles or trying to dazzle him. Maybe because she'd finally figured out a little dazzle went a long way with him. Or more likely, she'd figured out how messed up he really was.

"We should get back," he said.

"It's cold. And it's been a while," she agreed. She uncoiled, graceful and effortless, and held out a hand to help him up. Her skin felt right against his.

He didn't know how it had happened, that she'd ended up tending him, but he figured he owed her at this point.

~ 25 ~

T

HE LIGHTHOUSE PULSED through the misty night, regular as a heartbeat. A slow, sleeping one. Evoking the gritty rhythm of the melody that haunted her. Not the one she'd sung for Joe to talk him out of his tree, though how odd for that long-ago-discarded verse to bubble up in her mind at that moment. Somehow it connected to the new one that had come to her as he slept. The one that had wound through her sated drowsing with its insistent whispered song. Full fucking circle. A ray in the dark. Hope in the absence of despair.

Or the wrenching struggle against encroaching night, the fragile attempt to stop yet another shipwreck.

Both of them hung up on the rocks, in their own ways.

Joe held her hand still, but otherwise seemed far away and quiet, as he had been since the PTSD incident. Whatever had been too much for him, it had backed off. He wasn't exactly his relaxed self, but better. If it were Katey, she'd tuck her in bed with comfort movies and cherry sours. Or peppermints. What did normal guys do? She had no idea. The ones she knew either fucked groupies or trashed hotel rooms.

She'd already fucked Joe and while it had helped, it didn't seem like the thing now.

The beam of light swept over them and away. Then several more times, with him still saying nothing. Fully retreated into a taciturn silence.

"The lighthouse," she said, as a way of reaching out, like singing that song for him, "it has a rhythm. Different than the surf, but almost in sync, like counterpoint."

To her surprise, he replied immediately, as if he hadn't been deep in thought. "Like in the song you wrote."

And not how she expected. "The random fragment, you mean."

"Why did you call it crap and off brand? Or that new verse to 'Pinocchio.'"

She hadn't meant to wade back in to this boggy territory. Leave it to Joe not to let it drop. "That verse isn't exactly new. I made it up a long time ago."

"I liked it."

"It reminded me of you." The resonance befuddled her. It couldn't have reminded her of him back then, of course, but she'd sung it to him because it did. Like a kind of déjà vu, only backward.

"Because it's…crap?"

"No!" She punched his biceps with her free hand and he grinned at her. "Okay, maybe they're not crap exactly." In fact, she loved both with a savage despair. Not unlike she'd felt fucking Joe just then, her back against the proverbial hard place. Or was it the rock and he was the hard place? Whatever. She sighed. "But they might as well be. I can't use the new thing on the album for the same reason we cut that verse from 'Pinocchio.' So drop it already. I can't use it. Not on this one and not on the next seven."

"Why not?"

"Gah! You don't get it, Jack."

He stopped her. "No, I don't. Explain this to me."

She threw up her hands. Clearly he wouldn't budge until she did. "A crash course in the record biz? Okay, while I was still a minor, my ever-loving mother signed me into a 360-degree contract. One of the seventeen reasons I hate her. Basically, it means the label gets a piece of everything I do—touring, concerts, merchandise, endorsements, movies, TV—which also means they dictate what that is. My songs. *Everything.* Basically they own Ava. They own me."

"It sounds like a bad deal, but—"

"Four more years, two records a year. I don't deliver, they can take everything. Because it all belongs to them anyway."

"Okay." He stuffed his hands in his pockets, probably cold, but didn't move. "That doesn't explain why you can't use the song."

"Because, Jacky boy, the contract is for Ava the pop star princess, not for a bluesy, gritty song about wounded people and the shit the world dishes out." Lighthouses and shipwrecks. What the hell had she been dreaming about?

"Your fans love what you have to say, however you say it. Why not give it a try? Play it for Nona. I loved it. I bet she will, too."

Abruptly weariness crashed over her. Maybe the shadow-side aftermath of the fantasy romantic weekend. Or of everything. The lighthouse shone one moment, went dark the next. Bright hope, swallowed by the fog of grief and dread. "I can't just give them something in an entirely different genre. I'd be in breach of contract."

"So?" He shrugged. "What's the worst that can happen?"

Her eyeballs felt tight in her head, her nails cutting into her palms. "Seriously? You're asking me that? The person who fucked over her sister in the worst kind of betrayal, just to have what I have, be who I am today."

"Yeah, I am."

It gave her the spins to contemplate it. "You'd have me be nothing. Broke and without a job."

"Would you really be broke, though? You're already rich.

And nothing would stop you from singing your songs."

A ragged laugh cracked her chest. "And *what?* Sing them in shitty bars for tips and drinks? Because—make no mistake—I would be dead broke. They'd sue me for everything I have and then some."

"It seems to me," he said slowly, "that you'd find a way to get by. And that anything would be better than a life and career that makes you this miserable and crazy."

It stung more than it ought that he finally recognized the crazy. "Oh, you mean like you, melting down and needing a service dog to keep you from losing it entirely? Maybe I need an Arlin, too."

His eyes glinted, the lighthouse beam sweeping across his hard face before leaving it in the dark again. "Maybe so. Seems to me that he helped you, when he sat with you in the limo."

"If he were my dog, I wouldn't do him the disrespect of pretending that he's just a pet, making him stay at home or in the car when he could be with me."

"Oh, you mean like you leave your sister at home?"

She screeched and launched herself at him, but he met the attack, stopping her before she could swipe her nails across that smug mouth. She struggled to punch his chest while he held her by the wrists. "Fuck you for saying that! You have no fucking clue. She *won't* leave the house. Katey has panic attacks—worse than yours—and goes psycho if anyone tries to make her. Last time was Henry's funeral—which she insisted on attending—and she utterly lost it and stayed in bed for days. Even I couldn't get her to eat and we had to bring in home health care and put her on an IV and—" She ran out of words, her breath sobbing in dry heaves. "So… just… let me go."

He released her wrists and she wrapped her arms around herself, turning her back on him. No tears this time, just wracking rage and heartache. They stood there, neither saying anything. The apology she more than half expected never came. Finally, unwillingly—because he wouldn't just leave her there, would he?—she looked over her shoulder, to find him crouched by Arlin, scratching under the collar to the dog's obvious full-bodied delight. Joe, however, was watching her. "Done?" he asked.

She pulled off the knitted cap and raked her fingers through her hair. Who had she become? Someone totally different. "I have no idea," she replied, further taken aback when he smiled.

"An honest answer."

How was he not pissed at her? "I've never lied to you, Jacky boy."

"Except every time you call me a name that isn't mine."

"Fine. You want to know why I call you that? Because you remind me of that guy in the Jack and Diane song, an American guy, wanting to be a football star. The kind of guy I would have dated if I'd gone to high school or whatever. Henry really liked that song." Henry would have liked Joe, too.

He mulled that, picking something from Arlin's fur. "Seems to me that song is about empty dreams that go nowhere. Meaningless sex and a life not worth living even though it keeps going on."

Damn, the man had a knack for gobsmacking her. Empty dreams. Fuck. "Well." She blew out a breath. "Maybe I am Diane then."

He shook his head slightly, not in a no, but dubiously. "You love your sister."

She'd lost the thread entirely. "Katey?" she asked stupidly.

"Yeah," he replied, not giving her shit for it, coming close and taking the hat from her hand, resettling it on her head. "You'll catch cold and won't be able to sing. You said you don't know how to love anyone, but you love her. And you loved Henry. It must have been really hard to be alone in that grieving, that Katey collapsed and couldn't support you."

She grated out the laugh at that. "I never expected her to. It goes the other way. I do what I can to take care of her—I owe her."

"Forever?"

"I took what should have been hers." Just saying it made her throat crack into pieces. Maybe she would lose her voice and never sing again. Cosmic justice.

"You were a kid."

"I told you, I was never a kid. You don't—"

"You were a kid who'd been groomed to think only one thing mattered. Winning. Getting that tiara and the prize. Right?"

"Yeah." *Winning spirit.* She couldn't get anything more out. Not without crying again and… fuck it all to hell, she already was.

Joe wiped her tears away with gentle thumbs, holding her face in his hands. "And you didn't steal anything. You're who you are, with or without the fame and the wealth. Nobody can take who you are away from you. Ava."

"They call me human lip gloss." She said it like a confession, like picking a scab off a wound. It both hurt to say the words out loud and came as a relief to finally tell someone else.

"Who does?"

"A columnist in—"

"Fuck them. Whoever it was. I don't care. That's a heinous thing to say about another human being. You're a person. Don't they get that?"

The violence of his outburst shocked her, though his hands remained gentle on her. "What she meant was—"

"Oh, I get what she meant. It's just flat wrong. I should know."

"You should?" She felt a beat behind.

"Don't you get it, Ava? All that time I spent laid up in the hospital, you were a comfort to me. You. Your songs. They got me through and that's not something fucking lip gloss could have done. That's not insulting just you—it's an insult to all of us who love you."

"Oh." She didn't know what to say.

"If you won't finish the song for you, do it for me. It's my song, right?"

He watched her so earnestly, steady, but with a kind of hope that it made her chest tighten around her heart. So many emotions, it seemed impossible to feel them all. "Only for you, Jacky boy," she whispered, and felt like she'd promised something else entirely.

✦　✦　✦

SHE WOKE ALONE, morning light filtering through the half-curtains, reaching for Joe before it came back to her. Of course, he wouldn't be there. They'd returned to the quiet, dark house and found everyone abed. He'd gone to his room and she to hers.

She couldn't even tell how she felt. Rested, maybe. And a little hollow inside. But that melody nested within it, turning its circles, light into dark and back again. She'd promised to finish the song for Joe. Just like Henry had asked for a song.

Okay, there the feelings rushed over her. Not panic though, for once. Not that bitter regret.

Only a little sadness.

Joe hadn't left her a little note this time. No reason for it—and not like he was going to risk getting caught sneaking into her room just to leave a stupid note, so it didn't mean anything. She showered and dressed in cigarette leg jeans, flats and a cotton sweater. It bared her midriff, but whatever. At least she felt like herself, though also a weird kind of shyness, going down the shadowed hall alone and peeking into the living area. No Joe anywhere in sight. Nor Arlin. But he wouldn't have abandoned her with his family. He must be around somewhere.

She nearly snuck back to the bedroom, but Joe's mother spotted her and offered coffee. Because she really wanted it, Ava took the mug and, smiling, ignored the narrow glare at her belly-button piercing. Calling it a need for fresh air, she retreated, taking her precious out to the deck, where watery sunshine filtered through the autumn leaves.

The surf had settled and she leaned on the deck rail, cupping the mug, enjoying the view that finally deigned to show itself. The ocean glittered blue in the morning light, and it was pretty. But she kind of missed the raging tumult, the steady beat of the constant lighthouse cutting through. It all pulsed inside, though, winding with the incipient song.

"I think these must be yours," Nona said, coming out of the cabin. She set the scarlet Manolos near Ava's feet. "I found one under the coffee table and the other kicked under the couch."

Oops. She winced theatrically and tried an abashed, oh-silly-me smile she'd used countless times with fictional parents. "I wondered where those ended up when I kicked them off while I was dancing."

Nona rolled her eyes and leaned on the rail next to her. "My dad and brother went into town to do errands."

Ah, that explained that. "And your grandmother?"

"Morning constitutional. Walks five miles every day, rain or shine."

"Wow."

"Right?"

"Definitely. I'm way too lazy for that."

"Yeah, me too." Nona chewed her lip. "Sometimes I go with her, though, 'cause—you know—she's my grandmother and I won't have her forever."

"Smart. If I had a grandmother, I hope I'd be good to her like that, too." *You mean like you leave your sister at home?* She winced internally at Joe's accusation. It had been such a relief to be away from Katey.

"You're different than I expected." Nona cut into her thoughts.

"What did you expect?" Ava turned to put her elbow on the rail, bracing for whatever the teenager might say, realizing she'd forgotten to ask what Nona's favorite song was. The girl had put her hair in a ponytail and looked terribly young, kind of like they'd all been back on *Tween Hangout*. Except Nona was the kind of girl who'd go on walks with her grandmother, not give head to a producer in exchange for a part. She sipped her coffee, swallowing down that particular unsavory memory.

"Well, I didn't expect to find you in our family cabin banging my big brother." Nona gave her a sideways look.

Ava choked on her coffee. Apparently she hadn't braced enough.

"Don't worry. I won't say anything. I just wondered—why did you say you're not dating?"

Normal life was impossible. That's all there was to it. "Because we're not dating," she said it as gently as she knew how. She owed this much to Joe. Besides, she didn't know what they were doing. "I know how it must look from the outside, but... I don't have a real life as a person. It's hard to explain, but I just don't do things like date. I never have."

"You dated Tyler. I voted yes on Twitter that you should totally take him back." She frowned, clearly tripping on the disloyalty to her brother. "But that was before I knew... But you say you're not..."

The girl was floundering, so Ava had to say something. "Tyler... You know, when I first met him, I was young and stupid.

Much younger than you are now. But I never really dated him, like actual dates, or had a relationship. It was kind of like, um, for the cameras. For publicity. Made for good pictures. Sold a lot of magazines, generated tons of clicks. I know that sounds mercenary, but that's how it works." Everyone around her had understood it—why did it seem so bizarre only now, standing on this rustic deck, talking to a girl who was more innocent than she'd been at five.

"So, you didn't ever…" Nona trailed off with a light blush that hadn't manifested when she'd thrown down the "banging my brother" gauntlet.

"Bang Tyler?" Ava arched her brows, trying to keep it light. Such a mix of naïveté and brashness she'd had back then. Sex had seemed so easy. And fun. "Sure I did. Lost the V-card to him, which means *he* pretty much banged me." She sipped at the coffee, not sure why she'd felt compelled to put it that way. This being an honest person who had conversations had its draw-backs. She regretted doing Tyler in the limo that last time. Right, only last week. She barely remembered it. But Joe did. He'd been right there. What the hell had he thought? "I would be stupid to take him back, especially based on a Twitter poll."

"That's not being stupid. You'd be the luckiest girl in the world." Nona had an actual starry look in her eyes. "No disloyalty to Joe, but Tyler is dreamy."

"He's a narcissistic asshole, is what he is," she blurted and Nona goggled in shock.

"What?" She plunged on, something driving her to say it out loud, though she was probably not supposed to use language like that with the teen. "Are you shocked to hear that Tyler isn't what the hype says? I'm not that much older than you are, but I can spare you the truth, if you prefer." The coffee helped clear the bitterness from her mouth. "But if you do want to know— my song 'Monster in the Mirror'?—totally about him. Even if he never figured it out."

Nona gaped for a moment longer, then shook her head. "This is the real you, isn't it?"

"Yeah, sorry. I got in the habit the last couple of days with Jack, and now it's hard to go back to saying what I'm supposed to."

"My brother isn't a narcissistic asshole." Nona lifted her chin, as if daring Ava to argue.

"No. No, he's not." She found herself smiling, a giddy sensation behind it.

"So I don't get why you can't date him if Tyler is such a loser. I mean, I know my mom is a pain, but she's really not that bad. She just wants grandbabies and ever since Sheila broke off the engagement, Mom has been on the warpath to get Joe married and producing the next generation."

"He was engaged?"

Nona rolled her eyes. "Omigod, since right after high school graduation. She stuck with him when he enlisted and he was faithful to her, but when he came back..." She shrugged off what must have been a devastating betrayal.

"Because of his injury?" Ava cupped her mug, surprised by the vicious impulse to find this stupid fucking Sheila and beat the brains out of that pustulant cunt.

"Well, yeah. You know about his leg? You don't care?"

"Of course I don't care." Probably she shouldn't say she found the prosthesis oddly beautiful, even erotic. "Why would I?"

"Some girls do, is all. You know—like he can't dance at their wedding. And it can get worse, like the bone could dissolve and he could end up in a wheelchair. That's part of Mom's deal— that he should ensure his legacy by having babies before he can't anymore. Mom should be happy he's doing you because that means..." Nona looked embarrassed. "Okay, no more thinking about my brother's sex life."

Ava rolled the warm mug against her temple. Poor Joe. A legacy. Like he needed to sire the heir to the throne or something. And having everyone speculate on his ability to get it up. "Well, your mom is right about one thing," she said. "I'm not wife and mother material." A laughable thought, so it shouldn't make her heart twinge like that.

"Why not? You have plenty of money. And Joe is your biggest fan. He even took me to one of your concerts."

Oh, did he now? Sly dog.

"He'd be a great husband," Nona enthused, eyes all starry again. "And then—oh."

"What? 'And then' what?" Ava prompted, when she faltered.

Nona rolled her eyes at herself this time, ponytail bobbing. "It's selfish, but I was going to say we'd be sisters and you could get me concert tickets and stuff. Maybe let me borrow your seriously rocking shoes."

Ava laughed then, which felt better. Never in her life had she imagined having a conversation like this. Not even with her real sister. "These are a 7 ½—want to try them on?"

+   +   +

JOE AND HIS dad returned, both apparently bemused to find Nona wobbling across the deck in her shorts, sweatshirt and Ava's sky-high scarlet Manolos.

"I'm explaining that she has to learn to walk in them," Ava told them. "No—put the weight into your heels, not the toes. Trust they'll hold you. Feet closer together and let your hips compensate." *Don't waddle like some fucking pregnant dachshund*, her mother's voice sneered. "My mom used to make me practice going up and down stairs in heels, with a stack of books on my head."

"I'm totally trying that!" Nona teetered off for the stairs to the cliff walk.

"Not in those—" her father called after her, but Ava stopped him.

"It's okay. I can buy more if they get messed up and she's having fun."

He shook his head. "I hate to think how much those cost."

"Not much at all. They're knock-offs." That lie came easily enough.

He still watched after his daughter. "She's growing up, but I keep seeing her putting her little feet in heels five times too big and wearing a princess tutu. There's a special hell in raising a daughter. You'll see." He clapped Joe on the shoulder and went into the cabin, calling out as he went, "Reggie—I brought you what you wanted!"

Joe smiled after his sister, full of genuine affection. Then he sobered as he faced Ava. Was he mad at her for the things she'd said? She couldn't even remember where they stood with each other. He carried a large bag from Target. A *really* large bag. "I brought you something," he said.

Very close to what his dad had just said. Her heart warmed to it, another storyline to add to her fantasy of the weekend. *He'd be a great husband.* A great dad, too, like his, who worried about his daughter trying on sexy shoes. Joe would be that for some lucky girl. And he'd brought her a present. That should make her happy, not sad. "What did you bring me?"

"It's not Joan Jett's Gibson, but..." He pulled a small pink guitar out of the bag. Tags proclaiming it a "Daisy Rock Pixie Acoustic Guitar" and "great for girls!" hung off the neck.

Her heart stilled and she took it, turning it over in her hands. No words.

"It's just a kids' guitar," Joe continued, sticking his hands in his pockets, "but there's nowhere around here to buy a real guitar on Sunday morning and the big box stores don't carry them. You have to order online. But the Target—they had this one that someone ordered for store pickup and never came to get, so they let me have it. And it seemed right, kind of."

It was small and light—not even five pounds maybe—made of mahogany and rosewood, with a veneer of bubblegum pink. A bag of decals came with it, inviting her to *Personalize!*

She had no words at all.

"It's dumb, isn't it?" Joe sounded annoyed with himself. "I kind of thought it was small enough that you could play it in the car, work out the song—or whatever you feel like—but I can see it's dumb. What would you want with a little girl's guitar? We can just leave it here and my dad will return it."

"No." Tears yet again, hot on her cool cheeks. Oddly they felt good this time.

"No?" Joe bent over to peer into her face. "No, you don't want it?"

"No, I do want it." She smiled at him, feeling the wobble. "I had one a lot like this, forever ago, only it was blue. I drew purple flowers on it with some permanent ink pens and my mom had…well, such a huge fit." She rolled her eyes and blew out a breath with it. Her mom hadn't hit her often, because the bruises showed and hurt her audition chances, but that time… *Don't you fucking waste my money, ever!* "I love this. So much."

He shuffled, uncomfortable. "It wasn't expensive. It's not a fancy gift or anything."

"This is the nicest thing anyone has ever given me." So much so that she had no idea how to express that to him.

"There's more." He rummaged in the bag and brought out a journal, also pink, with a tethered matching pen. "I didn't know what you usually like to write stuff down in, but my grandmother would take exception if you stole her grocery pad."

"This will work just fine." Though it looked awfully permanent. Not the corners of sticky notes and cocktail napkins she'd usually jotted songs down on for someone else to transcribe, if Dwight approved them. A gulf of careful, polite space stretched between her and Joe. "Thank you. I—" Too much emotion in her, with all this family love and honest conversations. "I really, really appreciate it."

"So," he said, breaking the awkward moment. "I think it would be best to go. You about ready to get out of here?"

"Yes." Much as she hated to leave their retreat, she wanted to be alone with him again. Away from the girl who offered to be her sister like that would be a good thing, and a mother who recognized a bad influence on her son when she saw one.

And the dad and grandmother she'd never have. She turned the watch on her wrist. Forever stuck at 10:39.

~ 26 ~

A VA KEPT A death grip on the guitar, only relinquishing it temporarily by tucking it into the passenger seat for safekeeping while they said their goodbyes. Joe wasn't sure what she'd been thinking about when he'd handed it to her. She'd been laughing with Nona, bright eyed and glowing. Then the way her eyes had gotten that bruised look when she held the guitar made him regret the gesture. The girlishness of it made him think of that young her, hitting her sister with a tiara and feeling guilty about it still. *I was never a kid.*

He'd almost not bought it, but his dad had told him to quit dithering and follow his instincts. Always better, he said, to buy your girl the maybe wrong present than none at all.

None of them believed he only worked for Ava—they knew him far too well. But they'd never understand either, how terribly wrong it was for them to think of her as his girlfriend.

"You watch yourself, Joseph," his mother said, hugging him too tightly while Ava hung back, pretending she wasn't watching the scene in that avidly curious way of hers. "And you call me and tell me when you get home, so I won't worry."

"Yes, Mom." He gave Nona back her phone. "No texting anything until we're at least two hours down the road. I mean it."

"Do you think I'd do anything to hurt Ava?" she answered, all wounded indignation, though she immediately thumbed it on, scanning her messages. "Besides, I have no evidence. No one will believe me."

"I can take care of that," Ava said, surprising him by taking the phone and sliding an arm around his sister's waist. She held it up and out, leaning her head against Nona's and assuming her trademark smile. "Sparkle, Shirley," she said, and Nona smiled, too, beyond revved.

Ava handed the phone back to her. "I took several—make sure to pick the one we look best in."

His sister clutched the phone, bouncing with her excitement. "Thank you! You are fucking aweso—"

"Language!" Their mother cut in.

"*You* are awesome." Ava hugged her. "Tag me when you post it and I'll make sure to look for it and share, okay? If I miss it, text your brother with the link." She slid him a significant look, meaning she wanted him to remind Katey to do it. "But make up a place you met me—like at a mall or something. It doesn't matter, as long as it's not the truth."

Once in the car and on the road, Arlin in the jump seat, and Ava seat belted in before he reminded her, she laid the guitar across her lap and tore into the bag of decals.

"What are you doing?"

"Personalizing my Daisy Rock Pixie Acoustic Guitar, of course."

She looked so pleased that he nearly reached out to touch her, but he managed to restrain himself. They were in a strange place, with too many things said in the night on the cliff walk that didn't stand up well in the light of day. He couldn't believe he'd said some of what he had. But he'd awakened early, missing her lithe body and effervescent presence, heart sick for that kid she'd never been. The guitar… it had been a gamble. A silly thing to make her so happy, that he'd managed to make her happy. It gave him a strange kind of giddiness that he had. Like he was fourteen again, asking a girl to the dance and she smiled and said yes.

And now they headed back to real life, where he would be fired and he'd go back to the grind of shuffling people back and forth from airports. A week ago that comforting routine had been what he needed. Now the prospect seemed utterly lifeless.

"So, I'm wondering something," Ava said as she worked, and his heart skidded to a stop. Here it came, where she'd ask him where he got off calling her out on her life and choices. What the hell had possessed him to say all that shit last night?

"Yeah?" He braced himself.

"How did your Kentucky family end up with a cabin all the way up here? I can't believe they drove all that way."

Not at all what he'd expected. She never was. He blew out a breath, realigning his scattershot thoughts. "Well, they do it in two days, so it's not that bad. Grandmother won't fly, so we've always driven. Her second husband, my Grandpa Lester, he was from this area, though she met him in Kentucky. He wanted a place here, so we made the drive, three-four times a year. Thanksgiving, Christmas, Easter and summer vacation. You get used to it."

"A driver, even then."

"I suppose so." He hadn't thought of it that way, but he had learned to drive on those long interstate trips, his dad offering patient instruction. "It wasn't my life's ambition or anything. I just fell into it."

"What is your life's ambition?"

Didn't he wish he knew? He sure couldn't say that it was her. It seemed he'd found the perfect job in his chosen career of Avaology. And it would be over. Maybe as soon as that night, when they returned to reality and Manning figured out he'd disobeyed direct orders. "Not everyone has one, Sova." He must have sounded forbidding on the topic, because she was quiet for a while and he wasn't sure what else to say.

"Why won't your grandmother fly?" She positioned a purple flower, then peeled off the backing and precisely applied it.

"How my grandfather died—he flew planes in the war, and that's how he died."

"Oh. How awful for her."

She listened. More, she remembered. Ava might spend a lot of time trying to convince him she lacked compassion. *I'm a stone-cold bitch, Jacky boy. Don't ever forget it.* But she wasn't. No one who claimed to care as little she did paid that much attention to other people's stories. More of her masks, the roles she assumed, to cover up a tender, impossibly battered heart. He'd like to wring her mother's neck.

If the woman did show her face again, he'd take great pleasure in seeing her well away from Ava. And not gently, either.

"Did I say the wrong thing?" Ava had her head cocked, studying him.

"Just thinking. I probably shouldn't've put them through it. But I was young and stupid—thought I was immortal. Going wasn't difficult. Coming back, though, seeing their faces, how my mom reacted, was the absolute worst part of the injury."

"Not Sheila?" She wasn't looking at him, tuning the strings instead, cocking one ear as she plucked.

Great. Just wonderful. "Let me guess—Nona told you."

"Since you neglected to mention you'd been engaged."

"I told you I'd been in a three-year, long-term relationship. That was Sheila."

"Engaged is different than 'long-term.'"

"Says the woman who, according to the press, has been engaged at least twice. Possibly three times."

She tucked her hair behind her ear and wrinkled her nose. "*Not* the same thing, as those were the romantic fictions of marketers."

"Hmm." He nearly asked about Tyler. Left it alone as the Kryptonite it was.

"Did you love her—Sheila?" Ava, on the other hand, left nothing alone.

"Would I have asked her to marry me if I didn't?"

"I don't know, would you?"

Once he would have said of course he'd loved Sheila, but that guy seemed like someone else. And if he was honest, he'd given Sheila the ring in hopes she'd stay faithful and wait for him, not because he'd really wanted to marry her. He'd been thinking like the dumb kid he'd been. When she'd given it back, that had just been one pain among many and far from the worst. By then he'd had Ava to occupy his thoughts.

"She didn't love you," Ava commented, wadding up the empty packaging and stuffing it into the side pocket, still plucking the strings and tweaking the tuning.

He turned the snort into a cough. "Now you're the expert on love?"

"Look, Jacky boy, I might not know much about normal people and love and shit, but I do know that if you love someone you can't just walk away from them when they're in pain."

"Like you can't walk away from Katey."

"A clear example of my cold, black heart as I did exactly that this weekend."

He glanced at her, but her face was serene, intent as she listened to the tuning of the strings. "A few days away isn't walking out on her. You needed a break. Maybe the space was good for her, too."

"Maybe." The way she said it sounded like a definite no.

"She isn't kind to you," he said.

Ava looked up, eyes a startled owl in flight. "What?"

"Katey. The way she talks to you—she's cruel."

A long, slow blink as she considered. He had to look back at the road. "Maybe I deserve that from her."

"Years later? At some point people have to let go and forgive. Especially family."

"Like you do with your mother?"

Yeah, his mom took the cake sometimes. "Exactly. She pisses me off, worrying herself to death about me, but me being mean to her would only hurt her. My other choice is to cut ties entirely and I'm not going to do that. So yeah, I keep my distance most of the time and when we're together I try to remember that she's a flawed person, just like any of us."

"You're so still waters run deep." She sounded amused, so he took his eyes off the road to check, but she looked solemn.

A little embarrassed—if she only knew how fucked up he was—he looked away again. "Not so much. They make us do counseling, you know, in rehab and all, and my mother's infamous and bloodcurdling scream made that day's topic. My counselor laid it out for me."

Ava went quiet, trying a few chords. The guitar had a surprisingly rich tone for the size and pinkness. Or maybe that was the Ava magic at work.

"Will you tell me about when you got hurt?" she asked softly, a chord like the ocean framing the question.

"I have."

"No—the story. You don't have to, but I'd like to hear the whole story. Your dad said you got a special medal for saving an officer's life."

That caught him off guard. "He did?"

She nodded, modulating the chord, bringing in a hint of that melody she'd been humming when he roused from sleep the rainy afternoon before. "While you were packing the car. He's really proud of you."

Huh. Not something his dad had ever said to him. Why had

he told Ava? "It's not much of a story. We used to do these drills, drive in these caravans back and forth across Kabul in armored Humvees. Afghanistan is all open, rolling country—like northern New Mexico, if you've ever seen it."

"I did concerts in Albuquerque a few times, and filmed *Trouble in Double* around Santa Fe."

"That's it. So you can imagine. It looks all peaceful. Beautiful, but it got old, driving back and forth, day after day on these same patrols."

"And you were the driver."

"I was the driver." The smell came back to him, the oiled metal, men sweating, dust in the air. "I'd gotten a rep for being steady. Keeping alert without cracking. It's this weird combination of utter boredom and subtle fear. You gotta keep watching for anything to happen, and yet…"

"Most of the time nothing does." She picked a rhythm around it, an echo of the car tires, rolling endlessly.

"Right—until it does. There was nothing about that day. No buzz about threats. Nothing to indicate activity on our route. Then, boom." The flash. White hot agony. Screams.

"What was it?"

"They, ah—It's okay, buddy, I got it." He patted the nose Arlin poked between the seats. "See, they plant these homemade bombs under the road and pack the dirt down so you can't see it. I drove right over one. On the left side, so it shattered my leg, sent shrapnel into my buddy's face, burning shit all over us. It didn't disable the vehicle, though, so I kept driving."

She'd turned in the seat to face him, cheek leaning against the headrest, the guitar at an angle. "Steady," she said, and for a moment he thought she was giving him advice. But no, commenting on his reaction.

"More in shock, maybe. Mostly, I didn't want us to sit there while they came in and picked us off. I screamed plenty once we got clear and the medic worked on me." He tossed her a grin, but she didn't smile. His leg ached where it no longer existed.

"It hurts when you talk about it." She ran her slender fingers over the strings, white-tipped nails flashing, the guitar whispering back. "Your leg does."

Taking his eyes off the seductive movement of her hands, he made himself watch the road. "That's just the phantom pain. It hurts the most below the amputation. Like my brain thinks it has to keep telling me that something whoa-nasty has happened down there, flashing that emergency signal."

"Phantom pain," she mused, darkening the chords so they echoed the phrase. "I've been thinking about that since you mentioned it the other night. It's like there's some part of you forever living in that moment of utter shit storm and that past self keeps calling out for help. Only present you can't help, because that's over. But that trapped past self never gets it, just keeps screaming. And all you can do is try to tell yourself that there's something outside that dark place. Like a lighthouse, reaching back into the past, flashes of light to guide all your wounded selves to the future."

"Man." He shook off the way that raised the short hairs on the back of his neck. "The way you pull words out of the air— that's another song, right there."

"Not any of them ones I need to be writing."

"Just do it. Put them down and worry later. It makes you happy. That's something, isn't it? More than you had when we left the city. If you're happier, maybe it will be better recording the songs they have lined up for the album."

The strings murmured under her hands, the sound of storm-tossed surf and rain. "Maybe." It sounded a little less like a no that time. "Henry asked me to write him a song and I never did."

"You still might."

"Yeah, but…" She laughed. Not the musical one, but more a sound of disgust. "It won't matter. He's dead."

"It would matter to you and you're still alive."

"Hmm." She modulated the chords, then stopped to rub Arlin's ears. "What does he feel, that he knows when we're upset?"

"I don't know. He always does, though."

"Like he's telepathic. Or senses vibrations. They say cats can sense earthquakes hours before they happen. Maybe it's like that. Emotional earthquakes."

"Yeah." Like the nowhere zone, eating the ground out from under his feet.

"What's that face? You're thinking something."

"Nothing in particular." He gave her a smile. "At least, nothing listening to you sing won't cure."

She rolled her gorgeous eyes, but smiled back. Rich, warm and real. "You do my heart good, Jacky boy. You really do."

~ 27 ~

B Y THE TIME they got back to the city, she'd put down drafts of three songs in the little pink notebook, and had the bones of two more. Maybe even some hints of one for Henry, though she didn't want to examine that too closely, lest it retreat behind that wall again.

The drive seemed to take a lot longer going back. On the way up, of course, she'd slept a lot and been in kind of a fugue state the rest of the time. Still, she knew Joe made sure the trip went slowly. He claimed he was avoiding traffic—taking long, winding back-road routes, driving in his steady way, listening to her work up the songs. Happy to have her sing them to him, not seeming to mind the repetition.

He stopped often, too, taking Arlin for walks and runs around tiny obscure parks in small towns, parking her at a picnic bench or old bandshell to work. Keeping her always under his watchful eye, but giving her yet another gift—the time and space to noodle with the lyrics and music. No one looking over her shoulder and pronouncing it good for the album or not.

She hadn't had that since… well, since she wrote "10:39."

With the skyscrapers of Manhattan at last looming overhead, she finally put away the guitar, wedging it next to a disgruntled Arlin, her fingers nearly bloody and definitely aching.

"I've lost my calluses," she said, examining her fingertips. "And my nails are way too long to play. You could hear them

283

catching all the time."

"I didn't mind it," he replied. "I liked hearing the scratches here and there, the sound of you working. Real."

"Maybe because it broke the boredom of hearing the same thing over and over."

He slanted her a smile. "I don't want to play I-can-top-your-pain, but you don't know boring."

"Ha ha."

"Seriously—it's amazing hearing you dream up those songs, and how you wove in flashes of the last few days. 'Lighthouse' is going to be a huge hit."

"Jacky boy." The impatience with his obstinacy unfurled, like a cobra spreading its hood. "It won't be a hit because it will never be recorded. The label will never let me. How many times to I have to explain this?"

"But you have to follow your art, right? This is where it's leading you. In everything I read or hear about creative people, they say that."

She laughed. "I kind of want to be in the room and hear you explain that to the label."

"No." He threw her a determined look. "I'll be in the room when *you* tell them that. What's the point of being a crazy artistic genius, if you can't do that?"

"I can't even with you."

"You don't know until you try. They might like it."

"I can promise they won't. And then they'll sue me and leave me destitute." The prospect made her feel ill. By the determined set of Joe's jaw, however, he'd never listen to reason. "I don't want you saying anything about these songs to anyone."

He threw her a look. "NDA, remember?"

Yeah. She'd meant because she asked him, but whatever. "How come you're not touching me?"

"I'm not supposed to, remember? Back to the real world and

all." He said it evenly enough, but…

"Then I'll touch you." She knelt on the seat and wound her arms around his neck, kissing his cheek. Then nibbled on his ear for good measure. Much better than thinking about what the next day would bring.

He patted her arm across his throat. "This isn't safe."

"You going to save me, Jacky boy? Like you do with everyone."

"I don't—stop that."

But she had his fly open before he could stop her, his already hard cock springing free, hot and velvet smooth in her hand. She wanted him in her mouth. "I'll show you unsafe."

He fisted a hand in her hair, but groaned and didn't pull her away when she took him in. "I swear to God, you'll be the death of both of us."

"Want me to stop?" She licked the head, salt and sweet together.

"Yes."

"No you don't. Besides, if you can drive a blown-up vehicle with your leg gone and your buddies screaming, you can keep steady through a little ol' blow job."

He muttered something, thighs flexing under her hands, then caught his breath as she increased the suction, driving him in that hard rhythm that always took him apart. A car horn blared, he hit the brake, and his hand tightened in her hair, painfully yanking at her scalp as he pulled her away from his groin.

"No. I mean it, Ava. No more of that."

"It wouldn't have taken much longer."

He huffed a ragged breath she took as agreement. "I'm not going to risk you. And don't think I don't know you're using sex to distract me from a conversation that makes you uncomfortable." With one hand, he fastened his jeans again, eyes on the traffic.

Just as well, as it gave her a moment to assemble her addled thoughts. "There's nothing wrong with sex."

"I'm not saying there is. I'm saying you turn to sex to make yourself feel better when something scares or upsets you."

"Are you Dr. Phil all of a sudden?"

"No." He firmed his mouth. "Way too much group therapy. Some guys go down that path. It's not a pretty one."

And here she'd been feeling good. Happy, even. Now the fluttering churned in earnest. Making her stomach ache. Arlin put his nose into her hair, nuzzling her neck.

"You okay over there?" He slid her a glance, reached to put a hand on her knee, but she moved it. "Hey … talk to me."

"I'm fine." She shored herself up. *Sparkle, Shirley.* "Perfectly good."

"Shit," he muttered, and changed lanes, moving over to the side of the busy road.

"No, don't pull over. Just—just take me home, okay?"

He did as she asked, but his jaw had gone tight, his expression remote. "I'm sorry, Sova. I didn't mean to hurt you. I'm on your side. You know that."

Unexpected rage filled her. Far better than feeling like he'd slapped her. "Fuck you, Jack. Nobody is ever on anybody's side but their own. You know that."

He didn't answer immediately. Calm. Steadily maneuvering through the other vehicles. "You're wrong," he finally said. "And it's fucked up that you believe that. I've been in places where having the right people on your side is all that matters, all that saves you."

"Well, congratulations, I guess you're just stronger and less fucked up than I am. Shocking," she spat.

"That's not what I'm saying," he answered, still patient, still steady.

She wanted to thump on him with her fists, hurt him back.

No, to drive him into one of those states where he forgot the safe lines and just took her, hard and fast and furious. *You turn to sex to make yourself feel better when something scares or upsets you.* Well fine, if that was true. Better than the drugs. Right? *It's not a pretty one.*

"Sova?"

"Don't call me that. Just … don't talk to me right now."

And so he didn't, letting the silence stretch unbroken. He *would* have to be the one guy who took that seriously, who didn't try to explain it all away and cozen her out of her sulk. Neither of them said anything all that last half hour until he dove the car into the maw of the underground garage at her building.

Even on her best days, it made her think of being eaten alive, consumed into some mass grave of empty cars, the bones beneath her, no matter how high above them she lived. *Well, hello, morbid thoughts.* Apparently they'd simply waited to ambush her when she returned, like gibbering ghouls hanging onto the edges of the garage mouth, leaping onto her and chewing.

"Let's go to your place."

"What?" She'd surprised him out of some sort of deep thoughts.

"Your place. You live somewhere, right? Somewhere normal. Let's go there."

He set his jaw. "Absolutely not."

"Why not? You can bring me home in the morning."

"Not going to happen, Sova. Besides, we're here."

Soon Joe would leave her and this whole time would be over, like it never happened. The fantasy come full fucking circle, ending with a whimper. She'd just had to pick a fight with him, always having to ruin everything at the end. If he loved her really, like he loved his family, then it wouldn't matter that she'd pissed him off. He'd love her despite her flaws.

She really needed him to love her.

"Please don't be mad at me," she said, not moving even though they'd come to a stop and he'd unbuckled his seat belt.

With a sigh, he turned to her and took both of her hands in his. Strong and warm. "I was never mad at you. You were angry with me and justifiably so. I'm sorry that what I said hurt you."

She didn't know how to explain it wasn't that at all. *I'm just a girl standing in front of a boy.* "Where's a fucking Chagall when you need one?" she said. Or a script. No one fell in love over a weekend except in movies and romance novels.

"What are you talking about?"

"I want you to stay with me."

"Sova—"

"No, really. What you said is probably true. Because, look! I'm feeling all upset and I really want you to come upstairs and fuck me senseless."

He hissed through his teeth, shaking his head ever so slightly. "That's a bad idea."

"Only Katey will be there. No one else. The ravening hordes won't descend until morning."

"Including your manager."

"You want me to defy the label, risk losing everything, but you won't go against Dwight's stupid rule?"

"It's more than that. This thing between us—it was for the weekend. We're back and now it has to be over with. You know that as well as I do."

Wow, did that hurt. She knew she'd asked for the fantasy, but just like that? All of it a lie? At least no tears welled up. Her eyes burned, dry, searing. Back to her usual self. "Why did you give me the guitar?" she found herself asking.

He frowned a little, those dual lines between his brows forming. "So you could play in the car, write your songs."

Maybe. Maybe that's all it was. "I say the weekend isn't done. Not until tomorrow morning. You promised to pretend. Was that a lie?"

He sighed and rubbed his eyes. "No. The furthest thing from it."

She opened her mouth to ask what he meant, but he dropped his hand and shook his head briskly, like Arlin shedding rain and sea water. "I'll take you up and then come back to get the stuff."

Making her wait in the car while he checked out the garage, Joe even secured the elevator, Arlin helping all the while. Her boys. If only she could keep them with her forever. Maybe she wouldn't feel so fucking alone then. They rode up in silence, but Joe held her hand. It reminded her of that night, after the concert, when she'd leaned on him while he talked to Tyler.

Such a fucking mess.

She should maybe apologize for that. But then, what would she say? She and Joe hadn't been together then. Hell, they weren't even together now. All a sham. Yet another movie where she played the role because that's all she knew how to do.

Just a slut who slept her way to the top, clinging to the fame she didn't deserve. Every day holding her breath for the hard fall. *Anything would be better than a life and career that makes you this miserable and crazy.* Would it? Maybe so.

The elevator doors slid open.

"The prodigal daughter returns home." Katey stood in the middle of the hall, looking both smug and strained. Something was up. She held up Ava's phone. "Do you want to see it yet or extend the *mental break* until morning?" She made the words sound downright filthy.

"Anything calamitous?"

"Nothing I didn't handle for you—or that can't wait for your Monday morning meeting prep." Katey surveyed her, flicking at glance at Joe and Arlin behind her, then back to her face. "How was the fuck fest?"

"Mind if we come in?" Joe asked, his hand on the small of her back, and she loved him for calling Katey on her obstruction tactics.

Katey hesitated, and not out of obstinacy for once. The TV sounded loud from the other room and Katey glanced back, then at Ava. Her eyes were their real brown. And they were full of conflicted emotion, a hint of the old her in there.

"Um. There's something you should know, actually. I—"

"Hi, baby girl." Like a horror movie monster appearing from the shadows, her mother stood in the doorway.

Ava's skin went to ice, and she took a step back, colliding with Joe's solid frame. His arms wrapped around her, making her safe. He would always make her safe.

"No hug for mama?" Her mother's voice took on a mocking tone. "And who's this handsome young man? Someone has a boyfriend." The singsong grated in her ears. Katey stared at the floor, guilt and shame in every line of her body.

"You let her in?" Her voice sounded incredibly steady.

Katey's gaze flew to hers. "She's my mother, too."

"And she fucked you over, too. We agreed on this."

"You left me alone!" Katey screamed it, fists clenched by her sides. "What happened to *those* promises?"

"That's right, Ava." Krystal stroked Katey's hair, full of self-satisfaction. "I've been keeping Katherine company and we've been having some long conversations. Sharing old family stories. Seems there's things you neglected to tell her."

"I should have known." Katey's face burned with fury. "What you did. I never thought even you would be that low."

Oh no. But the knowledge was there in Katey's face, in her mother's. The trump card she'd finally played. Arlin leaned into her leg. Earthquake alert. "Joe, would you excuse us, please?"

"I can't do that," Joe replied evenly. "Ma'am, I'm going to have to ask you to leave. I believe there's a restraining order preventing you from being here."

"I was invited to be here and I'm staying. Ava, darling, tell him you agree or your new lover will hear the truth about you, too."

"What do you want?" Ava ground out, and her mother smiled, with a flirtatious wink at Joe.

"What I've always wanted. To take care of my girls. Your career is foundering without me. I've moved back into my old room. You'll lift the order and let me stay."

"Fine." It came out dully. Katey's betrayed face all she could see. She couldn't bear for Joe to know that about her, too.

"No way." Joe pulled out his phone and moved in front of her. "I'm calling Manning and the police.

"Joe—don't."

He paused, thumb poised. "It's my job. I can't do otherwise."

"Don't let him, or I'll tell," her mother warned. "Katherine and I have been talking a lot while you abandoned her. Is this one special? He must be. Does he know about the naked photos Tyler took of you?"

"*Everyone* on the fucking planet has seen those, Mother." Ava clenched her fists. Katey shifted, clutching the phone. Ava's phone. *Oh. My. God.* "It was you?"

Katey flinched, guilt all over her. She flung the phone away from her and buried her face in her hands, sobbing. Krystal cuddled her close, making cooing noises. "You needed to be taken down a notch. Getting too uppity."

"Tyler didn't do it," she breathed. Joe watched her, still waiting. Why that mattered, she wasn't sure, but it helped somehow. And this… this endless cycle of manipulation. She couldn't do it anymore. *Anything would be better than a life and career that makes you this miserable and crazy.* "Go ahead and call," she told him. A smile flicked on his face and he pressed the button.

Her mother's face creased in dismal rage. "That's a big mistake. I'll tell him. I'll tell everyone. You'll be ruined."

Katey pushed back her hair, so one baleful eye showed. "Whore," she hissed.

Joe stepped back. "The police are on their way. Maybe you should leave, ma'am, if you don't want a scene."

"I mean it, baby girl. I'll tell."

She would, too. It was all over. Had been for a while. "Joe—remember how I told you that I screwed Katey over for that part in *Little Girl Lost*, when she was laid up?"

"Sova, you don't have to—"

"Tell you the rest?" She shrugged. "You might as well hear it from me. I dressed up sexy, sang, danced, did the monologue." Joe watched her in growing horror, Arlin leaning against her leg, so she ruffled his ears, feeling oddly numb and detached from it all. "And then I stripped naked and let him touch me. While I gave him a blow job. My first one! He said I wasn't half bad."

Silence fell. Only the murmur of the TV in the other room. *Black Swan* again. Just perfect. Maybe she would run out in traffic.

"Anything to add, *Mother*? After all, you were there."

Her mother glared. "Just that you were a natural."

"Like mother like daughter."

Krystal shrieked and leapt at her. Before Ava could even flinch, Joe had her mother face to the wall, arm locked behind her. "You're going to want to leave," he was saying.

Krystal screamed obscenities. Katey sobbed.

And Ava walked down the long hall to her bedroom, Arlin close to her side.

~ 28 ~

H E FOUND HER there, curled into a ball in the middle of her enormous bed, looking like a child sent to her room. Arlin lay with her, head on her hip, eyes bright. His tail thumped softly at Joe's entrance and he thought Ava must be asleep.

"Did you bring the vodka?" she asked.

So, he toed off his shoes and crawled onto the bed behind her, wrapping himself around her back and ruffling Arlin's ears. "Good boy," he said.

"I guess he goes with whoever needs him most," she said.

"He's a smart dog. And you don't need vodka right now."

"I used to keep a bottle or three stashed in here. Then I stopped because, well, that's kind of scary behavior, right? I've been lying here seriously regretting that choice."

He kissed her hair, glad not to have found her passed out from drink. "You're a smart woman."

"Do I want to know what went down?"

"About what you'd expect. Manning and the rest of the team arrived. The police arrested your mother. She said her phone call would be to Candy Conway. Hilda is working up several responses, depending on how you want to present the story. She wants to talk to you but I said it could wait until the morning meeting."

"And they bought that?" Ava sounded incredulous. At least not so dispirited.

"They all agreed you'd do better then, once you had time to recover from the shock." After he'd gone nose to nose with Manning. And gotten fired, not incidentally. Not that it mattered. "Katey… She wasn't doing so good. They had to sedate her and take her to the hospital."

Ava moaned, so he pressed closer to her. "The psych ward. They can help her. Believe me, I know."

"You don't know. Those places are awful."

"Yeah, I do know. I was in one awhile." Ava was silent, so he continued, rubbing the silky spot between Arlin's eyes. "VA, of course, but after the injury I had night terrors and waking delusions. They had to sedate the hell out of me. That's why Sheila left. It wasn't the leg. The docs told her I might not ever get my brain working right again. I still have to take meds."

"I never saw you."

He shrugged a little. "I didn't want you to. But that's part of why I keep the duffel bag with me. Medication. Change of clothes in case I… well, need them."

She was quiet. Just the sound of her breathing. The faint noise of the city outside. He missed the ocean, but it was good to be there with her. "But you're okay now," she finally said.

"Not really." He stroked her hair back from her brow, and she rolled onto her back some, looking up at him. He'd expected to see signs of weeping, but her makeup remained perfect, her eyes clear, though haunted. Twelve. Just a little girl when they did that to her. *I had my first drink at nine, began smoking pot at ten, and took cocaine at twelve.* No fucking wonder. "The meds help, but it never quite goes away, you know? There's this feeling—I call it the nowhere zone in my head." He laughed, self-conscious to admit it, but she watched him solemnly. Owl eyes.

"What does it feel like?" She whispered. "The nowhere zone."

"Like… my skull is coming apart, and like the ground is

dissolving beneath my feet, and I can't—" He had to catch his breath. It helped when she reached up to run fingers through his hair. "Arlin kind of… reminds me of what's real. That I'm not actually coming apart."

"The nowhere zone. Yeah, I get that."

He turned his face, pressing a kiss to her fingertips.

"Don't you hate me?" Her lips were parted, vulnerable uncertainty on her face.

"For what—being a victim?"

"I wasn't. I mean, I did all that willingly. I even kind of liked it. The power. Winning."

"Oh, Sova." He kissed her forehead. "You survived a terrible thing, but you weren't any more willing than I was when I got exploded in my own Humvee. I can see it in your eyes. I always could."

"My white knight," she murmured. "You and Arlin. How is it that it hurts so much now when it didn't then?"

"Sometimes you don't feel the injury right away. At first you're numb. Shocked. Then, as sensation returns, you feel the pain."

"Phantom limb. Only I lost what made me real."

"You didn't lose it."

"A prosthetic soul?"

"Good line for a song."

She smiled, ever so slightly. "Besides longing for vodka, I've been thinking. Will you help me do something?"

"Anything."

✦　✦　✦

THEY USED KATEY'S abandoned tablet to record the song. Ava didn't even have to work hard to guess the password. 'Violet' opened it right up. She still couldn't quite process that Katey had been the one to leak those photos, though… of course it had been her. *Violet.*

She strummed the chords, unaccountably nervous. "Katey's not a bad person, you know."

"I never thought so," Joe replied. He sat on the couch, arm stretched along the back, Arlin belly-up beside him.

"You called her cruel."

"Yeah. Cruelty can come from being broken. Not necessarily from being a mean person. Seems like she suffered her share of shit, too."

"Yeah." She took a breath. Let it out. "I can't believe I'm going to do this."

"It's your call. Don't do it for me."

"But I am. Or maybe because of you. I don't want to go out with a whimper."

"Then let's do it. Ready?"

No. But she nodded and he hit record. They did it in one take. Then played it back. There she was, singing "Lighthouse," her voice rougher than usual, none of flash and glam. She looked and sounded full of emotion. Shattered to the bone. Different.

Definitely not human lip gloss. So there was that.

She wanted to go back and fix it, polish it up. Tweak the lyrics. Joe held his ground—along with the tablet—insisting that it would be more convincing if the song remained a little uneven.

"The story is you just happened to be sitting around on a Sunday evening, playing the guitar, having fun with friends. I video you singing "Lighthouse," and you accidentally post publicly instead of just to your private YouTube channel."

"I feel sick."

"Remember, everyone believes it's always been you on these accounts. They won't blink. We give it thirty minutes. Then you broadcast an apology to your fans. An honest mistake. Tell them we didn't mean to post it and that you're taking it down." He grinned. "And wait just long enough for everyone to race to download it and spread it around,"

"You think they will?"

"Hell," his fingers flew on the tablet, "I would have done it, if I were out there. This kind of news travels like wildfire. The fans who miss it will get it from others who post it to their own sites. It will be all over by morning."

"I don't know. What if they hate it?"

He shrugged like it wouldn't matter. "Then it won't go anywhere. Nobody will share it. It will fade into nothing and then you'll know. But at least you did what you wanted to."

She had. She'd really done it.

"Best case, your fans love it, rally to the cause and demand more," he said. He handed her the tablet. "But it's your call. All you have to do is hit 'upload.'"

She hovered her finger over the blue button. The last time she'd done this, actually posting to the internet, she'd been coked up and furious, Katey egging her on to take Mr. Wonderful down. *You were getting too uppity.* Her mother had played them both. Clearly her great talent.

"You can be trusted," Joe said.

All she needed to hear. She pressed the button. Swallowed hard.

"Feel good?"

"I don't know what I feel."

He scratched his chin. Getting bristly in the late evening. "Seems to me that's okay, too."

Setting the pink guitar aside, she got up and straddled Joe on the couch. He settled hands on her hips, eyes lighting with desire, a smile on his lips. "Are we moving to the distraction phase?"

"Please," she murmured, kissing him.

His mouth turned avid, drinking her in. Her head swam with

him, dizzying as a heat wave rising off black asphalt under a desert sun.

"Joe." His name came on a gasp as he took advantage of her breaking the kiss to nip under the delicate shadows at the corner of her jaw, the thudding pulse beat there. "You know what I want. Will you give it to me? No being careful or safe."

"You want it rough?" His growled question melted her.

"Yes. Hard. Fast. Whatever it takes," she replied, sinking her teeth into the muscle in his neck. "Anything you want to do to me. Obliterate me."

He swept her up in his arms and her head whirled at the sudden movement, blood thudding through her at the fixed set of his face, the stern line of his jaw. That shimmer of barely contained violence that always shot her over the edge into oblivion. Where she desperately needed to be.

Carrying her into the room, he kicked the door closed behind them, surveying the sitting area. A few sconces softly illuminated the space, all as the interior designer intended. Most of the light, however, came from the brilliant constellation of city lights from the skyscrapers around them, the floor-to-ceiling windows filled with her personal galaxy. They made her feel less alone.

"Can anyone see in?" Joe asked, his voice rough with restraint.

"No." She went wet at the question. Went wetter, that is, continuing the arc started when he seized her hands in that firm grip, taking her over. No, before that, since earlier that day, with all the hot licks of thoughts of him in the interim.

Obliterate me.

You turn to sex to make yourself feel better when something scares or upsets you.

Maybe so. But then she'd own it, like she owned everything else twisted and broken in herself. She'd asked and he'd answered. Her Joe. What would he do?

"You're in for it now then." His tone made her shiver and, before she knew it, he'd set her on her feet and bent her over the high back of one of the armchairs, holding her in place with one firm hand. She squirmed a little, just to feel him press her down. To her titillated shock, he smacked her on the ass, hard and stinging. "Don't fight me. You're going to stay still and take it. I still owe you from yesterday. Your turn to be tormented, little Sova."

She dug her fingers into the arms of the chair, beyond excited, delirious with anticipation, her hair falling around her face, screening everything from sight but the blue and silver damask pattern of the silk. She couldn't see what he was doing behind her and the cushioned back of the chair at the crease of her hips held her so precariously high she stood barely on tiptoe.

Then Joe pressed up against her, his cock a hard ridge against her bottom, his big hands spanning her waist, squeezing, sliding up her ribcage and pushing her sweater with it, so the loose-weave cotton tented over her head. She moved to pull it off, but he stopped her.

"No. Your job is to hold still."

She shuddered, his touch all the more devastating with sight and sound muffled. He flicked the back clasp on her bra and pushed that over her arms, too, further constraining her, leaving her breasts bare to him, vulnerable to his rough grasp. Tweaking and rolling her nipples, he leaned over her, bridging her body with his, trapping her against the chair.

His breath came harsh in her ear. "I'm going to take you apart, rip you at the seams until you're screaming for mercy." His fingers vised on her tender flesh and she whimpered. "That's right. So sweet, my Sova." With one last pinch of her nipples that made her sob, he released her to undo the button and zipper of her jeans, yanking them down her hips, leaving her lace panties in place. Holding her with that implacable hand in the small of her back, he tipped her forward so her feet kicked free of the floor, the blood pooling in her head. Dizzying, arousing, astoundingly out of control.

He pulled her pants free and settled himself between her spread thighs, not letting her touch her feet to the ground again, the denim of his jeans rough against her naked skin. Sliding his fingers inside her panties, he yanked them so they penetrated her slick folds, the lace rough against her sensitive tissues. With a wail she thrashed against him, needing more, and he rewarded her with a sharp slap on her flank that forced her breath from her lungs.

With his hand wrapped in the delicate lace, he scraped it over her clit, finding the pressure and rhythm that kept her from regaining that breath, desperately panting, the stimulation not quite enough to make her come, the grinding ridge of his erection only a tease for what she really wanted. She cried out, a long groan of despair and he had the nerve to laugh, smacking her bottom again.

Pulling the lace to the side, so it cut into her hip, he plunged his fingers inside her, dragging the fluids up her bared crack, over and over, so she wriggled, beyond words, reduced to helpless pleading. Mews of frustration that turned to a dark moan of pleasure as he worked his thumb into her anus, stretching and invading, sending a boneless shudder of surrender through her. He grunted his approval, thrusting his thick digit in and out of her tight orifice while sawing the lace over her clit.

She fisted her hands in the sweater, holding onto that, her brain going into that drugged dreamscape where only he existed, holding her suspended outside of reality. Only him and the all-encompassing ache of pleasure. "Joe…" she sobbed. "Please."

"Dirty girl," he growled, yanking the panties down her thighs and—ouch!—smacking her right on her open pussy.

She screamed. Then orgasmed. The climax wrenched through her, and she convulsed, speared on his invading thumb as she spiraled into the abyss. The impatient thrust of his cock caught her, yanking her back into impossible arousal, climbing with him as he slammed into her slick channel. He had her in three places, driving his thumb and cock into both passages, his other hand pinching her clit. His dark voice chanting guttural taunts and praises.

Until she shattered completely.

The galaxy of stars falling through her brain until they vanished into bloodred night.

Obliterated.

Thank God.

~ 29 ~

S HE CAME TO as he carried her to the bed, laying her on it with tenderness as exquisite as the brutality he'd treated her to. Loving the feel of it though, the caring way he stretched her out, she pretended to be asleep—or fainted?—still. In *Daddy's Girl*, the actor who played her father had carried his sleeping daughter to bed in one scene, tucking her in and kissing her forehead. She'd had to pretend to be asleep this same way, while he confessed how he was leaving her and her mother. They'd had to do several takes, as it was a critical, emotional monologue and the actor kept forgetting his lines. She hadn't minded a bit, loving the feeling of being held, pretending he really was her daddy, all broken up that he had to leave her.

Joe went into the bathroom, the sound of the faucet running, and he returned with his inevitable warm washcloth. Running it first over her cheeks, he brushed her hair back from her brow and kissed her lightly, whispering her name.

Tempted to luxuriate longer, she relented to the sound of worry in his voice and let her eyes flutter open and smiled at him.

"Are you okay?"

"Oh yes." *Obliterated.*

"You passed out."

"Job well done, Specialist."

He laughed softly, stroking the cloth over her breasts and

belly, down her thighs to clean her. "I was rougher than I should have been."

"I like it when you forget the 'shoulds.' Correction—I love it. You could go a lot further than that and I'd still like it."

"Until you didn't," he said in a somber tone, his caresses beyond gentle. "What if I really hurt you?"

"Hey." She tugged on that lock of hair that always fell over his forehead. "You'd know. Besides, if you did, I wouldn't care anyway."

He frowned at that. "I won't contribute to your self-destructive ways."

He was so adorable. Heartbreakingly so. "Oh, Joe, you're saving me from them. Remember? Just like you save everyone. Come here."

She twined her arms languidly around his neck, urging him into the kiss, and he willingly stretched himself beside her. He was still dressed, his jeans hanging open. Touching that he'd hurried back to her fast enough not to bother to fasten them. Drowsiness overtook her and, though she wanted to tell him to take them off so she could feel his skin against hers, she couldn't muster the words. He was bathing her again, smoothing over her curves with the cooling cloth, pressing kisses in its path. Reaching her wrist, he moved the watch aside.

"Sova?"

"Mmm."

He chuckled. "You're asleep. Let's get you under the covers."

"No." She forced her eyes open. "What were you going to ask me?"

"Why the watch?" He spun it around her wrist. "I used to think it belonged to your grandmother or something, and the fan sites always guess about it. But now I know your history and…" He trailed off, searching her face in the dim glow of the track lights. "You don't have to say."

She held up her arm, the silver glint of the watch sliding down with the movement. "You really want to know?"

"Only if you want to tell me."

So many times she'd been asked about the watch and she'd never said. At first it had worked as a mysterious feature for fans to speculate about. Especially when she'd come out with "10:39," one of her early big hits. The song was basically a red herring. More of a word game than anything, a fun way to try to rhyme "thirty-nine" as many ways as she could come up with. Only she had known what it really meant.

Turning it on her wrist, she tapped the cracked crystal, the hands forever frozen in place. "I bought it at a thrift shop in Florida. When we went to Orlando to do the *Tween Hangout* live show."

His finger joined hers, tracing the lightning-bolt-shaped flaw through the face. "You bought it broken?"

She nodded, meeting his gaze. No mockery in it, only thoughtful interest. "I was twelve." She waited, and he got it immediately.

"This was after…"

"My infamous audition, yes. I dunno. I was happy I got that part, even though Katey was really upset. She had to stay home and Mom stayed with her. I was on my own for the first time ever—surrounded by keepers, of course—but not the same. Anyway, maybe I did feel kind of broken inside without realizing it because I saw that broken thing and…"

"Had to have it?"

"Exactly. You know, there were all these old ladies there, in Florida. I'd never seen so many in my life. There aren't many old people in the business, and already they were worried about me aging, Mom making me do all this stuff to prevent lines. And these old ladies everywhere, they didn't act embarrassed or ashamed about their wrinkles. They seemed a lot happier than anyone I knew. And the watch only cost five bucks, so I bought it. I wouldn't take it off, even when they tried to make me, and I wrote that song really quick, so I could keep it."

"Kick me off the dirty vine, I won't be your flirty mime, yanked across your qwerty line, gimme gimme ten-thirty-nine," he sang softly.

More meaning in there than she'd realized. She held up the covers. "Get naked and get in."

He obliged, still looking thoughtful, keeping the prosthesis on. "I'll have to take Arlin out one last time, so if you feel me get up, don't worry."

She wouldn't. With his strong, warm body curled around her, she snuggled against him. Funny to think of that time, the near desperation to keep a cheap, broken watch.

"It wasn't a stupid whim, you know." He spoke against her hair, then pressed a kiss there. "You were a little girl all alone except for a mother who stood by while the unthinkable happened to you."

"She didn't just stand by," she whispered. "She suggested it."

He swallowed audibly. "How…"

"She just told me that he'd like seeing me naked and I should offer to suck his lollipop and he'd take it from there. Show me what to do. He did."

"Oh, Sova." He rubbed her belly in slow circles. "I hate to think that you—what we've done together—"

"No. It's not even the same. I like sex. I like it a lot. I won't let them take that, too."

"Okay." He didn't sound convinced, but she'd bring him around.

"I used to pretend—with the watch—that my imaginary grandmother had given it to me, a family heirloom. The grandmothers in the movies, you know, they did things like bake cookies and held your hand when the girls at school were mean.

It was only acting, I know, but sometimes…" *Everyone comes from something, child, even if they don't know what it is.*

"Sometimes you imagined how nice that would be."

"Yes." The word came out soundlessly, but Joe nodded and kissed her hair again.

✦   ✦   ✦

AVA HADN'T BEEN kidding when she called her staff ravening hordes. Arlin's growl woke him, then the sound of voices, speaking in the loud tones of people who'd been up for hours and had no concerns about waking anyone else. Grabbing his phone from the bedside table, he peered at it, eyes still blurred from sleep. Only six thirty. Damn.

Snuggled up against him like a kitten seeking warmth, Ava stirred and groaned. "No," she murmured. "It can't be Monday already."

"'Fraid so." Because it was there and too enticing to resist, he kissed the back of her neck, wishing he had time to make love to her. He'd had vague ideas of doing that last night, to give her some tenderness to counteract the violence of the way he'd taken her over the armchair. But they'd both fallen asleep so fast. He'd only briefly awakened to Arlin's whining reminder at the door, taken him out and locked up, then tumbled straight back into the sleep of the dead, barely taking time to shuck the prosthesis.

"Mmm." She nearly purred it, turning in his arms to sleek up against him, all hot, willing woman. "Put that mouth to better use than saying mean things."

A brisk knock interrupted their kiss, startling Joe when the door popped open and a tall, slender black man in a bright green, skin-tight suit walked in. "Ava, darling, get your adorable ass out—oh my!" The man fluttered his hand over his heart and sized up Joe, who'd sat up and put himself between the man and Ava. "Hellooo, sailor."

Behind him, Ava giggled, then levered herself up and put her chin on his shoulder. "Soldier. This is Joe, new driver and bodyguard. Joe, Cinna, my stylist in all things."

"And, girl, you seriously need my help today. What did you do to your hair? No!" He held up a dramatic hand, eyeing Joe's bare chest. "Never mind. Thinking about it is only making me hot and bothered and I'm guessing this one only goes for pussy, more's the pity. Out of bed, darling, shower off that man-spunk and report. Soldier Joe, if you want a shave and shampoo, I'll be cooling my heels for Miss Fabulous." He waggled his eyebrows and left as abruptly as he'd swept in.

"Wow." Joe couldn't think of anything else to say.

"There's a reason we nicknamed him Cinna. Though he's all flamboyance and no rebellion." Gloriously naked, Ava strode to the bathroom, stretching and dragging her hands through her tangled hair. Figuring it was the better part of discretion, Joe hastily dressed, just in case Ava's overly familiar stylist made another appearance.

Taking Arlin out to the rooftop terrace to do his business— definitely handy having that access, though less exercise for them both—Joe found the starkly quiet penthouse of the evening before transformed into jabbering chaos. Hilda, dressed and polished, sat at a table with a laptop and several flashing phones. Manning and two other women he hadn't met before all talked on their phones, not seeming to notice the others. Catching sight of Joe, Manning stabbed a finger at him, face contorted with anger, then flipped him off—never losing a beat in what he was saying.

Shit. The video. Joe had actually forgotten all about it. Needing time to reassess, he took Arlin out to the terrace. The predawn air settled crisp and damp around his shoulders, so he did a few jumping jacks to fend off the chill and get his blood moving while Arlin nosed around, taking his time in revenge for being locked out of the bedroom the night before, however briefly.

Then he thumbed his phone to social media.

Ava was trending on Twitter and Facebook. Over a hundred thousand YouTube hits before someone—not him, as he'd clean forgotten in the whirl of Ava—yanked it. His favorite fan sites had all grabbed and posted it.

The glass door crashed open, Manning standing in the opening. "Ivanchan. What in the name of the God of all the fucks did you do?"

"Sparkle, Shirley," Joe muttered to Arlin, and they went in to answer questions.

✦   ✦   ✦

PROMPTLY AT NINE, they all sat down at a huge conference table in a room on the far side of the penthouse. Ava's team consisted of a core of six people—five now, with Katey hospitalized. Besides Manning, there were Hilda, her publicist; Betsy, who seemed to handle the daily details of Ava's life; the nutritionist, Celine; and her stylist, Cinna—whose actual names he still didn't know. Manning dismissed Joe along with Celine and Cinna as not needed for the day's meeting, but Ava, sweeping in last, intimidatingly gorgeous in full glamorous mode, wearing a sleek black suit, complete with a man's white shirt and scarlet tie to match her lush mouth and wicked heels, said she wanted him to stay.

No secret smile or flash of eye-contact. She simply announced the preference in a tone that no one argued with. Diva mode. Feeling awkward, he seated himself at the end of the conference table, ignoring Manning's glare. The better he grew to know the man, the more it seemed that irate was his default emotional setting.

"Let's start with last night's SNAFU—" Manning began.

"Which one?" Ava snapped.

Her manager steepled his fingers. "Ava, darling. Are you aware that—"

The bodyguard Ava called Igor poked his head in. "Label rep is on the way up."

"Who?" Ava asked, studying her nails, crimson now, to match the rest, with some kind of rhinestones glittering on them. She made a good show of seeming not to care.

Igor put his hand to his earpiece. "Jessica."

Hilda winced and Manning threw up his hands. "Great. Just great. Fuck you for this, Ivanchan. Why are you even here? I clearly remember firing you."

"Don't you talk to him like that." Ava spoke as coolly as before, but the lethal fire in her golden eyes should have seared her manager on the spot. "I did it, not him. I'll take responsibility with the label."

"Oh you will, will you?" Manning sneered the question. "And will you pay the tab when the label sues for breach of contract and we're all out of a job?"

"Obviously," Ava replied, her tone pure ice. Joe could have kissed her it, if that had been possible.

Several people began speaking at once, though not Ava, all falling silent when the door opened again and a woman glided into the room, cutting the tension like a shark fin through water. Her black hair was tamed into a sleek knot and she wore a killer suit that made it immediately clear why Ava had chosen hers— and that of everyone in the room, Ava alone had anticipated exactly who the label would send. The woman immediately fixed on Ava and held out her hands, ignoring everyone else. "Ava, darling! Don't you look gorgeous."

Ava stood, took the woman's hands and then embraced her. "Jess! You always say the nicest things. We didn't expect you."

"No?" Jessica raised a perfectly penciled eyebrow. "You've been a naughty little pop star. You should have anticipated my visit."

Ava furrowed her brow as she sat, looking completely baffled, then beyond chagrined. Never forget what a good actress she could be. "Because I'm so behind on the album. You know what a perfectionist I can be. As soon as this meeting is over, I'm heading to the studio and getting this thing done. I promise."

Jessica meanwhile gracefully lowered herself into the chair next to Ava and poured herself coffee from the carafe on the table. "That's not what I mean. What's with this song that's everywhere this morning?"

"Song?" Ava looked around the table. "Did we post something?"

"On YouTube, Ava?" Hilda prompted, an eyebrow raised. "I think you posted something last night. Something… off the cuff?"

Ava gasped, a hand flying to her heart. "That little song I recorded last night for a lark when we had too many martinis? I saved it. I couldn't have posted it to YouTube."

"You could and did," Jessica replied in a very dry tone.

Ava spun her chair to Jessica. "Omigod. Is it awful—have you seen it?"

"We got the host to remove it this morning," Manning said. "To minimize the damage, and we feel—"

Jessica held up a hand to stop him. "I'm not talking to you right now. It doesn't matter that you pulled it. That horse is well and truly out of the barn. The thing is everydamnwhere." She pulled out her phone, queued something up and set it on the table. "Lighthouse," tinny in the poor reproduction, but with hints of its richness, poured out, transfixing the room. Jessica cut it off. "Our people are hitting it with DMCAs, but you know that's like playing whack-a-mole. Your fans are spreading it like wildfire. For free."

"Oh no." Ava pressed a trembling hand to her heart. "This is terrible. What can I do? I can have a press conference. Appeal to my fans. They love me. If I ask, they'll take them down."

Jessica laughed. "The fuck they will. They love it. The chatter is unreal."

Ava blinked at her, long and slow. His sova, reassessing, allowing a smile to illuminate her face. A sun everyone in the room reflexively brightened to. "They do?" she asked in hushed surprise. "But it's so not my style. Not produced at all. Just for fun."

Hilda had been working her tablet. "It hit big all right. Trending everywhere. Want some numbers, Jessica?"

"I've seen them. That's the only reason you have me and not the lawyers."

"They love it." Hilda shrugged. "I don't know if we can put the lid back on this one."

"Of course we can't," Jessica snapped. "There's a single solution and, by God, if you fight me on this, Ava, I will let the lawyers gut you."

"They can try," Ava answered, waving a negligent hand, not looking at him. "But I'm listening."

"You're recording that song today. With *us*. We're putting an official version out there on the retailers by COB and I don't want any of your drama. We're calling it a teaser for the album, which you *will* finish at the speed of light."

"Okay, Jess," Ava said, sounding meek as hell. "I'll try."

"But the songs she's already recorded," Manning argued, "they're nothing like whatever that was."

"Then she's writing more like that. Aren't you?" Jessica fixed

Ava with a predatory stare that made even Joe want to shift in his chair. "This is how you're making things up to us. At least seven more, just like that. And you will get your sensational ass into the studio nonstop and get this done. No more fucking around."

"I will, Jess." Ava maybe sounded *too* obedient, because Jessica's eyes narrowed in suspicion. Ava caught it, too, throwing a concerned glance at Hilda and giving Jessica a significant look. "Whatever it takes to smooth this over, right?"

The woman softened, patting Ava's hand. "We have your back. You know that. Just fix this on your end and I'll handle it on mine. Deal?"

Ava took the woman's hand in both of hers, holding it and treating her to the full wattage of her charm and charisma. Full on star, right there. "Deal, Jess. And thank you so much for handling this in person. *You* are a rock star."

Jessica shook her head and stood again, a reluctant smile on her face. "I'm expecting a generous thank you for the shit I'm going to have to shovel today because of you. Get me that recording." She swept out again, leaving everyone quiet for a moment.

"Okay," Manning said. "I want to know how the hell this happened."

~ 30 ~

AVA TOOK A deep breath, finally risking a glance at Joe. He nodded, eyes somber, but full of light. How had she ever thought him stoic? "That doesn't matter," Ava replied.

"The hell it doesn't! What the—"

"I want an update on Katey." She didn't have to make her tone steely. It just came out that way.

Betsy spoke up. "She was admitted to the hospital last night and she's resting comfortably under light sedation. Her doctors report that she's dangerously underweight, so they're keeping her on the IV for a while. We can discuss treatment options, but they want to keep her under for at least today, to at least get her hydrated and her vitals in better shape."

"Okay." Ava smoothed her cheekbones with her fingertips to relieve the pressure there, crimson nails flashing. A good choice for today. "Thank you, Betsy. Would you mind keeping an eye on her for me?"

Betsy seemed surprised, her cheeks pinking, but she nodded. "I'd be happy to, honey. You know we all love Katey, too. I'll go to the hospital now. How can I get in touch with you?"

Ava tapped her phone. "Text me updates."

"Now, Ava, darling—" Dwight began, yet again.

"Stow it, Dwight. I'm trying to take some responsibility here. I want the data plan activated. I'll take over social media while Katey is laid up."

"Are you certain, dear?" Hilda raised her brows. Not in criticism. Concern. *Having the right people on your side is all that matters, all that saves you.*

"I am certain," she answered, with more bravado than she felt. "Though not confident. I need to do this, though, so I'm hoping you'll help me."

"Of course. I'll get that plan activated now." She tapped out something on her own device, ever efficient.

Okay, the worst part. "What about the debacle with my mother. Jess didn't mention. Is the trending stuff about what she's said?" She looked around the table at the stricken faces. "Come on people, does anyone know?"

Dwight scrubbed his face. "She's telling the story. It's early yet for the papers, but the gossip sites have it. We can be sure it will get worse."

"But she lacks credibility," Hilda said, speaking to Ava. "There's no evidence. No photos. No corroboration. Alan certainly won't cop to it, whether he did it or not."

"He did," Ava said, before she knew she would, a hum between her ears. She caught Joe's eye and he dipped his chin, then glanced down beside him, gesturing. In the next moment, Arlin was at her side, eyes bright, tongue lolling in a doggie smile. She rubbed his ears. "I'm not actually coming apart," she murmured to him, and Arlin thumped his tail in agreement.

She looked around the table. "So I could deny."

"Yes," Dwight agreed. "I'm glad you agree, with that settled then we can—"

Ava held up a hand. She loved how Jessica could do that, silence a room with a sweep of her elegant fingers. Ava had been braced for Jess to clean her clock. Funny that the executive— despite being pissed—had been almost amused. Maybe even on Ava's team. Though the fan response had made all the difference. *They love you. It's real.* As if he'd heard the though, Joe nodded.

"What if I go public—tell my story?"

Dwight groaned and dropped his head on the table, but Hilda smiled. "It will be a major shit storm. Alan, the studio, everyone will deny. They'll try to smear you."

"And you're already in the shitter, publicity wise," Dwight said, lifting his head and stabbing a finger at her.

"Enough, Dwight," Hilda broke in with quiet conviction. "This song is the best publicity Ava has had in a long time. The memes with her mother are already out there, so this is just follow on. We can finally come clean on the reasons for the restraining order and Ava's emotional outburst. She's the victim here. You go shore up the legal end for our Ava, which is your job, as I recall."

Dwight braced his head in his hands, shaking it slowly. "What a clusterfuck." Then he dropped his hands and stared at Ava. "You could have told me, you know. I would have killed that motherfucker."

Her throat closed up, eyes welling with tears. For once, though, she didn't resent them. "Thank you, Dwight."

"I didn't know," he insisted, looking at his hands, opening and closing them where they lay palm up on the table.

"I know you didn't," she told him. "You'll handle this for me. I trust you to do it right."

Dwight's eyes gleamed with some of his usual spirit. "I'm going to ruin him for this."

"Go get 'em, tiger." She smiled, feeling surprisingly good. "Come on, Joe. I need to get to the studio. I have an album to record." Joe stood and moved to the door, opening it for her.

"About him," Dwight started.

"Shut up, Dwight," she said over her shoulder, quite sure she heard Hilda and Betsy snicker.

"Fine, fine," he muttered.

✦   ✦   ✦

J OE DIDN'T SAY anything until they were in the elevator. "He did fire me, you know."

"Good." Maybe it was all the emotions of … hell, the non-stop ride the last week had been, but she felt positively giddy. She'd faced ruin on every front and survived.

"Okay…" Joe said slowly, and she stabbed the elevator to a stop and took his hand.

"I want to start over and I don't know how to do this. I don't want you to work for me anymore."

He looked away, nodding, lips pressed firmly together. She held on to his hands when he tried to pull away.

"It got in the way," she persisted. "I know I'm crazy and messed up, the last thing from normal, but I want to… date you."

"Date me," he echoed, brows drawn together.

"However we can do that. Go for cheeseburgers. Visit your family. Whatever. I'm not good at that kind of thing, I know, but you can teach me."

Finally, he softened and smiled. "Believe me, Sova. You're good at it."

"I want to get better. I'd make some kind of grand gesture to prove it, like in the movies, but I don't have a Chagall to give you."

"Love isn't love without a violin playing goat," he said, very seriously.

She rolled her eyes. "I can't believe you know that movie."

"It's a great movie. Anna Scott is hot and the regular guy gets to bed her—what's not to like? I just didn't get the reference the first time."

She gripped his hands. "Do I have to make the speech?"

"No." He leaned in and kissed her. "Let's give it time. Take it slow."

Blowing out a breath, she nodded. "That sounds good."

"But I still want to drive you," he added. "I can get my old job back and arrange my schedule around yours."

"You want to be my driver still?"

"And bodyguard," he added in his steady way. "It makes me happy to take care of you."

"Okay." She found herself grinning, silly with it. "We'll work out the details."

"Sounds good to me." He started the elevator again, settling a hand at the small of her back. "Let's get you going on your damned job."

Arlin thumped his tail in enthusiastic agreement.

~ 31 ~

JOE DROPPED AVA at the studio, making sure she was safely inside—and receiving enthusiastic hugs from the staff and musicians. Andy Goldsmith was tearing out his hair at the prospect of producing the new sound, but seemed nearly manic with delight at the challenge, too.

Most important, everyone seemed to love "Lighthouse," and Ava glowed with the success of it.

He left the limo at the studio and took the subway to his apartment. The place seemed musty from being closed up, even for the few days. With it cool enough outside, he opened the windows to let the chill autumn air in, and set to work.

First to go were those prints of the naked photos. He made a little ritual of it, feeding them one by one into the shredder he'd borrowed from Mrs. Lassle. If he imagined shredding Tyler's face with them, well that was just emotional purging, right?

One by one, he took the photos down from the walls, popping them from their frames. As the machine consumed each, he thought of them as Wilson Alan—and all the others who'd bought and sold Ava—screaming, falling into the maw of destruction.

With ruthless determination, he destroyed it all. Even the mint GQ that started it all, Ava looking over her shoulder, naked back framed by the glittering gown, golden eyes wide and haunted.

Then he emptied the contents of the shredder into a trash can and piled in the movies and videos. Carrying it out to the alley, he set it in a clear spot and let it burn, the smoke rising acridly while Arlin nosed around the various pee spots, adding his own.

The music though—he kept all of that.

That was the part that mattered.

The part that was real.

Whistling for Arlin, he ruffled the dog's ears and they went back up. The apartment looked barren without Ava's eyes everywhere, but also clean. A fresh slate. Joe got out Arlin's service dog harness and suited him up, rewarded by a determined and enthusiastic tail wag.

"Both of us have jobs to do, huh, buddy?"

Joe locked up, and they went to see how Ava was doing.

Titles by Jeffe Kennedy

✦   ✦   ✦

CONTEMPORARY ROMANCES

MISSED CONNECTIONS
Last Dance
With a Prince
Since Last Christmas

CONTEMPORARY EROTIC ROMANCES

Exact Warm Unholy
The Devil's Doorbell

FACETS OF PASSION
Sapphire
Platinum
Ruby
Five Golden Rings

FALLING UNDER
Going Under
Under His Touch
Under Contract

EROTIC PARANORMAL

MASTER OF THE OPERA E-SERIAL
Master of the Opera, Act 1: Passionate Overture
Master of the Opera, Act 2: Ghost Aria
Master of the Opera, Act 3: Phantom Serenade
Master of the Opera, Act 4: Dark Interlude
Master of the Opera, Act 5: A Haunting Duet
Master of the Opera, Act 6: Crescendo
Master of the Opera

BLOOD CURRENCY
Blood Currency

BDSM FAIRYTALE ROMANCE
Petals and Thorns

FANTASY ROMANCES

A COVENANT OF THORNS
Rogue's Pawn
Rogue's Possession
Rogue's Paradise

THE TWELVE KINGDOMS
Negotiation
The Mark of the Tala
The Tears of the Rose
The Talon of the Hawk
Heart's Blood
For Crown and Kingdom

THE UNCHARTED REALMS
The Pages of the Mind
The Edge of the Blade
The Snows of Windroven
The Shift of the Tide
The Arrows of the Heart (Coming 2018)

SORCEROUS MOONS
Lonen's War
Oria's Gambit
The Tides of Bára
The Forests of Dru

OTHER WORKS

Birdwoman
Hopeful Monsters
Teeth, Long and Sharp

Thank you for reading!

About Jeffe Kennedy

Jeffe Kennedy is an award-winning author whose works include novels, non-fiction, poetry, and short fiction. She has been a Ucross Foundation Fellow, received the Wyoming Arts Council Fellowship for Poetry, and was awarded a Frank Nelson Doubleday Memorial Award, and recently received the Rita® Award for paranormal romance.

Her award-winning fantasy romance trilogy *The Twelve Kingdoms* hit the shelves starting in May 2014. Book 1, *The Mark of the Tala*, received a starred Library Journal review and was nominated for the RT Book of the Year while the sequel, *The Tears of the Rose* received a Top Pick Gold and was nominated for the RT Reviewers' Choice Best Fantasy Romance of 2014. The third book, *The Talon of the Hawk*, won the RT Reviewers' Choice Best Fantasy Romance of 2015. Two more books followed in this world, beginning the spin-off series *The Uncharted Realms*. Book one in that series, *The Pages of the Mind*, was also nominated for the RT Reviewer's Choice Best Fantasy Romance of 2016 and won RWA's 2017 RITA® Award. The second book, *The Edge of the Blade*, released December 27, 2016, and was a PRISM finalist, along with *The Pages of the Mind*. The next in the series, *The Shift of the Tide*, released in August, 2017.

She also introduced a new fantasy romance series, *Sorcerous Moons*, which includes *Lonen's War*, *Oria's Gambit*, *The Tides of Bàra*, and *The Forests of Dru*. She's begun releasing a new contemporary erotic romance series, *Missed Connections*, which